W9-APS-613

THE HERO'S GUIDE TO

Storming the Castle

THE HERO'S GUIDE TO
Storming the Castle

Written by

CHRISTOPHER HEALY

With drawings by

TODD HARRIS

WALDEN POND PRESS
An Imprint of HarperCollinsPublishers

Walden Pond Press is an imprint of HarperCollins Publishers.

Walden Pond Press and the skipping stone logo are trademarks and registered trademarks of
Walden Media, LLC.

The Hero's Guide to Storming the Castle

Text copyright © 2013 by Christopher Healy

Illustrations copyright © 2013 by Todd Harris

All rights reserved. Printed in the United States of America.

No part of this book may be used or reproduced in any manner whatsoever without written

permission except in the case of brief quotations embodied in critical articles and reviews.

For information address HarperCollins Children's Books, a division of HarperCollins

Publishers, 10 East 53rd Street, New York, NY 10022.

www.harpercollinschildrens.com

Library of Congress Cataloging-in-Publication Data.

Healy, Christopher, 1972-

The hero's guide to storming the castle / by Christopher Healy ; with drawings by Todd
Harris. — First edition.

p.   cm.

Sequel to: The hero's guide to saving your kingdom.

Summary: "The four princes erroneously dubbed Prince Charming and rudely
marginalized in their respective fairy tales have to once again save the kingdom from a great
threat." —Provided by publisher.

ISBN 978-0-06-211846-2 (pbk.)

[1. Fairy tales.   2. Princes—Fiction.   3. Heroes—Fiction.   4. Characters in
literature—Fiction.   5. Humorous stories.]   I. Harris, Todd, illustrator.   II. Title.

PZ8.H345He   2013   2012050668

[Fic]—dc23   CIP

                                                                                        AC

Typography by Amy Ryan

14 15 16 17 18   OPM   10 9 8 7 6 5 4 3 2 1

❖

First paperback edition, 2014

For Noelle

►TABLE OF CONTENTS◄

◄ MAP OF THE THIRTEEN KINGDOMS ►

Eisborg

Svenlandia

Frostheim

Frigidian Sea

Tortoiseshell Bay

Jangleheim

Yondale

Harmonia

Lake Dräng

Hithershire

Sylvaria

Sturmhagen

Erinthia

Rauberia

Aurelian Sea

Avondell

Valerium

Carpagia

Dar

Aridia (Desert)

THINGS YOU DON'T KNOW ABOUT HEROES

A true hero plays the flute.

A true hero always carries an eyebrow comb.

A true hero smells faintly of melon.

Are any of these things true? It depends on the hero you're talking about, of course. But you can find all these definitions of "hero"—and many more—in the how-to-be-a-hero instruction manual being written by one Prince Duncan of the kingdom of Sylvaria. Duncan's original title for his book had been *The Hero's Guide to Saving Your Kingdom*, but he decided that was too specific. So he changed it to *The Hero's Guide to Everything in the Whole World*. But that had kind of the opposite problem. He eventually settled on *The Hero's Guide to Being a Hero*.

Now, you may be asking yourself, Who is this Prince

Duncan, and what makes him such an expert on heroes? To which I will respond by saying that perhaps you may have skipped a book on your way to this one. You should probably check on that.

But even if you know who Prince Duncan is, you may still be asking yourself, What makes him such an expert on heroes? And that is a very good question. Duncan is a former Prince Charming, sure; but he is barely more than five feet tall, gets distracted by squirrels, and has a tendency to walk into walls. Does that say "hero" to you? Not that any of Duncan's colleagues in the League of Princes would necessarily fit your definition of "hero" either: Prince Gustav has anger management issues; Prince Liam gets easily flustered by bratty princesses; Prince Frederic collects fancy spoons and considers "dirt" his archenemy. And yet the League of Princes did manage to save not one but *five* kingdoms from the diabolical plans of an evil witch. Does that make all

Fig. 1
DUNCAN, author

of them heroes? Duncan certainly thinks so, as evidenced by the introduction to his book.

Hello! I'm Prince Duncan of Sylvaria. You may remember me from bard songs such as "The Tale of Snow White" or "Cinderella and the League of Princes." Although that first one never mentions my name and the second is full of factual inaccuracies. For instance, I did not escape the Bandit King by donning a magical "ring of flight" as the song suggests; I simply fell off his roof.

But at least it gets one thing right: I'm a hero. But did you know there was a time when I didn't even realize I was a hero? It's true. In fact, I thought I was kind of a loser. That's what everyone always told me, anyway. But then I joined the League of Princes, and along with my good friends Liam (the one from "Sleeping Beauty"), Frederic (the one from "Cinderella"), and Gustav (the one from "Rapunzel"), I outwitted the trolls, vanquished the giant, tamed the dragon, and destroyed the evil old witch, What's-her-name, without even breaking a sweat. Because sweat is gross.

—*from* THE HERO'S GUIDE TO BEING A HERO *by*
Prince Duncan of Sylvaria, aka Prince Charming
(the one from "Snow White")

Admittedly, Duncan's description of events skims over quite a few details. But at least his account is more accurate than the version of the story told in the popular bard song about that episode with the witch (referenced by Duncan above) that initially earned the League its fame:

Listen, dear hearts, to a tale most alarming,
'Bout a gathering of princes, all formerly charming.
'Twas fair Cinderella who bade them unite
For help with a powerful witch she need fight.
The nameless old crone held us bards as her captives
And threatened to silence our melodious octaves.
A world without music! That was her aim.
But Cind'rella would stop her at her wicked game.
She knew for this mission the allies she must have:
Prince Liam, Prince Frederic, Prince Duncan
*   and Gustav.*
Not one was a coward who shudders or winces.
These were the men of the bold League of Princes.
With the maid as their leader, the heroes set off
Into the dark woods with a grin and a laugh.

—from "CINDERELLA AND THE LEAGUE OF PRINCES" by Pennyfeather the Mellifluous, royal bard of Harmonia

Hardly any of that is correct.

Not that it matters. While Pennyfeather did indeed turn the former Princes Charming into household-name heroes with that particular bit of verse, he very quickly went on to embarrass them all with his next story-song, aptly titled "The Embarrassment of the League of Princes."

The celebration for these mighty warriors
Ended abruptly—and they couldn't be sorrier.
For the Bandit King (who deserves forty whacks)
Had pilfered the League's statue from behind their backs.
The Bandit had played with these princes like toys—
Appropriate, since he's a ten-year-old boy.
    —from "THE EMBARRASSMENT OF THE LEAGUE
    OF PRINCES" by Pennyfeather the Mellifluous

That one's basically true. While the princes were busy touting their victory over the witch, Deeb Rauber, the young Bandit King, humiliated the team by brazenly stealing their victory monument.

The League of Princes dropped out of sight after that. They never officially disbanded, but they all thought it best to stay out of the public eye for a while. Gustav decided to tough it out in Sturmhagen, even while his brothers continued to get credit for *his* heroic deeds. Duncan nestled back into his woodland estate in Sylvaria to work on his book (a choice his wife, Snow White, was quite pleased with). And Liam, still on the run from his wedding-hungry fiancée, Briar Rose, returned to Harmonia, home of his friend Frederic—and Frederic's fiancée, Ella (aka Cinderella).

But don't worry. It wouldn't be long before the princes reunited and put the fate of the entire world in peril. That's just sort of what they do.

It all begins in Harmonia, where one prince's moment of distraction starts a chain of events that will force the whole League to tackle a perilous quest—a quest during which both lives and pants will be lost. And if you're really worried about whether our heroes will succeed on this mission, you may not want to look at the title of Chapter 28.

Fig. 2
STATUE, pilfered

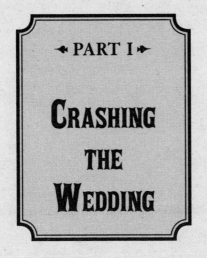

PART I

CRASHING
THE
WEDDING

1

A HERO HAS NARROW FEET

The path to hero-hood will be fraught with danger, risk, and adversity. But it will all be worth it in the end when someone writes a factually incorrect song about you.

—THE HERO'S GUIDE TO BEING A HERO

Frederic wasn't always helpless. Sure, he'd spent most of his life having his servants cut the crusts off his toast, and he once fainted after merely *thinking* he had a splinter in his finger (it was really a biscotti crumb). But then he joined the League of Princes and managed to hold his own against bandits, giants, trolls, and witches. And if you had seen him throw himself under a falling stone pillar to save the life of a friend, you would have assumed he'd gotten over his general Fear of Everything. But only ten months after that near-death experience, there Frederic was, fleeing madly down the corridors of his own royal palace, squealing like a startled piglet.

"You can't run forever," his pursuer called out. "I can hear you panting already."

"I'm aware of that," Frederic wheezed. The pale, slender prince ducked into a corner, squatted behind a large ceramic flowerpot, and poked the tip of his sword out from behind a lush, green philodendron.

"Aha!" he shouted, peeking between the feathery leaves. "I win."

Prince Liam stopped right before the big ornamental planter, lowered his sword, and shook his head. His long, burgundy cape fluttered down behind him. "Frederic," he said. "You know that if this were a real fight, I could easily cut through that shrub and get to you. It's a bush, not an iron shield."

"I think the philodendron might technically be a tree, but I concede your point," Frederic said, standing, hiking up the waistband of his gold-trimmed slacks, and straightening out the collar of his baby-blue velvet jacket (his "workout suit"). "However, this is not a real fight. And in this particular situation, the philodendron is a perfectly safe place to hide. So I'd say I outwitted you."

"No, you didn't," Liam retorted. "You won because you changed the rules. You knew I wouldn't attack the plant because I don't want to hear your father lecturing me again about 'defacing his royal foliage.' But in these training exercises, I'm not *me*; I'm playing a bad guy. A bad guy who wants to hurt you. How will you learn to defend yourself if you don't treat these bouts like real fights?"

"He's right, Frederic," said Ella, Prince Frederic's fiancée and Prince Liam's other sword-fighting pupil, who had raced down the hall to witness the climax of Liam and Frederic's "duel." She shook her head. "You weren't even supposed to leave the training room."

"But there's nowhere to hide in the training room," Frederic said.

"That's the point," Liam and Ella said in unison. They smiled at each other and laughed.

"Watch," Ella said to Frederic. "This is what you can learn when you apply yourself." She quickly drew the rapier that hung at her side and leapt at Liam.

"Whoa," Liam sputtered. He was taken off guard but raised his sword in time to parry Ella's stroke. "Nice speed," he said as he slashed back at her.

"Thanks," Ella replied, deftly blocking his strike. Swords clanged as she and Liam traded blows. But Liam was faster; he started to back Ella down the corridor.

"Watch that lamp!" Frederic yelled. "My great-

grandmother made that! Well, bought it. Had a servant buy it, actually. . . ." His voice trailed off.

Ella was up against the wall. But as Liam swung his sword, she dove under it, sliding across the polished marble floor on her knees and hopping back onto her feet several yards away.

"Nice move," Liam said with a raised eyebrow. "I don't think I could get that much distance from a single slide."

"Thank the pants," Ella said, gesturing toward her billowy satin trousers. "I made them myself." She cartwheeled toward Liam, her braid of brown hair whipping through the air. Liam leapt up and grabbed onto a chandelier to swing over Ella and avoid her assault.

"That's real crystal!" Frederic yelled.

Liam dropped down behind Ella. "Boo," he said.

Ella kicked her leg backward into his gut and sent him stumbling against the opposite wall.

"Careful with that tapestry," Frederic called out. "It depicts my great-grandmother's servant buying the lamp."

"Sorry," Ella said to Liam. "Did I hurt you?"

"Ha," Liam said with a wincing smile. "Good reflexes, though. You've come a long way."

Ella straightened the tapestry, plucked a piece of lint from it, and then charged at Liam with a quick barrage of blows—all of which he parried with ease. "A long way, perhaps" he said. "But not all the way."

As Ella's energy began to flag, Liam decided it was time for a little showboating. He performed an agile spinning maneuver, his cape flowing out behind him. Ella grabbed his cape as it fluttered past her and yanked him off balance. He fell to his knees, and Ella, grinning, touched the tip of her sword to his chest.

"Looks like I finally beat you," she said.

"No fair," Frederic interjected. "Didn't we just establish that he's not Prince Liam right now? He's playing a bad guy. You can't use his cape against him."

"A villain can wear a cape," Ella said.

"Of course," Liam added. "Plenty of them do."

"Who? Nobody we've ever faced," Frederic said. "Are you also going to tell me that villains regularly compliment you the entire time they're trying to kill you? And that they show off with fancy pirouettes in the middle of battle? You cannot honestly say you were taking that fight seriously just now, Liam. I don't think you're judging me and Ella equally."

Ella walked over to Frederic and put her muscular arm around his bony shoulders. "Come on, Frederic," she said playfully. "Don't be jealous."

"Jeal— um, what? Jealous?" Frederic stuttered. "Why would you say that? Jealous of whom?" For months now, Frederic had been trying to ignore the fact that Liam and Ella seemed like an ideal match for each other. They shared all the same interests (monsters, swords, monsters with swords). They shared all the same hobbies (rescuing people, climbing things, doing spontaneous push-ups). They had the same bold and daring spirit. But Ella was supposed to be *Frederic's* fiancée. She was the Cinderella made beloved by the bards' songs and stories, and Frederic was the Prince Charming who had swept her off her feet at that famous ball. But he was also the man whose life was so dull that Ella had left him in search of some real action.

It had been Frederic's quest to reunite with Ella that brought the League of Princes together in the first place. He'd wanted to impress Ella with his heroics—and he succeeded. But on that adventure he also introduced her to his good friend Liam. And now both she and Liam lived in the Harmonian royal palace with him, neither of them sharing Frederic's interests (artists, crumpets, artists who paint crumpets) or Frederic's hobbies (fancy spoons, poetry, spontaneous embroidery). Still, Frederic wanted Ella to notice him. Of all the women he'd ever met—and there had been dozens lining up to dance with him at the royal ball every year—none but Ella had ever made a real impression. No woman he'd met anywhere had. Well, actually, there was one other . . . but Frederic didn't know if he'd ever see *her* again.

"I'm just saying you don't need to be jealous of my sword-fighting skills," Ella explained. "I've taken to it quickly. But you'll get better, too. I'm sure of it."

"*I'm* not so sure," Frederic said. "Look, I may never become a good duelist. But that's okay. I've been telling you two for months: I'm not a sword guy. But that doesn't mean I can't be useful. *Wit* is my weapon. *Words* are my ammunition. You yourself helped me to realize that, Liam."

"You're absolutely right," Liam said. "No one is better than you at talking his way out of a fight. But if an enemy doesn't provide you with the opportunity for chitchat, you need to be able to defend yourself."

"That's when you let your *steel* do the talking," Ella said through clenched teeth.

Both Frederic and Liam gaped at her.

"And to think I was worried when she went out into the woods alone," Frederic said.

Liam gave Frederic a pat on the arm. "Come on, let's give it another try," he said. "Look, we've been living like hermits here for almost a year. I'm sure that 'Embarrassment of the League' song is a distant memory for most people."

"Cook was singing it at breakfast this morning," Frederic said.

"I said *most* people," Liam said. "My point is that it's about time we went out there and started redeeming ourselves. And if you're going to come adventuring with me again, I need to know you can handle yourself in a fight. Swords up."

Liam took a fencing stance and waited for Frederic to do the same.

"We should at least go back to the training room," Frederic said. "I think this hallway has probably seen enough action for one day." (This was, without doubt, the most excitement ever experienced in that particular corridor. Previously, the most suspenseful thing to have happened there was when two footmen hunted down a lost cuff link. It took them forty-seven seconds to find it.)

"You worry too much, Frederic," Liam said.

Frederic sighed and lifted his blade. "All right, but I want to state for the record that—*eek!*"

Liam took several quick swipes at Frederic, and— much to everyone's delight—Frederic managed to block them all. He had a giddy smile on his face as he whipped his sword back and forth to knock away each of his friend's attacks. And then his father showed up.

"What on earth is going on here?" King Wilberforce barked as he strode down the hallway.

The sound of that deep baritone voice completely broke Frederic's concentration. "Father," he blurted, and turned his head at just the wrong moment. The tip of Liam's blade sliced across Frederic's cheek. Frederic yelped, dropped his weapon, and brought his hand up to cover the wound.

"I'm so sorry!" Liam gasped.

"Are you okay?" Ella called, running to her fiancé.

The king marched up to them in a fury, dozens of medals jingling on his chest with every stomping footstep. "What have you done to my son?"

"It was an accident," Liam sputtered.

"It's just a scratch, Father," Frederic said. He checked his fingertips, relieved to see only the slightest dot of red. If there had been any more blood, he would likely have lost his composure—which he did *not* want to do in his father's presence. "And frankly, it would never have happened if you hadn't yelled and distracted me."

"What did I do to deserve such disrespect?" King Wilberforce said, sounding appalled. "I, ruler of this realm, see my only son being assaulted by some hooligan and demand that the violence come to a stop. For this I deserve scorn?"

"*Some hooligan*, Father?" Frederic asked. "Liam's been living with us for almost a year."

"I know who he is," the king said with disdain. "A supposed Prince Charming in exile from his own people, hated the world over because of the horrid manner in which he treated his Sleeping Beauty. A man to whom I have—against my best instincts—offered nothing but hospitality. And a hooligan who repays my kindness by fileting my son."

"Your Highness," Liam said. "I appreciate all the kindness you have offered me. And as I've tried to explain before, the rumors about me and Briar Rose are untrue. She spread those lies to get back at me because I refused to marry her. And surely you know I never meant to hurt Frederic. I was merely—"

"Oh, I know you probably didn't *intend* to hurt him," Wilberforce said. "But that's the problem with you. You think Frederic can do things that he simply can't. Putting my son in harm's way appears to be a hobby for you. Are you going to deny that you almost got Frederic killed in that whole unfortunate witch fiasco?"

Liam said nothing. Nor did Frederic, who, if he were a turtle, would have slipped happily into his shell at that moment.

The king looked down his nose at the three friends. "There will be no more swordplay within these walls," he stated. "Or anywhere on palace grounds, for that matter."

"But, Father," Frederic began.

"Sir," Liam stepped in. "Frederic is getting quite . . ." He couldn't bring himself to say "good." "Well, he's improving. With more training, he could—"

"There will be no more training!" Wilberforce snapped. His perfectly groomed mustache quivered as he spoke, and a fleck of saliva hit a purple silk ribbon on his chest, leaving a tiny wet spot the likes of which no one had ever before seen on any king of Harmonia. "Push me too far, Erinthian, and I won't hesitate to revoke the invitation I have so graciously extended to you. If I see you—*any* of the three of you—with a weapon in your hand, I will have you forcibly removed. Not just from my palace, but from the entire kingdom of

Fig. 3
King WILBERFORCE

Harmonia." Wilberforce spun on his heels and marched down the hall. "Frederic, get to the nurse immediately," he added as he left. "Make sure that horrible gash doesn't scar."

Frederic slumped down and sat on the edge of the philodendron pot. "I'm sorry," he said.

"You have nothing to apologize for," Ella said, sitting next to him. She put her arm around him and gave a tight squeeze. "You did nothing wrong. And, hey, any time you need me to jump in and help out against Old King Grumpy-pants, just say the word."

"Thanks, Ella," Frederic said, resting his head on her shoulder. "You're very sweet."

Liam looked away. Sensing his discomfort, Frederic stood up.

"I'm just embarrassed by the whole thing," he said. "I'm going to bed early. You two have fun." He hurried down the hall, leaving Ella and Liam alone.

Liam opened a pair of glass doors and strolled out onto an ornate marble balcony. "I shouldn't be here," he sighed, watching the quickly setting sun. "I've outstayed my welcome."

"But you can't go back to Erinthia," Ella said, joining him outside. She looked at Liam in the warm glow of the lanterns that were being lit all along the palace grounds below. He was almost ridiculously perfect as the image of a hero: mocha-tan complexion, piercing green eyes, chiseled cheekbones, a fashionable cape *and* lustrous black hair, both billowing behind him in the late-spring breeze. He was standing, as he often did, with his hands on his hips and his head turned to one side, as if he were waiting for some invisible sculptor to carve a statue of him. It was the kind of thing Ella usually enjoyed teasing him about, but she was too concerned to joke around.

"I mean, you still don't want to marry Briar Rose, right?" she asked.

"Do you really have to ask that question?" Liam replied. Princess Briar Rose of Avondell, to whom he'd been betrothed since the age of three, was quite possibly the worst person he'd ever met (and Liam had met a lot of nasty people, including a witch who wanted to explode him in front of a live audience). But no one in Liam's kingdom of Erinthia (except his little sister, Lila) seemed to care about his happiness—they only cared about Avondell's vast network of gold mines, which Erinthia would have access to once Liam married Briar. Now, understand that the Erinthian people were plenty rich already—but they'd always been second best next to Avondell. And when you're as greedy and petty as the average Erinthian, second place isn't good enough. "I have no idea when I'll ever be able to set foot in my homeland again. And I'm staying as far from Avondell as possible. I'm not going to let Briar's family or mine force this wedding on me."

"Where would you go, then?" Ella asked. And she started doing what she did whenever she got anxious: She cleaned.

"You know, they have servants to do that," Liam said when he saw her scraping bird droppings off the railing.

"Sorry, old habits die hard," she said. She turned to look him in the eye. "Just stay here."

"Things have gotten a little awkward, don't you think?" he asked sheepishly.

"What do you mean?" Ella asked in return, though she knew all too well what he was referring to.

Liam sighed. "What's the situation here? I assume you and Frederic are still getting married."

Ella glanced down at the servants locking up the palace gates three stories below. "To be honest, he and I haven't talked about it in ages. It's kind of an odd question to casually toss at somebody over lunch: *Hey, remember that time you proposed to me and I said yes? Are we still sticking to that?* I don't know—maybe I haven't asked because I'm not sure what I want his answer to be."

"I understand," Liam said. "You two are still engaged. Just like me and Briar."

"Oh, come now," Ella said, narrowing her eyes at him. "It's *nothing* like you and Briar. I love Frederic. He's a dear friend and a wonderful human being."

"I know that," Liam said quickly. "I love the guy, too. Which is why hurting him is the last thing I want to do." Liam turned away from her and stared off at the stars that were beginning to dot the indigo sky. "My mind's made up. I'm leaving in the morning."

"But . . . ," Ella started. There was so much she wanted to say to Liam—and so much she felt she couldn't say. "But we had so many plans. We were going to drive the rat-owls out of West Thithelsford; we were going to track down the Gray Phantom in Flargstagg; we were going to break up the hobgoblin gangs in East Thithelsford. . . ."

"Yes, *you and I* were," Liam said. "Do you really think Frederic will ever be ready for dangerous work like that?"

"But—"

"Don't worry. I'll come back for the wedding."

Ella stepped back inside. She couldn't let Liam walk away like this, but she knew he was too noble to put himself in the way of Frederic's relationship with his father—or

Frederic's relationship with her. *I'll never convince him to stay on my own,* she thought. *He needs to hear it from Frederic.*

In his very grand bedroom, Frederic sat in a cushy chair by his vanity table, his head tilted back as Reginald, his lifelong personal valet, dabbed at the cut on his cheek with a gooey substance he referred to as tincture of thistle-thyme.

"Do you really need to use that stuff?" Frederic asked. "It's sticky. I've never handled stickiness well. I'm sure you remember the infamous cotton candy incident."

"The ointment will aid in the healing of your wound, milord," the tall, thin servant said. "But I suspect this little scratch is not the greatest of your concerns right now."

Frederic looked his old friend in the eye. "Why is my father so cruel?" he asked. "I thought I'd proven myself to him. But he still treats me like a child. He still wants me penned in, to keep me afraid."

Reginald sat down on the edge of Frederic's elaborate four-poster bed. "Why does that matter? *You* know what you're capable of now. So do your friends. And Lady Ella."

Frederic shook his head. "I'm not so sure about Ella. I still don't think she's very impressed by me. How can she be when Liam . . ."

"When Liam what?" Reginald asked.

"Nothing," Frederic said. He absentmindedly began fiddling with a cologne spritzer. "It's just that Liam is trying to turn me into a true hero, so *naturally* my father can't stand him. It's only a matter of time until Liam gets banished. Father will stoop to anything to make sure I don't mar his perfect royal image."

"The king is not all *that* bad," Reginald said with sympathy in his voice.

"You're talking about the man who kept me in check as a child by hiring a circus tiger to terrify me."

"Point taken," Reginald said. "But what I'm trying to say is that the king's *motives* may not be as cruel hearted as you think. It's about time you learned the truth about what happened to your mother."

"I already know. She died when I was an infant," Frederic said. "A fatal dust allergy. It might be hereditary, which is why I wash my hands fifteen times a day."

"No, Frederic. That's just the story your father gave the public," Reginald said. "Adventure may not be welcome in these palace halls today, but that wasn't always the case. Queen Anabeth regularly strapped a sword to her back and went running off in search of one lost treasure or another."

"You can't be serious," Frederic said, turning the idea

over in his head. "*My* parents? *Adventurers?* At least that would explain how Father got all those medals."

"Ha!" Reginald couldn't help but laugh. "Your father awarded all those medals to himself. They're meaningless. Have you ever read what's engraved on them? One is for hopscotch.

"No, your mother was the only thrill seeker in the family. The king hated it. But even his objections couldn't keep Queen Anabeth reined in. Shortly after you were born, she heard a legend about a solid gold duckling that was supposedly hidden away in an ancient ruined temple on the wastes of Dar. She wanted that priceless idol for you."

"I do like ducklings," Frederic said in a bittersweet tone.

"She took a small team of soldiers with her, trekked off to Dar, and never came back."

"Never came back? Does that mean it's possible she's still alive?" Frederic asked hopefully.

"Sadly, no. One of her men limped back here weeks later, the only survivor. He explained how they'd accidentally set off a trap and the temple collapsed on top of the whole party. He only escaped because he was carrying your mother's bags and lagging far behind. Your mother never packed light."

"I can't believe this," Frederic said. "It's like something out of a Sir Bertram the Dainty story."

"It is *nothing* like a Sir Bertram story," Reginald said. "Sir Bertram's 'adventures' revolve around things like sorting socks and adding the proper amount of pepper to a casserole. Your mother lost her life! While treasure hunting. In booby-trapped ancient ruins. And I'm positive that her death has a lot to do with why your father is so overprotective. He doesn't want to lose you the same way."

"Wow," Frederic said. "Now I feel kind of guilty."

"Don't," Reginald added quickly. "You need to live your own life and do things your way. After all, you've got your mother's blood in you. You need to know that. And it was time for you to finally hear the whole story."

A knock at the door interrupted them. "Frederic?" It was Ella.

Reginald let her in. "Good evening, milady. I was just going." He gave Frederic a formal nod and exited.

"Shut the door and come here," Frederic said in a giddy whisper. He was standing by the corner of his bed, vibrating.

"What is it?" she asked, curious as to what had Frederic in such a state.

"My mother died trying to steal me a golden ducky!"

"Oh, my. That's . . . I'm sorry, I don't actually know how to respond to that."

"I only just found out," Frederic went on. "She was an adventurer, a real hero type. *My* mother—can you believe it? It's fascinating. You know, this is probably why I'm so drawn to people like you and Liam."

"Liam! He's why I came to you. He's leaving tomorrow!"

"Tomorrow? But where will he go?"

"Nowhere," Ella answered. "He's going to wander the world or something. He thinks he's outstayed his welcome here."

"Well, with my dad, maybe. But certainly not with me," Frederic said. "I should share this new revelation about my mother with him. It might help him understand why my father acts the way he does."

"Let's go," Ella said. She grabbed Frederic by the hand, and they hurried back toward the balcony where she'd left Liam.

Maybe Gustav could use a roommate, Liam thought as he stood on the balcony gazing at the dim sliver of moon in the sky. *Nah, who am I kidding? He'd cut up all my capes while I slept.*

A sudden clinking sound snapped him out of his

musings. He looked to his left and saw something shiny glinting by the balcony railing. On closer inspection, he saw that it was a metal grappling hook.

"What the—?"

Liam peered over the edge. A rope hung down to the gardens below, but there was no one on it. He put his hand on his sword, but before he could draw it, he was clonked on the head by a short, heavy club.

Ella and Frederic appeared at the balcony door just in time to get a glimpse of a hooded man scaling a rope up to the terra-cotta-tile palace roof. The intruder had Liam, unconscious, slung over his shoulder.

"Liam!" Ella shouted. She dove out onto the balcony and grabbed the intruder's rope. "Drop him," she snarled as she yanked the line back and forth.

"Stop that," the stranger moaned as his boots slid from the wall. He was left dangling momentarily but quickly managed to regain his footing. He glared down at Ella. "Think. You don't really want me to drop your friend from this height."

In a second he was over the roof's edge and out of sight.

"Frederic, hold the rope steady," Ella said. "I'm going after him."

"I should call the guards," Frederic argued, but he

grabbed the rope nonetheless. Ella made it halfway up to the roof before the kidnapper kicked the grappling hook from its perch. Ella, the rope, and the iron hook all tumbled down onto Frederic.

"Crud," Ella muttered. "We'll catch him on the other side!" She jumped to her feet and drew her rapier. But she was stopped in her tracks by King Wilberforce and four royal guards.

"Swordplay. I knew it," the king said. "As soon as I heard the noise, I said to myself, 'There they go again.' I knew you would disobey my orders, but frankly, I'd hoped you'd be able to restrain yourselves for longer than twenty minutes."

"No one's playing here, Your Highness," Ella said urgently. "This is real. Liam was just kidnapped."

King Wilberforce chuckled. "I sincerely doubt that. Crimes do not occur within the walls of the Harmonian royal palace."

"We saw it, Father," Frederic insisted. "A hooded man just grabbed Liam and swooped onto the roof."

"Oh, so he's a flying kidnapper?" the king said with a sarcastic smile.

"You're letting him get away," Ella barked.

"Seriously, Father, please send your guards out to the

gates!" Frederic begged. "You might be able to catch the criminal before he gets off the palace grounds!"

Wilberforce let out a long, slow breath. "If it means so much to you." He turned to his guards. "You two: Step outside and look for any signs of a magical winged bogeyman."

A pair of guardsmen bowed and marched off.

"And we'll go this way," Ella said as she began to leave in the opposite direction.

"Stop her," Wilberforce said, and the remaining two guards stepped in front of Ella to block her exit.

"What are you doing, Father?" asked Frederic.

"If there's anything dangerous going on, my men will handle it," the king said. "Neither of *you* will be involved. And to make sure of that, I'm confining you both to your rooms for the night. Guards, take these two to their quarters and stand watch outside their doors until morning."

Ella considered trying to overtake the men. But she knew it would only cause more trouble. She reluctantly sheathed her sword as the guards nudged her and Frederic down the hall.

"He wore a cape," Ella said as they walked.

"Who?" Frederic asked.

"The kidnapper. He was a villain with a cape. See? I was right."

"Actually, it had a hood," Frederic said. "So technically, it was a cowl."

Ella sighed.

King Wilberforce watched them disappear around a corner. Then he closed and locked the balcony doors. *That was convenient,* he thought. *With that Erinthian gone, it's one nuisance down, one to go.*

Frederic was sitting slumped on his bed. His father had won again. *Why do I turn into a helpless infant every time that man raises his voice,* he thought. *How does he do it to me?* He was startled by the sound of his window creaking open.

"Are you coming?" Ella asked, poking her head inside.

Frederic jumped to his feet and ran over to her.

"What are you standing on?" he asked.

"The ledge."

"It's so narrow!"

"Don't act like you've never heard of tiptoeing, Frederic—I've seen you sneak behind the drapes every time Liam suggests going for a run. So, are you coming?"

"Where?"

"To find Liam. I figured out who took him."

"I suspect my father is behind it," Frederic said sorrowfully.

"No, it's Briar Rose!" Ella blurted. She blinked her wide eyes repeatedly as words spilled from her mouth at a rapid pace. She couldn't have looked more wired if she'd just guzzled an entire pot of double-strength Carpagian Wide-Awake Brew. "I know who the kidnapper is; I put all the clues together. The hood, the little gray beard, the mumbly voice like somebody just killed his puppy: That's exactly how Lila described Ruffian the Blue, the bounty hunter. And who does Ruffian the Blue work for?"

"Bri—" Frederic began to answer.

"Briar Rose! Exactly!" Ella shouted (and then shushed herself). "Briar is still bent on marrying Liam; and now she's going to force the wedding to happen, and you and I have to go to Avondell and stop it. So, are you coming?"

"Right now?" Frederic asked. "Can't we just wait until morning and leave through the front doorway?"

"Do you really think your father's going to let us?"

"No, you're right." He took a deep breath. "Okay, let's do it. I think I'm pretty much ready to go."

Ella frowned when she noticed how Frederic was

dressed: a pale yellow suit with a royal-blue sash across the chest and tasseled shoulder pads. "You changed into formal wear?" she asked. "When you thought you would be locked in your room all night?"

"It helps me relax."

"Suit yourself," Ella said.

"I just did." Frederic laughed.

"Did what?"

"Suit mys— Never mind."

"Okay, let's head out," said Ella. "Take your sword, though."

"You know," Frederic hedged. "Like I said before, I'm not really a sword person."

"Take your sword," Ella repeated.

He attached the sword to his belt along with a pouch of coins and a small satchel of writing implements, then he climbed through the window to join Ella on the ledge. He wobbled a bit when he got a view of the lantern-lit walkways three stories below. "I'm not really a heights man either."

Ella put her hand under his chin and raised his head to look him in the eyes. "You're my hero, Frederic. You can do this."

"Of course I can," Frederic said. "I've got narrow feet."

As the two shimmied along the ledge, it occurred to Frederic that he was finally doing what Ella had always wanted him to: going on an adventure with her.

And she asked me to, he thought. *She didn't run off to rescue Liam on her own. She wants me by her side. Perhaps there's hope for us yet.* The pair sidled around a corner and onto the balcony where the kidnapping had taken place. As Ella had hoped, the bounty hunter's rope and grappling hook were still lying there in a pile. She tossed the barbed hook up to the roof, where it caught onto the side of a chimney.

"Shall we?"

Climbing up onto the roof, running along the ramparts, descending into the gardens behind the palace, and hopping over the exterior gates all took much longer than Ella had hoped—Frederic moved with the speed of a wobbly toddler wearing shoes for the first time. By the time they were off the palace grounds, the sun was coming up.

"I am so tired," Frederic said, collapsing on the grass.

"Well," Ella said, sitting down next to him, "we need to pause and figure out a plan anyway."

"Oh, I *have* a plan," Frederic said. He pulled two pieces

of parchment and a quill from his satchel. He quickly dashed off two notes, rolled them up, and stood. "Let's head into town and hire a messenger to deliver these. It's time to get the League of Princes back together."

2

A Hero Is a Carnivore

Mere words cannot defeat a true hero.
Unless they happen to be the words to some sort
of Instant Death spell. Magic is scary.
—The Hero's Guide to Being a Hero

Six months before Liam's kidnapping, Prince Gustav exploded. Not literally. Although there was quite a mess. You see, Gustav did not share the same taste in music as his sixteen older brothers. The elder princes, for example, adored "The Sixteen Hero Princes of Sturmhagen." That song had *everything*: an evil witch, five kidnapped bards, sixteen strong, young heroes. The only thing it didn't have was Gustav, the seventeenth and youngest of the Sturmhagen princes—which was unfortunate, as Gustav was the only one of them actually involved in saving the bards. Suffice it to say Gustav didn't care for the song. Nor was he a fan of "The Embarrassment of the League of Princes," a tune his brothers couldn't get enough of. After a full year of mocking Gustav for his failure to rescue Rapunzel, they were pleased to have a new reason to taunt him.

And taunt him they did. They never let Gustav forget that the Bandit King—whom the world now knew to be a ten-year-old boy—managed to rob him in full view of about a thousand people. Prince Sigfrid (#7) spattered Gustav with baby food. Osvald (#5) startled him with shouts of "Don't look down! There's a toddler crawling after you!" Alvar (#3) even pinned a sign to his back that read PROPERTY OF BANDIT KING. IF FOUND, PLEASE RETURN TO TOY BOX. Every time something like this happened, Gustav gritted his teeth, grumbled unseemly things under his breath, and stomped away—which, for him, showed incredible self-restraint. Despite being six-foot-five and having biceps the size of watermelons, he was the smallest member of his family. His older brothers teased him through most of his life; and in the past Gustav responded to their jibes with flying fists, thrown furniture, and sometimes even a good, old-fashioned head butt. The past year had changed him, though. Gustav was more mature now. He vowed that he would not let his brothers get the better of him.

But he was fooling himself. Gustav couldn't swear off tantrums any more than a volcano could promise not to erupt. It was on the day of his brothers' birthday party (all sixteen, having been born in two sets of octuplets exactly one year apart, had the same birthday) that Gustav finally lost it.

The entire kingdom came out for the big celebration, which was held in the big cobblestone courtyard outside Castle Sturmhagen. HAPPY BIRTHDAY banners were hung everywhere, bands played, food vendors handed out turkey legs and ostrich eggs, and crowds of Sturmhageners danced merrily in their leathery, fur-lined suits and dresses. All the birthday boys, from Henrik (#1) to Viktor (#16), were seated at the lengthy table of honor on a central stage. Only Gustav sat by himself, at a tiny round table-for-one that had been set for him on the outer edge of the courtyard. Behind the crowd. Under a drippy rain gutter. Next to a stinking barrel with a sign that read PLEASE DEPOSIT BONES AND OTHER UNCHEWABLES HERE.

Gustav watched glumly as his parents, King Olaf and Queen Berthilda, led a procession of bakers up onto the stage. The bakers carried an eight-foot-by-four-foot, seventy-pound sheet cake, topped with marzipan sculptures of all sixteen princes. The colossal dessert was

Fig. 4
GUSTAV, celebrating

set on a viewing platform near the edge of the stage so the crowd could marvel at it.

Then Lyrical Leif, Sturmhagen's royal bard, was introduced. The round-bodied musician pranced onstage wearing his usual green tights, puffy gold blouse-shirt, and floppy feathered hat. He took a proudly over-the-top bow and announced—to great applause—that he would serenade the birthday boys with his hit, "The Sixteen Hero Princes of Sturmhagen."

As Leif began strumming his lute and singing ("Dear hearts, listen well to a tale most sublime / of sixteen strong princes—that's seven plus nine"), Gustav decided he was done being ignored. He stood up, kicked the barrel of unchewables at an oblivious trio of swaying Leif fans, and shoved his way through the crowd to the stage. He climbed up and stood face-to-face with the bard (or bellybutton-to-face, really—Lyrical Leif wasn't very tall). A tense quiet fell over the square.

"No one wants to hear that song anymore, Featherhead," Gustav declared. "Sing the one about me." In his heavy, fur-lined armor, with his shoulders heaving and his long blond hair hanging over his face, Gustav was an undeniably imposing figure. But the roly-poly Leif was undaunted.

"Oh, 'The Song of Rapunzel'? In which you got beaten by the old lady and Rapunzel had to rescue you?" Leif asked sarcastically. He turned to the audience: "Who out there wants to hear 'Rapunzel'?"

Scores of people raised their hands and hooted.

"You know which song I mean," Gustav growled. "The one where I'm a hero."

"Oh. You're talking about that song in which you play the part of Cinderella's little helper." Leif made an over-the-top frowny face. "I'm afraid we don't get many requests for that tune. It's a tad too unbelievable, I think."

His brothers crowed with laughter. As did most of the crowd.

"Starf it all," Gustav cursed under his breath. If he couldn't get people to like him, maybe he could at least get them to hate him. Anything was better than being laughed at.

Gustav abruptly reached out, grabbed Lyrical Leif's floppy hat by the brim, and yanked it down to the bard's shoulders. The cap split down the middle as Leif's head burst through the shimmery fabric. Gustav then grabbed the bard by the seat of his tights and hoisted him up in the air with one hand. With the other hand, he reached down and scooped up a handful of richly frosted birthday cake—which he proceeded to smoosh all over Leif's shocked face before dropping the singer on his ample belly.

As horrified gasps and shouts of derision sounded from all around the square, Gustav grinned and wiped his hands clean. "Maybe now," he declared, "you'll show some respect to the mighty Prince Gustav."

He turned to walk away, slipped on a dollop of icing, and flopped face-first into the giant birthday cake. As Gustav slowly staggered back to his feet, covered from his tangled hair to his big steel boots in buttercream frosting, uproarious laughter echoed throughout the courtyard.

King Olaf gave Gustav a new job after that, one that would conveniently keep him away from Castle Sturmhagen for a while. "Go check on the trolls," he ordered. "We need an ambassador out there, and since you're the reason we had to turn over a hunk of our land to them, you should be the one to fill that position."

"With pleasure," Gustav said. Minutes later, he was riding his big gray warhorse, Seventeen, out to troll country.

As he approached a wide swath of farmland on the outskirts of Sturmhagen's thick and wild pine forests, Gustav was suddenly encircled by what appeared to be hulking mounds of overcooked collard greens. But these were no shambling piles of vegetation; these were living creatures—nine feet tall with scraggly green fur, enormous clawed hands, frighteningly large teeth, and, in some cases, a horn or two. Or three. Trolls. And they were closing in on the prince.

Gustav hopped from his horse and waited with his massive battle-ax at the ready. Clad as he was in heavy plated armor rimmed by thick tufts of boar and bear fur,

Gustav's mere silhouette would have been an intimidating sight to most humans. Most monsters, too, really. But the trolls showed no fear.

It had been a long time since Gustav had been among the trolls and he'd been bald the last time they saw him, so most of the creatures didn't recognize the long-haired human standing before them. One did, though: the single-horned troll who went by the name of Mr. Troll (all other trolls simply went by Troll—a practice that made taking attendance in troll schools either very difficult or very easy, depending on whom you ask).

"Prince Angry Man!" Mr. Troll shouted, gleefully calling Gustav by his "troll name." "Troll so glad Angry Man come back!" The monster threw its furry green arms around Gustav and, much to the prince's displeasure, lifted him off the ground in a bear hug.

"Enough, enough," Gustav grunted, and Mr. Troll put him down. The other trolls, realizing this was their beloved Prince Angry Man, joined in with celebratory hoots and howls. Gustav couldn't help smiling. Sure, the trolls were monsters, but they were happy to see him. And that felt pretty good.

"Trolls never thank Angry Man for giving trolls farmland," Mr. Troll said in his low, gravelly voice.

"Yeah, that's okay," Gustav said. "You guys give the place a name yet?"

"Yes," said Mr. Troll. "Trolls call place Troll Place."

"I should've guessed that," Gustav said. "So, um, I'm here as an ambassador."

"That fantastic," Mr. Troll said. "Troll not know what that mean. But it sound fancy. So Troll happy for you."

"To be honest," Gustav said, "I don't really know what it means either. But I am a big hero, so I suppose I can teach you trolls a thing or two while I'm here."

Mr. Troll looked ecstatic. "Prince Angry Man come to help trolls," he explained to his fellow monsters. "Him teach trolls all sort of amazing things!" The trolls cheered.

"Yeah, sure," Gustav said, crossing his arms and nodding. He was getting his old confidence back. "I'm great at all kinds of stuff. Hunting, fishing . . ."

Several of the monsters stopped smiling and glowered menacingly at Gustav.

"Ha-ha," Mr. Troll said. "Angry Man joking. Angry Man remember trolls is vegetarian."

"Oh, yes," Gustav mumbled. "How could I forget?"

"Angry Man will teach trolls how grow veggies," Mr. Troll announced as if it were an established fact.

"You've had this farm for months," Gustav said. "You

haven't grown *anything* yet?" He surveyed the scene around him. The field was completely bare except for a few rickety troll stick-houses and a large rock with a log tied to it (which one helpful troll pointed to and identified as "plow").

"No, nothing," Mr. Troll said. The monster looked down, embarrassed (at least Gustav thought he was embarrassed; it's hard to tell when you're dealing with a creature that has a face like a demonic mulch pile). "Trolls not know how grow stuff. That why trolls still steal food from humans."

"You're still stealing food?" Gustav asked, flabbergasted. "The whole reason we gave you this farmland was to stop the food raids. Do you want to start a war?"

"No. Trolls just want eat. That why Angry Man must teach trolls grow veggies."

Gustav paused. He knew nothing about farming. Although, to be honest, he didn't really know anything about hunting or fishing either. But being a farming instructor was better than going home. "All right, trolls," he said. "Let's do some farming."

Gustav taught the trolls everything he knew about growing fresh produce. He spent day after day out in the fields, imparting every bit of knowledge he had about preparing soil, sowing seeds, and keeping plants well watered. And after months of working under Gustav's tutelage, the creatures were able to head out for a harvest and gather up a fresh crop—of exactly two potatoes. Each of which was approximately the size of a peanut.

Let me reiterate: Gustav knew nothing about farming.

"How 'bout I teach you trolls to fight instead?" he suggested.

The trolls greeted this new idea with enthusiasm. And that was when Gustav really started enjoying himself. He put together a lesson plan (Ramming Your Enemy, Throwing Heavy Objects, Pummeling for Beginners, and so on), and the trolls proved to be excellent students. In reality, trolls were natural fighters and didn't need the instruction—but they had a blast taking Gustav's classes.

One afternoon, Gustav and Mr. Troll sat together in the house that the trolls had built for their teacher (five precariously balanced logs with some loose straw thrown on top). "Troll think Angry Man better fighter than farmer," Mr. Troll said.

"I guess you and I have something in common then, Leafy," Gustav said.

The troll let out a harsh, retching laugh. "Maybe Angry Man be better as troll than human."

"You know, there's a lot I can appreciate about you trolls," Gustav said. "You pack a solid punch, you're not scared of anything, and you've got no love for fancy doohickeys and dingle-dangles. That's why I've been able to tolerate you beasts for months now. But I still think I make a pretty good human. And anyway, I miss meat."

"Troll understand. Troll not be happy living with humans either. Human houses have too many parts; make Troll claustrophobic." Through the "walls" of Gustav's dwelling, they could see the other trolls gathering for their next lesson. "But Angry Man inspire Troll," Mr. Troll went on. "Troll going to be first troll hero. Trolls always bad guy in songs by Itty-Bitty-Guitar Men. Troll want Itty-Bitty-Guitar Men to write song 'bout Troll save the day."

"Yet another thing we've got in common," Gustav said.

"Huh?" the troll grunted.

"Never mind," Gustav said. "It's time for class." He stood up, bumped his head against a log, and knocked the entire house down. It was the fourth collapse that week. Mr. Troll started to pick up a log to rebuild it, but Gustav told him not to bother. The two of them stepped out to the field to join the rest of the trolls.

"Okay, furries," Gustav announced. "Today's lesson is brawling. Everybody start beating up your neighbor."

Dozens of the enormous monsters started attacking one another, slamming their hairy bodies together and grabbing each other in wet, sweaty headlocks. "Nice," Gustav said, and dove into the fracas himself.

It was then that a messenger ran up. He was a skinny, gap-toothed thirteen-year-old in a heavy sweater, wool hat, green knit scarf, shorts, and tall leather boots. He was undeterred by the raucous fray going on before him. He produced a rolled-up piece of paper from the satchel at his side and cleared his throat.

"Excuse me," he said, his voice cracking. The brawl came to an abrupt stop, all the combatants panting and staring at the messenger. "I'm looking for a Prince Gustav. Which of you is Prince Gustav?"

Gustav cocked his head. "I'm the only one here without spinach growing out of my skin and you need to ask which one I am?"

"Sorry, sir, Your Highness, sir," the messenger said. "But I have strict instructions to deliver this message only to Prince Gustav. I went to Castle Sturmhagen, but Prince Gustav wasn't there. They told me that if I wanted to find Prince Gustav, I had to come here. So are you Prince Gustav?"

"Gimme the note," Gustav said.

The messenger shook his head.

Gustav huffed. "Yes, I'm Gustav. Now give me the note, Captain Specific."

The messenger hurried over to Gustav and handed him the letter. "Here you are, sir, Your Highness, sir," he said. "I sense you were probably being sarcastic when you referred to me as a captain, but just to be clear, I am not one. I'm merely a messenger. My name is Smimf."

"Sorry to hear that," Gustav said. He unrolled the note and read, his eyes growing wide as he took in everything that Frederic had written. "Criminy Pete! Capey went and got himself kidnapped. Hey, Message Kid, go back and tell Tassels not to do anything stupid without me. Tell him I'll be there."

Fig. 5
SMIMF

"Right," Smimf said. "Only, the name is Smimf."

"Whatever," Gustav said.

"And by Tassels, I assume you mean Prince Fre—"

"Yes!" Gustav said. "You

assume right. Go." But by the time he was finished, the messenger had already vanished.

"Angry Man got to go, huh?" Mr. Troll asked.

"Duty calls, Swamp Fuzz," Gustav said. He'd never admit it to anyone, but he'd been waiting for months to hear from his old friends. He was somewhat annoyed that it was Liam they'd have to rescue, but the thought of a real quest got his blood pumping in a way it hadn't in ages. "Don't worry, though. I'll be back. You're in charge of lessons while I'm gone."

"Ha-ha, excellent," Mr. Troll said. "Troll going to do class on smacking with tree stumps."

"Good call," Gustav said. He gathered his things as quickly as he could, mounted Seventeen, and tore off down the long road to Avondell.

3

A Hero Doesn't Remember What He Did That Was So Special

As hard as this may be to believe,
some people may not like you. These people
are called villains. Everyone else will like you.
—The Hero's Guide to Being a Hero

"Okay, people, let's try it again from the top," Prince Duncan called out.

He and Snow White had returned to their woodland estate in the forests of Sylvaria shortly after the League of Princes disbanded. And ever since, he'd been working day and night on his guidebook for would-be adventurers. After his exploits with the League, he figured he was the perfect person to write such a manual. Unfortunately,

Duncan had a very difficult time remembering *why* he'd done any of the things he did. To help himself figure out the motives behind his own actions, he started having the local dwarfs act out his past so he could relive it all from a spectator's point of view. The dwarfs were not happy about this.

"From the top," Duncan repeated. Clad in his puffy red-and-yellow pantaloons, green felt jacket, and fluffy white neck ruff, he sat on a small chair in his backyard, ready to witness a reenactment of his and Liam's attempted escape from a heavily guarded bandit camp. He had a quill pen in hand, prepared to take notes. "That means you should start again," he added.

With heavy sighs, two tired-looking dwarfs plodded out from behind some shrubbery.

"You're supposed to be running," Duncan said.

"Imagine it faster," grumbled Frank, the first dwarf. Sylvarian dwarfs are notoriously cranky by nature, but these particular dwarfs had been dealing with Duncan all day and were in worse moods than usual.

"Can you at least *pretend* to run? It would help me visualize the scene better," the prince said. "After all, what you do here today, you do in the name of all hero-dom."

Flik, the second dwarf, simply pulled down the earflaps

of his cap and pretended not to hear.

"All right, then. Carry on," Duncan said. "Um, enter the Big Bandit!"

A third dwarf, Frak, appeared, dragging slowly behind the first two. He shook his fist halfheartedly at Flik and Frank.

"Don't forget your line," Duncan whispered.

"I'll get you, princes," Frak said in a flat monotone. Then he paused to pull a beetle out of his beard.

"Oh, no," Flik recited without emotion. "We're surrounded."

Two more dwarfs, Frid and Ferd—playing the entire bandit army—entered on the opposite side, stepping out from behind a birchwood gazebo. Duncan bit his lip in excitement.

"Don't worry . . . Liam," Frank said to Flik. "I . . . Prince Duncan . . . have an idea. Throw me at him."

Flik gave Frank a one-handed shove. Frank shuffled over to Frak, waving his arms limply and mumbling, "Oh, I'm flying through the air." He stopped and faced Duncan. "Okay, you get all that?" he asked. "We done?"

Duncan leaned back in his seat and scratched his chin. "I *still* don't know why I did that," he said. "Hmmm. 'Throw me at him.' Why in the world did that seem like a good idea at the time? We'll have to try it again. Maybe in reverse this time."

"Nope. I'm outta here," Frank said. He and the other dwarfs began to walk away.

"Okay, good idea, Frank," Duncan said. "We could all use a break. Nice energy, by the way, Frak. And Flik, good line reading, but next time maybe you could sound a little more heroey. Let's all meet back here in, say, ten minutes? Johnny Peppercorn!" That last bit was Duncan getting distracted by a chipmunk he suddenly decided should be named Johnny Peppercorn. Spontaneously naming random animals was only one of the many odd traits and hobbies that had made Duncan an outcast for most of his life. In fact, until the previous year, there had really been no one other than Snow White whom Duncan could call a friend. But joining the League of Princes changed that. Frederic, Liam, and even Gustav (to an extent) seemed to genuinely care for Duncan. He'd gone from one friend to several in a very short period of time. It was an undeniably positive step for his social life, but it also gave him a false sense of popularity. He believed he was a superstar. And since he never traveled very far outside his own yard, he never ran into any of the Sylvarian citizens who told jokes about him and referred to him as "Prince Dumb-can."

"I don't care if it's going to get Snow White upset—we've got to put an end to this," Flik grumbled to Frank as they walked around a hedge for some privacy. "I'm beginning to lose whatever trace of self-respect I have left."

"It's not just these pointless reenactments either," Frank said. "Everything he does gets on my nerves. I still don't know why we answer to these stupid names he invented for us."

"So annoying," Flik agreed. "Though I suppose it's an improvement over the old days when Snow White didn't use names for us at all. She just referred to us by personality traits."

"Hey, at least Duncan gave *you* a different name. They *both* called me Frank!"

"You've all got it better than me," yelled Fork, another dwarf who'd been hiding from Duncan in a nearby wheelbarrow.

"We need to choose our battles wisely," Flik said. "We can tolerate the name stuff. But this reenactment business needs to stop. Let's go talk to Snow."

The dwarfs found Snow White at a picnic table on the other side of the garden, weaving a vest out of sunflower petals. A petite woman, she was practically swimming in a voluminous pink dress adorned with dozens of violet ribbons.

"Good day, boys," she said cheerily. She was one of the only people alive who seemed to be able to make her eyes twinkle at will. "Having fun?"

"No, we're not," Frank said. "We need you to talk to Duncan for us. Tell him to stop making us perform these ridiculous scenes for him."

Snow shook her head (and then readjusted the wreath of daisies that sat atop her black hair). "As long as Duncan is working on his book, he's not tempted to wander off— and that's a *good thing*," Snow said. "My husband hasn't gotten lost in ten whole months—a new record, by the way—and if you fellows stop acting out his memories for him, he's likely to traipse off into the woods and try to make some bears do it."

"But he's been so insufferable ever since he started thinking he's a hero," Frank said. "You can't tell me it doesn't annoy you, too."

"Oh, pishposh," Snow said. "Duncan's just got more self-confidence now, and I like that."

"It's Duncan's fault we lost our dragon!" Flik griped.

Just then a call rang out from the front garden gates. "Make way for the royal family of Sylvaria!"

Snow burst from her seat and darted over to where Duncan still sat pondering his past. "Dunky, your family is here," she said.

Duncan stood up and grimaced. "Oh, no. Not them. Not here. They'll embarrass me in front of the dwarfs," he whimpered.

Snow put her hands on Duncan's shoulders and looked him in the eye. "They're your parents and your sisters," she said. "Be nice."

Duncan slumped. "But I'm popular now," he said. "And they're so . . . not."

You see, Queen Apricotta (named after her mother's favorite fruit) and King King (whose parents liked to keep things simple) were shunned by the very people whom they supposedly ruled. And Duncan's teenage sisters—twins Mavis and Marvella—were no better off. Those two girls turned weirdness into an art form (dancing to imaginary music, walking pet crickets on leashes, constantly sniffing each other's hair). Of course, Duncan was just as unpopular as the rest of his family, but he didn't realize that, which is why, for the past several months, he'd turned down every one of their invitations to come visit the castle. But he couldn't avoid his family forever.

"First of all, who cares what the dwarfs think?" Snow said. "And secondly, you don't know for sure that your family is going to do anything embarrassing."

"Oh, Duncan!" King King called out. "Where are you? I want you to taste this pea I found under my bed."

The king—who had announced the family's arrival himself because no servants were willing to travel with them—strode into the yard wearing his favorite pillow-top crown and long, zebra-striped robe. A blue jay zoomed by and snatched a tiny green pea from between the king's thumb and forefinger. "Oh, well," King King said.

He opened his arms and beckoned for a hug. Snow nudged Duncan toward him.

"Hello, Dad," Duncan said as his father wrapped him in a tight embrace.

"Son," King King said happily. "You've grown. Or perhaps I've shrunk."

Queen Apricotta stepped in alongside her husband. She wore her red hair in long pigtails that flopped against her silver gown as she walked. "Hello, hello! It's nice to see you, Snow," she said. "Ooh, that rhymed! That was fun. I should say hello to you more often."

"Good afternoon, Your Highnesses," Snow said with a curtsy. "And you, too, Mavis. Marvella."

The stoop-shouldered, inky-haired twins stood behind their mother, both wearing feathered shirts and homemade wings strapped to their backs. Their noses were painted yellow. "We're owls," the girls said in unison.

"Fantastic," Snow said, because that was the best thing she could think to say at the moment. "Would anyone like some tea?"

"Tea!" the king shouted as he finally released Duncan from the hug.

"Tea!" the queen echoed.

"*S!*" yelled Mavis.

"*Q!*" yelled Marvella.

"Okay," said Snow.

"*P, X!*" added Marvella, who assumed that the game had now changed to calling out two letters at a time.

"*D, A!*" said Mavis.

"*B, K!*" said the king.

Duncan leaned over to Snow and whispered, "This could go on for a while."

"Ooh, the dwarfs are here," Queen Apricotta noted with delight. "They're fun."

"Dwarves," Frank corrected.

King King crouched down in front of Frak. "Show

me how you fellows do birdcalls. You do such wonderful birdcalls."

"He's squatting," Frak complained to no one in particular.

"I can do a crow song. Want to hear?" the king said. He stood up and puffed out his chest. *"Ka-caw! Ka-caw!"*

"I learned a song about dwarfs," the queen announced.

"Dwarves," said Frank.

"I think it goes like this," Apricotta continued. "Dwarfs, dwarfs, dwarfs, dwarfs! Dwarfs, dwarfs, dwarfs, dwarfs!"

The twins started pulling feathers from each other's costumes and blowing them at Frid and Ferd.

Duncan whispered to Snow again, "I can't tell if this is going well or not."

Flik walked over to Frank and pointed to the garden gate. There was another person standing out there.

"I'll handle it," Frank said, and eagerly darted away from the chaos.

Smimf, the messenger, was waiting at the entrance to the yard. Frank eyed him suspiciously.

"Excuse me, sir," Smimf said. "I'm looking for Prince Duncan."

"He's busy," Frank said. "What do you want?"

"I have a message here for Prince Duncan." He held up the note.

"Give it here," Frank said.

"I have strict orders that the message is only to be delivered to Prince Duncan."

"Oh, yeah, that's me," Frank said. "I'm Prince Duncan."

"Then here you are, sir, Your Highness, sir." Smimf handed over the note.

Frank's eyes lit up as he read Frederic's letter. "Hey, kid, wait here," he said, and he started back into the yard.

"Yes, sir, Your Highness, sir," the messenger said. "And my name is Smimf."

Frank stopped. "Duncan gave you that name, didn't he?"

"I thought *you* were Duncan, sir, Your Highness, sir," Smimf said with a tinge of horror.

"Nah, but I'm gonna go get him." Frank dashed off.

Smimf swallowed hard. *My second job ever, and I've already muffed it up,* he thought.

Frank returned several minutes later with Duncan and Flik.

"What's this all about, Frank?" Duncan asked as the dwarfs pulled him to the gate.

"Read this," Frank said. He shoved the note into Duncan's hands.

"Sorry, sir, Your Highness, sir," Smimf said. "I thought the other gentleman was you."

"Really?" Duncan asked, looking up. "But I'm famous."

"Just read," Frank urged.

Duncan finished reading the letter. "Does this mean what I think it means?" he asked.

"Knowing you, probably not," Frank said. "It means one of your Prince Charming buddies got kidnapped. And you need to go help rescue him."

"That's sort of almost what I thought it meant," Duncan said, feeling rather happy with himself.

"So, go," Frank said. He handed Duncan a small sack. "I'm sure this bag has whatever you'll need."

"Well, I'm not certain how to get to Avondell," Duncan said. "Although I'm sure I can figure it out."

"Oh, no," said Flik. "We don't want you getting lost and circling back here."

"That's why you're gonna go with this kid here." Frank pointed to Smimf.

"Oh, um, yes, sir, Your Highness, sir," the messenger said. "The name's Smimf. I can lead you there. But I'm pretty fast. I hope you can keep up."

Flik dashed off to the stable and came back leading a dappled brown-and-white horse.

"Ah, Papa Scoots Jr.!" Duncan said. "He's a speedy steed. I'm sure he can keep up with your horse, Mr. Smimf."

"It's just Smimf, sir, Your Highness, sir. And I don't use a horse."

"No horse?" Duncan questioned as Flik and Frank hoisted him up onto Papa Scoots Jr. "Walking will take forever, though."

"Not for me, sir, Your Highness, sir," Smimf said. "I've got these special boots. Seven-league boots, they're called."

"Seven leagues! We princes only have one," Duncan said. "Do the members of all seven leagues get to wear such snazzy boots?"

"A league is a measure of distance, sir, Your Highness, sir. Three miles. The boots let me take very long steps. But I can go slower so you can follow me."

"That is so neat," Duncan said. "And please, tell me about the rest of your ensemble. I'd never considered wearing short-pants with a scarf and hat, but I admit it's quite fetching."

"Oh, well, the boots make me run really fast," Smimf answered, "which makes my legs get hot, so I wear the shorts. But when I move with that kind of speed, the wind makes my upper half rather cold. So I wear the woolens. It all works out quite well when I'm running. Though it can get uncomfortable when I'm standing still. Like now." He pulled off his hat and rung out a bit of his dripping, sweaty hair.

"You two can chat about fashion on the way," Frank said impatiently. "You're wasting time. Leave now."

"Yeah, before Snow White sees," added Flik.

Duncan winced. "Ooh, Snow. I'd better talk to her about this before I go."

"There's no time; your friend is in danger," Frank said. "We'll talk to Snow for you. Don't worry."

"You sure?" Duncan asked. "But what if—"

"This is hero business, remember?" Frank said. "The world needs you. Or something like that. She'll understand. Now go."

"Well, you *are* right about my hero responsibilities," Duncan said. "But—"

"Go!" Frank barked.

"All right," Duncan said. "Lead the way, Mr. Smimf."

Smimf took one step and seemed to vanish into thin air.

"Huh? I didn't even see which direction he went," Duncan said, stunned.

Smimf reappeared. "Sorry, sir, Your Highness, sir. I've got to remember to keep it slower. Let's try again." He ran off at a startling speed, but Duncan was at least able to see him this time.

"Onward, Papa Scoots Jr.!" Duncan shouted, and rode off after the messenger.

Frank rubbed his hands together. He'd gotten rid of Duncan. And the royal family had Snow in such a tizzy that it would probably be hours before she realized her husband was missing. Frank and Flik did something very rare for Sylvarian dwarfs: They smiled.

4

A Hero Doesn't Appreciate Good Comedy

You're never too young to start being a hero.
Practice dueling one-handed so you
never need to drop your blankie.
—The Hero's Guide to Being a Hero

"How do you like your new throne?" asked Princess Briar Rose. She looked as smug and superior as ever, standing on the red carpet of her statue-lined royal reception chamber in Avondell Palace. She wore a ruby-studded gown and sapphire-tipped shoes. Her arms were covered by long silk gloves that were only slightly whiter than her bone-pale skin, and a diamond tiara was tucked into the mountain of thick auburn hair piled atop her head. She crossed her arms and flashed a self-satisfied grin at Liam, who sat before her in a gold-plated, velvet-cushioned super-seat.

"I'd like it better if I wasn't chained to it," Liam said. Iron shackles bound his ankles to the legs of the throne. "Seriously. My feet are going numb. Can we loosen these cuffs a bit?"

"Sorry if your tootsies are sore, Tough Guy," Briar snickered. "Better get used to it. How else can I make sure you don't try to run before the wedding?"

"I don't understand any of this," Liam said. "You obviously hate me. Why would you want to be tied to me for the rest of your life?"

"Haven't we been through this before, Lover Boy?" she said. "It's destiny. You were promised to me when we were both eensy-weensy babies. And when something is promised to me, I make sure I get it."

Liam couldn't argue those facts. Back when Briar was an infant and he was only three years old, their parents made arrangements for the two to someday be married. But Briar ended up spending the majority of her life hiding from an evil fairy's curse, and when Liam woke her from an enchanted slumber and finally got to meet her in person, he discovered she'd become a spoiled brat. He called off the wedding—and in doing so earned himself the scorn of *both* their kingdoms.

"But I still don't get why you *want* to marry me. You spent the last year spreading lies about me and destroying my reputation," Liam said bitterly. "Your people despise me. Do you think they'll be happy to see me by your side?"

"They will feel however I tell them to feel," Briar said. "I'm pretty much a goddess around here. And besides, nobody cares about your precious little reputation. You're just here to be eye candy."

That comment struck a nerve (not the eye candy bit—the part about Liam's reputation). "You've tried to take everything from me just to be spiteful," he said coldly. "But no matter what people may think, I know who I am. Being a hero is all I have lived for—ever since I was three years old and I saved the lives of *your parents*."

Briar chuckled. "Oh, yes, that's right—those two professional assassins you managed to beat up when you were just a toddler," she said. "Nothing about that story ever seemed—oh, I don't know—a wee bit fishy to you?"

"Look," Liam said, "if you're going to force me to marry you, why drag it out? Why aren't you calling a cleric in here right now to perform the ceremony and get it over with?"

Briar shook her head in disbelief. "I'm a princess,

darling. And not just any princess. I'm heir to the throne of the richest kingdom on the continent. I am having a proper royal wedding: platinum coach pulled by two dozen white horses, ninety-eight-piece marching band, cannons blasting a salute, thirty-foot-tall bouquets of flowers most people thought were extinct, little mesh bags of those pink and white candied almonds—*everything*!"

"And the groom in chains?" Liam asked.

"Why not?" Briar said dismissively. "I'm going to look so fabulous, most people won't even notice you anyway. Seriously, look at us next to each other." She sat down in the throne next to Liam's and struck a regal pose.

"Adore me, people," she commanded.

The dozens of servants and guards who had been standing silently along the marble walls suddenly came alive with awestruck gasps and murmurs of admiration. Several clasped their hands to their chests or fanned themselves. A few pretended to faint.

One man did nothing.

"Ahem! Ruffian," Briar scolded. "I don't hear any oohing and aahing coming from under that dreary hood of yours."

Ruffian the Blue, the most notorious bounty hunter alive, stood stoically between two bronze statues of dancing goddesses. "I'm not paid to ooh," he said. "Or to aah."

Briar scowled at him. "But I pay you to do a lot of other things, Grizzle Face," she sneered. "And if you'd like to receive the gold you're due for those tasks, I'd better start hearing some adoration."

Ruffian took a deep breath. "Ooh," he said flatly. "Aah."

"You're not impressing anyone, Briar," Liam said.

"I beg to differ," she said. She looked to her guards: "Men?"

"We're impressed!" they all shouted in unison.

Liam shook his head. "I pity you, Briar. I can't imagine how hollow I would feel if I knew that none of the praise or admiration I got was genuine."

Briar's eyes lit up. "You know what, Hubby-to-be?" she said. "Since you don't seem to appreciate your insanely gorgeous throne anyway, I'm going to set you up with cozier accommodations. Guards! Unchain the prince and take him down to Dungeon Level B. Cell 842. And throw in some extra rats."

"Do your worst, Briar," Liam said as a pair of guards unshackled him from the throne and began to haul him away. "Go ahead and try to wear me down. You'll never get me to say 'I do' at that wedding."

"Oh, I will. I have ways of getting people to do what I

want," Briar said with assurance. "And after the wedding, it will be even *easier*," she added, almost to herself.

As Liam was dragged away, Briar lounged back in her throne and thrust her arms out to either side. "Buff me!" she commanded.

Two servants rushed to her and vigorously began shining her overlong fingernails with baby seal pelts.

Liam was led down a gorgeously tiled corridor, the walls of which were festooned with ribbons of spun bronze. The people of Avondell prized ornamentation and beauty above all else. Absolutely nothing in the palace was allowed to look plain or ordinary. Even the soldiers in Avondell were natty dressers: The two guards escorting Liam wore blue suede jackets and silver pin-striped pants. On their way to the stairwell, they passed a cleaning boy who was hard at work sweeping.

"Don't step in the dirt pile," Liam helpfully warned his captors. As the two guards looked down, Liam quickly reached out, snatched the broom from the cleaning boy's hands, and bashed it over the heads of his two armed escorts, cracking the long handle in two.

"Aw, man," the cleaning boy griped. "They make us buy our own brooms, you know!"

"Sorry!" Liam shouted as he dashed away down the corridor. While the two disoriented guards struggled to their feet, the fugitive prince zipped around a corner. Straight ahead of him was an open window, an easy path to freedom. But before leaping through it, he paused.

Briar is planning more than just a wedding, he thought. *I've got to figure what.*

As the footsteps of the pursuing guards echoed from around the corner, Liam abandoned the window and darted up the nearest staircase. He'd heard Briar brag about the view from her top-story bedroom, so he headed straight to the upper level. As he dashed down hallways looking for a room that could be hers, he ran past several surprised servants and even a few befuddled guards.

"New prince here," he announced as he sprinted by and waved. "Just taking a tour of the place!"

He turned down a corridor that dead-ended in a door that was framed by a twisted border of thorny vines and bright red roses. *Thank you, Briar, for having just as little subtlety as I'd hoped.*

He strode up to the two sentries flanking the door and said, "How goes it, my good men?"

"Um, okay?" one answered.

Liam slammed their heads together, sending both men

to the ground. He opened the door and stepped over the unconscious guards into Briar's room. *I've got to make this quick,* he thought as he glanced around the room. He saw a carved ivory bed, platinum-plated vanity, dress dummies draped in extravagant gowns, framed portraits of Briar doing things she obviously never did (like taming a panther and throwing a spear into the moon). *If Briar had some diabolical secret, where would she hide it?* he asked himself. *Someplace not even her maids would go. But someplace that has special meaning to her. Hmm. What has special meaning to Briar? Briar has special meaning to Briar!* "The mirror!"

He dashed to Briar's full-length dressing mirror, reached behind it, and instantly found the latch to a hidden compartment. "Man, I'm good," he said as he pulled out what appeared to be the princess's personal journal. What he saw when he flipped through the pages made him shudder. There was a map, which Briar had labeled "The Kingdoms Fall." On it, the nations surrounding Avondell had all been numbered and X'ed out. The notes scribbled beside each eliminated nation were as baffling as they were unsettling. Next to Erinthia (#1) was scrawled, "Marry in. Simple enough." But by Valerium (#2) Briar had written, "King abdicates throne"; and by Hithershire (#3) it said, "Royal family imprisoned." Liam saw his friends' kingdoms on the list as well: Sturmhagen—"Army disbanded"; Harmonia—"Scandal ousts king"; Sylvaria—"Monarchs disappear into wilderness." But none of these events had occurred. Was Briar able to see the future? Or was she planning on making these things happen herself? Was she plotting a takeover?

It made sense, Liam thought. Briar never stopped *wanting*. And when you already own a kingdom, what is there left to yearn for but more kingdoms? The only question was how she planned to do it. What was the key to her scheme?

He turned the page and saw: "The key is *JJDG*!"

Well, that sort of *helps,* Liam thought. *But what the heck does* JJDG *mean?*

He kept reading.

"I'm so close I can taste it. It all begins with the wedding. Then *JJDG*. Then—"

Liam was startled by the sound of footsteps running up the hall outside. He quickly shut the diary and slapped it back into its hiding place behind the mirror as his two frustrated prison guards rushed into the room.

"Here I am, gentlemen," Liam said, holding up his hands in the air. He was going to have to play along with Briar until he could find out more. "I give up. Take me back to Briar Rose. I'll do whatever she wants."

The men grabbed Liam's wrists and pulled them behind his back. "We'll give her the message," said one prison guard. "But you're crazy if you think we're not following through on her orders first. She said dungeon, so dungeon it's going to be."

"Yup," said the second guard while holding up a squirming burlap sack. "I've got the extra rats right here."

Liam went quietly this time, and moments later he was thrown into cell 842 on Dungeon Level B, a tiny stone room containing nothing more than a pile of hay on the floor and a few lovely landscape paintings on the walls (this was still Avondell, after all). The guards emptied a bag of live, skittering rats into the cell with Liam and then slammed the iron-bar door shut with a loud *clang*. A second later, the rats all scampered back out between the bars and ran off down the hall. The guards shrugged and walked away.

"That happens every time," came a rickety voice from the cell across the corridor. A scrawny older man with a wild, knee-length beard waved to Liam from behind iron bars of his own. A second prisoner, just as hairy and emaciated as the first, stood by his side.

Fig. 6
CREMINS and KNOBLOCK

"They always seem to think the rats will stay in the cells for some reason," the second man said. "But of course they don't. If I were that size, I'd have slipped through these bars ages ago. I don't know why *you* don't leave, Kippers." That last bit was addressed to something sitting on the floor of the men's cell.

"Is he talking to that piece of straw?" Liam asked cautiously.

"Shhh," the first man whispered. "He thinks it's a wiener dog. We've been in here a *very long* time."

"Hah! You ain't kidding," the second man said, picking up the piece of straw and petting it. "You know, I was clean-shaven when they first put me in here. Had a chin so shiny it could light up a room. Ain't that right, Kippers?"

Wow, these men must have been jailed here since long before Briar Rose's reign of terror, Liam thought. "What are you two in for?" he asked.

"Attempted assassination," the first man said. "We're innocent, of course—but I got tired of saying that after about the eighth or ninth year."

"Ooh! And now we get to guess why *you're* locked up!" the second man hooted, hopping up and down on his calloused feet. "We don't get to play this game very often; it's exciting. Okay, lemme see. . . . You're wearing a cape, so . . . I've got it! You're a cape thief! They don't tolerate stealing another man's cape around these parts."

"Nah, you're all wrong, Knoblock. Look at him," the first man countered. "Flowy shirt cuffs, spiffy belt buckle—not to mention that lustrous head of hair. He's the swashbuckling type. You were doing a stealing-from-the-rich thing, weren't you, kid?"

Liam shook his head. "I'm sorry, but no. I'm just here

for safekeeping until Briar Rose marries me."

The two old prisoners gaped in astonishment. "Could it be?" the first asked, his frail voice quivering. "Are you the kid from Erinthia?"

Liam took a step closer, peering through his cell door at the other men. "I *am* Prince Liam of Erinthia. Who are you?"

The prisoners gripped the bars of their cell and howled with glee.

"Well, I'll be dipped in griffin dung!" the man named Knoblock cried. "Finally!"

"You've got to get us out of here," the other said with desperation.

"Well, if you really are innocent men, I'll do what I can," Liam began. "But I'd need proof that you're not actually assassins before I—"

"Of course we're not really assassins!" Knoblock hollered. "You were practically a baby! Your father hired us!"

"My father? What are you talking about?"

The slightly more rational of the two men put his hands on Knoblock's shoulders to calm him down, then said to Liam, "I'm Aldo Cremins. This is Varick Knoblock. We were actors. And good ones, too. We had fantastic careers in the Erinthian theater. People would line up around the block to see us onstage."

"Cremins and Knoblock. You must have heard of us," Knoblock said. He dropped into a goofy, bowlegged stance, elbowed his partner, and said in a fake nasally voice, "Hey, Cremins, what's the difference between a goblin and a hobgoblin?"

"I don't know, Knoblock," Cremins replied in an equally ridiculous voice. "Please enlighten me. What *is* the difference between a goblin and a hobgoblin?"

"A goblin will eat your cat," Knoblock said. "And so will a hobgoblin."

Both men spun around to face Liam with big smiles and waggling jazz hands. Liam simply stared.

"Did we do that right?" Cremins asked, dropping the silly voice. "I don't think that was the original punch line."

"That would explain why it wasn't funny," Knoblock said.

"Could you please just finish your story?" Liam asked.

"Well, anyway, we were hot stuff once upon a time," Cremins said. "But that was all before King Gareth hired us to make sure *you* won a certain contest."

"I don't know what you're talking about," Liam said.

"You couldn't have been more than three at the time," Cremins said. "People from all over the world were showing off their kids here in Avondell so the king and queen could pick a future husband for their baby princess, Briar Rose."

"Well, of course I know that," Liam said. "That's how I ended up engaged to Briar in the first place. But no one helped me win. The royal couple picked me because I saved their lives. That was the most important day of my life—the day I first became a hero. I single-handedly stopped two masked assassins from attacking . . ."

The two men pulled their beards up to cover their faces.

"Oh, man. Two assassins. It was you."

They nodded.

"You were actors?" Liam asked, his horror growing by the second. "And my father . . . ?"

"King Gareth set the whole thing up," Cremins explained. "He said it was the only way he could be certain you would be chosen to marry Briar Rose. We always enjoyed a challenge, so we took the job. Of course, Gareth also assured us we'd get away somehow."

Liam's mouth hung open as he shook his head silently.

"We also assumed he would have told you about our little charade at some point," Cremins said. "To be honest, I feel kinda bad for you right now. You look like a kid who just had his pet goldfish served to him for dinner."

"I've based my entire life around that moment," Liam said, his voice hushed and his words slow. "My first act of heroism was really an act of deception. It's all a lie."

"Yeah, we feel all sorry for you and everything," Knoblock said. "But you're gonna get us out of here now, right? You're gonna tell everybody we didn't do it?"

"You *are* gonna make sure we're freed, right, kid?" Cremins added hopefully.

Liam sat down on his pile of hay and said nothing. "Why couldn't I see it before?" he mumbled as his mind flooded with thoughts of his past escapades, every flub and blunder suddenly seeming like a colossal failure. "So many mistakes . . . I lost to the bandits, to the witch, to the dragon, to Briar, to a ten-year-old boy. . . . I never actually *saved* any of my friends, did I? In fact, I almost got each of them killed. Several times. Everybody looked up to me and believed in my plan. But my plan didn't work. I'm no strategist. I've based everything I've done around a skill I don't even have."

"Kid?" Cremins called gently.

But Liam didn't hear him. "Briar Rose is going to take over the world. I'm the only one who knows about it. The people need a hero. But all they've got is . . . me."

5

A Hero Cries at Weddings

*Planning is an essential skill for any hero. If you begin
something and don't know how to end it, then, well . . .*
— THE HERO'S GUIDE TO BEING A HERO

"Do you think they'll show?" Ella asked. She and
Frederic crouched within a small circle of elms
outside the back gates of Avondell Palace.

"I hope so," Frederic said. "I've been seeing guests go
in through the front gates all morning. The wedding is
probably going to begin soon."

"C'mon, where are you guys?" Ella muttered under
her breath as she peered anxiously between the trees.

"Well, whatever happens, these past few days have
been quite enjoyable," Frederic said. "You and I, dashing
across the countryside together, holding secret meetings
and such. Very exciting, no? Almost makes me wish it

didn't all have to end in a perilous prison break."

Ella was barely listening. "Look, Frederic, the others are no-shows. You and I have to do this alone." She patted the sword hanging at her side and saw Frederic tremble slightly. "Take it easy, Frederic. We can—" A figure appeared suddenly between them as if erupting from the very air itself. Ella reacted on instinct, shoving Frederic out of the way and hauling off with a gut punch that knocked the intruder flat on his back.

"Your messages have been delivered, sir, Your Highness, sir," Smimf wheezed from the grass where he lay.

"Oh, my goodness," Ella exclaimed. "I'm so sorry!"

"My fault," Smimf said, holding his belly. "Got to learn not to startle people like that. I did it to my grandmother once, and she reacted the same way. Only she's got a metal hand."

A second later, a dappled horse galloped out of the trees, with Duncan at the reins. "Oh, dear!" Duncan cried when he saw Frederic and Ella bent over the fallen messenger. "That boy ran so fast he melted, didn't he?"

"I'm fine, sir, Your Highness, sir," Smimf said as Ella pulled him back to his feet.

"Duncan!" Frederic shouted.

"Frederic!" Duncan exclaimed. And promptly fell off

his horse. He scrambled to his feet and enveloped Frederic in a hug.

"It's so good to see you," Frederic said.

"Likewise," Duncan replied. "You're exactly how I remember you. But in different clothes."

"Thank you for coming, Duncan," Ella said.

"Oh, I'd do anything for my friends," Duncan said with a goofy grin. "Um, what are we doing again?"

Ella pointed to a large wall just outside the trees that was decorated with huge mosaic rainbows. "We have to break into that palace garden before Briar Rose marries Liam," she said.

"Weddings always make me cry," Duncan said.

"Duncan, we're not here to *see* the wedding," Frederic said. "We're here to stop it."

Duncan shrugged. "I still might cry."

"Oh, by the way, sir, Your Highness, sir," Smimf said. "Prince Gustav told me to tell you that he would be here as well."

"Timely news delivery, Short-Pants," Gustav said as he rode up on his warhorse. The brawny prince's armor clattered as he jumped to the ground. "So when do we get to fight?"

Duncan rushed in for a hug, but Gustav sidestepped,

allowing his friend to face-plant into a nearby tree. Feeling slightly bad about this, Gustav treated Duncan to a pat on the head. Duncan was satisfied.

"Hey, Mr. Mini-Cape, I see you've got yourself a ride this time," Gustav said, noticing Duncan's horse.

"Ah, yes," Duncan said. "Allow me to introduce Papa Scoots Jr. As you surely remember, the original Papa Scoots ran away last year. I thought I'd never have a horse like that again. But as luck would have it, one autumn morning, this fine beast wandered into Papa Scoots's old stable. To make it even more of a coincidence, he looks *exactly* like Papa Scoots! So I had to name him Papa Scoots Jr. It's like fate."

"Um, Duncan," Frederic said tentatively. "Did you ever consider that maybe Papa Scoots just found his way back home? That this *is* Papa Scoots?"

"Impossible," Duncan said. "Papa Scoots hated me." And with that, Papa Scoots Jr. kicked Duncan into a bush.

"All right, we've got business to attend to," Gustav said. "Enough horsing around."

Frederic chuckled. "That was funny, Gustav."

Gustav frowned. "It wasn't meant to be. What are we waiting for? I heard you guys say the wedding was going to start any minute now. How do we get in?"

"Well, for that we need one more person," Frederic said. A rustling rose from some nearby shrubbery. "I hope that's her now."

Lila struggled between two bushes, snagging her very expensive-looking magenta gown on several branches as she did (not that it seemed to bother her at all). "Hey, you're all here," the girl said happily.

Lila, Liam's tweenage sister, shared her brother's coffee-toned complexion and green eyes. She had the sleeves of her gown rolled up, and her chestnut hair curled into tight ringlets that bounced like little springs when she walked. (The hairstyle was completely her mother's idea.)

Ella and Frederic introduced her to the other princes.

"Lila has a way to sneak us into the wedding," Frederic explained. "We knew that, as a member of the groom's family, she would have an invitation. So we figured she'd be the perfect inside man—or girl—for this job."

"Happy to do it," Lila said. "Follow me, everybody. We don't have much time. The music has started, and the circus people are already performing."

"Circus people?" Frederic asked, suddenly looking as if someone had a sword pointed at his heart. "What circus?"

"Oh, it'll be a great diversion, actually," Lila said. "Briar's got some acrobats from the Flimsham Brothers

Circus warming up the crowd for her."

"Flimsham?" Frederic gulped. He took a staggering step backward and gripped a nearby tree trunk for support. "I can't go out there."

"Why not?" Ella asked.

"El Stripo," Frederic said.

Ella, Gustav, and Duncan responded with a collective "Ahhh." They'd all heard the story of how King Wilberforce used El Stripo—the Flimsham Brothers' talented circus tiger—to terrify Frederic when he was a little boy. The experience of being engulfed by the mouth of a raging tiger (even a toothless one) had scarred him for life.

"Don't worry, Frederic. I'm sure that same tiger isn't still with the circus," Ella said. "Do tigers even live that long?"

"Not when I'm around," Gustav quipped.

"Let's work this out scientifically," Duncan said, tapping a finger to his head. "A tiger is what you get when a cat and a zebra have a baby. Cats have an average lifespan of about ten years, while zebras get about twenty-five—"

"Guys!" Lila said sharply. "Anyone who's part of this rescue needs to come with me now." She turned and began to head through the trees.

"She's right; let's go," Frederic said. He turned to Smimf. "I'll pay you a bonus if you stay here and watch our horses."

"Absolutely, sir, Your Highness, sir," Smimf said. "I don't think they're going to do much. But I'll watch."

Frederic and the others trailed after Lila as she sneaked along the palace's outer wall.

"I bribed a guard to open the back gate and then disappear, so that's your way in," Lila whispered. "The wedding is being held in the big garden behind all the animal-shaped hedges. They've already got Liam out there, chained to the altar."

As soon as they were on the palace grounds, huddled together on a cobblestone path, Gustav closed the gate behind them. There was a loud clink as its bolt-lock fell back into place.

Lila frowned. "I hope that wasn't your escape route," she said.

Awkward pause.

"Oh, man," Lila said, growing distraught. "You guys don't actually know *how* you're going to rescue Liam, do you?"

"Well," Frederic said. "We figured out how to get inside the gates."

"*I* got you inside the gates," Lila said in a harsh whisper. "Me—the kid! What are you going to do from here?"

"Liam's really the planner of our team," Frederic said, trying to hide his face in the collar of his jacket.

Ella cleared her throat. This was the kind of test-your-mettle challenge she'd been longing for. A year earlier, when she fled Frederic's palace in search of adventure, she had ended up getting more than her fair share of thrills. But despite several near-death experiences, she'd been aching for more action ever since. "Don't worry, Lila. I can think quick on my feet. Remember how you and I dealt with those goblins last summer? We'll figure this out, too. Trust me."

Lila did trust Ella. "Okay," she said. Suddenly the sounds of trumpets, drums, and glockenspiels filled the air, followed by explosive bursts of cannon fire.

"It's starting!" Lila said. "I've got to get back to my seat. Good luck!" And she dashed off to find her place among the wedding guests.

Ella surveyed the rows upon rows of hedges cut to resemble animals like bobcats, dragons, elephants, and guinea pigs (generations of Avondellian royal gardeners had been working toward the goal of having a shrub shaped like every animal in existence; after seven decades of working alphabetically, they'd only gotten as far as "iguana").

"Come on, we need to hurry," Ella said brusquely. She drew her sword and headed for the topiary bushes.

"Wait, who put you in charge?" Gustav asked.

"The bards did," Ella said.

Gustav huffed but scrambled after her anyway.

"What's the plan?" Frederic asked.

"See that tree in the far corner? That's our new escape route," Ella said in the gruff tone she imagined all military commanders used. "We bust Liam out of his chains, climb that tree, and head back out over the wall."

"And if anybody gets in our way?" Frederic asked.

"We knock them down," Ella answered.

Gustav grinned. "I think I like you, Boss Lady."

The quartet crawled between the legs of a buffalo-shaped hedge. From beneath the "belly" of the bush, they looked out on the

Fig. 7
Decorative
TOPIARIES

wedding. At least five hundred silver chairs had been set up in the enormous garden, and every one of them held a dignified, important, and very wealthy guest. Behind the audience, practically hidden by massive arrangements of roses, orchids, lilies, and snapdragons, stood dozens of musicians playing what was presumably a wedding march. (The song sounded more like a battle hymn than a bridal tune, but hey, that's Briar Rose. . . .) In grandstand bleachers behind the band there were at least a thousand more guests—ordinary citizens of both Erinthia and Avondell who had paid nearly a year's wages to attend the grand event.

Above the crowd, tightrope walkers—all of whom were costumed to look like Briar Rose, complete with giant wigs—sashayed along a pair of high wires that ran from the palace roof to the top of the wisteria-covered pergola behind the altar. Below them, along a long red carpet that ran down a wide center aisle, acrobats in formal wear cartwheeled in time to the orchestra music, while top-hatted clowns pretended to pluck large, lustrous rubies from the ears of audience members.

The red carpet ended at a raised altar, on which stood Liam, dressed in an exquisite royal-blue tunic and shimmering white cape trimmed with gold filigree. But his attire was the only elegant thing about him. His shoulders were slumped, his head drooped nearly to his chest, and his normally stylish hair hung limply over his face. His left leg was chained to the decoratively carved oak pulpit that rose up from the center of the altar.

"I love the cape," Duncan said. "But the rest of him looks terrible."

"He looks even more mopey than when we first met him," Gustav added.

In truth, Liam was in worse shape than any of them even realized. In the four days since he'd spoken to Cremins and Knoblock, he hadn't eaten so much as a crumb and had no sleep whatsoever. He was in such a stupor that a pair of attendants had to literally drag him down the aisle and prop him up at the altar.

Ella refused to dwell on Liam's sad state. "Gustav, do you think you could rip that pulpit out of the ground?" she asked.

"Without breaking a sweat," Gustav said.

"Then that's how we free him," Ella said.

"What about all those frowning men with long, pointy things?" Duncan asked. Soldiers armed with tall poleaxes were positioned throughout the garden, with several standing guard around Liam on the altar.

"There are too many. We can't take on all of them," Ella said.

"Aw, now I'm starting to like you less," Gustav muttered.

"We need a distraction," Ella said.

"My specialty!" Duncan beamed. He hiked up his pantaloons and crawled off toward the rear of the crowd.

"Wait!" Frederic said. "What if you get caught?"

"You guys are about to rescue Liam," he said as if it were the most obvious thing on Earth. "Once he's free, he'll just rescue me." He scuttled off on his hands and knees.

Just then a collective gasp rose from the crowd of wedding guests. A giant hot-air balloon had floated into view and was hovering over the altar. From the basket of that craft emerged the Archcleric of Avondell, the kingdom's highest-ranking clergyman. The red-robed, white-haired cleric stepped to the edge of the craft's basket, blew kisses down to the audience, and—to the sound of even louder gasps—stepped out into thin air. Or so it seemed. The holy man was wearing a harness, and two burly circus workers in the balloon were lowering him down by rope. The Archcleric descended to his spot behind the pulpit with his arms spread to the sides, like an eagle soaring down to roost on a tree branch. After landing, he adjusted his pointy, gold-flecked hat while another servant dashed up to disconnect his harness. Nearly everyone burst into applause, including Frederic.

"I know Briar Rose is the enemy here," he said, nodding appreciatively. "But she knows how to put on a show."

The Archcleric took a bow and gestured toward the far end of the aisle, where the bride was about to make her entrance. The guests turned to watch.

As the sound of thundering drums filled the courtyard, Briar Rose rode out of the palace on a unicorn. She wore a sparkling, diamond-studded bridal gown with a train so long that she was halfway down the aisle before the end of it finally emerged from the palace. An elaborate headdress— which included several live, tweeting tropical birds—was entwined around her swaying pillar of hair. Her fingers were covered with so many jeweled rings that it was impossible to bend a knuckle. The unicorn also wore a gown.

As Briar slowly made her way toward the altar, waving and blowing kisses to the audience, she allowed herself a moment to glare triumphantly at Liam. "I told you so," she mouthed silently at him, and she smiled as she saw him slump halfway to the floor. But when Briar was about two-thirds of the way down the aisle, Duncan burst out from under the chair of a monocle-wearing baron, pointing and shouting, "Jenny von Hornhorse!"

The unicorn stopped and reared, its dress billowing. The orchestra froze mid-note. Everyone stared, dumbfounded, at the strangely dressed little man who now stood in the center of the aisle like a roadblock.

"Isn't Jenny von Hornhorse the perfect name for her?" Duncan said, smiling.

"What are you doing, you idiot?" Briar hissed between her teeth. "Get back to your seat or I'll have you thrown in the dungeon with a sack full of rats."

Duncan didn't move. Briar tried to steer her mount around him, but each time she got the animal to take a step left or right, Duncan countered by leaping in front of it again. "It's like we're dancing," he said.

Several guards started to rush toward her, but Briar raised her hands to stop them. "Stay back!" she commanded. "No violence near the dress!"

She leaned down to snarl at Duncan. "Get. Out. Of. My. Way."

"I love unicorns!" Duncan cried, throwing his arms around the creature's neck.

While everyone's eyes were glued to the spectacle in the center aisle, Ella, Frederic, and Gustav crept to the back of the altar platform.

"Psst!" Frederic whispered.

Liam looked down and wondered if he was hallucinating. Ella held a finger to her lips. The guards at Liam's sides were still staring at Duncan—who was now running his fingers through the unicorn's mane and singing to it—but they and the Archcleric were blocking Gustav's path to the pulpit. The big prince had no idea how to get to it without causing a commotion.

Fig. 8
BRIAR, regal

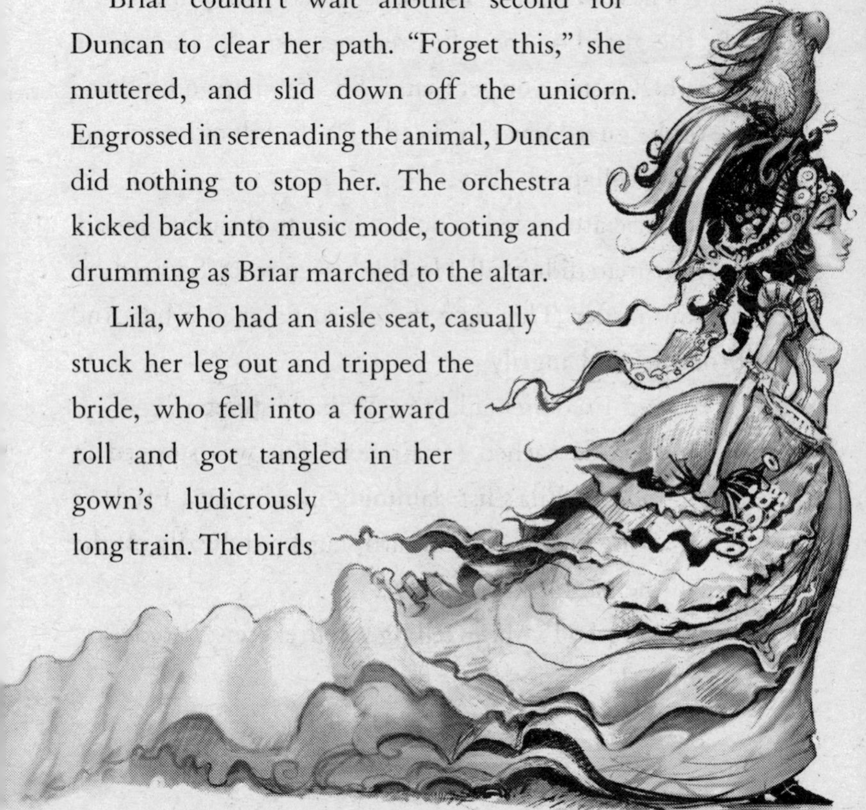

Briar couldn't wait another second for Duncan to clear her path. "Forget this," she muttered, and slid down off the unicorn. Engrossed in serenading the animal, Duncan did nothing to stop her. The orchestra kicked back into music mode, tooting and drumming as Briar marched to the altar.

Lila, who had an aisle seat, casually stuck her leg out and tripped the bride, who fell into a forward roll and got tangled in her gown's ludicrously long train. The birds in her hair squawked and flapped their wings frantically. Again, guards began to run to Briar's aid. But she poked her head out from under layers of twisted, sparkling fabric and barked at them, "No one touches the dress!"

"Are you all right, Your Highness?" the Archcleric asked from up on the altar.

"Never better," Briar snarled as she picked herself up. "Just start the stupid ceremony."

"It's now or never," Ella whispered to the princes. "I'll take the guard on the left; Frederic, you take the one on the right. Gustav, you get Liam." She stood up and clubbed one of the guards over the head with the hilt of her sword. The man collapsed.

Frederic attempted to do the same to the other guard. Only the man didn't fall. He didn't even react. So Frederic hit him harder. This time the guard flinched a bit. And turned around angrily.

"Sorry," Frederic said. "My, uh, hand slipped."

The guard reached for Frederic but was stopped in mid-motion by Ella's fist slamming into his jaw. Frederic let out a long breath as the guard staggered dizzily off the edge of the platform.

"This is why I've been telling you to exercise, Frederic," Ella chided.

"I do ten neck rolls every morning!" Frederic sputtered.

As shrieks rose from the crowd, Gustav leapt up onto the altar and hoisted the Archcleric over his head. He glanced left and right, not sure of what to do with the holy man.

"Unhand me," the Archcleric cried.

"Sorry, Church Guy, nothing personal," Gustav said, before hurling the old man into the front row. The Archcleric landed across the laps of Liam's parents, who toppled backward in their chairs.

"What is going on?" Briar howled.

As dozens of armed guards charged toward the dais, Gustav grabbed hold of the wooden pulpit and, with a grunt, ripped it from its foundation.

"Yes!" Ella cheered. A guard swung his poleax at her, but she was faster—a quick slice of her sword and the guard's weapon was in two pieces. She followed up by knocking the man from the dais with a powerful leg sweep—which wasn't easy to pull off, considering Frederic was crouched behind her, clinging to her waist.

In a daze of exhaustion, hunger, and melancholy, Liam blankly watched the chaos around him. "Is this real life?" he muttered to no one in particular.

Briar, assuming Liam had somehow arranged all this

chaos, climbed up onto the platform and confronted him. "This is a rescue attempt?" she scoffed. "What a joke. You're not going anywhere!"

A contingent of five soldiers reached the end of the aisle, their spears aimed at Gustav.

"Look out!" Frederic cried.

Gustav chucked the pulpit at the guards, bowling them over. Liam was still chained to the pulpit, however, and was whipped off his feet as it flew. He landed on the pile of very unhappy soldiers.

"Oh, starf it all," Gustav groaned, and smacked himself on the forehead.

Lila sank in her seat, shaking her head.

Duncan, finally noticing the predicament his friends were in, scrambled up onto the unicorn's back (taking note of how much easier it was to mount an animal that was wearing a dress) and charged up the aisle, shouting, "Tally-ho! Hero coming!"

The soldiers scrambled out of the animal's way, but Liam was unable to get very far. He was stuck at the end of the aisle, directly in the path of the charging unicorn.

"Whoa!" Duncan yelled. The unicorn skidded to a halt, narrowly avoiding Liam, but the force of the stop catapulted Duncan up in the air. He slammed into Ella just as she was about to finish off the guard she'd been dueling.

Out in the crowd, the monocle-wearing baron turned to his wife and whispered, "This is a very good wedding."

Seconds later, swarms of guards were on top of the wedding crashers. Duncan, Ella, Frederic, and Gustav were tackled and shackled.

"Well, this has been an interesting turn of events," Briar said. She stood, smiling down at Liam, who looked in every way like he'd just been chewed up and spat out by a dragon. "You know, I still hadn't been completely sure how I'd get you to say 'I do.' But now I don't think it will be a problem at all."

After the bedraggled Archcleric had been retrieved from the audience, the tattered bride and groom took their places once again on either side of the uprooted, overturned pulpit.

The old holy man cleared his throat, adjusted his hat, and began: "Dearly beloved, we are gathered here today to witness the joining in holy matrimony of Prince Liam of Erinthia and the fair, gentle, wise, generous, sweet-hearted, caring, artistically talented, pleasant-voiced, graceful, punctual, acrobatic—"

"Seriously?" Liam interrupted.

"—and lovely Princess Briar Rose of Avondell. This marriage shall forever unite their two kingdoms. What belongs to Avondell shall now belong to Erinthia; what belongs to Erinthia shall now belong to Avondell."

Liam's parents were dancing in their seats.

The Archcleric continued: "Do you, Briar Rose, take Prince Liam to be your husband?"

"I do," Briar said with a wide, wicked grin.

"And do you, Liam, take Briar Rose to be your wife?"

Liam looked past the cleric to Ella, Frederic, Duncan, and Gustav. They were on their knees in chains, with guards holding sharpened axes over their heads. His eyes lingered on Ella's the longest.

"I'm a madwoman, right?" Briar whispered. "What do you think I might do to your friends if you say no? Let your imagination run wild."

Liam eyed her with contempt. He took a deep breath.

"I do," he said.

"I now pronounce you husband and wife," the Archcleric said cheerfully.

Ella felt as if her heart had fallen out of her chest.

6

A Hero Has
a Fancy Closet

It is the villains who covet treasure, not the heroes.
Unless the treasure in question is a really snazzy
belt buckle, in which case, who can resist?
—The Hero's Guide to Being a Hero

"**M**ake way, people of Erinthia! Step aside for your new princess." Briar Rose was jubilant as she strutted through the bronze-plated front doors of her new husband's royal palace, while servants and noblemen alike scurried from her path. She rubbed her hands together hungrily as she surveyed the kneeling footmen, priceless urns, and jeweled chandeliers that surrounded her in the palace's grand entry hall. "My new home away from home," she said. *The first of many,* she added to herself.

King Gareth and Queen Gertrude, the rulers of Erinthia, hurried down a wide marble staircase to greet their new daughter-in-law.

"Greetings! Greetings!" Gareth bellowed. "Welcome to the family!"

"We've been waiting for this day since our Liam was three years old," Gertrude said. Just like most of the people in Erinthia, Gareth and Gertrude were interested in the Liam-Briar marriage solely because of Avondell's enormous wealth—a fact Briar was very much aware of. And she was willing to bet the royal couple would do just about anything to please her.

"Oh, I couldn't be happier," Briar said, dripping with false sweetness. "But, Papa— May I call you Papa?"

"Of course, my dear," said Gareth.

"Papa, I believe your inexcusably unclean entryway got my emerald slippers all dusty," Briar said. "Could you be a dear and do something about it?" She lifted her foot slightly to show off an elegant shoe that seemed perfectly clean.

"Oh, well, um, we can't have that, can we? I do apologize," Gareth said, flustered. He raised his arm and motioned to a servant. "Footman, come here and—"

"Oh, Papa," Briar said. "I don't think I need to tell you

how unique and valuable these slippers are. I couldn't trust their cleaning to a mere footman."

Gareth gulped. He looked over to Gertrude, who nodded vigorously. Gareth cleared his throat and bent down at Briar's feet. He blew gently on her shoe. "There we go," the king said. "All better."

When he began to stand, Briar put her hand on his shoulder and pushed him back down. "Not quite, Papa," she said. "They're still covered in dust."

King Gareth blew harder and harder at Briar's emerald slippers; his cheeks inflating like a puffer fish and his thick mustache flapping like a flag in the wind. Queen Gertrude, feeling panicky, crouched down next to her husband and began working on the other shoe, scrubbing at it with the lace cuffs of her gown. Briar grinned.

Liam, who'd been sulking far behind Briar on their journey from Avondell, finally entered the palace hall and saw his parents on their knees, polishing the princess's shoes.

"You two are pathetic," he said.

The king and queen quickly stood and smoothed out their clothing as Liam approached them.

"Son, it's so lovely to see you back home again," Gareth said.

"We're so happy you finally came to the right decision regarding this marriage," Gertrude added. She touched her hand to Liam's cheek, but he brushed it away.

He leaned over and whispered into his father's ear, "I know what you did, Father. All those years ago. With the actors whom you left rotting in prison."

"Humph," Gareth grunted and whispered back, "I don't see those two walking around free, so I guess you were smart enough to keep it to yourself."

"You're despicable," Liam hissed.

"I guess it's hereditary," the king spat back. And he returned his attention to Briar Rose. "Come, my dear," he said. "There is so much to show you. This vase back here, for instance, was imported from the treasury in Kom-Pai. It's over two thousand years old and—"

"Yeah, whatever, I don't care about that," Briar said. She walked away from the king. "Where's your treasure room?"

"It's on the third floor," the king said. "But there's so much to see before we get there."

"No, I'm going there now," Briar said. She started up the marble staircase. "Husband! Take me to the treasure room."

Liam jogged to catch up to Briar midway along the

flight of steps. "What's your rush, Briar?" he asked. "Up to something?"

"Yes, I'm almost up to the second floor," she replied. "And I'm going to keep going straight to the third. And you're coming with me so you can show me to the treasure room. Because you're my loving husband."

"I'm coming with you because my friends are in your prison," Liam said.

"Ah, togetherness," Briar said, and she blew Liam a kiss.

Lila was waiting for them on the second-story landing, standing with her arms crossed and a sour look on her face.

"Hi, sis," Briar smirked.

"Don't call me that," Lila sneered. "Nobody but Liam gets to call me that."

Briar knit her brow. "You'd better watch yourself, brat. I know you tripped me on

Fig. 9.
BRIAR and LILA

purpose at the wedding. The only reason I didn't throw you in jail with the others is because you and I are family now."

"I don't know what you're talking about," Lila said with mock innocence.

Briar sniffed and continued up to the third floor.

"Be careful around her, Lila," Liam whispered to his sister. "I wouldn't put anything past her."

"Oh, come now," Lila said, poking him in the belly. "You love it when I get spunky."

Liam tried to smile but seemed to have trouble working the muscles at the corners of his mouth.

"There's something wrong with you," Lila said seriously. "The Liam I know would treat this as a minor setback."

"I'm *married* to her," Liam said.

"Yeah, I know. And your true love is stuck behind bars."

Liam blushed. "My *friends*. My friends are behind bars."

"Yeah, your friends. And Ella. You're not fooling anyone, Liam. I've visited you in Harmonia. I've seen you and her together."

"Ella is Frederic's fiancée. And it's a moot point anyway, because I'm married to Briar now."

"Like I said, a minor setback," Lila said. "You'll figure a way out of this. You're still the same hero you've always been."

Liam winced at her words. *That's just the problem,* he thought. *I was never a real hero to begin with.*

"Buck up, big brother," Lila said, landing a playful punch on his arm. "And remember, I'm here whenever you need me. If you're ready to bust your friends out of prison—"

"Lila, stay out of this," Liam said. "I don't want you involved. And nobody's breaking anybody out of jail anyway."

"You're not going to let them rot, though. Right?"

"Of course not. I just . . ." He sighed. "I don't know what I'm going to do."

"You know where to find me," Lila said. "Let's talk later."

"Yeah, sure," Liam said glumly. "If Briar let's me." He trudged up the stairs after his new bride, who was waiting for him at the top, impatiently tapping her foot.

"Get a move on, prince."

"The treasure room is down this hallway," Liam said as he walked past her. *This is my life now,* he thought. *I've gone from Everybody's Hero to Crazy Lady's Puppet, just like that. But I deserve it. I'm a fraud.*

Halfway down the third-floor corridor, two armored knights stood guard outside a set of thick oak doors.

"Your Highness," both knights said, snapping to attention.

"At ease, men," Liam said. "And please open the treasure room for the . . ." He sighed. "For the princess."

The two knights each produced a key from inside their sleeves. They inserted the keys into two brass keyholes and turned them simultaneously. The heavy oak doors swung open, revealing museum-like rows of pedestals and glass cases, each displaying a jeweled idol, golden goblet, or some other valuable artifact. Briar rushed inside.

"Well?" Liam asked. "Does our treasury meet your standards?"

Briar scanned the entire room from wall to wall, floor to ceiling. She began to dart around, checking behind large framed oil paintings and lifting gold busts to peer underneath them. "Where is it?" she said, mostly to herself.

"Where is what?" Liam asked, growing increasingly curious.

"Shut up," Briar snapped. Her search became frantic. She yanked down silver plaques, sending them clattering to the stone floor. She kicked over crystal vases. She shoved aside a cabinet full of hand-painted porcelain eggs, several of which fell and shattered into countless fragments.

"This room is not that big," she growled. "Where is it?"

"What are you looking for?" Liam asked.

Briar turned and grabbed him by the shoulders. "The sword!" she spat. "The Sword of Erinthia! Where is it?"

For the first time in weeks, Liam laughed.

Briar stepped back. "What's so funny? What's going on here?"

Liam walked over to an empty display case that was mounted on the treasure room's back wall. "This," he said, "is where the Sword of Erinthia goes."

"Well, why isn't it there?" Briar's face burned a bright red. The veins in her neck throbbed grotesquely.

"It was stolen," Liam said, unable to hold back a smile. "A few years ago."

"WHAT?!" Briar's shriek was so loud, the knights in the hall winced in pain from the sound reverberating inside their helmets. For several minutes, Briar stood huffing and panting, then she took a deep breath, brushed a wayward strand of hair from her face, and addressed Liam in a calm, reserved manner.

"Why was I unaware of this?"

"Well, it was kind of an embarrassing theft," Liam

said. The Sword of Erinthia was the centuries-old symbol of his family, an heirloom that was encrusted from hilt to tip in rare jewels. "We didn't exactly advertise the fact that it went missing."

"Who stole it?" Briar asked.

"Deeb Rauber, the Bandit King. You know, I actually had a chance to win it back from him last year. But it . . . didn't work out. Why do you want that sword so badly?"

"It's priceless."

"So is half the stuff in here," Liam said. "Including those eggs you so casually destroyed just now. Why do you really want the sword?"

"Same reason I wanted you," Briar said. "I want what I want. That sword is the most legendary treasure your stupid family owns, so I want that sword. And as always, I will get what I want."

"You plan on asking Rauber to turn it over to you?"

"I'm not naive," Briar said. She half smiled. "No, I'm going to have you take it back from him."

"You want me to steal the Sword of Erinthia from the Bandit King?"

"That's right, genius."

"Why me?"

"Because you've dealt with Rauber before. Plus, you're

familiar with the sword. And also because I just like making you do things for me."

"I'd love to win that sword back for my family," Liam said. "But I don't know if—"

"Fine," Briar snapped. "If you're going to turn into Mr. Wishy-Washy, I'll just put Ruffian on the job."

"No, I'll do it!" Liam exclaimed, struck with a sudden epiphany. He was beginning to understand why Briar had wanted to marry him to begin with: The Sword of Erinthia must somehow play a key role in her plot for global domination. Could that be what the cryptic *JJDG* referred to? As far as Liam knew, the sword had never gone by a name other than the Sword of Erinthia, but that didn't mean it didn't have a mysterious past he wasn't aware of. In any case, he was certain of one thing: He had to get his hands on that sword before Briar did. The fate of the world might depend on it. *Drat,* he thought. *Looks like I picked a bad week to stop believing in myself.*

"I'll go after the sword for you," Liam said, finally getting a bit of oomph back into his voice. "But only on one condition: Ella, Frederic, Duncan, and Gustav come with me."

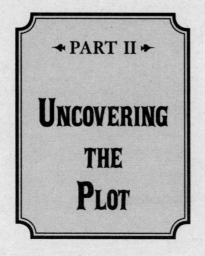

PART II

Uncovering the Plot

7

A HERO HAS NO IDEA
WHAT'S GOING ON

Knowledge is power. For instance,
don't you feel much more powerful now that you
have the knowledge that knowledge is power?
— THE HERO'S GUIDE TO BEING A HERO

Throughout history, the kings of Avondell would meet with their generals in the palace War Room in order to discuss combat strategies and hatch plots against their enemies. For this reason, you might not expect the War Room to be a very cheery place; but like most things in Avondell, it was really quite lovely. Springtime sun streamed through large picture windows, illuminating colorful murals that depicted the Avondellian army's many victory celebrations (showing the battles themselves was deemed too much of a downer). At the center of the chamber, under a shimmering crystal chandelier, was a large round table surrounded by twelve incredibly plush, high-backed chairs. Beneath it all was a plush red carpet that Briar's family servants kept impressively lint free. It was often said that no nation sent its soldiers to war with as much style and panache as Avondell.

While Frederic didn't care for the name War Room, he certainly appreciated the chamber's lively decor, which was a huge improvement over the prison cell he had been confined to ever since the wedding. He sat at the circular table in quiet trepidation, with Ella, Duncan, and Gustav beside him. Across from them were Liam and Briar.

Fig. 10 WAR ROOM

"Okay, this meeting may now officially begin," Briar said, banging a small golden gavel against the table. "First off, I don't care if this table is round; wherever I'm sitting is the head. Now that that's been established—go ahead, husband. You may speak."

Liam rolled his eyes. "Briar has asked me—"

"Ordered you," Briar corrected.

Liam shot her an icy stare, then turned back to his friends. "Briar wants me to go on a quest for her, and I . . ." He paused. Gustav was cracking his knuckles; Frederic was anxiously chewing his lower lip; and Duncan was sniffing the spaces between his fingers. *I've made a horrible mistake,* Liam thought.

Then he looked at Ella, who was listening intently. Her eyes met his and she nodded, urging him to continue.

"I need to ask the four of you to help me," Liam said.

"I hope it involves more unicorns," Duncan said. "I never even realized how much I *love* unicorns."

"You may remember that Deeb Rauber stole the Sword of Erinthia from my family," Liam said.

Duncan shook his head. "I don't."

"That's the sword with all the jewels on it," Frederic said helpfully.

"Ooh, sounds pretty," Duncan said. "But no, I don't recall this."

"The Bandit King tried to chop you to pieces with it," Frederic added.

"Hmm," said Duncan. "You'd think that would have stuck with me. But no."

Liam suddenly remembered how easy it was to lose track of a conversation with these guys. "It doesn't matter," he said. "The sword is a family heirloom; Rauber swiped it; the five of us are going to sneak into his castle and get it back."

"I'm not usually one for sneaking," Gustav said. "I'm more of a direct-attack kind of guy. But snatching this sword is bound to tick the little punk off, so I'm in."

"Well, I can't possibly say no," Duncan said. "Not after you've told me how pretty the sword is."

Frederic dabbed his brow with a handkerchief. "Oh, this is not a fun decision to make. I have absolutely no desire to face off against armed thugs again. But at the same time, I *really* don't want to spend another night on a prison cot with so many unidentifiable stains." He didn't realize he'd been drumming his fingers on the table until Ella put her hand over his to calm him. "Do we get to go home after we've gotten the sword?" he asked Briar.

"Ehh, why not? You'll all get full pardons," Briar replied. "But that's only *if* you get the sword. Which I wouldn't bet on. I've seen you people in action. Oh, man, I wish there were some way we could have captured a moving image of the wedding just so you fools could see how ridiculous you looked trying to play heroes."

"Listen up, Mount High-Hair," Gustav barked. "Say what you want about me, but lay off the rest of the team. I've been through a lot of stuff with these people. Nobody can tell me that Fancy Dancer and Lady Slick-Pants aren't heroes. Captain Gloom-Cape over there, too. And even Shrimp Charming has his moments."

Briar leaned back in her chair. "I admire your ability to insult your friends *while* you defend them. It's a rare talent."

"People!" Liam said forcefully. "Can we move on to planning this heist? It really shouldn't be too difficult. We've been to Rauber's castle before. We know exactly where he keeps his treasures. Gahh!"

Everybody yelped as Ruffian the Blue suddenly popped up from behind Briar's chair. "As I am receiving a consultant's fee for this mission, I feel it is my duty to correct some misconceptions," the bounty hunter droned.

"Don't sneak up on me like that," Briar scolded,

banging her gavel to underscore her displeasure.

"You *asked* me to be here," Ruffian grumbled indignantly.

"Yeah, I also figured you'd *walk through the door* like a normal person," Briar groused. "Now sit down."

"I don't like to sit," Ruffian replied.

"Excuse me, Ruffian," Ella interjected. "You always wear that cape, right? Because Frederic was insisting that villains never wear capes."

"I'm not a *villain*," Ruffian whined. "Bounty hunting is a legitimate profession. And anyway, I'm wearing a cowl."

"Aha!" said Frederic, sitting back and folding his arms in a very satisfied manner. "Thank you, Mr. Ruffian."

"I thought it was a cloak," Briar said.

"No. Cloaks are just long capes," Frederic said.

Briar rubbed the fabric of Ruffian's cowl between her thumb and forefinger. "Why aren't you wearing a cloak? I

Fig. 11
RUFFIAN, cowled

wanted a henchman draped in a mysterious cloak."

"How could the name of the garment possibly make a difference?" Ruffian asked.

"It sounds scarier," Briar said. "'Cowl' is the least terrifying word I've ever heard."

"Oh, I disagree," Duncan added. "It makes me think of cow-owls. And those are horrifying. *MOO-WHO! MOO-WHO!*"

"It doesn't matter. I'm not changing my outfit," Ruffian insisted. "I need my hood."

"Fine," Briar said. She banged her gavel against the table. "I hereby declare that capes with hoods are called cloaks."

"It's still a cowl," Frederic grumbled (few things could cause him to summon up his inner courage like improper word usage).

Briar slammed her gavel down again and glared at Frederic.

"Can we please get back to business?" Liam said. "Ruffian, you had some information?"

Ruffian sighed. "Deeb Rauber is not in the same castle anymore," Ruffian said. "Hasn't been for the better part of a year. He currently resides in a fortress at the foot of Mount Batwing. I believe you've been there before."

"The old witch's place?" Ella asked.

"Well, I suppose it *was* available," Duncan mused. "You know, since Old What's-Her-Name went *kccchggh!*" He let his tongue dangle out of his mouth, crossed his eyes, and fell sideways out of his seat.

"Who cares if the thieving brat has moved?" Gustav said. "Wherever he is, we'll go there and make short work of him."

"*Short* work," Frederic repeated with a smile. "Nice one, Gustav."

"Nice what?" Gustav asked.

Ruffian cleared his throat. "You cannot simply stroll into the home of a legitimate monarch and steal his possessions without having it considered an act of war."

"You're giving the kid too much credit," Liam said. "He calls himself the Bandit King, but he's not a *real* king."

"Yes, he is," Ruffian said flatly.

"No, really, he's not," Liam said.

"Yes, he is," Ruffian repeated.

"No, he's not," Frederic, Gustav, and Ella chimed in together.

Ruffian huffed. "Who at this table has been out and about in the real world for the past ten months, keeping up with current events?" He raised his hand.

Ella and the princes lowered their eyes.

"Nine months ago, Deeb Rauber founded his own kingdom," Ruffian said. "After the five of you vanquished that nameless old witch—"

"Um, actually, she did have a name," Frederic interjected.

"Pipe down, Professor Textbook," Gustav said. "Let's hear what the talking hood has to say."

"After his last run-in with you, Rauber rebuilt his army and marched his men into the area that was known as the Orphaned Wastes," Ruffian explained. "It was a no-man's-land, a barren stretch of gray earth that no kingdom ever felt the need to claim as its own. So Rauber claimed it. He renamed the area Rauberia and established himself as its monarch and sole authority."

"Can he do that?" Liam asked skeptically.

"I hate to say it, but based on the classes I've taken in interkingdom laws and regulations, it sounds plausible," Frederic said.

"Did you know about this?" Liam asked Briar.

"Of course I did; I'm a member of the ruling family of one of the most powerful kingdoms in the hemisphere," she said mockingly. "Oh, wait a minute—so are all of you. Losers."

"This doesn't really change our mission, though, does it?" Ella asked. "It just makes it a bit more complicated."

"That's right," Liam said. "First thing we'll need to do is have someone scout out Rauber's new digs. A lot of the witch's stronghold had crumbled by the time we left it, so I assume Rauber must have done some work on the place."

"He has erected an eighty-foot-high stone wall surrounding the entire castle," Ruffian explained. "Only a select few have seen what's beyond it."

"Ruffian, can you get in there, figure out where Rauber has the sword, and report back to us?" Liam asked.

"There's no way I could get farther than the gate," Ruffian said flatly. "It's common knowledge that I am in the employ of Princess Briar. And since you and she are married . . ."

"The whole world knows about our marriage, huh?" Liam asked.

"The bards have already circulated a song about the wedding," Ruffian said. "The League of Princes Fails Again.'"

"Seriously?" Gustav sputtered, slamming his hand on the table in frustration. "Every time we mess up, it has to become global news?"

Frederic flopped onto the table, burying his face in his arms.

Duncan didn't seem bothered by the idea that they'd once again been humiliated in song. "If I had my own kingdom," he said, "I would call it Pantsylvania."

"You *have* your own kingdom," Ella pointed out.

"Hey, you know what? I'm not letting this bother me," Gustav said, puffing up his chest. "Pretty soon, it's not gonna matter. Once we've stolen this sword from Bandit Boy, we'll finally have the bards singing about us as winners again."

"You really are clueless, aren't you?" Briar interjected. "No one will sing of your victory—no one can *know* about your victory. This is a *secret* mission."

Gustav kicked the table. "Never mind, I'm out," he grumbled.

"But, Gustav," Ella said. "You might still get the chance to punch someone."

"All right, I'm back in."

"We're all in on this," Liam said definitively. "We just need to get more information about Rauber's new place before we go storming in there."

"Wait!" Frederic said, jumping to his feet. "I know

who we can send to scout out the Bandit King's castle. And I'm going to feel very guilty if he's still where I think he is."

Smimf was indeed still standing—or rather weakly teetering—in the small grove of trees outside the Avondell Palace garden gates, watching the princes' horses. As Frederic and the others approached, the messenger snapped to attention.

"Sir, Your Highness, sir! The horses have done nothing interesting."

"Great job, Smimf," Frederic said. "I'm sorry we took so long."

"It was just a few days," Smimf said. He panted a bit, seeming very thirsty and overheated. "A job is a job, after all."

"Well, I don't know if this is the best time to ask," Frederic said, putting his arm around Smimf's shoulders, "but would you be interested in doing *another* job for us?"

8

THE VILLAIN REDECORATES

A warlord's home should inspire fear in all
who lay eyes on it. The walls should induce shivers;
the entryway should instill abject terror. Visions of the
welcome mat should haunt visitors in their nightmares.
—THE WARLORD'S PATH TO POWER:
AN ANCIENT TOME OF DARIAN WISDOM

It was eleven years earlier when a sweet and perfectly innocent nurse named Clara had the misfortune of delivering Prudence Rauber's baby.

"It's a boy," said the nurse. And then the infant proceeded to jab his toe into the poor woman's eye. As the nurse dropped the newborn into his mother's lap, Prudence looked at her son's wrinkled face and could have sworn he was laughing.

Six miserable years later, young Deeb locked his parents in

a cupboard and took off on his own to become a professional criminal. Two solid years of schoolhouse pillaging, mansion ransacking, and palace burglarizing followed. And by the time he was eight, Deeb Rauber was known worldwide as the Bandit King. He had an army of grown thugs at his disposal, and monarchs and peasants alike cowered at his name. Toward the end of his tenth year, he suffered a brief setback: The League of Princes ambushed him with a horde of trolls and decimated his army. But Deeb was resilient. He struck back a few days later and turned the League into laughingstocks by literally stealing their victory celebration out from under them. After that his notoriety peaked: Every cutthroat, footpad, and ne'er-do-well around lined up to join him. He was easily able to refill the ranks of his bandit army and went on a brazen crime spree across the Thirteen Kingdoms. He stole the giant bronze yeti sculpture from outside the royal palace of Eïsborg; he dug up the bones of the ancient kings of Carpagia and stripped them of their jewelry; he birdnapped every golden goose in the nation of Jangleheim. Only one month after publicly humiliating the League, Rauber was stronger, richer, and more powerful than ever.

But then, on his eleventh birthday, he decided he wanted more.

* * *

It was in the heat of early August (still ten months before Liam and Briar's wedding) that the Bandit King and his men celebrated Deeb Day.

"It's the big one-one," Rauber said as he lounged on his stolen throne in the treasure chamber of his dumpy little castle in Sturmhagen. He shoved a piece of red velvet cake into his mouth, sending a cascade of crumbs down the front of his tattered black vest. "I need to up my game."

"Let's steal more cake!" shouted one of the many bandits who were crammed into Rauber's Hall o' Loot for the celebration. Throughout the gray stone room, big, brutish men in black were rolling in loose coins, snacking on foot-long taffy strips, wrestling each other, and dipping chocolate-chip cookies into pints of foamy grog.

"Nah. Something different," Rauber said. He adjusted the edge of his crown, which had an annoying habit of sliding over his ears (as it was originally sized for the king of Hithershire), and sucked cream cheese frosting from his fingertips (the main reason he wore fingerless gloves).

"We ain't kidnapped nobody in a while," a buck-toothed bandit said before letting loose with an enormous belch.

"Ooh, what about snatchin' the hats off old ladies?"

another bandit asked. "That usually puts you in a good mood."

"Been there, done that," Rauber said. He sounded uncharacteristically somber, despite the fact that he was twirling a doughnut on his finger as he spoke. "No. I'm eleven now. I need to make sure I don't lose my spark with age. I need to do something big, something special. You know what I mean, Vero?"

"I fear, sir, that I do," replied a tall bandit who stood apart from the others, both literally and figuratively. It wasn't just that Vero didn't care to take part in the raucous carousing of his fellow bandits; he also carried himself in a way that was completely different from any of the other men. He dressed in black, as did all Rauber's men, but unlike the rest, Vero had style. His puffy-sleeved shirt and embroidered vest were the kinds of clothing you'd more commonly see on a nobleman than a thief. His pencil-thin mustache was impeccably trimmed,

Fig. 12
DEEB, bored

and his dark brown hair was tied back in a long, sleek ponytail. At his side was a slim, pointed rapier—a far more precise and graceful weapon than the thick broadswords favored by most bandits. And Vero knew how to use that blade; he was without doubt the most accomplished swordsman in Rauber's army and possibly one of the best in the world. The only thing he enjoyed more than dueling was relieving rich people of their money.

"I fear you are planning to pursue your vendetta against the League of Princes again," he said in a sharp Carpagian accent.

"And why is that a *fear*, Vero?" Rauber asked, eyeing his right-hand man with skepticism.

"This League of Princes is a distraction, sir. You have bested them already, ruined them. This is why I sought to join your forces to begin with. Why waste your time now going after men nobody cares about?"

"They're the ones that got away!" Rauber said, standing up on the seat of his throne. "Look, you're new, Vero, so you may not understand just how much I hate those fat-headed, snot-nosed princes." He flung his cake across the room, spattering several of his henchmen with it.

"I think I do, sir," Vero said. "You cannot even speak of them without losing control of your temper. This is part of the problem, no? These men, they will cause you to make mistakes. It is not worth the risk. It is, as we say in my country, *dangerous*."

"I don't lose control, Vero," Rauber said softly and clearly. He lifted his chin and dusted off his crumb-covered vest. "Not even when it comes to those sniveling, fart-monkey princes!" He let out an echoing scream of rage and kicked over a table of treats, which crashed down in a loud shattering of cups and dishes. The room fell into a sudden hush. Most of the bandits froze in place, silently praying that their boss was not about to have one of his famous tantrums. Several began to surreptitiously inch toward the exit.

"Of course you don't, sir," Vero said coolly.

Rauber plopped back down onto his throne and laughed. "I'm just joshing with you," he said. "You're honest with me, Vero. I like that. So tell me, what do you think I should do to really make my mark?"

Vero crouched down beside the throne and spoke to Rauber in a conspiratorial hush. "Well, sir," he said, "one of the many reasons you despise these princes is because you wanted to rule Sturmhagen, and the League—they got in your way."

"Yeah, them and an army of trolls," Rauber said in a near growl. "Stinking trolls."

"Yes, but that was *then*, and this is what we call in my country *now*."

"We call it *now* in this country too."

"The point I am making, sir, is this: You still want to rule your own kingdom, no? I say never mind Sturmhagen. There are other ways to become a true king, no? Other places to rule." Vero watched Rauber's expression carefully as the boy mulled over his advice. A wide grin spread across the Bandit King's face.

"You're absolutely right, Vero," Rauber said. "That's what I'm going to do! I'm going to become a real king. Of a real country. With a real flag and a real army and real laws and—I don't know—maybe a national bird or something. And the best part is, I don't have to conquer anybody to do it."

Vero returned the Bandit King's smile. "You are thinking of that no-man's-land, the Orphaned Wastes, are you not?"

"It's small, but it's totally free," Rauber said. "With that creepy old lady dead, the place is completely empty. Nobody wants it because it's ugly and nothing grows there, but I don't care about that. I just need a piece of land with real borders and I'm good to go: King Deeb!"

"This is a good plan, sir, no?"

"Darn tootin', Vero," Rauber said, bouncing in his seat. "This is going to change everything!"

"When shall we, as we say in my country, *do this thing*?"

Rauber looked askance at Vero. "You're from a *different* country, right?"

"That is correct, sir."

"Just wanted to make sure," Rauber said. "Anyway, we do this now! It's still my birthday—I'm going to celebrate by founding the sovereign nation of Rauberia!" He stood up and shouted to his men, "There are crates in the basement, boys! Pack everything up. We're moving!"

With about fifty tons of ill-gotten goods in tow, Deeb Rauber marched his army from his old castle in the pine forests of Sturmhagen, around the base of Mount Batwing, and into the Orphaned Wastes. He strode right into the old witch's abandoned fortress, planted his official Bandit King flag (which depicted a hunched, elderly king being kicked by a giant boot) on its parapets, and immediately sent messengers to all the nearby kingdoms announcing the founding of Rauberia.

The witch's castle was a wreck (its sky-high observatory tower had completely collapsed; broken broomsticks and half-smashed tarantulas were strewn about the corridors;

overturned cauldrons clogged the stairwells), so Rauber hired a skilled construction crew to clean the place up over the next few months—and make several structural improvements while they were at it, including an eighty-foot-tall Wall of Secrecy around the entire property. By late autumn (and still over six months before the wedding), the Bandit King had one of the most secure castles in the world. He thanked the builders by robbing them of their tools, stripping them down to their underwear, and leaving them to fend for themselves in the Nightkill Mountains.

Then Rauber set about the business of being a monarch. Noblemen and women from nearly every kingdom were invited to be guests of the unnamed king of the new nation of Rauberia. And you know how noblemen are: They can never resist a chance to rub elbows with a real monarch (it makes them feel important). Countesses, earls, duchesses, and barons lined up to spend a luxurious night in the newly dubbed Castle von Deeb. And while they were surprised to discover the identity of their host, any shock or suspicion fell by the wayside as the guests were flattered and pampered, and treated to lavish meals and accommodations. They all enjoyed their stays—until realizing upon leaving that their valuables had mysteriously gone missing. Even the queen of Svenlandia paid a visit—and headed back home wondering how she managed to misplace the spun-gold wig that had been sitting on her head when she'd arrived.

After pulling off his New King Swindle on rich folks far and wide, Rauber checked a map to see which kingdoms he hadn't hit yet. He spotted a land called Dar, way off to the east, barely visible along the rightmost edge of the map, and ordered that an invitation be sent to its king.

"It is not a king who rules Dar," Vero said, his words sounding more like a warning than an explanation. "Dar is run by a warlord."

"Neat," Rauber said. "Send the invitation."

"Are you sure you want to do this thing, sir?" Vero asked. "This Warlord of Dar, he is what we call in my country *not a nice man.*"

"I'm not a nice man either," Rauber said with a wink.

You are not a man at all, Vero thought, but was wise enough not to share this. "I am aware, sir," he said instead. "But the Warlord, he is reputed to be one of the cruelest rulers in the world. His whole country, this Dar, is noted for its violent nature. I have heard that in Dar, if you merely speak ill of the Warlord, you are sentenced to death. They will cut off your body."

"Cut off your head, you mean," Rauber said.

"No," Vero said. "Your head stays—they cut off the rest of you."

"I'm not sure how that's different."

"The point I am making is this," Vero continued. "These people from Dar, I do not think you want to get on their bad side."

Rauber laughed. "Wait till they get a load of *my* bad side." He turned around and wiggled his bottom at Vero. "Ha-ha!"

Rauber handed an invitation to a bandit named Gordo. "Take this to Dar," he told him.

"Sure thing, boss," Gordo replied. The bandit saluted before patting himself up and down, hoping to find a pocket somewhere on his clothing. Failing to locate one, he reached down to place the note in his shoe—and realized he was barefoot. Finally, he stuck the message between his teeth and left on the long journey to Dar.

And that was the last anybody ever heard from Gordo. (I hope you didn't grow too attached to him in that last paragraph.)

Rauber's message made it to the Warlord of Dar. But it was a very rare occasion when a messenger was allowed to leave the kingdom of Dar alive. Because Dar was an awful, awful place. Sandwiched as it was between a vast, foot-burning desert and a frostbite-inducing frozen tundra, Dar had just about the worst climate you could imagine. The very land itself seemed to hate the idea of living beings walking on it.

That's why the only things to survive in Dar were nightmarish creatures like ice wraiths, scorpiogres, giant sand snakes, and bone-moles—and really nasty people. Dar's entire culture was based on war and fighting. Even its name had a violent origin. Ages earlier, the first cartographer to attempt to draw a map of the region was killed before he could finish writing the name of the land. Historians believed Dar's true name may have been Darkhold Hollows. Or possibly Daredevil Barrens. Or perhaps even Darr, with two r's (though that would have been disappointing).

The Warlord to whom Deeb Rauber decided to send an invitation was considered to be one of Dar's most terrifying, brutal rulers ever. Lord Rundark stood six-foot-five, with a wrestler's physique that belied his fifty-odd years. He had a wild mane of black hair surrounding his face, which blended into a long, braided beard at his chin. His skin resembled a cracked desert landscape, and a ropy pink scar ran across his face from one ear to the other. The irises of his eyes were solid black.

Some people say Rundark was born out of a mad alchemist's attempt to distill the essence of pure evil. Others claim he emerged fully grown from an erupting volcano. Although it's also possible that he was the son of a used-cart salesman from Nebbish Village—they didn't keep very good records in Dar.

Whatever his origin, Rundark was not a man to be trifled with. He had risen to power in a bloody campaign of destruction that left a trail of broken bodies and demolished homes across the Darian countryside. When Rundark finally faced the previous warlord, he had no trouble at all taking the man's crown—with his head still in it.

As Lord Rundark read Deeb Rauber's invitation, he was amused.

"It is not often that some fool invites the forces of Dar into his home," the Warlord said. "We shall go. It is always fun to kill a novice king."

Fig. 13
Lord RUNDARK

* * *

With winter snows falling (and the wedding still five months away—don't worry, though, we're almost back in the present) the Warlord left Dar. With a small, handpicked contingent of bloodthirsty Darian soldiers, Rundark marched across the mountains of Carpagia and through the thick forests of Sturmhagen—stopping for pillage breaks every few miles or so—until he arrived in Rauberia, where he and Deeb met. Rundark wore bloodstained leather armor and a helmet made from the skull of a scorpiogre. Deeb sported an unnecessary eye patch and pants with holes in the knees. The two leaders talked. Rauber showed Rundark around his castle (and displayed his ability for yanking down his underlings' pants without them noticing). Then they shared a large, disgusting meal together (during which Rundark killed one of his captains for blinking too much). And a couple of interesting things happened.

Deeb Rauber decided not to rob Lord Rundark. It wasn't that he was afraid of the Warlord—he was *awestruck* by him. Rundark was not just the coolest world leader Deeb had ever met; he was the first adult Deeb had ever looked up to.

Even more interestingly, Lord Rundark decided not to kill Deeb Rauber. At least not yet. He was fascinated by the boy. Or more accurately, he was fascinated by the way this sloppy, obnoxious, immature eleven-year old managed to command the respect and devotion of an entire army. The bandits adored their king—and Rundark couldn't figure out why.

Rauber invited Rundark into a chamber that he identified as Scheme Central. The tall, powerful Darian glanced in disdain at the maps and blueprints that were covered in glops of jelly and smeared chocolate fingerprints—not to mention the half-dozen bandits lazing around the room, chewing noisily on caramels.

"Check it out," Rauber said, running to a torn-open sack of looted candy in the corner. "Can't make evil plots on an empty stomach. Am I right?" He offered a squishy brown cube to the Warlord. "Nougat?"

Lord Rundark stared at him in silence.

Rauber shrugged. "Whatever. More for me," he said, and tossed the nougat into his mouth. He threw a gum ball in, too, for added chewiness.

Rundark moved to the window and stared out at the dry, broken landscape before him. "This is a very nice country that you have chosen to take as your own," he said, his voice deep and hard-edged.

"You think so?" Rauber asked with his mouth full.

"It's pretty ugly out there."

"You've never been to Dar," Rundark replied. In reality, though, the scenery had nothing to do with Rauberia's appeal. It was the tiny kingdom's location that excited the Warlord. Rauberia was situated smack in the middle of the map, with *so many* wealthy kingdoms—Harmonia, Sylvaria, Sturmhagen, Avondell, and Erinthia, among them—just a day's march away.

"I am going to grant you an invaluable favor," Rundark said.

"Yeah, what's that?" Rauber asked.

"There is much potential in you, but your army is weak and undisciplined," Rundark said.

"No way, man," Rauber said. "I lay into my guys when they deserve it." He pulled the wad of wet gum from his mouth and shoved it into the nostril of a nearby bandit. "That's for not laughing at my awesome fart joke yesterday," he snarled at the man.

Rundark cleared his throat. "Nonetheless, my men and I will stay here in Rauberia. We will train your people in the ways of war. We will make a few . . . security adjustments to your fortress. And when we are done, my friend, *then* you will be a force feared worldwide."

"I'm already pretty feared," Rauber said, popping a

new piece of gum into his mouth. "But you might be right about my guys. They could use a few kicks in the rear. And I've only got two feet, so welcome aboard, Warlord."

Both Rauber and Rundark smiled, but for different reasons.

And then, on a late-June afternoon, three days after Liam and Briar's wedding (Yay! We're back!), two bandits standing guard outside the Wall of Secrecy were surprised to see a lone stranger running toward them across the wastes of Rauberia. They braced themselves for a fight. It wasn't often that anybody passed through these dead lands, let alone somebody on foot. And it was even more bizarre that this young man appeared to be wearing both a woolen winter hat and summery shorts.

"Excuse me, sirs," Smimf said. "I have a message for the king of Rauberia."

9

A Hero Makes It Up as He Goes Along

When writing down a plan, I suggest numbering the steps.
But just in case your plan falls into enemy hands, make sure
you number them in the wrong order.
— The Hero's Guide to Being a Hero

The four princes, along with Ella and Briar, sat at the round table in Avondell's War Room, waiting for a report from Smimf. Only one day had passed since the League of Princes sent the young messenger to Rauberia armed with a fake advertisement that would serve as his excuse for getting inside the castle gate ("SPECIAL DEAL FOR NEW MONARCHS! HALF-PRICE CROWNS! FREE ESTIMATES ON RESIZING!"), and already he had returned. He stood at attention before the group, loosened his scarf, and hiked up his shorts.

"What did you find out?" Liam asked.

"Well, I found out that the king is not interested in purchasing a new crown unless he can get at least *seventy-five* percent off," said Smimf.

"What did you learn *about the castle*?" Liam more specifically inquired.

"Oh, I saw everything, sir, Your Highness, sir," Smimf said. "I handed your pamphlet to the guards at the front gate; and while they were reading it, I zipped in past them and checked out every floor of the building."

"Nobody saw you?" Ella asked.

"Most people can't when I'm going my fastest, so I just never stopped running."

"Quit jibber-jabbing and make with the info," Gustav said impatiently.

"Right," said Smimf. "Well, first there's a wall—"

"I have a wall at home!" Duncan blurted. "Four, actually."

"Is this a good time to mention that I'm slightly afraid of heights?" Frederic threw in.

Liam stood up. "Okay, before we go any further,"

he began. "New rule: Do not interrupt Smimf. He's got crucial information, and we need to hear it. So, no talking until Smimf is done. Everybody got that?"

"But if it's a new rule," said Duncan, "shouldn't the lady with the cactus hair bang her little hammer?"

"He's right, you know," Briar said. "I'm the one who makes the rules here."

"Fine," Liam said, his eyes rolling. "Briar, would you please make it a rule?"

"Since you said *please* . . ." Briar pounded her gavel. "No one speaks until the weird kid is done."

"Thank you, sir, Your Highness, sir," Smimf said. "As I was saying: There's a wall—the Wall of Secrecy they call it. It's square: four sides and four corners. But I'm sure you all know what a square is." He chuckled uncomfortably.

"Anyway, it's real tall. And totally smooth, like my grandmother's ceramic leg." Smimf paused and swallowed. "Sorry, that was an unnecessary and possibly disturbing comparison. There's a reason I don't usually do this much talking. But anyway, the wall is pretty much unclimbable. Plus, there are guard towers at each of the four corners. So the only way in is through the main gate, same way I went.

"And once you're inside, you're totally in the open. There's a lot a distance between the gate and the castle itself—Castle von Deeb they call it. Oh, and the castle is surrounded by a moat—the Moat of a Thousand Fangs they call it. It's filled with bladejaw eels. But I got across when the bandits lowered the drawbridge; they were

Fig. 14
Wall of SECRECY

rolling in giant barrels of pudding. Or possibly poison. It's hard to read while I'm running that fast.

"Anyway, once I was inside I learned that the Sword of Erinthia is down on the dungeon level, locked in a vault—the Vault o' Fine Loot they call it. But here's the tricky part: The switch that opens the vault is up on the castle's roof. There's a strange man up there, a man covered with even more tattoos than my grandmother. And this man, it seems, sends a thirty-foot-long snake down into a hole— the Snake Hole they call it—to trigger the vault switch. The Snake Hole is very deep, and just wide enough for the snake to fit in. Granted, it's a pretty big snake, but even *I* couldn't squeeze into that hole. And I'm on the thin side. My grandmother used to call me Swizzlestick."

Smimf stood in silence for a minute while everyone simply stared at him. "Oh, I'm done," he finally said.

Everyone started talking at once until Liam hushed them. "One at a time, people," he shouted.

Gustav spoke loudly enough to make sure he was first to be heard. "A vault in the basement that can only be opened by a giant snake in a hole on the roof: Who thinks up something like that?"

"A ten-year-old boy, that's who," Ella said. "Remember that this is my cousin we're talking about. I knew Deeb when he was five. Even back then he'd create sadistic little traps to catch mice in—like a piece of cheese tied to a match so that when the mouse grabbed the cheese, it pulled the match across a flint stone, lit the wick of a tilted candle, and drizzled hot wax down onto the poor animal. I had to rescue so many trapped critters every time he visited."

"It doesn't matter that the castle's defenses sound crazy," Frederic said mournfully. "What matters is that they sound *impossible* to get past. I, for one, don't plan on doggie-paddling through a school of bladejaw eels."

"Oh, hey!" Duncan blurted out. "Wasn't there a Sir Bertram the Dainty story where he made a bladejaw eel soufflé?"

"Yes," Frederic said. "*The Battle for the Baron's Brunch*. Bladejaw eels are an incredibly rare delicacy. They're rare because the eels usually eat you before you can eat them."

"And they're only found in some very faraway country, right?" Duncan said, trying to remember the story. "Dorf?"

"Dar," Frederic corrected. "It's that horrible, scary land from all those terrifying old bedtime stories." *It's also where my mother died,* he thought.

"How in the world did Rauber get a bunch of eels that are only found in Dar?" Liam asked. "Smimf, are you sure that's what they were?"

"Almost positive, sir, Your Highness, sir," the messenger said. "When I was younger, my grandmother's favorite book to read to me was *101 Animals You Should Be Glad Only Live in Dar*."

"As I was saying," Frederic sighed, "this is an impossible mission."

"Unless . . . ," Ella said hopefully. "Smimf, can we borrow those boots of yours?"

"I'm sorry, sir, Your Highness, sir. I would gladly lend them to you if I were able to get them off. But I can't. They're magically bound to my feet. There's a curse on them, I think. At least that's what my grandmother said before that torch-wielding mob chased her out of town."

"Well," Duncan started, "maybe Smimf can just go back in there himself and—"

"Don't even think about it," Briar interjected. "I can't trust the retrieval of a priceless artifact to a mere messenger. Besides, there's no way a *true hero* like my Liam would allow an untrained teenager to risk his life like that."

"No, of course not," Liam said quietly.

"Um, Briar?" Frederic asked. "I don't suppose there's any other legendary treasure you might want us to steal for you instead? Perhaps something in a more convenient location?"

Briar sighed. "I knew working with you guys would be a waste of my time. I'll send a request to that team of ninjas from Kom-Pai."

"No!" Liam stood up. He alone knew they had no choice—they *had* to be the ones to recover the sword. But with Briar constantly hovering around, he couldn't exactly share that point with the others. "People, you're thinking about this all wrong. It's not impossible. Sure, there are a few obstacles, but we can get past them."

"Just tell us your plan, Liam," Duncan said. "You're our super-planner."

Everyone looked eagerly to Liam.

"All right," Liam said. He crossed his arms. "The plan. Yes. I will tell you the plan now." He looked off into the corner of the room and nodded to himself several times as if he were in the middle of some deep mental calculation. In reality, his mind was a blank.

Have you ever been so worried about something that it got stuck in your head and prevented you from thinking of pretty much anything else? Perhaps you're dreading the thought of eating an olive loaf sandwich your mother packed you for lunch, and when the teacher asks you for the square root of nine, the only answer you can come up with is *Olive loaf*. What's the longest river in the world? *Olive loaf*. How does the water cycle work? *Olive loaf*. That's how Liam was feeling at that moment in the War Room, only he wasn't thinking about olive loaf.

Each time Liam thought about how they could steal the Sword of Erinthia, his brain responded with *Hire actors to pretend they're criminals*.

No! he screamed at himself mentally. *Stop and focus, Liam. Get Cremins and Knoblock out of your head. They have nothing to do with this mission. You may be working through a little confidence crisis right now, but you can't let anybody else see that. Especially Briar. Because if she doesn't believe you can get the sword for her, she'll recruit somebody else to do it.*

"Hey, hubby," Briar said. "The rest of us can't hear your inner monologue, you know. You might want to use those vocal cords of yours."

"Huh?" Liam said. His team needed a plan, and he couldn't give them one. He was going to have to fake it. "Sorry, everyone, here we go. Let's start with that Wall of Secrecy. According to Smimf's report, going over the wall would be . . . difficult."

Pause.

"Soooooooooooo . . ." Liam drew out the word, praying one of his companions would jump in.

"So we'll have to go *under* it!" Ella said enthusiastically.

"Yes! Exactly!" Liam shouted, pumping his fist the way he did when he was six and had won his first Cross-Duchy Fencing Championship. "We need a tunnel. Thank you, Ella."

"Ooh! Ooh! Dwarfs are expert diggers," Duncan said, bouncing in his seat. "And Frank will do *anything* for me.

He and I are like *this*." He attempted to cross his fingers but couldn't quite figure out how to do it.

"That's just what I was about to say," Liam added. *Dwarfs digging tunnels—that's actually good,* he thought. *At least I think it is. Would I even know a good plan if I heard one? At least it doesn't involve actors pretending to be criminals.*

"And if I recall correctly," Liam added, "the dwarfs work fast, too."

"Oh, yes," Duncan agreed. "One time a gopher stole my pants, and the dwarfs tunneled after him in, like, ten minutes."

"Dwarfs are not invisible, though," Frederic said. "What about Rauber's lookout towers?"

"We just need a distraction," Ella said.

"Distraction, right," Liam said. "Something that will draw the attention of the guards from all four watchtowers." *Like actors pretending to be villains,* he heard in his mind. He ignored it.

Smimf timidly raised his hand. "Um, if I might interject, sir, Your Highness, sir. There was a moment of panic while I was at the castle. Someone shouted, 'Troll! Troll!' And every bandit in sight ran to check. Turned out it was just a tumbleweed, but still, the bandits were in quite a dither about it."

"Perfect!" Duncan shouted with excitement. "I know where we can get a tumbleweed!"

"I think what we actually need is a troll," Ella said, patting Duncan on the shoulder.

"Of course that's what we need," Liam said. "It makes sense that Rauber would hate trolls after he got trampled by about fifty of them last summer. An experience like that is bound to leave an impression."

Frederic chuckled.

"This is no laughing matter, Frederic," Liam said, stone-faced.

Frederic's grin vanished. "Sorry—*trampled* by trolls; leave an *impression*—I assumed you were joking," he said. "You actually plan to use a troll?"

Liam paused. *Hire an actor,* his brain told him. "No," he said aloud, rather angrily. When people looked at him strangely, he quickly corrected himself. "I mean, *yes*. If Rauber's men know he's afraid of trolls, we need to use a troll to get their attention."

"Leave that bit to me," Gustav said. "I can get us a troll, no problem."

"Great," Liam said.

Frederic eyed him skeptically. They'd befriended trolls before, but only because they were desperate. Trolls were violently unpredictable creatures—not the types of allies Liam typically hinged a plan around. "And once we're past the wall?" Frederic asked. "How do we cross the moat?"

Duncan's hand shot up in the air again. "I know! I know! A boat!"

"Duncan," Frederic said. "Even if the dwarfs dig us a tunnel under the wall, it's not like we can just squeeze a boat through with us."

"Why not?" Liam said. "We don't need a *big* boat. Sometimes the simplest solution is best."

"And once we're across the moat, we can scale to the roof of the castle with some of Ruffian's grappling hooks!" Ella added, slamming her fists against table.

Briar banged her gavel. "Hey, only *I* get to pound on things for emphasis."

"Okay, people," Liam said. He was slightly more at ease, his shoulders no longer at stiff right angles. "So at this point in the plan, we've made it to the top of Rauber's castle. Next we need to trigger the switch to open the vault, but none of us can fit down the Snake Hole to reach it. Ella, I bet you can guess how we solve that little problem."

"Um, let me think. . . ."

"Come on, Ella," Liam urged, counting on her to come up with an idea. "There must be some . . . tiny idea nagging at the back of your mind, right? Even an itty-bitty inkling of a thought . . ."

"You're hinting at that gnome I met last summer, aren't you?" Ella asked in a burst of enlightenment. "The one I rescued from those imps? He said if I ever needed help for anything, I should call on him."

"You're perfect!" Liam exclaimed. "I mean, you're perfect*ly correct*." He hoped he wasn't blushing too noticeably. "Your gnome friend will easily fit down the Snake Hole."

"*If* he agrees to do it," Frederic added sharply. "You realize there are a whole lot of assumptions in this plan, right? Have you considered the many ways it could go wrong?" *Or are you just showing off for Ella?* he thought.

Liam clenched his jaw. He locked eyes with Frederic and said, "The plan will work. Stop questioning it."

"But what about the fact that we'll be on *the roof* when the vault is several stories *belowground*?" Frederic asked.

"I will be down on the dungeon level with the vault, waiting for it to open," Liam answered in a semigrowl.

"And how in the world do you expect to get into the Bandit King's dungeon?" Frederic asked.

"Hire someone to pretend he's a criminal!" Liam slapped his hand over his mouth, but it was too late—the words had already escaped his lips. *That's it,* he thought. *Now they're all going to know that I've lost it.*

But instead, he heard nothing but wild enthusiasm.

"Liam, you're brilliant!" Ella exclaimed. "We'll hire an inside man—someone who's working for us but whom Rauber *believes* is on his side."

"That's right," Liam said with a weak smile. He'd just volunteered to be captured by his archenemy. And it was all because Frederic *had* to question everything; he couldn't just stand by and nod like a good number two. Liam took a deep breath. "The inside man can pretend to deliver me to the Bandit King for a reward," he said. "And then he'll free me once the vault is open."

"If anyone can pull that off, I know you can," Ella said.

And the way she stared at Liam was just a bit too moony-eyed for Frederic to take. "I'm going in the dungeon, too!" he blurted.

All heads turned to him. Frederic already regretted his outburst but was too embarrassed to take it back. "We can't leave that crucial step to just one person," he said. "There should be at least two of us in the dungeon. And . . . I volunteer."

"I suppose backup is a good idea," Liam said. "But maybe it should be Gustav."

"Nah," Gustav said. "I really want to fight that snake."

"A minute ago you asked me for my trust, Liam. Don't I deserve the same from you?" Frederic asked. "I risked my life for you, trying to save you from marrying Briar."

"And that worked out really well, didn't it?" Liam muttered.

"Ahem! I'm *in the room*," Briar said.

"Fine," Liam said grudgingly. "But, Frederic, you have to be ready to hold your own in there. I can't babysit you."

"I haven't needed a babysitter since I was sixteen," Frederic said defiantly.

"You don't have to do this, Frederic," Ella said, laying her hand on his arm.

"I know," Frederic sighed. "But I will."

"I just hope you guys find an inside man you can trust," Ella said.

"Oh, don't worry. We'll probably just go to the Stumpy Boarhound and interview random thugs and hoodlums for the job," Frederic said sarcastically.

Liam's eyes lit up. "Yes! That's what we'll do," he said. "The League has fans at that tavern. We'll be sure to find an eager accomplice."

"But wait," Frederic sputtered. "I was only . . ."

"What, Frederic?" Liam asked. "You were only *what*?"

"It's just that, well, the Stumpy Boarhound is in Flargstagg," Frederic said. "Is that really the safest town to visit right now? With the Gray Phantom terrorizing the place?"

"Frederic, the only reason you've even heard of the Gray Phantom is because of those recent bard songs," Liam said. "And you know how accurate the bards are. The Phantom's probably not as bad as they make him sound. He might not even exist. It's not a concern. The only remaining question is: When do we attack?"

"I know!" a voice called out. Everybody turned to see a curly-haired girl in a fraying gown climb in through the window.

"Lila!" Liam shouted. "What in the world are you doing here?"

"Spying," she said. "Do you have any idea how boring it is at home?"

"That's a second-story window," Liam went on. "How did you—?"

Briar stood, rushed over to the window, leaned out, and hollered, "A little girl just broke into my War Room! Anybody who can hear me right now is fired! Banish yourselves!" (Eight Avondellian soldiers dropped their weapons, lowered their heads, and began a long, slow

163

shuffle out of the kingdom.)

"Liam, look at this!" Lila shoved a scroll of paper into his hand. "It's a schedule. I snagged it out of one of the circus wagons after the wedding."

"The Flimsham Brothers are going to be performing for the king of Rauberia at four o'clock on the day of the summer solstice," Liam said as he scanned the paper.

"*That* is when you should stage the heist," Lila said excitedly. "During the circus. Rauber and most of his men will probably be watching the show, so there'll be a lot fewer bandits wandering around the castle."

"My sister is right," Liam said. "We attack during the circus." He turned back to Lila. "Now go home."

"But—" Lila began to object.

"Go home," he repeated.

Lila hopped back out the window and slid down a rain gutter to the ground below.

"Briar, what are you doing?" Liam asked. His wife was running her finger down the pages of a small datebook.

"Checking the calendar," she said. "We've got a big royal ball coming up, two days before the solstice. I would have liked to have had the sword *for* the ball, but, oh well . . . Okay. I approve of this circus idea."

"Ugh, the Flimshams again," Frederic muttered.

"Maybe it's a good thing I'll be locked away in Rauber's dungeon at the time."

"So, the solstice, huh? That means we have about six days to prepare, right?" Ella asked.

"Six days!" Gustav wailed. "I don't want to wait that long before I get to fight somebody!"

"Six days will barely give us enough time to recruit the allies we need for this mission, let alone train for it," Liam said. He took a moment to look each of his teammates in the eye. "But we have a solid plan. And we've dealt with Rauber's men before; they're not very formidable. He may have the numbers, but we have the heart—"

He was interrupted by the pounding of Briar's gavel. "No cheesy pep talks," she ordered.

Gustav leaned over to Frederic and whispered, "First chance I get, I'm going to grab that little hammer of hers and shove—"

Briar slammed the gavel even harder. "No whispering!"

Frederic massaged his temples. "This is going to be a long week."

"Briar, I'd like for us to get started first thing in the morning," Liam said. "And I think it's best if my teammates are able to get a good night's sleep beforehand. Would you agree to let them stay—"

"Yeah, yeah, I get it," Briar said. "I'll have the servants make up guest rooms for all of you. Servants!" She paused, waiting for a footman to appear at the door, but no one came. "Oh, that's right. I just banished them. Be right back." Grumbling, she got up and stepped out into the hallway.

"Oh, thank goodness we get real beds tonight," Frederic said. "I swear, some of the stains on that cot *moved*."

The moment Briar was out of earshot, Liam interrupted Frederic. "It's not just about the sword," he said quickly. "She's plotting to taking over the world."

"What?" the others all gasped.

"When were you planning on sharing this little detail?" Frederic asked.

"I'm *trying* to tell you now," Liam snipped. "If you'd let me speak."

"Guys!" Ella hissed. "She'll be back any second. Liam, talk."

"I got a glimpse at her diary," Liam said. "It includes schemes to dethrone every ruling family in the Thirteen Kingdoms. If she were to pull it off, she'd create a power vacuum that she could then step into."

"How could one bony little woman do all that?" Gustav asked.

"She's got '*JJDG*' written all over her journal," Liam said. "Does anyone know what that could stand for?"

"Jimmy John Digglesford Garbenflarben!" Duncan said.

"Who's that?" Liam asked hopefully.

"I don't know," Duncan said. "But if he exists, his initials would be J.J.D.G. We should check him out."

"Look, everybody; somehow Briar's plan all hinges around the Sword of Erinthia," Liam said. "The sword must hold some sort of secret."

"Maybe it's magic," Ella said.

"Could the sword be an actual key of some kind?" Frederic asked. "I remember a Sir Bertram the Dainty story about a hidden chamber that could only be opened with an ancient butter knife."

"I don't care what the sword does," Gustav said happily. "This is fantastic no matter what!"

"Why?" Frederic asked.

"Because we're *not* really on some secret mission nobody can ever know about," Gustav said. "We're out to stop a crazy tyrant lady. And *that* will be big news! You can't say this isn't gonna help us in the public image department."

"I think I hear my book sales skyrocketing," Duncan singsonged. "Nope, sorry, it was just Briar coming back."

They spun around to face the doorway, in which stood Briar, flanked by six new guardsmen. "What are you chatting about?" she asked. "Planning on double-crossing me?"

"Relax, Briar, we were just talking," Liam said. "It's not unusual for *friends* to talk sometimes. Not that you'd understand such things."

"Ouch," Briar said drily. "How about a little gratitude for the woman who just hooked you up with luxury suites at Avondell Palace? And to think they called you *charming*."

"Briar, we're all very grateful for the room upgrades," Frederic said. "Please forgive—"

"But none of us believes for a second that you're doing this out of the goodness of your heart," Liam butted in.

Briar smiled and waved him off playfully. "Oh, you're just saying that because I kidnapped you and threatened to execute your friends. Come on, people. Bygones are bygones, right? We're all working together now. And we have hours yet before sundown. Who's up for croquet?"

Duncan began to raise his hand, but Liam pushed it back down.

"So be it," Briar said, her demeanor returning to its usual iciness. "Guards! Take our guests to their far-too-posh rooms and lock them in until morning."

As Ella and the princes were escorted to five separate rooms, Frederic called out, "What now?"

Liam shouted the only reply he could think of: "We wait until morning. Then we go look for dwarfs, gnomes, and trolls!"

10

A HERO TAKES
NO FOR AN ANSWER

*I cannot overstate the importance of good allies. But I
will try: Good allies are more important than breathing.*
—THE HERO'S GUIDE TO BEING A HERO

THE TEAM

1. Liam ✓
2. Frederic ✓
3. Gustav ✓
4. Duncan ✓
5. Ella ✓

6. Dwarfs (for digging)
7. Troll (for distraction)
8. Gnome (for hole)
9. Inside Man (?)

"**N**o," Frank said without breaking his stride.

"But Frank, it's *me*," Duncan said, jogging through
his own backyard, trying to outpace the disgruntled dwarf.

"I'm your hero, your prince!"

"I can think of better words to describe you," Frank groused.

"Look, Mr. Frank," Frederic said, stepping into the dwarf's path to stop him. "We're here on a matter of utmost urgency. I had hoped that, in order to help us save the world, we could count on the courage and honor of the dwarves."

"*Dwarves,*" Frank barked out of habit. He was so used to correcting everybody's pronunciation of the word that it took him a second to realize it had not been necessary in this case. He eyed Frederic with a mix of skepticism and awe. "Hey, you said it right."

"Of course I did," Frederic replied. "I know how important proper grammar is to you and your people."

"All right, fine," Frank said. "You've got

Fig. 15
FRANK, unamused

thirty seconds. Convince me why I should do this for you."

Frederic was about to follow up with a rousing speech, but before he could utter another word, the back door of Duncan's house flew open and Snow White rushed out. She was wearing a garment of her own design— an overalls-sundress hybrid—accessorized with a headdress woven from marsh reeds. "Dunky!" She ran to her husband, hugged him, then pushed him away and waved her finger in his face. Then she pulled him to her and hugged him again. Then shoved him away, glared, and frowned at him. "Do you know how upset I am with you?"

"Well, I didn't at first," he answered. "But then I did. And then I didn't. And now I do again. But why? Did I do something wrong?"

"You vanished without a word!" Snow exclaimed, her wide eyes glaring. "You left me alone. With your family. For *days*. It was only yesterday that I finally convinced them you weren't in the outhouse all this time."

"But—But—" Duncan stammered.

Snow looked sternly at Frederic. "I should have known the Princes Charming were behind Duncan's disappearance," she said. "It was only a matter of time before he ran off on another of your crazy quests. I just thought somebody would have had the decency to *tell* me about it."

"But I did! Or, I mean, Frank did," Duncan said. "The quickety boy with the boots came for me. And I had to go stop Liam from marrying the shrill lady. Only I got arrested instead. And now we have to steal a pretty sword from the Bandit King. Frank was supposed to tell you everything. He promised."

Snow spun to face down Frank, who was trying to sneak around the corner of the house. The dwarf looked up at her sheepishly.

"Frank!" Snow said. The one word had the weight of an entire angry tirade.

"It's possible I may have said something to make Duncan believe that maybe I was going to tell you about his little outing," the dwarf mumbled.

At that moment, if beams of flame had shot forth from Snow White's eyes and flash-fried Frank, nobody would have been surprised.

"Um, Snow? Ms. White?" Frederic asked. "Duncan is in the middle of a very important mission, and we desperately need the dwarves to dig a tunnel for us. I'm wondering if you might speak to them on our behalf?"

"I believe Duncan and Frank each have a lesson to

learn," Snow said, thrusting her chin up in the air. "So I'm going to teach them." She marched back inside.

"What did she mean by that?" Frederic asked uneasily.

Both Duncan and Frank shrugged.

A few minutes later, Snow stepped back out, dragging two large baskets filled with all sorts of random odds and ends (a sewing kit, drumsticks, a wheel of cheese, a teapot, a marble paperweight in the shape of a chipmunk, about two hundred loose buttons, dominoes . . .). "Please put these in the wagon for me," she said.

"Why?" Duncan asked as he obediently carried one of the baskets to Snow's covered wagon, which was parked by the side of the house.

"I'm coming with you, silly," Snow said.

"That's crazy talk," Frank said immediately. "But if you insist on going, you can bet we'll be following right behind."

Frederic breathed a sigh of relief—prematurely.

Snow raised her right hand, putting the left over her heart. "I thought you dwarfs were my best friends, but you've betrayed my trust. It will take a lot to earn that trust back. I hereby vow that any dwarfs I see while I'm away will be banished from Sylvaria forever."

Frank growled in frustration. Snow White did not

make vows lightly. The last time she took an oath like that, she promised to never again overcook a brownie—and true to her word, every brownie she served after that was a drippy lump of raw dough. Frank backed down and walked off glumly.

"You know, Ms. White," Frederic said. "This mission could be quite dangerous. I'm not even sure why *I'm* on it."

"There's no talking me out of this," Snow said. She handed him another basket. "Here. I've just got nineteen more of these to grab and then we can go." She went back inside.

"On the bright side, I get to spend more time with my wife," Duncan said with a smile.

"Liam's not going to be happy about this," Frederic said queasily.

"I expect not," Duncan replied matter-of-factly.

"Do you think maybe she'll be able to help us figure out the secret of the sword?" Frederic asked, trying to be optimistic. "Maybe crack the *JJDG* code?"

"Snow? Pfft!" Duncan laughed. "She can't even find her shoes in the morning. She just makes a new pair every day."

Snow poked her head out of a window and shouted, "By the way, do either of you know how to drive a wagon?"

* * *

"Stuuuuuurm-hayyyyyyy-gennnnnnn!" Gustav shouted his battle cry as he spurred his horse and charged directly into a mob of growling, thrashing trolls. He leapt from his saddle only to be caught in midair by a large, one-horned troll that slammed him to the ground.

About a hundred yards behind, Liam winced. "I knew this was a bad idea." He drew his sword and galloped into the fray.

"Run, Gustav!" Liam yelled as he whipped his sword toward Mr. Troll. The big creature leaned back, dodging the blow but losing a few hunks of swamp-colored hair in the process. As the green fuzz floated to the ground, Gustav grabbed Liam's arm.

"What the heck are you doing?" Gustav snapped.

"Uh, rescuing you?" Liam said, right before Mr. Troll socked him in the face. The Erinthian prince flew through the air, landed in a heap of cape, and was immediately piled on by a dozen roaring trolls.

A short time later, Liam sat on a jagged tree stump (or troll chair) trying to soothe his swollen cheek with an herbal compress (aka, a handful of mud and pine needles).

"I'm sorry, Mr. Troll," he said with some difficulty. "I didn't realize you were just conducting a class." He turned to Gustav and added, "Why does it feel like we spend half of our adventures apologizing?"

"Speak for yourself. I don't apologize for anything," said Gustav. He punched Liam in the shoulder. "See, I'm not sorry for that."

"It okay, Squirmy Man," Mr. Troll said to Liam. "Any friend of Angry Man is friend of Troll. So, to what do Troll owe pleasure of this visit?" He leaned back on his stump and took a bite out of a pinecone.

"We hoped to offer you some employment," Liam said. "My team and I are about to embark on a very important, though possibly quite dangerous, quest. In order for us to succeed, there will be certain—"

"Squirmy Man talk too much," Mr. Troll said. "Angry Man explain."

"You wanna break into Bandit Boy's castle with us?" Gustav asked.

Mr. Troll stood up. "Troll just need get Troll's things." He looked around, picked up another pinecone, and said, "Troll ready. Let's go."

"It's got to be around here somewhere," Ella said, crawling on her hands and knees, pushing fern fronds out of her way to examine every large rock she could uncover.

"You've gotten us lost, haven't you?" Briar asked, sounding strangely delighted by the question. She stood several yards away, leaning against a tree.

Ella glared over her shoulder at her. "I am not lost. The gnome's house is definitely around here somewhere. The search might go faster if you help, you know."

"And ruin this dress? I don't think so." Briar was clad in one of her "travel gowns," meaning it had slightly fewer diamonds sewn onto its cuffs than usual.

"Why did you insist on coming with me if you're not going to do anything?" Ella asked.

"Everybody else partnered up; why shouldn't we? Besides, I thought it would be fun for us to have some Ladies Alone Time. So what's up with you and Frederic?"

"What?" Ella's palm slipped on a mossy stone, and her face landed in the dirt. She quickly picked herself up and brushed soil from her eyebrows. "We're engaged. What of it?"

"Oh, I don't know. You and him? I just don't see it."

"Well, no one asked you. And I suggest you keep your opinions—"

"I hate to interrupt a good rant, sweetie, but I think you just found something." Briar pointed to the rock that Ella had slipped on. With the moss out of the way, a miniature door was visible. Above it hung a tiny sign that read G. GNOME.

Ella set aside her anger and knocked on the little door, which opened a second later to reveal a wee, bearded man in a little pointed cap.

"Ella!" the gnome cried out cheerily. "It's so great to see you! I love visitors!"

"It's great to see you, too. . . . " Ella realized she had no memory of the gnome's name. " . . . pal."

"Oh, Ella," Briar said with feigned sweetness. "Why don't you introduce me to your friend?"

"I love introductions!" the gnome trumpeted.

Ella shot Briar a dirty look, then smiled at the gnome. "Um, Briar Rose, this is . . . G . . . Gee, it's just so fantastic to see you again, friend! Who cares about these formalities, right?"

"Sure, that's fine!" the gnome giggled. "I mean, I love formalities . . . but that's okay! I love being casual, too!"

"Great!" Ella shouted, trying to match the gnome's level of enthusiasm. (Not all gnomes were as sunny and agreeable as this one—like Ted, the gnome who got migraines—but in general, gnomes jumped at any chance to be helpful.)

"Well, buddy," Ella said. "Remember when you said I

could call on you if I ever needed a favor?"

"Absolutely! Whatcha got? I love doing favors for people!"

"Well, an important, priceless treasure was stolen from us," Ella said. "And to get it back, we need the help of someone who can fit into a very small, tight tunnel."

"Boy, did you come to the right gnome! I love tunnels! I'll put a snack together and then we can head off for some treasure snatchin'! I love treasures!" Before the gnome stepped back into his rock house, though, he stopped and turned back to Ella, suddenly serious. "There aren't going to be monsters, are there? I *don't* love monsters."

"Monsters?" Ella echoed. "No, there shouldn't be."

"Fantastic!" The gnome stepped inside his home.

"Wow," Briar said slyly. "I didn't take you for such an easy liar."

"I didn't lie," Ella said as she dusted away a few remaining strands of moss that were sullying the gnome's entryway.

"No monsters?" Briar said. "I seem to recall that the tunnel we're sending this tidbit into is called the *Snake* Hole."

"Snakes aren't monsters; they're animals."

"Even the giant ones?"

"Many snakes are naturally large."

Briar grinned. "I think I underestimated you."

The gnome reappeared with a picnic basket. "All right!" he said. "Let's go on our monster-free adventure!"

Frederic, Duncan, and Snow were the first group to arrive at the team's designated meeting spot: an empty tower that was littered with snapped mandolin strings and smelled oddly of rancid bacon. As the sun went down, Duncan lit a fire—unintentionally. But once the shrub was already ablaze, he figured they might as well roast the mini-sausages Snow had packed.

Fig. 16
Sausage ROASTING

"So Sleeping Beauty is going to take over the world unless we find this sword of yours, huh?" Snow asked. She took a wiener-on-a-stick and waved it rapidly over the flames as if she were trying to swat a bug with it.

"That's what Liam says," Frederic replied. "I sure hope he's right, or we're doing all of this for nothing. Or . . . No, I hope he's wrong, because that would mean there's really nothing to worry about. Except we'd still be putting our lives at risk. Oh, I don't know what I think."

"The important thing is that we stop the wedding," Duncan said.

"That was four days ago," Frederic said. "The important thing *now* is that we figure out the secret of the Sword of Erinthia. The abbreviation *JJDG* doesn't mean anything to you, does it?"

"My favorite sandwich!" Snow said. "Jelly, jelly, dragonfruit, and ginger."

"You put jelly on twice?" Frederic asked.

"I have to," Snow replied. "I hate the taste of dragonfruit."

"Well, I don't think that's it but . . ." Frederic stopped when he heard a rustling in the bushes. "Shhh! Here's Briar now."

"Oh, she doesn't look so horrible," Snow said loudly as

she stood to see the newcomers.

"Um, that's Ella," Frederic said, lowering his head.

Briar stepped out from behind Ella, scowling. "And who is this?" she asked bitterly.

"This is Snow White!" Duncan announced. He offered Briar a stick: "Weenie?"

"Why is she here?" Briar asked.

"I'm teaching Duncan a lesson," Snow said, and went back to swinging her sausage through the flames.

Ella leaned over and whispered to Frederic, "The dwarfs?"

Frederic shook his head.

"That's unfortunate," Ella said. "But at least we got the gnome." The gnome, who had been clinging to Ella's back, jumped down and waved.

"Hello, strangers!" he cried. "This is already so wonderful! I love fire!"

"Ella? Frederic?" Liam called out as he, Gustav, and Mr. Troll stepped from the trees. The troll burped out a small cloud of dandelion fluff.

"Monster!" the gnome screamed. He scrambled away with far more speed than his short legs should have allowed, tearing through the underbrush and leaving a trail of floating leaves in his wake.

"Wait!" Ella shouted. "Come back . . . *you*!" But the gnome's shrieks had already vanished into the distant woods.

"What was that?" Liam asked.

"That was our way down the Snake Hole," Ella said.

"He gone?" asked Mr. Troll. "That shame. Troll love gnomes."

It was a new moon and too dark to travel, so most of the team members retired for the night. Briar was resting comfortably amid a dozen down pillows inside the robin's-egg-blue tent that she made Liam set up for her. Duncan and Snow were curled together on a blanket, while Frederic was wrapped in a blanket of his own—enviously eyeing Briar's tent—and Gustav sprawled flat on the dirt. Mr. Troll, nestled into a pile of thistles, snored nearby. Liam, however, was pacing around the still-smoldering fire, wringing his cape.

"Can't sleep?" Ella asked as she swept up loose ashes with a small broom she had just constructed out of twigs and grass. "Me neither. I'm too keyed up. I wish we could just do this thing tomorrow."

"I'm in no rush," he answered. "There's a ticking clock here. The circus is hitting Rauber's castle in five days. How are we going to find replacements for the allies we failed to recruit today?"

Frederic tossed his blanket aside and crept over to them. "Plus we need to figure out why You-Know-Who wants the you-know-what."

"Shhhh!" Liam warned. "She might not be asleep."

"Sorry, sorry," Frederic whispered. "But we should be focused on solving that mystery, right?"

"Knowing what the sword does isn't going to matter much if we can't reach it," Liam said. "So filling in the holes in our plan has to take top priority."

"Actually," Frederic said, sitting on a tree stump, "I've been thinking about another person we might want to have on the team."

"For the tunneling part or the Snake Hole part?" Liam asked.

"Well, neither, but—"

"Then no, Frederic," Liam said, cutting him off. "This plan is too complicated as it is; we can't start adding new elements."

"Don't you even want to hear who I'm talking about?"

"Unless that person is a speedy digger or a skinny spelunker, it doesn't matter."

"Liam, you're not being— *Gahh!*"

Frederic yelped and leapt into Ella's arms as, without warning, a person fell from the branches of the tree he was standing under.

"Crud," grumbled the figure on the ground.

"Lila?" Liam asked in disbelief. "Where did you come from?"

"The *tree*," Lila said. "I thought that was pretty obvious." She stood up, wincing and holding her elbow. "I was hoping to make a smoother entrance than that."

"How long have you been following us?" Liam asked sternly.

"Since Avondell," Lila said. "I never went back to Erinthia."

"What?" Liam was aghast. "Why in the world would you do such a thing?"

"I've been away from home for half a week now. Have Mom and Dad sent anybody to look for me? No. I think that should be all the *why* you need," Lila said. "Let me come on the mission with you. I have no purpose at home. I want to be useful."

Liam gave an incredulous laugh. "I can't believe this."

"I'm very good at what I do," Lila said.

"What you do?" Liam gaped. "You're a child! *What you do* is hopscotch and math homework. We're talking about

a secret mission to break into the vault of the Bandit King. It's not kid stuff."

"Um, isn't the bad guy like ten?"

"I believe, based on the intelligence we've gathered, that's he is now eleven," Liam said.

"So? I'm still older," Lila said. "Please. I can do this." She clasped her brother's hand. "You can't send me back home to a life of eyebrow tweezings and impossibly tight gowns and not speaking until I'm spoken to. If I end up locked in the Bandit King's dungeon, it'll be a step up— believe me."

Liam was stewing.

"And besides," Lila added, "I can fit in the Snake Hole."

Liam froze with his mouth open and one finger up in the air.

"She's right, you know," Ella said, considering Lila. "I'll keep an eye out for her. I promise."

"She's my baby sister," Liam said. "How can I agree to this?"

"Look," Lila said. "If I can impress you right now, will you let me on the team?"

"It'll take a *lot*," Liam said.

"Hey, Ruff!" Lila called out. "I spotted you hours ago. Why don't you come out and show yourself?"

Liam, Ella, and Frederic all gaped as Ruffian the Blue stepped into the firelight from behind a tree. He grimaced at Lila from under his dark hood.

"For the record," the bounty hunter droned, "I saw you, too."

"Welcome to the team, sis," Liam said. Then, as Lila danced over to Ella, he turned to lash out at Ruffian. "And you! I don't appreciate being spied on! We've been fully cooperating with Briar, and we expect to be treated accordingly."

"I travel with Briar as a bodyguard, nothing more," Ruffian said. He was barely paying attention to Liam, his attention focused on a nearby cluster of trees. "I hide because it is the princess's preference that I stay out of sight. She finds my goatee unsightly."

"Oh, I'm sure that's all it is," Liam said, his jaw tight. "Although I can believe the bit about the goatee." He turned and snarled at Briar's tent. "Well, when 'Sleeping Beauty' wakes up, you can tell her that my team and I need a little privacy or this arrangement isn't going to work."

But Ruffian had already vanished.

"Hey, keep it down," Gustav groaned from his place on the ground, opening one eye to glare at the group by the fire. "Oh, hi, kid."

"I'm going down the Snake Hole," Lila said perkily.

"Aces," Gustav replied. And he was snoring again a second later.

THE TEAM

1. Liam ✓
2. Frederic ✓
3. Gustav ✓
4. Duncan ✓
5. Ella ✓
6. ~~Dwarfs~~ ? (for digging)
7. Troll (for distraction) ✓
8. ~~Gnome~~ Lila (for hole) ✓
9. Inside Man (?)
10. Snow White (for ?) ✓

11

A Hero Is Grossed Out by Sticky Floors

Sometimes a hero can be found in the most unexpected of places. That's when you must say to him, "Get out of my kitchen, silly! Don't you have some monsters to fight?"
— The Hero's Guide to Being a Hero

The next morning, while Briar applied her complicated daily regimen of face creams and Ruffian trekked off, reluctantly, to fetch her some fresh spring water, Liam took the opportunity for a private huddle with his team.

"It's time to head back to Avondell," he said. "We've got four days. You need to figure out what *JJDG* means. Do whatever you need to in order to get answers, but don't be obvious about it."

"Why are you speaking as if you won't be there?" Frederic asked.

"Because I'll meet you back in Avondell in two days. Right now, I'm going straight to Flargstagg," he said. "I've got to get to the Stumpy Boarhound to find our inside man. And I want Ella to join me as backup."

"*Love* that place," Ella whispered excitedly.

Frederic blinked fiercely. "Wait," he said. "I'm coming, too. If we're choosing the man who will have my life in his hands, I think I should be there."

"Frederic, I really hoped you'd be leading up the investigation back in Avondell," Liam said.

Frederic hesitated. Liam sounded sincere. But he couldn't be sure. "No, I'm sorry," he said. "I need to be between you and Ella—*with* you and Ella. And besides, I can help brainstorm new ideas for getting past Rauber's big wall."

"Don't worry," Gustav said. "I'll take care of business back at the Golden Palace. You guys haven't even seen my detective skills yet. If Miss Prissy Britches is hiding something, I'll get it out of her."

There was probably nothing Gustav could have said that would have worried Liam more. "You understand that we need to handle this subtly, right?" Liam asked.

"We cannot afford to have Briar figure out that we're on to her scheme."

"I know what *subtly* means," Gustav said.

"And don't worry, Liam," Duncan added. "I'm far more likely to give away our secrets than Gustav is. Ruby!" He pointed at a hummingbird that darted by.

Liam flipped his cape over his head and walked away.

The Stumpy Boarhound was, for the most part, just as Frederic remembered it. Despite the BIRTHPLACE OF THE LEAGUE OF PRINCES sign over the bar and the roped-off Official League Founding Table in a back corner, the tavern still made him feel uncomfortably out of place. Perhaps it was the various dead-animal-part trophies (reindeer antlers, warthog tusks, hippogriff wings, and the like) that cluttered every wall. Perhaps it was the long and sometimes dark-stained gashes that marred every surface—the obvious results of poorly aimed sword and ax swings. Or maybe it was the Boarhound's clientele: filthy, ill-mannered pirates, assassins, and thieves who, despite being huge League of Princes fans, were still filthy, ill-mannered pirates, assassins, and thieves. In fact, several of the customers were in the process of robbing one another when Frederic, Liam, and Ella entered.

"Well, I'll be soaked in porcupine oil," the crooked-nosed, stubbly-faced bartender shouted when he saw them. "If it ain't a couple o' our very own Prince Charmings come back for a visit! Oh, and Miss Cinderella, too!"

The criminals in the tavern took a break from stealing, gambling, and pummeling in order to gawk at the celebrities.

"Good day, Mr. Ripsnard," Frederic said with a polite nod.

"Ooh, he remembers my name," the bartender tittered. "I'm honored, I am. Let me get the Founding Table set for you." He sat them down and gave their table a halfhearted wipe-down with his filthy rag. Ella resisted the urge to snatch the rag away and clean it herself.

"Can I get you fellers any snacks?" Ripsnard asked. "Snake knuckles? Varmint nuggets? Perhaps a couple bowls o' meat stew?"

"What kind of meat?" Ella asked.

"Animal meat," Ripsnard answered. "At least, I'm pretty sure it's animal."

"Maybe just a few glasses of water," Frederic said.

"Coming right up!"

Ella glanced around the room at the various items that were on display to honor the League: Frederic's old mud-caked jacket, the charred remnants of Liam's original cape, a napkin on which Duncan had doodled a picture of himself riding a dolphin. "Wow," she said. "They really like you guys here. It's even more done up than it was the last time we stopped in."

"Yes," said Frederic. "Although I think they're pushing it a bit far with some of this so-called *memorabilia*. I'm pretty sure the 'Authentic Gustav Hair' over there is actually a piece of spaghetti."

Ripsnard reappeared and plopped three grimy mugs on the table. Each was filled with a thick and malodorous brown-green liquid.

"I'm sorry," Frederic said. "We just wanted water."

"Yeah," said Ripsnard. "We don't have any o' that." And he left.

Ella took a sniff of her drink, and her eyes immediately began to tear up. She pushed the mug off to the side and pointed to a Wanted poster hanging on the wall behind their table. "I can't believe we're actually here and we're not going after the Gray Phantom," she said. "Did you notice how deserted the streets were? The people of Flargstagg must be terrified of this guy."

Frederic studied the sketch of the mysterious criminal whose face was hidden by a creepy demon-face mask, complete with white, triangular fangs embroidered on it. "'Wanted for assault, theft, destruction of property, murder most foul, murder slightly less foul, and unlawful de-kidneying,'" Frederic read. "He actually sounds *worse* than the bard songs made him out to be."

"We need to get down to business," Liam said. "It's a long ride back to Avondell from here, but I'd like us to make it before nightfall. I'm still a bit worried about Gustav's idea of a 'subtle' investigation."

"Well, let's start then," Ella said.

"Okay, since we want the most skillful accomplice we can find," Liam said, "I think we start by asking around. Seeing who has the best reputation."

"Do you think that will work?" Frederic asked. "I doubt these people will have much nice to say about one another. I'm thinking we sit back and watch them for a while, see if anybody stands out as looking particularly trustworthy."

Ella stood up, stepped in front of the princes, and loudly announced, "Anybody who wants to work for the League of Princes, get in line!" The thugs and hoodlums practically ran over one another in their haste to queue up by the Founding Table.

"Or we could just do what she did," Frederic said sheepishly.

The first in line was a bearded pirate who was missing a couple of key teeth. Frederic and Liam remembered him from their first visit to the Stumpy Boarhound when he'd tried to rob them both. He was also one of the few people to have preordered Duncan's book.

Fig. 17
Cap'n
GABBERMAN

"Cap'n Gabberman at yer service," the pirate said in a gruff but friendly-sounding voice. "Whatever the task is that ye be needing done, Cap'n Gabberman can get it done for ye. I do sea. I do land. I don't do air so much, but it's not entirely out of the question. Do ye need some flying? If that's what ye need, I can make it happen. I'm a go-with-the-flow sort of pirate."

"Captain Gabberman," Frederic began.

"Please, call me Cap'n," the buccaneer replied.

"Captain," Frederic said.

"Cap'n," the pirate repeated.

"Cap . . . tain," Frederic tried.

"Cap'n."

"Cah." Long, deep breath. "Puhn."

"Cap'n."

"I'm sorry," said Frederic. "My mouth just doesn't work that way."

"Cap'n Gabberman," Liam said. "I'm not sure this is the right job for you. But if we're ever in need of a fast ship, we will definitely come calling."

"Aye," the captain said. "Ye do that now. If ye be in need of some seafaring, ye know where to find me. Me and my . . . *fast ship*." He gave a gracious nod and walked away, mumbling, "Note to self: Get a ship."

A bare-bellied barbarian strode up to take the captain's place. His hefty gut, which drooped over his thick rawhide belt, had more hair on it than his balding head. He folded his beefy arms, raised an eyebrow, and bellowed, "Do you need clubbing? 'Cause that's my specialty. Anything or anybody you need clubbed, I'll club it."

Liam was about to give him a speedy "No, thank you," but Ella jumped in. "Where's your club?" she asked.

"I got two clubs," the barbarian said, raising his ham-size fists. "Here and here. That's why they call me Two-Clubs."

Fig. 18
TWO-CLUBS

"Seriously?" Ella asked. "That's all you've got? Fists? You never use a weapon?"

"Don't need to," Two-Clubs said.

"Ella," Frederic said in a hushed tone, "we don't want to provoke these people."

"He's right," Liam agreed.

Ella ignored them. She never got to be around shady types like the customers at the Stumpy Boarhound. And whenever anything sparked her curiosity, she wanted to see more of it. "Show me how you use those things," she said to the barbarian.

The barbarian turned and, without warning, slammed his fist over the head of the thief who was standing behind him in line. The thief made a guttural noise like he had a hedgehog caught in his throat and crumpled to the floor.

Frederic jumped backward a few inches.

"Whoa," Ella said. "That was a bit more graphic of a demonstration than I expected. But impressive." She leaned over to Liam. "You sure we can't use him for *something*? Maybe if Briar gets too—"

"Maybe next time, Mr. Clubs," Frederic said.

The barbarian clomped off, and a tall, monstrously ugly half-ogre thug stepped over the unconscious thief to approach the table.

"Daggomire Hardrot," the half ogre introduced himself. He pointed to Liam. "We met previously when I was punching the back of your head."

"I remember," Liam said flatly. "What kind of skills do you have, Hardrot?"

"Skills?" the half ogre asked, his mouth crinkling into a frown. "Nobody said we'd need skills." And he sadly walked away.

"This is going to take a while, isn't it?" Frederic asked.

Fig. 19
Daggomire HARDROT

"No, it's not," Ella said. She slammed her palm on the table, causing drops of the murky nonwater to fly from everybody's mugs. "Most of you guys aren't even worth our time!" she shouted to the crowd (and both Liam and Frederic sank a few inches deeper into their seats). "So let's narrow it down: Last man standing gets to talk to us!"

It took three seconds for the tavern to devolve into total chaos. Robbers, pirates, and assassins throttled one another. A chunky thief crashed through a table, sending broken glass and critter bits flying, while Two-Clubs flattened a pair of twin assassins. An enormous bounty hunter picked up a scrawny pickpocket and threw him into a display case of Things Found on Prince Charming's Shoe. Cap'n Gabberman slapped a burglar across the face with a flounder.

"Gustav is going to be so sad he missed this," Ella said.

"What were you thinking?" Liam questioned as he ducked a flying alligator skull.

"That you two were never going to get your act together," Ella replied, and shoved away a dizzy buccaneer who had staggered her way. "We're on a tight deadline, right?"

"Wait! Look what's happening!" Frederic called to them (he was under the table). "Somebody new just came in."

The newcomer was a smaller man who wore glasses and dressed neatly in a vest and slacks. The Boarhound's front door had barely closed before the unsuspecting man was sucked into the fray, tossed from one thug to another. *That guy's going to die,* Liam thought.

But within seconds, the bespectacled stranger began defending himself—with nothing more than a needle and thread. He bounced about like an acrobat, rapidly winding his thread around his attackers to trip them up and bind them to one another (he also gave a few of them a good poke with his needle). One by one, brawlers began to drop, their hands and feet tied together. Eventually, only the stranger and Two-Clubs were left upright. The smaller man caught both of the barbarian's tremendous fists together in a loop of thread and yanked on the long string, forcing Two-Clubs to punch himself in the face. The brawl was over.

"Is this what a guy has to do in order to get a drink around here?" the stranger asked, wiping his rectangular eyeglasses clean on the bottom of his shirt. Liam got up and ushered the man back to the League's table, as Ripsnard the bartender came out with a pair of scissors to start freeing his patrons.

"That was incredible," Liam said.

"Thank you," the stranger replied, mending a loose button on his vest while he talked. "Thank *all* of you," he added, winking at Ella. He gathered the three untouched mugs on the table and chugged each of them, one by one. When he was finished, he slammed down the last mug and flashed a giddy smile. "I can't believe I'm sitting here with the League of Princes."

"Well, you earned it," Ella said. "You were great out there."

He lowered his glasses to the tip of his nose and batted

his eyelashes. "Why, thank you, Miss Cinderella. Name's Taylor. I'm a tailor. Folks in town call me Little Taylor, so as to distinguish me from Medium Taylor. He's also a tailor."

"Is there a Big Taylor?" Ella asked.

"No," Little Taylor said.

"The pleasure is ours, Mr. Taylor," Frederic said. "But I hope you understand that we'll need to ask you a few questions before we officially hire you."

"I can handle this, Frederic," Liam said, pulling his chair closer to Taylor's. "So what we need for this mission is—"

Taylor raised his hands in protest. "Whoa there, Prince Charming. Not to seem ungrateful, but I don't know anything about any contest or audition or whatever was going on here; I was just thirsty." He tilted his head way back, grabbed one of the mugs, shook it upside down to spill the last few drops of liquid into his open mouth.

"So you're not interested in the job?" Liam asked.

"Not unless it involves hemming your cape," he said. "I'm a tailor, not an adventurer."

"But all that amazing stuff you did—it was like . . . battle sewing!" Ella said.

"What can I say?" Taylor quipped, running his hand

through his slick, black hair. "I've got a way with a needle and thread. That's why I'm *a tailor*."

"Well, sorry to bother you then," Frederic said.

Liam sighed. "I guess we're back to square one," he said to Ella. "It's a shame, too. Taylor's skills would have come in handy against Rauber and his men."

Taylor was about to get up but stopped. "Deeb Rauber? The Bandit King? This mission of yours has something to do with him?"

"Yes, we're looking to raid Rauber's vault," Liam said.

"The Bandit King ruined my life," Taylor said. His eyes grew squintier, his face redder. "I used to be the busiest tailor in town until Rauber took everything from me. I lost my shop, my home, my life savings. I live for only one thing now: revenge against Deeb Rauber. I want in on this mission of yours."

"But I thought you were just a tailor," Frederic said.

"All right, I wasn't exactly honest with you guys," Taylor said. He began to roll a piece of thread between his fingers. "After Rauber destroyed my life, I taught myself String-Chi, a centuries-old combat technique that originated with the warrior-seamstresses of Kom-Pai. I've been using my skills to take down Rauber's bandits wherever I see them. Yesterday I took down seven with one blow."

"You're some kind of vigilante?" Liam asked.

"I prefer to think of myself as a freedom fighter," Taylor said. "And you're right; my talents *will* come in handy."

"But we want to get into Rauber's castle by having an accomplice deliver us there as prisoners," Frederic said. "If Rauber recognizes you as one of his former victims, he'll never believe you're on his side."

"What if he doesn't see my face?" Taylor said with a devious grin. "Have you noticed all the Wanted posters around town?"

"Yes, the Gray Phan-
tom," Liam said. "Even
back in Harmonia, we'd
heard about that mad-
man's crime spree. We
planned to put a stop to
it, too, until we got . . .
distracted."

"I'm not surprised.
That murderous madman
has done more damage to
Flargstagg in the last few
months than the Bandit
King has in his lifetime,"

Fig. 20
Wanted POSTER

THE
GRAY
PHANTOM
WANTED

DEAD OR ALIVE

Taylor said. "But my point is that the Phantom always wears a mask. Nobody has seen his face. I could make a copy of the mask. Rauber might not agree to an audience with Little Taylor, but I bet he'd open his door for the infamous Gray Phantom."

Liam took Taylor's hand and gave it a vigorous shake. "Welcome aboard, Taylor. Or should I say . . . Gray Phantom."

Outside the Stumpy Boarhound, Liam unhitched their horses, while Taylor ran off to collect his things.

"So you're happy with Little Taylor?" Frederic asked. "You think he's a good choice for our inside man?"

Liam nodded as he brushed the flanks of his black warhorse, Thunderbreaker. "I can't say I'm a huge fan of the way he . . . deals with other people," he said. "But yes, I think he'll work out fine for our purposes."

"I guess so," Frederic said. "Still, I think we should only fill him in on the parts of the plan he absolutely needs to know."

"I'm on top of it, Frederic," Liam said, a tad snippily. "I've finally got everything in place, so you can stop worrying about the details."

"Well, we still don't know how to get past the Wall of

Secrecy," Frederic reminded him. "That's a pretty big part of the equation."

"It's become clear that there is no way past the wall besides the front gates," Liam said. "That's how you and I are getting in. So everybody else will have to go in that way, too. They'll sneak in with the circus, hidden in crates or something, and then make their way to the roof."

"That's so risky, though," Frederic argued. "At least the original plan didn't require everybody to traipse through the castle and potentially run into bad guys."

"Yes, but that original plan required a tunnel," Liam said, his speech tight and clipped. "And we don't have anybody to dig that tunnel, thanks to *someone* who couldn't get his job done."

"Hey, that's not fair," Frederic said.

"You're supposed to be the talker, Frederic—the charmer," Liam said. "The only thing I've asked you to do so far is convince the dwarfs to help us. And you failed. If you can't even succeed in your own supposed 'area of expertise,' can you at least stop trying to outdo me at mine?"

"Hey, you're on the same side, guys," Ella warned. But both princes ignored her.

"Liam, your plan has holes in it big enough for a giant to step through," Frederic said.

"If you've got better ideas, spit 'em out!"

"As if you'd listen to anything I have to say," Frederic snapped, trembling with anger. "For days now I've been trying to make suggestions, and you shut me down every time I open my mouth. You're willing to entertain anybody's crazy ideas except mine. And I know why: It's because you're jealous."

"Me? Jealous of you?" Liam barked back. "I taught you everything you know. You'd still be cowering in the mud under a gorse bush in Sylvaria if I hadn't come along and showed you what it meant to be brave. If there's any hero in you at all, it's only because I put it there!"

Frederic stared at him with watery eyes before soppily muttering, "Excuse me. I have some business to attend to." He took his horse by the reins and stomped away with her down the sewage-strewn cobblestone street.

"Liam!" Ella said, aghast. "What is wrong with you?"

"Wrong with *me*?" Liam asked. "Frederic keeps trying to undermine me. Why can't he just let me lead?"

"Take a step back and look at yourself, Liam," Ella said, aggravated. "Frederic hasn't gotten in your way any more than Duncan or Gustav or I. He was right; you *do* judge him differently. And it's because of me, isn't it?"

"No, it's not," Liam quickly responded. "It's just . . . it's . . ."

They were startled by the sudden sound of loud hoofbeats. "Frederic?" Ella wondered aloud. She and Liam darted to the corner and saw Frederic galloping away.

"Frederic, wait!" Liam yelled.

"Should we get our horses?" Ella asked.

"By the time we do, he'll be long gone," Liam said. "We'll never find him in this maze of alleyways."

"He left a note," Ella said, picking up a folded Gray Phantom poster that was sitting on the fence post Frederic's horse had been hitched to. She grimaced as she read it.

"What does it say?" Liam asked. She handed it to him.

Liam—
You think you know better than I. And often you do—I'll admit that. But in this case, you're wrong. So I am taking matters into my own hands. I'll be back in Avondell in time for the solstice, and I will show you why you should have trusted me from the start.

Yours truly,
Frederic

P.S. I apologize for the lack of a proper salutation at the

head of this letter. I was quite incensed when I began writing, but that's no excuse for improper form. I didn't even indent—that's how upset I was.

"*Grr!* He's doing exactly what I told him not to do," Liam said, angry all over again. "And now what? We're supposed to put our mission on hold to wait for him? He's determined to show me up in front of everyone."

"I hate to say it, Liam," Ella said, "but you pushed him to this."

"Go ahead, take his side," Liam said. "He's your boyfriend anyway." He shoved the note back into Ella's hand and marched to his horse.

"What's Liam's beef?" Little Taylor asked, returning with a packed rucksack.

"You should take this," she said, passing the Wanted poster over to him. "Use it as a reference to make sure you duplicate the Gray Phantom mask perfectly."

"Hmm," Taylor said with a sly smile. "Smart *and* tough, eh? You don't see that combination in a lot of ladies."

Ella punched him in the stomach and headed for her horse.

Liam, Ella, and Little Taylor were all so distracted as

they left Flargstagg that none of them noticed the shadowy figure watching them from the roof of the Stumpy Boarhound.

THE TEAM

1. Liam ✓
2. ~~Frederic~~
3. Gustav ✓
4. Duncan ✓
5. Ella ✓
6. ~~Dwarfs~~
7. Troll (for distraction) ✓
8. ~~Gnome~~ Lila ✓
9. Little Taylor (Inside Man) ✓
10. Snow White ✓

12

A Hero Has No Sense of Direction

A responsible hero leaves nothing to fate. You never
know when you might be faced with a difficult decision,
so make sure you always have a coin to flip.
—The Hero's Guide to Being a Hero

Earlier that morning, the others had packed up their campsite and taken off for Avondell. They'd only made it a few yards before Lila yelled out, "Hey! Gustav! We're heading the wrong way!"

Gustav pulled back on the reins of his horse and let out an annoyed grunt. He trotted over to Lila, who sat in the driver's seat of Snow White's covered wagon. "You're messing with me, kid," he said. "I may not be able to tell a salad fork from a soup fork, but I know east from west."

"Shhhh." Lila pointed toward the covered portion of the wagon, inside of which sat Briar—squeezed among Snow's twenty-one baskets of "travel necessities." Lila motioned for Duncan (who was astride Papa Scoots Jr.) and Snow (who was next to her on the driver's bench) to lean in closer as well.

"I only said that for Briar's benefit," Lila whispered. "I don't want her to get suspicious when I turn the wagon around."

"Turn around? Why?" Gustav asked.

"Remember earlier when Briar excused herself to the woods to 'take care of some princess business'? I figured she was lying so I followed her," Lila said.

"You've got some guts, girl," Gustav said. "What if she'd been telling the truth?"

"Anyway," Lila went on, "I saw her having a secret powwow with Ruffian. I couldn't hear what they were saying, but when they were done, Ruff went off in the same direction as Liam and the others."

"Ooh, I know a mystery when I hear one," Duncan said excitedly. "Sounds like Ruffian's up to no good. Which would make sense, since he's a bad guy."

"I'm sorry," said Snow. "I don't know who this Ruffian is."

"He's a bounty hunter," Lila explained.

"I'm sorry," said Snow. "I don't know what a bounty hunter is."

"Um, it's a guy who hunts people down in order to earn a bounty."

"I'm sorry, I don't know what a bounty is."

"You know what?" Lila said. "I'll write it all down for you later. But now we've got to turn around and follow Ruffian."

"I don't know," Gustav said. "I've got one simple mission: go back to Avondell. I don't wanna mess it up."

"C'mon, Gustav," Lila urged. "My brother and your friends could be in trouble. How will you feel if something terrible happens to them just because you weren't willing to go a little bit out of your way?"

Gustav massaged his temples. "This makes my head hurt like when I suck down too many lingonberry ices. Okay, let's turn it around."

They all made a big U-turn and headed off along the same path Liam, Frederic, and Ella had taken.

"Should we tell Mr. Troll about Ruffian?" Duncan asked.

Gustav looked back at the green-furred behemoth who was shambling behind the wagon and bending over to taste a new shrub every few yards or so. "Nah, he's fine."

They traveled slowly, with Lila pointing out broken branches, flattened grass, and other telltale signs that someone had passed through. These were all skills she'd picked up by watching Ruffian track her brother the previous summer, and the thought that she was now using them against the bounty hunter himself made her beam with pride.

After a distance, the trail turned south, and the thick shrubbery and fat vines gave way to dried-out branches and brittle brown leaves. The road slowly turned into dead and dusty earth, obstructed in spots by rubble from age-old landslides.

"Never too late to turn back," Snow offered.

Both Lila and Gustav shook their heads and plowed on.

They were in the mountains now, bouncing over jagged terrain (with Briar cursing each and every bump as she tried to prevent Snow's stack of overpacked baskets from tumbling onto her). When they emerged from the rocky pass, they found themselves on a wide plain of barren earth. In the distance was a tall, curved peak. And at its base stood a monstrous fortress surrounded by an eighty-foot-high stone wall.

"Starf it all," Gustav groaned.

"Uh, Gustav," Lila said, pulling the wagon to a halt.

"That's Mount Batwing. We're in Rauberia!"

"So the hood is working with the bandits," Gustav quietly surmised.

"Not necessarily," Lila said. "His trail doesn't head to the castle. It veers east, back toward Sturmhagen."

"Flargstagg is that way," Gustav whispered. "He just took a shortcut so he could ambush the others at the Boarhound!"

"Maybe. But why?" Lila said. "Briar wants Liam to get the sword. . . . Unless she doesn't! Unless it's all a trap of some kind!"

"What's going on? Why have we stopped? Where are we?" Briar grouched, poking her head out of the back of the wagon and peering at her surroundings. "You've got to be kidding me! Here? You brought us here?!"

"We took a wrong turn, Briar," Lila said quickly. "Don't worry. We're changing course now." She steered the wagon in a wide arc and found herself blocked off by a scouting party from Rauber's castle: three black-clad, sword-wielding men on horseback. "Crud," she said.

"Hello," said Vero. "I believe you people are, as they say in my country, *trespassing*."

"Sorry, sir," Lila said. "We just took a wrong turn. We'll be leaving right away."

"No," said Vero. "I am afraid you will have to be coming back to the castle with us."

Gustav assessed the situation. He could take three bandits, he thought. Especially with Mr. Troll. Wait a minute—where was Mr. Troll? The big, hairy thing must have wandered off at some point. And then it hit him that Duncan was missing, too. "Great," he muttered.

"The castle is this way," said Vero. "So if you would be so kind as to follow us."

Briar stuck her head out again, ready to lash into the bandits with one of her patented "Do you realize who you're talking to" speeches, but quickly thought the better of it and ducked back inside. *If I'm seen here, the entire plan is kaput,* she thought.

The bandit scouts—one bald with pasty white skin, the other hairy and covered in metal facial piercings—tried to peer in past the stack of baskets that Briar had quickly piled in front of herself.

"Who is your passenger?" Vero asked. "An individual of great wealth, no doubt. Her taste in hairstyles is *mwah*!" He made a kissing sound and nodded approvingly.

"Dunky?" Snow called as she looked around anxiously. "Where are you, Dunky?"

"I am sorry, miss, but your donkey will have to wait,"

Vero said. "Please reverse the direction of your vehicle. We will be starting back to the castle immediately."

"Maybe some other time," Lila said.

Vero raised a finger disapprovingly. "I do not think you understand me, young lady."

"I'll give you something you don't understand!" Gustav shouted. Without warning, he rammed Seventeen into Vero's horse, knocking the swordsman from his saddle.

"Flee, girl!" Gustav cried.

Lila didn't need to be told twice. She cracked the reins and sped off with the wagon.

Gustav leapt to the ground, drew his battleax, and faced Vero.

"I will take care of this one," Vero told the other scouts. "You two follow the wagon." The bandits on horseback sped off after Lila, Snow, and Briar.

"Now, my long-haired friend," said Vero. "We shall fight, no?"

The wagon barreled along the mountainside, churning up a trail of billowing dirt and dust behind it. Every few feet another sharp, jutting rock would jar everyone on board. Lila tried desperately to hold on to the reins, while next to her, Snow dug her fingernails into the wooden driver's bench to keep from flying off. Inside, Briar's voluminous mound of hair became flatter and flatter each time her head hit the roof, and random knickknacks and tchotchkes spilled from Snow's baskets.

The bald bandit rode up next to Lila and smiled at her. She flinched when she realized the man's teeth had been filed into pointy fangs. He reached out and tried to grab on to the speeding wagon, but Lila kicked his hand away, grateful for once that her mother made her wear such pointy shoes.

As the first bandit lost ground, the second was quickly catching up to them on the opposite side, his eyebrow, nose, and lip rings jangling as his steed bounded along. He sneered at Snow White.

"Throw something at him," Lila shouted.

Snow puzzled over her options for a second. Then, with a high-pitched little "Ooh" (which was, frankly, too adorable for the circumstances), she bent down and pulled off her shoes. She tossed one shoe and then the other at the pursuing bandit. Each hit him square in the face, causing him to growl in fury but not really slowing him down.

Snow slid open a small window to the wagon's interior. "I need more stuff," she called.

Briar put aside her indignation at being told what to do

by a "lesser princess" and reached into the nearest of Snow's baskets. She grabbed the first object her fingers touched: a feather duster. She passed the duster out to Snow, who tossed it, handle first, at the bandit. It flew like a dart and lodged itself through the loop of the man's big nose ring. His horse swerved as he tried to see past the feathers that were now sticking up in front of his eyes.

"More stuff!" Snow yelled.

Briar handed one item after another up to Snow—a ball of yarn, wooden spoon, a HOME SWEET HOME pillow, a bottle of ink, a pouch of potpourri. Snow whipped each of them at the bandit, and each item gave the man an annoying slap in the face. Finally Snow reached down and found a lopsided ceramic mug placed in her hand. She paused, staring wistfully at the mug, which she'd crafted herself as a gift for Duncan (she'd painted a picture of a flute on it, although Duncan assumed the image was supposed to be an alligator named Fluke). But this was no time for sentimentality.

She hurled the alligator/flute mug and watched it crash between the eyes of the pursuing bandit. The man toppled backward off his horse.

"Did you see that?" Snow asked, turning to Lila. But Lila was too busy trying to fight off the pointy-toothed bandit, who had leapt from his horse onto the speeding wagon.

"Get off, Freakface," Lila grunted as she tried to push the man away. The bandit's foot slipped and he tumbled downward, but not before grabbing hold of Lila's arm. Snow yelped as Lila disappeared over the side.

"That is a very big ax you have," Vero said. He faced Gustav in a dueling stance, his sword held out in front of him. "Impressive to look at. But not so graceful as my rapier, I would think."

Gustav roared and let loose with a swing of his ax that could have cut down three full-grown trees. Vero ducked it easily and swiped upward with his sword, slicing through one of the leather straps that held Gustav's armor in place.

Gustav raised the battleax high overhead in preparation for another strike. Vero danced around him and—*thwick, thwick*—two more straps popped loose.

"Surely you can do better than this, no?" Vero asked. "You are, as my people say, *not so tough*. Yes?"

Gustav huffed and slammed his ax down hard. Vero casually sidestepped it, and the ax planted itself firmly in the rocky ground.

"This duel—it is not nearly as much fun as I had

hoped," said the swordsman. "Perhaps you would like to start over?"

As Gustav struggled to pull his ax free, Vero swung at him, severing yet another strap. Gustav's armor clanged to the ground, leaving his upper half clad only in a light undershirt.

"Starf it all."

"I am sensing you are not much for conversation," Vero said with disappointment.

Gustav charged the swordsman. Vero tripped him and then pointed his blade at the chest of his fallen opponent.

"This is so often the mistake of the rich," Vero said. "They hire for their bodyguards such large and muscular brutes—no offense. But strength alone will not protect these wealthy people. Wits and skill will always win over pure muscle."

"Hey, look what we found! This rock totally looks like Frank!" Duncan appeared from behind a large boulder, holding up an oddly shaped stone. Mr. Troll was by his side.

Vero's attention snapped to the newcomers. "Troll!" he shouted, a dire look on his face. "Troll! Troll!" He reached for a horn on his belt to call for reinforcements.

Before Vero could sound the alarm, however, Gustav kicked upward as hard as he could, slamming his steel boot into a very sensitive area of the bandit's body. The swordsman crumpled to the ground, and Gustav scrambled to his feet.

"Nice to see you, Hairy Scary," Gustav said to Mr. Troll. "Where were you when I needed you?"

"Rock really is very funny," Mr. Troll offered by way of an explanation.

"Seventeen!" Gustav called, and quickly hopped into his saddle. "This way, everyone! Hurry!"

Duncan, who was beginning to grasp the situation, climbed up onto Papa Scoots Jr. and followed, with Mr. Troll sprinting right behind.

About a half mile away, Snow's driverless wagon was careening out of control.

"Take the reins!" Briar shouted through the small window.

Snow hesitated. "Frank usually drives our wagon! I don't know how!"

"Learn fast," Briar yelled. "You're the only one up there!"

Snow reached for the reins and gave them a hard yank. The well-trained horses slowed in an instant. "Ha!" Snow said with a smile. "That wasn't so hard."

"Great," Briar said. "Now steer us west. Take the first pass you find back through the mountains toward Avondell."

"But we have to go back for Lila," Snow said.

"Argh," Briar growled. "That girl wasn't even supposed to be part of the plan. Fine! Turn around!"

Snow experimented with the reins, and by pulling them hard in one direction, she discovered the miracle of the U-turn. A few minutes later, Snow and Briar could see the pointy-toothed bandit walking along the wastes, pushing Lila in front of him as he went. Briar rifled through Snow's baskets and came across one of Duncan's old trophies: a bronze statuette of a prancing man covered in birds, on the base of which was etched MIDWINTER REGIONAL BIRD-FEEDING CHAMPION.

"Go slowly and get as close to him as you can," Briar said.

The bandit heard the wagon coming up behind him and whirled around angrily, his hand on the hilt of his sword. But he paused when he realized the vehicle wasn't trying to run him down; it was rolling right past him. Very slowly. He never imagined Briar would suddenly lean out from the back and swing a bird-feeding trophy at his head like a club. But she did. The bandit dropped to the dirt with a thud.

"Victory!" Briar sang out.

Snow brought the wagon to a stop.

"Thanks, Briar," Lila said breathlessly.

Briar snorted. "I couldn't have you ruining the mission, could I? Now hurry up and get back on the wagon. We need to be out of Rauberia *this instant*." She slunk back inside.

Lila was uneasy but climbed up onto the driver's bench next to Snow.

Briar peered up at her through the little window. "Oh, and west is *that way*," she said, pointing.

"Yeah, I know," Lila muttered, and slid the window shut. She took the reins back from Snow and was about to crack them when she saw Gustav, Duncan, and Mr. Troll heading toward them in the distance. Lila flashed Gustav a thumbs-up to let him know they were all right. He responded by nodding and pointing westward. Then he took Duncan and Mr. Troll and turned back the way they'd come.

"They want us to go back without them," Lila whispered to Snow.

"But where will *they* go?" Snow asked.

"They're going to try to find Ruffian on their own," Lila said, and felt an unpleasant gurgling in her belly. But Briar knew exactly where they were now; Lila had no choice but to take her home. She cracked the reins and headed west. "Gustav, Duncan, and a troll. That's not going to turn out well." She didn't know the half of it.

"Great," Gustav said. "The girls are okay, and we've finally ditched Miss Prissy-Britches. Now we just need to hustle on to Flargstagg so we can ambush that bounty hunter before he ambushes our buddies."

"Ah." Mr. Troll smiled. "Troll finally get to try out techniques Angry Man taught in ambush class."

"You got it, Awful Clawful," Gustav said, spurring his horse. "Let's move before Rauber's anti-troll brigade comes gunning for us."

As they went, Duncan rode up alongside him.

"Seriously, Gustav, you've got to see this rock," he said, holding the odd stone out to his friend. "Doesn't it look *just* like Frank?"

Gustav glanced over at the stone and couldn't help chuckling. "Yeah, it does."

13

THE VILLAIN FEEDS THE FISH

A successful warlord demands loyalty from his followers
but gives his loyalty to no one. This may mean
that the birthday cards you receive from your henchmen
are not written out of genuine emotion, but that
is a small price to pay for supreme power.
—THE WARLORD'S PATH TO POWER:
AN ANCIENT TOME OF DARIAN WISDOM

"What do you mean, 'There were trespassers'?" Deeb Rauber stood on his throne so he could literally get in Vero's face. He flipped up his unnecessary eye patch in order to give his swordsman a full, unabridged stink-eye. "That can't possibly be true," the boy continued, "because if there really were trespassers, you would have captured them and brought them to me."

Vero didn't flinch. Nor did the two scouts, both

transplants from Dar, who stood behind him. "This is, of course, what we attempted to make happen, Your Highness," Vero said casually. "However, apprehending these particular intruders—it was, as they say in my country, *not to be*. Still, I thought you should know."

"I'm disappointed, Vero," Rauber said. "You blew it big-time. You're supposed to be my right-hand man. I can't have you embarrassing me in front of the Warlord."

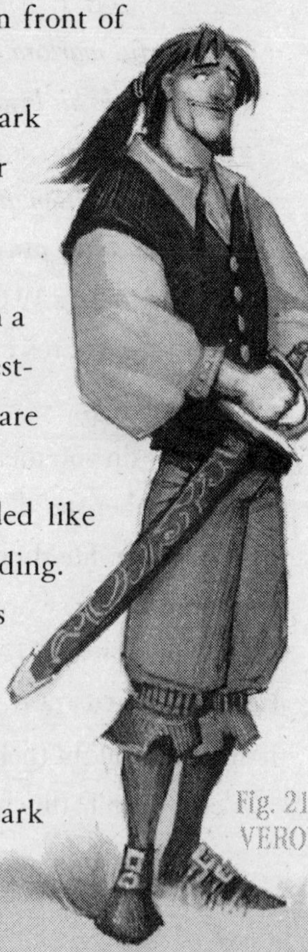

"Too late for that," Lord Rundark intoned. The dark-eyed warrior strode in, his beard-braids bouncing on his wide chest as he walked. "Where I come from, such a misstep is unacceptable. Your highest-ranking officer has failed you. You are right to be embarrassed."

Rauber bit his lip. This sounded like scolding. He didn't like scolding. Scolding was what got his parents locked up in a cupboard.

"However, in Dar we say that a leader can be forgiven the mistakes of his followers," Rundark

Fig. 21
VERO

continued. "Provided the underlings are properly punished." He folded his arms, watched, and waited.

Rauber stroked his preteen chin as if it were covered with the beard he was still years away from growing. He had to think about this carefully. He liked Vero; he didn't want to do anything too harsh to the guy. But if he wanted to keep Rundark and his men around, he knew he'd have to impress the Warlord.

"Who were these people that you and your two buddies here couldn't manage to capture, Vero?" Rauber asked.

"We did not get their names," Vero said. His eyes darted over to Rundark, and the sheer intensity of the Warlord's stare made him recoil just a bit. "It was a rich lady in a wagon driven by two girls," Vero admitted. "They had a bodyguard with them."

"One bodyguard!" Rauber shouted in exasperation. "Oh, Vero, that's pathetic. I might have to send you down to Wrathgar."

Vero went white. The two Darian scouts behind him swallowed hard.

"Surely, Your Highness, you do not need to do anything so drastic," the swordsman said. "If I might remind you, there have been some men who have never recovered from the . . . *adjustments* Wrathgar made to their bodies."

Rauber glanced over at Rundark. He couldn't read anything in the Warlord's cold, hard stare. "Sorry, Vero," the Bandit King said. "You bumbled."

"There was a troll," Vero blurted. "There was a troll, Your Highness. This is why we could not apprehend the trespassers."

"A troll?" Rauber began breathing in loud, heavy snorts.

The two scouts nodded, backing up Vero's claim.

"Repelling trolls from Rauberia takes top priority: This you said yourself, sir," Vero argued. "When the troll appeared, I focused my attention on the beast. It was only then that the intruders were able to flee."

Rauber was still seething but managed to slow his breath and appear a bit calmer. "Well, this changes things," he said. He looked to Rundark. "It's true. My men have a standing order to drop everything if they see a stupid, stinking *troll* slopping its way onto my property. I hate those broccoli-headed, onion-reeking, marsh-faced, cruddy-eyed, lemon-knuckled—"

"Sir?" Vero interjected.

"Where was I?" Rauber asked. "Oh, yeah. Vero, you're off the hook. For now."

Vero breathed a sigh of relief.

"*Your* men may have to follow this rule about trolls," Lord Rundark said as he strolled over to the quivering Darian scouts. "But mine have no such order. And a lesson still must be learned."

The Warlord lifted the nose-ringed scout by his throat. He carried the man, flailing, to an open window, where he held him outside and dropped him into the moat three stories below. The man's shrieks echoed across the wastes as the bladejaw eels went to work.

Rauber was agape, unable to decide whether Rundark's act had been terrifying or awesome. "You gonna do the guy with the pointy teeth, too?" he asked.

Lord Rundark shook his head. "No, Falco will be spared for the moment," he said. "I doubt he will make such a mistake again."

The bald scout stood at attention, blinking sweat from his eyes.

"Come, Falco," Rundark said. "It's time for barracks inspections." The Warlord strode from Rauber's throne room, with Falco scurrying at his heels.

Rauber, filled with unfocused energy, paced around snapping his fingers rapidly. His heart was pounding.

"Sir, if I may," Vero ventured. "Having the Darians here—you still think this a good idea?"

"Good idea?" Rauber burst out. He leapt from his seat and grabbed Vero by the shirt. "It's the best idea I've ever had! I've been playing this king thing all wrong. I thought I was tough—but I can't begin to compare to Rundark. That man is the real deal. He's heartless. He'll stop at nothing. A guy like that could rule the whole world someday. And that's no good. Because *I* wanna rule the world someday."

"What is it you are saying, sir?"

"I've gotta take Rundark down. He thinks he's so big and scary and impressive—"

"He *is* big, scary, and impressive," Vero said.

"But he won't be after I embarrass him in front of my entire army." Rauber fell back into his throne and started cackling with glee. "Vero, the circus is coming in a few days. And I'm going to make sure the grand finale is the utter humiliation of Warlord Rundork! I'm talking cow pies in the face, bucket of slime over the head—maybe even a good ol' pantsing! When I'm through with him, he'll be too embarrassed to ever show his face around here again. And to think—he said I wasn't a serious villain!"

14

A HERO STARTS
NEW TRADITIONS

Know your enemy. If you don't,
who will you aim your sword at?
—THE HERO'S GUIDE TO BEING A HERO

Crouched behind the smoke-spewing chimney of the Stumpy Boarhound, Ruffian the Blue watched Liam, Ella, and Little Taylor ride away through the dark, ramshackle streets of Flargstagg. He crawled along the uneven roof, grabbed the rickety gutter, and flipped himself down into a slime-drenched alley, where he found Duncan and Gustav waiting for him.

"Did you get *this* badly lost?" he asked drolly.

"Oh, we're exactly where we want to be, buddy," Gustav said, swaggering up to the bounty hunter. "I'm Gustav the

Mighty. I don't get lost."

"You appear to have lost most of your clothing," Ruffian said. Gustav tugged his undershirt down a bit to make sure his belly button wasn't showing.

"We know you're up to no good," Duncan said, squinching up his face in an attempt to look intimidating. "Lila saw you being sneaky and tracked you here."

"Ah, the young girl," Ruffian said, nodding to himself. "That makes more sense."

"Yeah, but we sent her home," Gustav said, cracking his knuckles. "'Cause we caught you. And what's gonna happen now isn't kid stuff."

Duncan pulled out his flute. "Yes," he said in what he hoped was a sinister voice. "Prepare to hear the worst concerto ever composed for a wind instrument."

Gustav turned to Duncan and threw his hands up. "Seriously? *That's* what you meant when you said you had a weapon?"

In a flash, Ruffian pulled a small square of mesh from one of his belt pouches and tossed it. As it flew up in the air, it unfolded into a large net and landed over Gustav.

"Get it off me!" Gustav cried, and Duncan tried to comply. "You're poking me in the eye!" Gustav howled. "Drop the flute first!"

"I'm not dropping my flute on this disgusting street," Duncan insisted. "I have to put it in my mouth!"

Ruffian turned to leave. That was when Mr. Troll entered the alleyway and leveled him with an enormous clawed fist.

As soon as Gustav was free, he and Mr. Troll wrapped the unconscious bounty hunter in the net, and Duncan secured it with fifty-seven different types of knots.

"One thing you learn from living with Snow White," Duncan said, "is how to tie a whole bunch of bows."

Gustav hoisted Ruffian up and tossed him through the broken window of an empty building across the street from the Stumpy Boarhound. "You know, I think I tossed an unconscious guy through this same window last time we were here," he said. "Maybe I can make a tradition of it."

"My favorite tradition is seeing how many blueberries you can fit up your nose on New Year's Day," Duncan said.

Gustav, Duncan, and Mr. Troll stood in a small circle.

"Gentlemen," Gustav said. "Everyone may think of us as the B Team, but we did nice work here today." He and Mr. Troll exchanged high fives. Duncan attempted one as well but only succeeded in slapping Gustav across the face.

"I'm just going to pretend that didn't happen," Gustav said. "Go, B Team!"

* * *

Lila, Snow, and Briar were waiting at the gates of Avondell Palace as Liam, Ella, and a small man in glasses approached on horseback. The sun had already set, and the sky was darkening by the second.

"Hey, guys," Lila said. "My brother's already kinda nervous about me being on this trip, so maybe we could just not mention the part about me being caught by the bandits."

"Relax, sweetie," Briar said, patting her on the back. She turned to the two pin-striped guardsmen who stood nearby and yelled, "Open it up!"

The men snapped to action, and the polished pewter gates swung open. Little Taylor rushed past Ella and Liam to be the first inside. He did a backflip off his horse and took a bow. "Hel-*lo*, ladies," he said.

Ella shoved him into an aardvark-shaped shrub and marched past everyone.

Fig. 22
Little TAYLOR

"What's wrong with her?" Lila asked.

"She's miffed at me. It's nothing," Liam said, dismounting. "Wait, what happened to you guys? Where are Duncan and Gustav?"

"Oh, it was terrifying. Your sister got kidnapped by some of Rauber's men," Briar said. "She was almost killed." Lila shot Briar the dirtiest look she could muster.

"What?" Liam gasped.

"Oh, she's fine, though," Briar said proudly. "I saved her. Me. I made sure she got back alive." She crossed her arms and held her head high, waiting for thanks and praise to be showered upon her. None came. Everyone rushed to greet Gustav, Duncan, and Mr. Troll, who had just appeared on the path up to the palace. Nobody even noticed when Briar walked away alone.

The Avondellian princess was back to her usual "perky" self the following morning as she joined Liam—or rather insisted that he join her—for a hearty breakfast.

"Svenlandian truffle honey?" Briar offered as she smeared a hearty dollop of golden goop on a crumpet. "Gotta eat this stuff while you can; the species of bee that made it is extinct."

Liam frowned. "I'm not hungry." He hadn't touched

the piles of glistening wildebeest bacon, bowls of poached green eggs, or stacks of Briar-shaped pancakes that sat between him and his wife at the breakfast table. "Can we please just get this over with? There are only two days before we have to launch this mission, and we've got a lot of training to do." And by "training" he meant snooping around the palace to uncover Briar's secrets.

"My team is waiting for me," he added. *Well, most of my team.*

"Just update me on your plan," Briar said, biting into a grapefruit. "You keep changing it around, and I want to make sure it's sound before I send you off to recover the object I desire most in the world."

"It's the same basic idea," Liam said. "We just had to alter a few details. Little Taylor, disguised as the Gray Phantom, is going to deliver me to Deeb Rauber and ask to stay for the circus as his reward. While I'm being placed in the dungeon, Duncan and Snow will bribe two clowns and take their places. Then they'll load three crates onto the circus wagons—crates that contain Gustav, Ella, and Lila. Once inside the castle, those three will make their way to the roof, where Lila will slide down the Snake Hole and hit the trigger to open the vault. Halfway through the circus show, Little Taylor will excuse himself, go down to the dungeon, and free me so I can grab the sword from the open vault. Then we all meet by the circus wagons and slip out with them when the performance is over. It's pretty straightforward."

Briar gnawed on a piece of bacon. "Where does the troll come in?"

"We *were* going to use him to cause a distraction while the dwarfs tunneled us under the big outer wall, but since we're not tunneling anymore, I sent Mr. Troll home. He wasn't very happy about it. Which reminds me, your gardeners will have to carve a few new animal hedges—the cheetah, chimera, and chinchilla didn't survive his exit."

"There's one bit of the plan I'm a little unclear on," Briar said. "Your friends in the circus crates—how exactly will they make it up five stories to the roof without being seen?"

Liam didn't answer right away because he didn't know. He closed his eyes, pictured the situation, and hoped a solution would come to him. All he got was: *Hire an actor to pretend he's a bad guy.*

"Still?!" he griped aloud.

"Yes, Liam, I am *still* asking this question," Briar said, assuming he was responding to her. "And I will until you provide me with an adequate answer."

"We'll make this plan work," Liam said.

"Not good enough," Briar said forcefully. "I want the Sword of Erinthia, and the upcoming circus performance provides the perfect chance to get it. I'm not going to waste the opportunity on a group of losers with no real plan. You have two days to tell me how your teammates are getting onto that roof. Otherwise I'll dump your pals back in prison and send someone else after the sword." She sat back and dunked a green hard-boiled egg into a glass of cranberry juice before taking a bite of it. "Now go play with your friends and let me finish my morning meal in peace."

Liam left, and Briar craned her neck to look all around the room. "Ruffian!" she called. "Ruffian, where are you?"

She threw her egg angrily to the floor. It landed with a barely audible *whump* and wobbled slightly, which was very unsatisfying. So she hurled the rest of her breakfast to the ground as well. Once everything was shattered and splattered in a delightful mess that would take a servant hours to clean, Briar took a deep breath and smiled to herself. "Ah, now I feel ready."

And she stepped outside.

The door to Avondell Palace's Royal Gymnasium opened slightly, and Gustav poked his head out into the hallway.

The two pin-striped guards standing in the corridor stared at him. "Can we help you, sir?" one asked.

"You guys gonna be there all day?" Gustav asked.

The men nodded.

Gustav pulled his head back in and slammed the door. He walked over to Liam, Duncan, and Lila, who were huddled in the center of the vast marble chamber. "They're not leaving," he reported.

"Okay, we've got to make it sound like we're practicing for a fight in here," Liam said.

"I'm on it," said Duncan. He jogged near the door and began making loud puffing, grunting, snarling, and moaning noises. He grabbed himself by the hair and threw himself to the ground, where he rolled around and barked like a rabid seal.

"That'll do," Liam said. He looked over to Ella, who sat by herself, sour faced, against the far wall. "Are you going to join us?" he asked.

"I suppose I must," she grumped. She let out an exaggerated sigh as she stood up and walked over to the others, making sure Liam knew she was still steamed at him.

"It doesn't feel right doing this without Tassels," Gustav said.

"Look, people," Liam said, annoyed. "Frederic *chose* to leave. We can't put the entire mission on hold. And if any of you are mad at me for moving on without him, get over it. There are more important things at stake here than any of our personal feelings."

The others all nodded silently.

"So, listen," Liam continued. "We've got to figure out what Briar plans to do with the sword, but so far we have no idea where to even start looking."

"I do," Lila said. "I've been spying on Briar before she goes to bed at night, and I've seen some interesting things."

"You did what?" Liam gasped. "You're going to get yourself caught. Or killed. You cannot keep putting yourself into situations like that."

"Jeez," Lila griped. "Do you ever listen to your own advice? What happened to all that stuff you just said about putting personal feelings aside?"

Liam shut his mouth, his cheeks reddening.

"Lila, tell us what you've learned," Ella said. "And make it fast, because—let's face it—Briar's going to walk through that door at some point. The woman won't leave us alone for long."

"That's why I stationed Snow outside her room as a lookout," Liam said.

Ella, Lila, and Gustav all stared at him oddly.

"What?" Liam asked. "Bad idea?"

Briar stepped out of her bedroom and recoiled at the sight of Snow White standing directly in front of her, wearing a homemade sombrero with strawberries dangling from the brim like fringe.

"What are you doing here?" Briar sneered.

"Nothing sneaky," Snow said.

"Where are Liam and the others?"

"Down in the gym, taking lessons in hand-in-hand combat. Or maybe it was hand-*to*-hand combat. I hope not, because hand-*in*-hand sounds much sweeter."

Briar pushed past her and started on her way to the gymnasium, striding purposefully down her mirror-and-marble corridors. This was never going to work if she couldn't get Liam and his friends to trust her. She'd been trying for days now to work her way into their group, to spend time with them, become—*ugh*— friendly with them. But they continually shut her out. It infuriated her.

More than she thought it should.

She began to walk faster.

"Every night, Briar has Reynaldo, the bard, come sing her a *lullaby*," Lila told everyone. "That's a bit suspicious for someone her age, no?"

"Not necessarily," said Ella. "Frederic does the same thing back at home."

"But with the same song every time?" Lila asked. "I watched Briar twice before your little field trip and then again last night. It's been the same tune every time."

"What's the song?" Liam said. "Any mention of *JJDG*?"

"I don't know. I've been kind of . . . dangling outside her window," she said, glancing at Liam to see if he'd turned completely purple. ". . . so I haven't been able to hear the lyrics clearly. But I've caught snippets—something about a thief and his wife."

"At least it's not 'The Song of Rapunzel,'" Gustav said. "I half expected it to be. Every time there's something bad in my life, that woman ends up being part of it somehow."

"Gustav, shush!" Ella scolded. "Lila, go on. Quickly."

"Okay," Lila said. "After the song, her behavior gets even more peculiar. As soon as the lullaby is over, she kicks the bard out of her room and starts reading some old book."

"Her diary," Liam said. "I've already seen it."

"No," Lila said. "This is something called *Remembrance of Kings Past*. It looks ancient. Big, yellowing pages with lots of portraits of old-timey people. She always flips straight to the same section toward the back. And she gets all evil-looking while she reads it." Lila hunched her shoulders, curled her fingers like claws, and arched her eyebrows to demonstrate.

"Very good likeness," Ella said.

"I'm telling you," Lila said, "that book and that song have something to do with whatever Briar is planning."

"All right, people," said Liam. "Looks like we know what we have to do: break into Briar's room to snatch the *Kings* book and spy on her again tonight to hear the bard's song."

Everybody was nodding when the gymnasium door flew open. As Briar stepped into the chamber, Duncan hurled himself into her path, tripping her. Each of the others quickly grabbed the person standing nearest to them and pretended to wrestle.

"Sorry, sorry!" Duncan said as Briar picked herself off the floor. "Messy business, this handy-dandy combat."

"So is this your plan? *Shove* your way up to the roof?" Briar asked. "I've already sent a messenger to Kom-Pai.

The ninja team is probably on its way here as we speak, ready to take your place if it must."

"No need for that," Liam said. "We've come up with a foolproof way of getting onto the roof without ever needing to step foot inside the castle." He was lying, of course.

"Tell me," Briar said flatly. "I'm on pins and needles."

Liam paused. He was blanking out again.

So Gustav stepped in. "Catapults," he said.

Briar started to chuckle but soon realized he was serious. "Catapults?"

"Yes, that's right," Liam said haltingly. "We're going to use your army's catapults to launch Ella, Gustav, and Lila over the wall and onto Rauber's roof."

"Without dying?" Briar asked.

"Mm-hmm," Liam said, nodding. "They're going to use, um, glider wings. To land safely."

"Intriguing," Briar said, mulling over the idea. "Okay, you'll have full use of Avondell's catapults. But in the meantime, practice is over. The party is this evening."

"Party?" Gustav asked, unhappy just to hear the word.

"Yes, the royal ball," Briar said. "I mentioned it days ago. Jeez, you people pay no attention to me."

"No, we heard you," said Liam. "We just didn't think we'd be attending."

"Oh, but you have to," Briar said with a hint of a smile. "It's our annual June Junior Debutantes' Gala. The best of Avondellian society will be there. It's a very big deal."

"We'll skip the party, Briar," Ella said. "We've got a lot of work to do."

"What work?" Briar asked. "You've got your plan figured out. And big, famous heroes like you shouldn't need to waste time *learning* how to fight. No, I'll see you all at the ball."

Everybody slumped simultaneously.

"But wait," Ella said. "Can't we as least train until the dance?"

"Oh, you won't have the time, dearie," Briar said. "You schlubs can't attend one of my royal galas looking the way you do. I'll have attendants get you prepared. It shouldn't take more than four or five hours. By then the party will be starting."

There was a long, awkward silence.

Then Snow burst into the room and shouted, "Briar is coming!"

Briar smiled at her and left.

"Catapults, Liam?" Ella asked. "Really?"

"Yeah, um, I'm the science fair champion here," Lila said. "And we'll die if we try that."

"What's wrong with catapults?" Gustav asked.

"We're not using catapults," Liam said. "I just had to agree to *some* way past the wall so Briar wouldn't replace us as her strike team. We need to come up with an alternative before the morning of the solstice."

"Which is the day after tomorrow," Lila reminded them.

"Plus we also need to get that *Kings Past* book," Gustav said.

"And we need to somehow hear Reynaldo's song," Ella added. "It's so much to do."

"We're not really going to this ball tonight, are we?" Lila asked.

"We can't miss it!" Liam said. "The dance might be the next step in Briar's plan: June Junior Debutantes' Gala? *JJDG*." The others nodded in understanding.

"Plus," Liam said, "we're going to use the ball as a cover to steal Briar's book."

And at that, a platoon of silk-suited wardrobesmen and frilly-skirted dressmaids flooded into the gymnasium, ready to drag the heroes off to their rooms, powder their faces, truss up their hair, and squeeze them into outfits that made them look like the display window of a hoity-toity bakery.

"I can't believe we're going to a ball," Ella moaned as she was whisked away. "Where are you when I need you, Frederic?"

Fig. 23
WARDROBESMEN
and DRESSMAIDS

15

A Hero Has a Ball

Solving a mystery is just like solving a crossword puzzle.
You look up and down and back and forth and fill in all the
answers you already know; then you hand the rest over
to a dwarf and ask him to finish it for you.
—THE HERO'S GUIDE TO BEING A HERO

Pretty much any royal ball is a big event—orchestra
music, elegant suits and gowns, scores of people
dancing quadrilles, onion dip—but Avondell's annual
royal ball was the event of the century (in part because
Briar legally declared each one the Event of the Century
and threatened to jail anyone who disagreed). It was set in
a grand hall that was big enough for twenty bull elephants
to run figure eights without crossing one another's paths.
A two-hundred-piece band—containing every instrument
from bagpipes and didgeridoos to steel drums and hurdy-

gurdies—plinked, zummed, and tooted its way through waltzes, minuets, and rumbas. More than a thousand candles lined the walls on platinum sconces, and the glow of their flames was caught and scattered by a ceiling full of dangling crystals, turning the floor into a sea of twinkling lights. A hundred-foot-long buffet table was laid out with delicacies such as pegasus kabobs, sea serpent caviar, and basilisk fritters. And amid all this extravagance, countless noblemen and ladies hobnobbed, snacked, and danced.

"I'm so glad to see you all made it," Briar said to Liam, Gustav, Ella, Lila, Duncan, and Snow—who were crowded behind an hors d'oeuvre table, wriggling uncomfortably in the excessively frilly outfits they'd been made to wear.

"Wouldn't have missed it for the world," Liam said with an obviously fake smile.

"Well, what is everybody waiting for?" Briar said. "Dance."

She grabbed Liam by the hand and pulled him to her. Liam grudgingly began doing a two-step; and as soon as he took her hand in his, he noticed a strange bit of jewelry around her wrist: a diamond bracelet from which dangled a tiny silver key.

The others watched the newlyweds waltz off into the center of the enormous dance floor.

"Okay, she's busy. Let's go," Lila said.

"It's not going to be easy," Ella warned. "Look at her; she's peering at us over Liam's shoulder. And have you noticed the guys along the walls? The ones who aren't dancing?"

"You mean the statues?" Snow asked.

"No, the ones in the striped uniforms," Ella said. "They're guards. We're going to have to be really careful."

"Hey, Gustav," Lila said conspiratorially. "Dance with me!"

"No way," he grunted. "I don't dance. And anyway, I'm not stepping out from behind these crab rolls. I can't be seen looking like this!" His shimmery lavender suit was so tight that it threatened to burst if he so much as flexed a biceps. Flapping lace cuffs spilled over his hands from the ends of his jacket sleeves, and the fluffy ruffles at his collar tickled his chin when he spoke. His hair had been curled.

"Get over it, big guy," Lila said. "I need you to be my cover. Keep your back to the center of the room while you and I dance over to that window. I'll slip out, and you just keep on dancing as if I'm still there."

"Excellent plan," Ella said. "Okay, shoo!"

"But I don't even know how to dance," Gustav moaned as he waddled away, awkwardly holding Lila's hands.

"You two," Ella said to Duncan and Snow. "Go ahead

and dance. Act as normal as possible but watch for my signal. If you see me raise my hand *like this*, that means I need you to cause a distraction."

Crash! A plate of crab rolls hit the floor.

"No, I don't need a distraction *now*," Ella said. "I was just showing you what the signal would be."

"Oh," Duncan and Snow said in unison. Then they clasped hands and sashayed into the whirl of dancing couples.

While cleaning up the spilled crab rolls, Ella lost track of Liam and Briar. As she scanned the ballroom for them, she felt a tap on her shoulder.

"May I have this dance?" Little Taylor asked, posing with one hand on his hip and the other behind his head to show off the gold lamé suit he was wearing.

"Oh, you were invited, too?" Ella said with very little enthusiasm.

"Of course," Taylor said. "So, hey, I just asked the orchestra leader to play a sweet tango. What say you and Little Taylor show these rich folks what we've got?"

Ella closed her eyes. *Frederic, where are you?*

In a secluded valley far to the south of Sturmhagen, Rapunzel returned to her small wooden cottage after a long and tiring day of healing the sick and injured. She'd spent most of the morning mending the broken toes of a farming family whose cow had gone on a stomping spree. Then, before she had even finished her lunch, a trio of tiny, flying, blue-skinned messengers—Rapunzel's helper sprites—came and told her about a poor leprechaun who had been shoved into a beehive by a gang of mischievous imps. After that it was an elf with swamp flu, a troll with gastrointestinal distress, and a little girl who sizzled the tip of her nose while trying to see a "magical world" inside a match flame.

Rapunzel was exhausted. But such is life when your tears have the mystical power to heal. The sun was going down, and Rapunzel was looking forward to a quiet evening at home with a book and a bowl of turnip soup. But alas, it was not to be. She knew she was in for some overtime as soon as she saw a headdress-wearing show horse trot out of the woods with a man draped across its back.

Holding up the hem of her plain white dress, Rapunzel ran to the horse to check on the sickly-looking man. As soon as she got close enough to see his dusty brown hair and pale cheeks, she recognized him.

"Frederic!"

Frederic opened his eyes and sat up, almost losing his balance. It took him a second to get his bearings, but as soon as he noticed the long-haired blond woman running toward him, he stopped his horse and hopped down. "Rapunzel! Hello!"

"Are you okay?" she asked. She eyed him up and down. "I thought you were almost dead again."

"Oh, no, I'm in perfect health," he said as Rapunzel held him by the chin and looked skeptically into his eyes. "Except maybe for a little saddle chafing. Not that I need you crying magical tears for that!"

"I got scared seeing you slumped over the way you were," she said.

"Sorry," he said, slightly embarrassed. "I was just, um, really tired. And I found a way to sleep on the horse."

"It's good to see you," Rapunzel said. She'd only met Frederic once before—for only a few minutes nearly a year earlier—but he'd made quite an impression on her.

"It's very nice to see you, too," he replied. And Rapunzel threw her arms around him.

The hug took Frederic by surprise. And at first he let his hands hover tentatively above her shoulders, afraid to fully embrace the embrace. Ella's hugs always had a bit of roughness to them—they made him feel safe and protected, but tended to hurt just a bit. Rapunzel's hug, on the contrary, was warm and soft. It made him feel safe in a completely different way. He let his hands come down to rest on her back.

Rapunzel stepped away. "Sorry," she said, her round cheeks reddening. "I was just relieved to see that you were all right."

"Oh, no worries," Frederic said. "The, um, you know . . . the hugging . . . that was fine. Definitely. I mean, well, you know. Anyway, I apologize if I gave you a fright."

"If you don't need healing, what brings you here?" Rapunzel asked.

"Well, I was hoping to ask for your help with something. Can we talk?"

Fig. 24
RAPUNZEL and FREDERIC

Rapunzel led Frederic into her cottage, where the two shared a tiny wooden table. Frederic sat on a storage trunk, since Rapunzel only had one stool. She lit a lantern and ladled out a mug of turnip soup for Frederic, eating her own portion directly from the pot (she only owned one mug).

As they ate, Frederic told her everything: about Liam's forced marriage to Briar Rose, about their plan to steal the Sword of Erinthia back from Deeb Rauber, about their need to reach it before Briar does. Rapunzel listened intently, kneading a handful of her waist-length blond hair.

"That's an incredible story," she said when Frederic was done. "And you are so courageous for attempting such a quest. But I'm still not sure how I could help. . . . Why are you smiling like that?"

"I don't hear people calling me courageous very often," he said. "But anyway, I'm afraid someone could get hurt in the process of this mission. So I would feel much better knowing we had a healer standing by. Just in case."

"That's exactly how the people and creatures of this forest feel," Rapunzel said. "They're very secure knowing they have me nearby."

"So . . ."

"I'm needed here," she said apologetically. "You should have seen that poor leprechaun today; he looked like a walking sticky burr. What if I hadn't been there for him?"

Frederic nodded, though he couldn't hide his

disappointment. "What you do here is incredibly noble and important," he said. "I won't take you away from it."

"Thank you for understanding," she said.

"Absolutely. Now . . . what was I saying?" Frederic noticed the dimples that appeared on her cheeks when she smiled, and he temporarily forgot what they were even talking about.

Rapunzel laughed. "You were complimenting me on my good works."

"Ah, yes, brilliant job with that," he said.

Speaking solely in terms of dancing, Liam and Briar made a very nice couple. With great poise and flawless stepping, the pair weaved their way through the other dancers.

"I never knew you were this good," Briar said.

"I took lessons when I was Lila's age," Liam grudgingly revealed.

"And you haven't forgotten a thing. See, this is why I chose you to sit by my side. Can't you picture us as queen and king of the whole realm? We will be so adored."

"You may have the upper hand right now, Briar. But I'm not beaten yet."

"Do you get lines like that from a book somewhere? Because you spout out far too many for me to believe it's all off the top of your head." She grabbed Liam's hand and looked at his palm. "Do you have them scribbled down? Are you cheating?" She flashed a flirty little smile and waited for a reaction. But Liam merely looked away and took a deep breath. Briar rolled her eyes. *I don't know why I even bother.*

Liam's gaze landed on Gustav, who was bobbing strangely in front of an open window.

A few minutes earlier, Lila had slipped through that window and began scaling the outer wall of the palace up to Briar's bedroom. Liam prayed she'd be safe. And successful. And as the orchestra kicked into a tango, he prayed she'd be fast.

Fig. 25
The DANCE

* * *

Hanging from a fourth-story ledge, Lila used a stolen pickle fork to pry open a stained-glass window. She pulled herself up and over the sill, and tumbled into Briar's dark bedroom. As she landed, her foot knocked into a small ceramic globe, which tipped off its wrought-iron stand, dropped a few inches onto Briar's desk, and began rolling across the polished mahogany surface. Lila scrambled to stop it, but the skirt of her gown was snagged on the corner of the window. The globe slipped off the edge of the desk.

"Hhrrnh!" Lila grunted as she dove and caught the globe in her hands just before it hit the ground. Panting softly, she looked toward the door. It stayed shut; the guards outside hadn't heard anything. *Thank goodness Briar likes her privacy enough to install thick doors,* she thought.

Then she noticed that her legs were clad only in ruffled, knee-length bloomers; the bottom half of her ball gown had ripped completely off. And was presently flying over the Avondellian countryside in a strong breeze.

How am I going to go back to the party like this? she thought. *Liam will never trust me again. I can't— No. Snap out of it, Lila. Who cares if you're in your underwear? There's work to be done and no time for little-girl worries.* She carefully set the globe back onto its stand and rushed to the desk drawer into which she'd seen Briar put her mysterious book. She pulled on the knob.

"Crud," she whispered. The drawer was locked. And she'd stashed her lock pick in her skirt.

"So, rumor has it you appreciate a man with a good cross-stitch," Little Taylor said as he and Ella tangoed through the sparkling ballroom. "Ouch! You know, that's the fourth time you've stepped on my foot."

"Really, I thought it was five," Ella mumbled, staring over Taylor's head to watch Liam and Briar swaying a few yards away. She noticed the pained look on Liam's face, and as angry as she'd been with him, she couldn't help feeling sorry for him at that moment.

"You've got to loosen up, Cindy," Taylor said. "Let Little Taylor show you how it's done."

"Do not call me Cindy," Ella said. She dropped Taylor's sweaty hand from hers and wiped her palm on the side of her gown. That's when she noticed Gustav, standing by a window, waving his arms wildly to get her attention. She shook her head. *Subtlety, Gustav,* she thought. She gave him a quick wave back to let him know she'd seen him—and unwittingly signaled Duncan to overturn a punch bowl.

"Oh, jeez," Ella muttered. She speedily dragged Taylor

over to a powdered-wig-wearing countess who had just entered the ballroom and practically pushed him into the bewildered noblewoman. "You'd like to cut in?" Ella asked. "Sure. Take him."

She ran over to Gustav. "What's wrong?" she whispered. The big prince pointed toward the window. Ella leaned out to see Lila crouching like a gargoyle on a narrow ledge.

"Her drawer is locked," Lila said.

"Drat," Ella grumbled. "Well, okay, you'd better come back in before someone notices you're gone."

"I can't," Lila said. "I'm only wearing half a dress."

"I'm not even going to ask," Ella said. She had to talk to Liam. She strode straight to the center of the dance floor and raised her hand high over her head. This time Duncan and Snow hip-checked an old, monocle-wearing baron into a table full of salted phoenix tongues. As the unfortunate man tumbled to the ground, taking three other guests and loads of grotesque appetizers with him, Briar spun to face the commotion. "What in the world is going on?" she fumed.

Ella grabbed Liam by the arm and tugged him back to the window with her. "Lila's stuck out there," Ella blurted. "And Briar's desk is locked."

"She's wearing the key," Liam said, remembering

262

Briar's bracelet. "We need someone to—"

"Someone to what?" Briar asked as she walked up to them. "To rein in your clumsy backwoods buddies, I hope. They're ruining my ball."

"Yes," Liam said. "I'll talk to Duncan and Snow. Gustav, you dance with Briar in the meantime."

Gustav barely had time to yelp out a "But!" before Liam shoved him into Briar's arms. The band started playing a lively mazurka, and Briar reeled off into the crowd with the very unhappy Sturmhagener.

"Now what?" Ella asked.

Liam brushed his hair from his eyes. "We need to get the key."

Ella darted around the ballroom until she found Little Taylor, who was rubbing his red, stinging cheek, which had just been slapped by a very offended duchess. Ella pulled him away by his slick gold sleeve.

"We need you to do something for us," she said.

Briar stumbled, trying desperately to keep her feet out from under Gustav's. "It's like you've never danced before in your life," she said. "A dead yak has more grace."

"Is there a dead yak around?" Gustav asked bitterly. "'Cause I'd happily change partners."

"Ooh, nice one," Briar snarked. "Which of your biceps thought up that zinger?"

"Jealous, Lady Twig-Arms?" Gustav shot back.

"Me? Jealous of a man shaped like an upside-down triangle?" Briar smirked. "Don't flatter yourself."

"I wouldn't dream of it," Gustav said. "Flattering yourself is what *you* do best."

Briar was so thoroughly engaged in bickering with Gustav that she didn't notice Ella and Taylor dancing right behind them. As soon as they got close enough, the tailor deftly looped a thread through Briar's bracelet. As Ella "accidentally" bumped into Briar from behind, Taylor yanked the bracelet—and the key—from the princess's wrist.

"Watch it," Briar barked, but immediately returned her attention to Gustav. "Where was I? Oh, yes. You call that an insult? I've heard wittier barbs coming out of the cribs at a nursery school."

Ella placed the key into Liam's palm and whispered, "Good luck."

Liam cleared his throat and looked at Little Taylor, who was hovering next to Ella.

"Oh, thanks, Taylor," Ella said. "You can go now."

"C'mon. I helped you out," the tailor whined. "Tell me what you need that key for."

"Hey, look over there," Ella said, pointing. "Isn't that the Baroness of Bartleby?" She not-so-gently shoved Taylor away, and Liam slipped out the window.

Liam looked up to see his sister, in her bloomers, clinging to a second-story windowsill. "C'mon," she whispered, and skittered up the wall, brick by brick.

"This is how you got to Briar's room?" Liam asked, somewhat awestruck, as he followed her.

"I'm good with heights," Lila said. She slipped back into Briar's window, and Liam swung himself in after her. The siblings crawled quietly to the desk, unlocked the drawer, and opened it to reveal a thick book with a cracked, peeling leather cover: *Remembrance of Kings Past*. Liam lit a candle as Lila carefully started leafing through the yellowed pages.

"It's a history of *our* family," Liam said.

"Wow, we're related to somebody named Humperdinck?" Lila asked.

"You were right, Lila. This must have a connection to the sword," Liam said.

Lila flipped pages faster. "Here! There's a chapter called 'The Jewels of the Sword of Erinthia.' Jeez, there's a story in here for every single stone on the sword. There are like fifty of them!"

"Just skim," said Liam. "See if anything stands out."

"Let's see," Lila said as she ran her finger along the lines of text. "Diamond from a mine, ruby from under the sofa, amethyst that was traded for a herd of pegasi . . ."

"Ha! I have a toy poodle with more bite than you." Briar laughed.

"A poodle? Is that who does your hair?" Gustav tossed back.

"Oh, you want to bring hair into this?" Briar grinned. "Eat any good porridge lately?"

"Are you calling me a little girl? 'Cause I'll—"

"Hey, that reminds me," Briar said. "Weren't you dancing with young Miss Lila earlier? Where is she now?" Briar glanced all around the room.

"She just went to the, uh, you know, the powder room," Gustav said.

"She's been gone a long time, hasn't she?"

Gustav shrugged. "Don't ask me. I have no idea what girls do in there."

"Hmm," Briar said. "I'd hate to think my sister-in-law got into some sort of trouble. I'd better go check on her."

"I'm sure she's fine," Gustav said. "Stay and . . . dance some more. With . . . me."

At that moment, the final notes of a waltz faded out and the orchestra stopped for a break. "We'll be back in five minutes," the bandleader announced. "In the meantime, everybody enjoy some crispy pixie wings."

"Perfect timing," Briar said. And she left the ballroom.

"Found it!" Lila said, almost too loudly. "Look! *JJDG!*"

She'd just turned to a story titled "The Orange Jade," beside which Briar had jotted the four mysterious letters. The tale revolved around Prince Dorun, Liam's great-great-great-great-great-great-great-grandfather (give or take a few "greats").

"Could one of those *J*s stand for 'jade'?" Lila asked. She and Liam feverishly read on.

Several hundred years ago, it seemed, Prince Dorun embarked on a long and hazardous journey to the desert land of Aridia. Up until that point in history, no member of the Erinthian royal family had ever left his or her kingdom. But the plump Prince Dorun had a notorious sweet tooth, and when he heard rumors of an Aridian treat called a *maldente*—consisting of twelve different kinds of sugar molded into a solid sugar nugget that was topped with powdered sugar, dipped in sugared cream, and filled with a liquid sugar center—nothing could hold him back. Sadly for Dorun, he never got a chance to taste the legendary *maldente*; he and his party were caught in a violent sandstorm and became hopelessly lost among the dunes.

They wandered for weeks, until they happened upon a half-buried temple: cracked columns and broken slabs of granite rising up from the sand. At its center lay a skeleton draped in tatters of magenta silk, clutching a glistening object in its bony hand. When the starving Prince Dorun saw what he thought was a big, sparkling jelly bean, he pried it from the corpse's long-dead fingers, took a tremendous bite, and instantly broke his four front teeth. Because he'd actually chomped down on a rather large orange gemstone. Disappointed that it was not candy but still rather happy that he'd discovered a priceless-looking treasure, Dorun pocketed the strange, glowing jewel and continued his search for a way out of the desert.

Months later, Prince Dorun crawled back through the gates of the Erinthian royal palace alone. The fate of the other members of his traveling party remained unknown (though quite a few people wondered why the prince hadn't lost any weight after months of wandering in the desert). Dorun presented the eerie, orange-hued gem to his family. As a reward, the king and queen gave him total control over the royal kitchen and its menu. It was not an honor Dorun had asked for, but one he'd dreamed of since he was a child. "It's like you read my mind," the prince said.

At that time, the palace's royal craftsmen were completing work on the Sword of Erinthia, a jeweled sword of intricate splendor such that the world had never seen. And Dorun's unusual piece of orange jade was given a place of honor at the base of the blade.

Liam shut the book and looked at his sister. "If I'm reading Briar correctly, the sword itself means nothing," he said. "It's this gem she wants, the orange jade."

"And I bet that lullaby will tell us why," Lila said. "We've got to listen to it tonight."

Liam nodded. "For now, though, put the book away. We've got to get back downstairs."

The clack of Briar's tall heels echoed down the empty hall as she strode toward the ladies' washroom. She put her hand on the knob and paused. Had she heard someone else's footsteps?

"Ruffian?" she whispered into the silence of the corridor. There was no reply. She huffed and turned the knob. But before she could open the door, there was a loud crash from up above, followed by a cry for help.

Briar abandoned the washroom door and darted to the staircase across the hall. She began running up to investigate but was stopped at the second-floor landing by a trio of guardsmen speeding past her.

"Go back downstairs, Your Highness!" a guard barked. "It's the Gray Phantom!"

Just as Lila turned the key to relock Briar's desk drawer, she and Liam heard the screams from outside the room.

"Go back down quickly!" Liam whispered urgently. "Make sure to drop the key on the dance floor somewhere!"

"But I'm in my bloomers," Lila protested.

"Go!" Liam repeated. Lila slipped out the window, taking Briar's key with her. Just then the door was kicked open from the outside, revealing a man dressed in gray with two unmoving guards at his feet. Liam recognized the stranger's intricate demon-face mask immediately.

The Gray Phantom wavered when he spotted Liam.

"Not who you were expecting?" Liam asked. For lack of a better weapon, he grabbed a silver hand mirror off Briar's vanity table and swung it. Surprising Liam with his speed, the Phantom caught Liam's arm, bent it behind his back, and pushed him painfully out into the hallway. He slammed Liam into the wall and sent him to the ground with a hard kick to the small of his back.

Lying on the floor, Liam heard the sound of many approaching footsteps. "Stop! Thief!" guards yelled as they rushed down the corridor. With a crash of shattering glass, the Phantom dove through a window at the end of the hall and disappeared into the darkening night.

"Your Highness, are you all right?" one guard asked as he helped Liam to his feet. Liam ignored him and rushed to peer out through the window. There was no sign of the Phantom. He knelt for a quick check of the guards on the ground; they were barely alive.

"Get these men medical help immediately," he said, and sped to the stairs.

A few seconds later, Liam burst back into the ballroom. While the orchestra played a slow ballad, he darted over to Gustav, Ella, Duncan, and Snow.

"Thank goodness you're back," Ella said when she saw him coming. "Briar left and—"

"Someone attacked us upstairs," Liam said breathlessly. "Someone wearing a Gray Phantom mask."

"The Gray Phantom is here?!" Duncan screamed. Violins screeched and oboes fizzled as the orchestra's music abruptly cut off—only to be replaced by shrieks of fear. "Wait," Duncan continued. "Who's the Gray Phantom?"

Before anyone could explain, the royal ballroom turned into total bedlam. The formerly dignified guests shoved past one another as they scrambled and clawed their way to the exits. A white-haired earl belly flopped into the onion dip, and a beauty-marked duchess skidded on her bottom through a puddle of cocktail sauce. Spit valves spilled and xylophone sticks flew through the air as band members fled. The monocle-wearing baron leaned over to his wife and said, "This is not as good as the wedding." Then somebody pushed him into a bowl of pudding.

In minutes, the majority of the guests had run off, and the ballroom looked like the aftermath of a tornado. Shattered plates, broken clarinets, and squashed rhino nuggets littered the dance floor. Briar walked in from the hall and began pulling at her hair.

"Hey, Briar," Lila called out, after stealthily slipping back in through the window. "Look what your rotten guests did to my dress!"

In one corner of the ballroom, an overturned table shifted as Little Taylor crawled out from under it. His gold lamé suit was spattered and dripping with red wine.

"What happened?" he muttered. "I thought I'd finally won that countess over and then—*bam!*"

"Taylor," Liam asked, "could anyone have stolen the Gray Phantom mask you made?"

Taylor shook his head. "Impossible." He reached inside his jacket and pulled out a gray cloth mask, onto which only half of the Phantom's elaborate demon pattern had been embroidered. "I haven't even finished it yet."

Liam looked at the others. "That means it was the real Gray Phantom. He must have followed us from Flargstagg."

"Now I'm kind of glad Frederic isn't here," Ella said.

"Well, I should probably be going," Frederic said.

He stood up, gave a gallant bow, and headed back outside. Rapunzel followed.

"It's dark," she said. "Are you sure you don't want to wait until morning?"

"It's okay. Tomorrow's our last day to dig into Briar's secrets before the mission," Frederic said. "I'll just sleep on the horse." He walked over to Rapunzel's stable, put one foot into a horse's stirrup, and began to climb onto the saddle.

"Wait," Rapunzel called. "That's the wrong horse!"

Her red-brown mare, Pippi—with whom Frederic's Gwendolyn had been sharing the stable—was spooked by the stranger mounting her in the dark. She reared up onto her hind legs and sent Frederic spilling to the ground.

"Frederic, are you all right?" Rapunzel called as she ran into the stable.

"Yes, I think—OW!" Frederic was hit with a powerful jolt of pain as he tried to pull himself up. "No. That would be a no. Not all right. My leg. Ow-ow-ow."

Rapunzel knelt next to him and rolled up his left pant leg to check the injury.

"Oh, my goodness," she gasped. "That looks awful. It's bending in a *very* wrong direction."

"That would explain the immense pain," Frederic said, blue faced.

Rapunzel lowered her head. "Be still," she said.

Frederic tried hard to calm himself. He watched as Rapunzel's shoulders shuddered and a single tear fell from her eye and splashed onto his shattered leg. In less than a second, an eerie humming sound filled the air. Frederic's leg began to vibrate and slowly pulled itself back into a normal position. The pain was gone.

"Thank you," Frederic wheezed as he tried to catch his breath.

Rapunzel wiped her eye. "You did that on purpose," she said.

"What?" Frederic asked, incredulous. "Me? Break my leg on purpose? You obviously need to get to know me a little better. I avoid pain at all costs. When I'm sewing, I wear thimbles on all ten fingers."

"So this wasn't just a way of playing on my emotions? Making me feel guilty if I'm not there to save you when you get hurt again?"

"No, of course not." Frederic looked hurt by the accusation. "I meant everything I said tonight. I would never be dishonest with you."

Rapunzel looked into his watery eyes, and she believed him. "I'm sorry," she said. "I guess I just haven't come to expect the best from the men in my life. My father sold me for turnips, and, well, you know what happened with Gustav."

"It's okay," Frederic said. "I understand."

She grabbed a blanket off a nearby shelf and handed it to Frederic. "I'm not letting you leave in the dark. Sleep here. I hope you don't mind using a horse blanket."

"This will be fine," Frederic said. He found a corner away from the animals, piled up some hay, and lay down with the blanket. "Thank you. And good night."

"What do you think you're doing?" Briar asked sharply.

Ella was mopping up some spattered cheese sauce in the wrecked ballroom.

"Where did you even get a mop?" Briar said. "My staff will clean up. All of you are being escorted back to your rooms."

"Fine with us," Liam said.

"And as a safety precaution, everyone will have guards posted outside their doors," Briar continued.

"We don't need—" Gustav began.

"Stop," Briar commanded. "The Gray Phantom just attacked my palace. He could still be around here somewhere. I'm doubling the amount of guards around the palace, inside and out. And until the Phantom is apprehended, everyone will remain in their rooms."

"But what if he's never caught?" Liam asked. "What about the mission?"

"Of course you'll be allowed out for the mission—I want my sword," Briar said, rolling her eyes. "But you'll stay locked up until then if need be. Oh, and don't worry; I've informed General Kuffin about your need for catapults. He'll have them ready for you on the morning of the mission." Before anybody could argue, she marched out of the ballroom. Liam and the others could see the guards waiting for them in the hall.

"Catapults?" Snow asked, her lip quivering slightly.

Liam turned to Taylor. "When you're done with that mask, I may need you to make some glider wings, too."

Taylor shrugged. "I'll get started on them now." And he walked out into the hall, where two soldiers immediately took him by the arms and led him to his room.

"Guys," Liam said, stopping the others before they left. "We found out that it's not really the sword Briar wants; it's one particular gem on the sword. Orange jade."

"I like lemonade better," Duncan said.

"Not orangeade," Liam said. "Orange jade."

"I thought jade was green," Ella said.

"Normal jade is," Lila explained. "The orange stuff is incredibly rare."

"Well, why does Briar want this particular stone?" Ella asked.

"We don't know," Liam said. "We need to hear that bard song."

"And it won't be tonight, now that we're all grounded,"

Lila grumbled.

"I have a question," Snow said. "Why did you ask the sewing man to make glider wings?"

"Because if we don't also come up with a better way past the Wall of Secrecy," Liam said, "Briar is going to shoot us out of catapults in twenty-four hours."

16

A HERO FORGETS THE LYRICS

*Never underestimate the power of music. A mandolin over
the head can really knock someone for a loop.*
— THE HERO'S GUIDE TO BEING A HERO

The next morning, Frederic awoke to hot, wet horse
breath on his neck. Gwendolyn was snuffling her
nose against him.

"Good morning," he said drowsily to the horse.

"Good morning," he heard Rapunzel reply brightly.

Frederic opened his eyes and sat up to see Rapunzel
standing with her horse, Pippi. She was wearing a clean
white dress and had her hair tied back into a thick ponytail.
Apples and bread peeked out of Pippi's overstuffed
saddlebags.

"Ready to go?" Rapunzel asked. "I packed some
breakfast for the road."

"You're coming? Are you sure about this?" Frederic asked.

"Well, I'm not going into the Bandit King's castle with you," Rapunzel answered. "It's not like I've suddenly become a whole new person overnight: So long, Rapunzel, Healer of the Ill! Hello, Rapunzel, Smiter of the Wicked! No, that's still not me. I don't fight. But I can be there for anyone who needs my help afterward."

"What about your patients?"

"They can wait," Rapunzel said. "They don't call them *patients* for nothing."

Frederic chuckled. "But seriously, they'll need you, right?"

"I've given the sprites some pointers in basic first aid. I think they can handle things here for a few days."

"I . . . I, um . . . I don't know what to say," Frederic stammered.

"I'm sure you'll think of something," Rapunzel smirked. "You have a way with words."

"Are you teasing me?" Frederic said with a grin. "I had no idea you could be so . . . lively. Please don't take offense to that. It's just that you usually seem—"

"So serious?" she said. "Well, healing the sick and injured isn't the most lighthearted of professions. Maybe that's why I was so happy to get a visit from someone in good health. Oh! Speaking of health . . . Here, take this." Rapunzel took a small glass vial of clear liquid and tucked it into the inner chest pocket of Frederic's jacket. "It's a little backup supply of my tears. Just in case you need it before you can reach me."

Frederic was suddenly, terrifyingly aware that his hair, after sleeping in a barn, was a complete mess. "I should freshen up before we go. Do you have a mirror?"

"Sorry," Rapunzel said, shaking her head. "Oh, but my dish is pretty shiny. You can probably see your reflection in it if you needed to. It's in the cottage by the washpot."

Frederic excused himself and jogged inside. As he cleaned up and straightened his bed head, something sitting in the corner of the cottage caught his eye. He called Rapunzel inside and pointed to the incredibly odd-looking . . . well, for lack of a better word, let's call it a statue. The figure's body was a warped tree branch. It had broken pinecone arms, a round pebble nose, a crookedly carved smile, and a hearty handful of ragweed hair.

"Where did you get that?" Frederic asked.

"Nice, huh? It's supposed to be me," Rapunzel said. "It was a gift from a patient—a giant who had an incredible blister on his big toe. Sweet guy, but . . ."

"Was this giant's name Reese, by any chance?"

"Yes," Rapunzel said with surprise. "How did you know that?"

"He crushed me once," Frederic said. "Not the time you fixed me up—that was a different crushing. I guess I get crushed more than the average person."

"You're making me feel much better about my decision to join you, you know," Rapunzel said.

"Anyway," Frederic continued, "all that crushing notwithstanding, Reese and I came to a sort of understanding." He paused, a thought striking him suddenly. "Rapunzel, do you know where Reese is now?"

She nodded.

"Then we need to make a detour on our way back to Avondell," Frederic said. "I think I finally know how we're going to get past the Bandit King's wall."

After an entire morning of wringing his cape in angst, Liam had worn the edge of the garment down to bare frayed threads. He opened his window to get some fresh air and spotted Gustav leaning out of his own window one room over.

"Ah, you're going stir-crazy, too, huh?" Gustav said. "I can't take it anymore. I'm gonna make a jump for it."

"Don't be ridiculous, Gustav," Liam said. "First of all, the fall would kill you. And even if you managed to climb down safely—well, take a look. There are guards all over the place: dolphin hedge, harpy hedge, *guard*, crocodile hedge, troll hedge, *guard*, clam hedge, hedgehog hedge, *guard*. There's no way to avoid being seen."

"Well, come up with one of your famous plans," Gustav said.

I wish I could, Liam thought.

Suddenly, Duncan's head popped out of the window next to Gustav's. "Hey, did somebody mention clams?" he asked. "Because I am famished."

"We're trying to figure out how to get out of here," Gustav said.

"It's not looking good," Liam added.

"What's not looking good? The clams?" Duncan asked, leaning farther—and completely tumbling over the edge of his windowsill. That was when the garden's troll-shaped hedge sprung to life and caught the falling prince in its grassy green arms.

"Thank you, tree," Duncan said.

"Hairy Scary, is that you?" Gustav called down.

Mr. Troll waved up to him.

"You were supposed to leave," Liam said. "I told you

we didn't need you."

"Troll disagreed," the creature said. "So Troll stayed."

The three nearest Avondellian guardsmen left their posts and ran at the troll with their long poleaxes.

"Explain that it was an accident," Liam instructed. But Mr. Troll proceeded to clobber all three pin-striped soldiers, knocking them out. "Or not," Liam sighed.

"Hey, Troll, I'm coming down, too!" Gustav called. He leapt from his window. Mr. Troll caught his Prince Angry Man with a gleeful grin.

"What do you think you're going to do?" Liam yelled down.

"We can't wait till bedtime. With the lockdown in place, this might be our only chance," Gustav said. "We're gonna find the bard and get the song out of him." He turned to Duncan and Mr. Troll. "It's B team time. You ready for some investigative action?"

They nodded eagerly.

"No, Gustav!" Liam shouted. "Wait!"

"It's now or never, Capey," Gustav said. "We've already knocked out three guards." He had a point.

Liam briefly considered jumping down to join them but was honestly afraid the troll wouldn't catch him. And the trio was already on its way, creeping through the forest of shrubbery. He couldn't stop them.

"*Subtly*, Gustav," Liam called. "*Subtly*!"

Gustav gave him a thumbs-up as he disappeared around a corner.

"He has no idea what that word means," Liam muttered.

Liam pounded on his locked bedroom door, praying that Gustav and Duncan hadn't already ruined everything. "Guard! Guard!" he shouted. "Please, you've got to let me out! It's an emergency!"

"Emergency?" he heard the guard ask from out in the hall. "It's not the Gray Phantom again, is it?"

Liam thought for a second. "Yes," he shouted back. "I saw the Phantom outside. Let me out. I can help stop him!"

"The Phantom's back!" the guard called to his comrades along the corridor. Through the door, Liam heard a lot of murmuring and commotion, then the pounding of a dozen booted feet running off toward the stairwell.

One good hard kick later, Liam's bedroom door burst open, and he rushed out into the now empty hallway. He dashed straight to the opposite end of the corridor and rammed his shoulder into another bedroom door, breaking the lock and knocking it open. Ella jumped up with a start when she saw him.

"I need your help," he said. "We may have a big problem."

"For someone the size of my living room, you're very good at sneaking," Duncan said as the trio crept through the garden, freezing behind Mr. Troll any time a guard passed by.

"Oops Man not so bad either," Mr. Troll replied.

"Okay, guys," Gustav said. "Since everybody in the palace is supposed to be locked in their rooms, we can assume Mr. Sing-Song is in his room as well. And all the bedrooms seem to be on the top floor of the palace."

"That's really smart thinking, Gustav," Duncan said.

Gustav paused and grinned. "You're right, it is," he said. "But we don't know which room is the bard's."

"You know who we should ask?" Duncan said. He pointed to a high window. "Whoever lives in that room with the music-note curtains."

Gustav's eyes brightened. "That's got to be the one! Time to go back to the top floor."

"How?" Duncan asked.

"Same way we got down, only backward," Gustav said. "Awful Clawful, how strong is your throwing arm?"

* * *

Reynaldo, Duke of Rhyme, was (as Liam liked to point out to people) not really a duke. He was, however, Avondell's royal bard and one of the most famous bards in the Thirteen Kingdoms. His "The Tale of the Sleeping Beauty" was the biggest international hit of its day—or at least it had been until that Harmonian hack, Pennyfeather the Mellifluous, started flooding the market with his "League of Princes" songs. What was so special about Pennyfeather's songs anyway? Was it because he *named* the princes? A cheap gimmick! And one that, if it caught on, would mean more work for the bards. Reynaldo couldn't imagine how annoying his life would become if he had to start making sure his stories contained *facts*.

But he was going to beat Pennyfeather at his own game. Reynaldo's song about the wedding, "The League of Princes Fails Again," was already gaining in popularity— and he didn't mention a single real name in it (other than that of Briar Rose, of course). No, Reynaldo went back to calling all the men Prince Charming. It made the story incredibly

Fig. 26
REYNALDO,
Duke of Rhyme

difficult to follow, but nobody seemed to care—the people were just happy to hear about a familiar character they already knew. Or thought they knew.

Reynaldo was sitting on the edge of his bed, strumming his lute and composing a song about himself out-barding Pennyfeather, when a gigantic blond man flew in through his window—and landed on a rack of tambourines. Gustav growled as he shook one of the jingling rings off his foot.

Reynaldo shrieked and dropped his lute. He ran to his door and pulled on the knob, forgetting it was locked. "Guards! I'm being attacked!" he screamed. But his guards, like all the others, had run off in search of the Gray Phantom.

"Are you the Gray Phantom?" the bard whimpered, pressing himself against his door as if he hoped to squeeze himself through the keyhole.

"Jeez, you bards don't pay attention to anything, do you?" Gustav groaned. "I'm Prince Gustav, one of the guys who rescued you from that witch."

"One of the sixteen hero princes of Sturmhagen?" the curly-haired bard asked, crouching in a corner and shielding his chest with his floppy feathered hat.

"No, I'm the seventeenth, and for your information—" Gustav was cut off as Duncan flew in through the window and bowled over a set of music stands. The much smaller prince staggered to his feet, holding his head. "Now I know why penguins prefer to walk."

Reynaldo tried to scramble under his bed, but Gustav grabbed him by the pantaloons and yanked him back out. "I'm too talented to die!" the bard whined.

"Hey," said Gustav. "All you've gotta do is sing for us and we'll leave you alone."

Reynaldo didn't need to be asked twice. He immediately jumped into song: "Listen dear hearts to a tale most upsetting, four bumbling Prince Charmings who destroyed a wedding—"

"Not that song!" Gustav growled.

"And it's *Princes* Charming," Duncan added pointedly. "How many times do I have to remind people of that?"

"But Princes Charming just sounds wrong," Reynaldo said. "No one would request my songs if I used stiff grammar like that."

Gustav picked Reynaldo up by his ankles and held him upside down.

"Okay, *Princes* Charming," the bard shrieked. "*Princes* Charming!"

"No, I actually agree with you on that point," Gustav said. "I just don't want to get off topic. Sing us the lullaby—

the one you sing to Princess Sourpuss every night."

"'The Tale of the Jeopardous Jade Djinn Gem'?" Reynaldo asked, his face turning bright red as blood rushed to his head.

"The Jepperjajinjam?" Gustav asked quizzically.

"Jeopardous Jade Djinn Gem!" Duncan shouted triumphantly. "We've found it, Gustav! *JJDG*!"

"Hate to break it to you," Gustav said. "But that would be all *J*s."

"No, it's *JJDG*," Duncan insisted.

Gustav mulled it over. "All right, I've heard of *G*s making a *J* sound, but not *D*s."

"The *D* in 'djinn' is silent," Duncan explained.

"Stupid language," Gustav grumbled. He dropped Reynaldo and ordered, "Sing us the Jeopardy Jewel song!"

"And try to stay on-key this time," Duncan added, squinting in an attempt to look tough.

"Sorry," said Reynaldo. "My vocals aren't at their best when I'm terrified for my life." Reynaldo cleared his throat and trilled, "Listen dear hearts to a tale of mayhem, of death and destruction all caused by a gem. . . ."

Gustav and Duncan listened to the bard's ancient tale, and while I could simply repeat all the lyrics for you to read right here, I'll do you the favor of just summing the story up instead. Believe me, there are only so many times you can hear someone rhyme "gem" with "phlegm" before it becomes really annoying.

In the tale, a nameless adventurer opened a mysterious bottle and freed a long-captive spirit: a "djinn," or genie. The djinn offered to grant the man one wish, but the man thought he could outsmart the spirit by wishing for two things at once. "I wish for wealth *and* power," he said.

The djinn responded by presenting the adventurer with an extraordinarily rare piece of orange jade, the most valuable gem in the world. "What about the second half of my wish?" the man asked angrily.

"That stone is not just priceless," the djinn replied. "It grants its bearer the power to control the mind of another. While you are in physical contact with the gem, anyone in your presence can become your puppet. Simply think what you want that person to do, and he will do it, regardless of his own will. Only one person at a time, though, and only while you can see him."

The greedy adventurer rushed home and immediately began using the jewel to make others do his bidding. But as he was not a very imaginative person, he mostly used it to make street vendors give him free coconut drinks. And that was when a thief swiped the jade from him.

The thief was much smarter than the adventurer, and he used the gem to great advantage. All his enemies conveniently decided to kill one another—after turning over all their treasures to him, of course. Suddenly, this petty pickpocket had the largest house the land had ever seen, the fastest horses, and the finest magenta silk robes. Before long, he ruled his town.

But there was one thing the thief did not have: love. He'd been pining after a lovely barmaid for years, but the girl had always rebuffed his advances. So one day the thief went to the barmaid, proposed marriage, and used the gem to make her say yes. But he'd never heard the djinn's rules for using the magical stone. As soon as the pickpocket grew tired, closed his eyes, and could no longer see his new bride, his control over her was broken. She fled into the desert. Blinded by his desire to find the girl, the thief trekked into the dunes after her. But he was unprepared, with no food, no water, and no map. He soon became lost. And it was there, somewhere in the desert sands, that he died.

Reynaldo finished his song and took a bow as Duncan applauded.

"That was rather dark," Duncan said. "But I liked the part about coconut drinks."

Before Gustav had a chance to roll his eyes, the door was bashed in. Liam and Ella surveyed the wrecked bedroom—broken tambourines, toppled music stands, quivering bard—and both smacked their hands to their foreheads.

"*Subtly*, Gustav," Liam said. "I've been telling you for days—we needed to do this *subtly*."

"And I did!" Gustav retorted. "Subtly. Everything's quiet, the bard suspects nothing, and then subtly—*BOOM!*—we attack."

"Gustav?" Duncan said gently. "I think you were thinking of 'suddenly.'"

"No," said Gustav. "Suddenly is when . . . Oh. Yeah. Well, uh . . . who cares? Because we heard the song. And now we know what *JJDG* is!"

"The Jeopardous Jade Djinn Gem!" Duncan announced.

"Even though it sounds like all *J*s," Gustav added.

"Jade," Liam said. "Is it orange jade, like the jewel on the sword?"

Duncan and Gustav nodded.

"But what's so special about this gem?" Ella asked.

"It's a spooky magic jewel that lets you control other people's minds," Duncan explained. "You could make them do whatever you want: squawk like a chicken, wear a funny hat. . . ."

"Turn over an entire kingdom to you," Liam added, his face turning unnaturally pale. "It's all coming together. That's how she plans to take over the world."

"Who's taking over the world?" a shrill voice asked from the hallway. Briar Rose pushed her way into the room past Liam and Ella and repeated her question. "Who's taking over the world?"

"We're on to you," Liam said. "We know why you want the Sword of Erinthia: the Jeopardous Jade Djinn Gem."

Briar stared at him fiercely but said nothing.

"With the power of the gem, you plan to take down every government in the Thirteen Kingdoms, one by one," Liam continued. "Force the king of Valerium to abdicate his throne, make Gustav's parents disband Sturmhagen's army, trick Duncan's parents into getting lost in the wilderness. . . ."

"You read my diary!" Briar fumed. "I thought you had more respect for personal property than that, Prince Charming."

"So you're not denying it," Liam said.

Briar walked over to Reynaldo's harp-shaped bed and sat down on the edge of the mattress. "Growing up in hiding from an evil curse can be pretty dull," she said. Her tone was softer than usual. "Even humiliating your servants becomes tiresome after a while. So you know what I did? I read a lot. And since I already knew I was destined to marry you, Liam, I read your family history. When I came across the story of that oaf, Prince Dorun, I immediately connected it to one of my favorite old bard songs, 'The Tale of the Jeopardous Jade Djinn Gem.' So much death and doom in that one—how can you not love it? Anyway, the orange jade, the skeleton in the Aridian desert, the magenta silk robes, the story about the royal menu—it didn't take a genius to realize that Dorun's gem *was* the Djinn Gem. And—"

"And now you want the gem for yourself, so you can take over the Thirteen Kingdoms," Ella said.

Briar gritted her teeth. "I'm explaining—"

"You can't explain your way out of this, Briar," Liam said.

"Believe what you want," Briar said. "Just let me know right now whether you're backing out of the mission or not. Because the ninjas from Kom-Pai just arrived. And I'll happily send them to Rauberia tomorrow if you guys aren't willing to go."

Ella and the princes all looked at one another.

"No, we're going," Liam said.

"Good," Briar said, standing up. "Because, one way or another, that sword has to be taken out of Deeb Rauber's hands." She walked to the cracked doorway and turned around. "I find it fascinating how you're all so worried about me when all I've done is enforce a preexisting marriage contract and arrest a handful of people who assaulted my palace. And yet you don't seem concerned in the slightest that this powerful gem is already sitting in a castle full of known criminals. There are worse people in the world than me, you know."

17

THE VILLAIN JUST WANTS TO HAVE FUN

If someone stands in your path to glory, crush him.
If someone holds you back from achieving your goals,
crush him. If someone peppers his speech with too
many "ers" or "ums," crush him.
—THE WARLORD'S PATH TO POWER:
AN ANCIENT TOME OF DARIAN WISDOM

The Warlord of Dar closed the door to his guest suite: a posh room carpeted with pilfered animal-skin rugs and furnished with sophisticated armchairs and armoires that Rauber had stolen over the years. He turned to address the Darian soldiers he had gathered there. First in line was Madu, the Keeper of the Snake. Tall and lithe, Madu wore a tattered kilt and a loose vest that hung open to reveal scores of serpent tattoos covering his skin.

Beside the snake handler stood a stocky bodyguard named Jezek, who was clad from collar to boots in spike-studded armor. And next to him was Redshirt, a thick-necked barbarian with a penchant for licking the edge of his ax.

The final member of Rundark's cabal was Wrathgar, the dungeon master. A walking mass of muscle, Wrathgar was larger than the Warlord himself (larger than all Gustav's brothers, too—in case you're keeping score). A red-and-black mask covered the top half of his face, while below it, a freakishly long mustache hung down to his chest like a pair of face-ponytails. Tied to each end of his mustache was an unidentified bone: the remnant of a lion's claw, perhaps, or a human finger, or maybe just a chicken leg (it's not like anybody was going to ask).

Lord Rundark had discovered Wrathgar years earlier. The Warlord had been leading a platoon of barbarian soldiers to raid and ransack the Darian village of Hocksnath, but when he arrived, he saw that the town had already been reduced to a blackened field of burning timbers and smoking rubble. Standing in the center of all that debris was Wrathgar. As the Warlord approached the masked behemoth, Wrathgar simply said, "The people of Hocksnath didn't like my facial hair." To which Rundark responded by offering the man a job. Wrathgar had been Rundark's secret weapon ever since.

"Tell us what you need, Lord Rundark," Wrathgar said. When he spoke, it sounded like his mouth was full of broken glass (which it often was—he liked to chew on bottles in between meals).

"As we have discussed," the Warlord said, "Rauberia will soon be ours. And once we have transformed this most perfect of all geographical bases into New Dar, the rest of the nations of the world will be waiting for us to skewer them like so many kingdom kabobs. But the boy remains an issue."

Fig. 27
Rundark's
HENCHMEN

"So we take him out now?" Wrathgar asked.

"No, I cannot eliminate the Bandit King until I understand the core mystery that surrounds him," Rundark said. "I cannot comprehend his popularity among his men. Nor his notoriety among the people of these nearby kingdoms. Rauber is a floundering mess of a criminal. He is sloppy, stubborn, and, from what I can tell, he doesn't have the stomach for true evil. In short, he is a child."

"Have you all been on the roof?" Madu, the snake handler asked. "He's got a little golf course up there. Where you have to hit the ball between the legs of an elephant that squirts water at you. I don't get it."

"His dungeon disgusts me," Wrathgar bellowed. "To see the things he calls 'torture devices'—a funnel to drip saliva into one's ear, a machine to stretch a prisoner's undergarments—it is pitiful." He picked up an armchair, bit it in half, and spat the pieces onto the floor.

"I understand you are all frustrated, but you will need to tolerate the boy's insufficiently villainous behavior a while longer," Lord Rundark said. "As powerful as the five of us are, I doubt we can hold back a rebellion of three hundred bandits. We need to win Rauber's men over to our side first."

"We need bards," Redshirt suggested. "Rauber's got

so many of those songs about him. That's why he's so infamous. People hear those bard songs, and they either want to join Rauber or flee from him. I've been saying for years that Dar should have a bard."

Rundark grabbed Redshirt by his red shirt and hurled him out through the fourth-story window. More eel food.

"Bards are good for nothing more than brainless entertainment," Rundark said to his remaining henchmen. "It is not men wielding tiny guitars who tell the world what they should fear; it is men of true power like myself. We have been schooling Rauber's men in the ways of Dar; eventually they will realize what true villainy looks like.

"It is to this end that I have gathered you four . . . er, *three* here today. We must begin working on Rauber's bandits, sowing the seeds of discord among them. Pay extra attention to the swordsman, Vero. If we can turn him, others will follow."

There was a quick knock, and Falco—the bald, sharp-toothed sentry—opened the door and slipped in, looking agitated.

"What is it, Falco?" Rundark asked.

Falco got down and walked on his knees and made a goofy face.

"Rauber is coming?" Rundark said.

Falco nodded.

Seconds later there was another knock at the door—a loud banging this time. Falco opened it to reveal Deeb Rauber, picking his nose.

"Yes?" Rundark intoned.

"I'm hosting a circus tomorrow—four o'clock," Rauber announced. "It's gonna be sweet. Clowns, dancing bears, cat jugglers—I think they've even got a monkey that throws darts at a pig."

Jezek stepped up to the doorway. "I'm supposed to be teaching your men spear technique tomorrow afternoon," he said.

"It can wait, Spike," Rauber returned. "Did you hear what I said? *Cat jugglers!*"

"What does that even mean?" Jezek asked with disdain. "Is it men who juggle cats or cats that juggle other stuff?"

"Like it matters?" Rauber retorted.

"Fall back, Jezek," Rundark said. He stepped up to Rauber. "My men and I will not be attending this circus," he added with barely disguised disdain.

"No way, man" Rauber said. "You can't skip it. I mean, you'd totally regret it if you did."

The Warlord let out a long, slow breath. "If it means so much to you, I will try to stop by at some point."

"And chance missing the best part?" Rauber said. "No, you're gonna be sitting right next to me in my private viewing box. Best seats in the house. Especially for the finale. It's gonna be awesome."

Rundark eyed the boy in silence for several seconds. Then his mouth curled into something resembling a grin. "You win," he said in his friendliest voice (which was still pretty scary). "I will be there at four on the dot."

"Excellent," said Rauber. "You're not gonna regret this. Circuses rule." And he left, whistling loudly and very much off-key.

As soon as the Bandit King was out the door, Rundark's men began grumbling. "A circus?" Jezek asked skeptically.

"Rauber was unnaturally insistent that I not only attend, but that I sit in a specific seat," Rundark said. "The boy thinks himself my equal, my *rival* even. It was only a matter of time before he tried to eliminate me. And he's making his move now. He plans to assassinate me at the end of this . . . *circus*." He spat the word. "I will let him try," Rundark continued. "And after he has failed in front of everyone, I won't have to worry about winning over his men. I will do so right then and there—by killing the boy."

18

A HERO HAS FRIENDS
IN HIGH PLACES

There is no "I" in League of Princes.
—THE HERO'S GUIDE TO BEING A HERO

"So, what do you say, Reese?" Frederic asked. "Will you help us?"

The giant squinched up his massive face. "Ehhhhhhh . . . I think not," he said. After nearly a full day's travel, Frederic and Rapunzel had finally found Reese along the shores of Lake Dräng, just across the border in the kingdom of Jangleheim. The hundred-foot-tall man was sitting in the sand, wearing a shirt and pants sewn together from thousands of discarded flour sacks. He held an entire tree in one hand and whittled at it with a knife he'd created for himself by welding thirty iron shields together. All around him, sloppily carved wooden figures were displayed against the rocks. They had hair of swamp reeds, moss, or straw; faces that were painted on with berry ink or constructed out of seashells. Some had long, scrawny, tree branch arms; others had stiff, splintery limbs that were once the oars of abandoned rowboats. None looked even remotely lifelike, yet several had SOLD signs around their "necks."

"Don't get me wrong, sir," Reese continued. "I'm honored that you've come to me with this request. But I've been enjoying the peaceful life up here. I've got beautiful scenery everywhere I look, I'm doing what I love, and business is booming."

By almost any assessment, the giant was a terrible artist. But he was lucky enough to settle in Jangleheim, a nation whose people had notoriously poor taste. Which just goes to show: There's a place for everybody.

Frederic respected that Reese had given up his dangerous and violent henchman work and was now living an eminently honorable life. He took a deep breath, feeling a little guilty about what he was about to say.

"I understand your reluctance, Reese," he said. "Really, I do. I guess I was just hoping that, after *saving your life* ..."

"And healing your blister," Rapunzel threw in, flashing Frederic a quick smile.

"Yes, after the help we've given you," Frederic continued, "we hoped you'd be gentleman enough to return the favor."

"It's true," Reese said. "If you hadn't convinced me to run when I did, I would be a big pile of bacon right now. I do owe you for that. And that blister—ooh—that was quite nasty; but still, I can't do any dangerous stuff. I promised my mum."

"And how do you think your mum would feel if she knew you were so callously denying a friend in need?" Frederic asked.

"Hey, you're just trying to guilt me," Reese said.

"That's right, Son, they are," a thunderous voice boomed from the woods behind them. "Good for you, not falling for it."

Frederic and Rapunzel spun around to see a titanic woman even taller than Reese standing on the beach. She was clad in a tunic made from the hides of what seemed to be at least a thousand animals. Her teeth were like tombstones, her eyebrows untrimmed hedges. Entire families could get lost in her forest of spiky gray hair. "Let me get rid of these pests for you."

The giantess lifted her humongous bare foot.

"No, Mum, wait!" Reese shouted, jumping up and

causing a rockslide that buried several of his art pieces. "Please, don't crush these people. They're not so bad. I swear it."

She gently lowered her foot back to the sand. Then she squatted and peered suspiciously at the pair of puny humans.

"You must be Reese's mum—I mean, mother," Frederic said.

"The name's Maude," she replied in a gruff yet feminine voice. "Because my son asked me nicely, I'm not going to squash you. But stop harassing the boy. He's a good kid. I don't want him getting involved with the wrong crowd. So leave before I decide to exfoliate my toes with your faces."

"Ma'am," Frederic said. "Reese has always spoken highly of you. I know you are a wise and compassionate woman. If you could just hear us out . . ." He went on to explain their mission and the plan he had come up with to have Reese lift Gustav, Ella, and Lila over Rauber's Wall of Secrecy. "So, as you can see, we *need* Reese."

"No, you don't," Maude replied. "You need a giant. And this sounds like *my* kind of job."

"Mum, you can't be serious," Reese blurted. "You said you were retired from this sort of thing. You wanted a quiet, peaceful life now."

"I want that for *you*, Reese," the mother giant said. "But me? I miss the old days." She stared wistfully up at the emerging stars.

"Excuse me, ma'am," Frederic said. "'Old days'?"

"I was quite a wild one in my youth," Maude said. "Stomping down villages, wrestling dragons, biting the roofs off palaces. I had more knights and adventurers trying to slay me than I could shake a tree at. I hit the peak of my notoriety after that beanstalk incident."

"I didn't know the giant from that story was a woman," Rapunzel said in awe.

"Well, the bards don't always nail the details, do they?" Maude replied. "But that's all in the past, anyway. Once I became a parent, I wanted to settle down and set the right example for my boy."

Reese flashed a sweet smile.

"But, hey, my job here is done, right?" Maude continued. "Reese has turned out okay. Mission accomplished. Let's go crush some stuff."

The enormous woman began doing warm-up stretches.

"Um, you know, we don't really need you to crush anything," Frederic said.

"Yeah, yeah—don't worry," Maude said dismissively. "I'll do what you need me to: carrying people places, dropping them over walls, crushing whatever."

"No, really," Frederic said. "No crushing."

Maude waved him off. "Seriously, don't worry. I won't crush anything too big." She bent down and scooped the pair of humans into one hand—Rapunzel clasping onto Frederic's shoulder to steady herself—and their horses into the other.

"Um, before we go," Frederic said, nodding toward the lake. "Maude, could you please also grab one of those old rowboats?"

As the sun rose over Avondell Palace on the morning of the summer solstice, Ella looked out her bedroom window and was infuriated by what she saw. Liam and Little Taylor were heading out through the front gates—by themselves. Still in her bedclothes, Ella burst from her room and ran down after them.

"Where do you think you're going?" she snapped when she caught up to them on the road away from the palace. "Running off on your own? Doing the exact same thing you were so mad at Frederic for?"

Liam stopped. "This is different," he said. "I'm doing this to prevent the rest of the team from dying."

"Gee, thanks for your faith in me," Ella said bitterly.

"Did you see those catapults lined up outside the palace?" he asked. "I'm not letting you or my sister—or even Gustav—get shot out of those things."

"You know, I did make the glider wings you asked for," Taylor said. But he was ignored.

"No catapults—got it. So . . . then what? You're planning to pull the heist off by yourself?" Ella asked, trying to decide whether she was more incredulous or offended.

"Well, not just him," Taylor said, tossing his arm around Liam. "Little Taylor will be there, too."

"Look," said Liam. "You know as well as I do that Briar was lying to us last night."

"Lying about what?" Taylor asked. Ella shushed him.

"But she was right about one thing," Liam continued. "We've still got to snatch that treasure from Rauber."

"When we say 'treasure,' are we talking about one particular treasure?" Taylor asked, tapping Liam on the shoulder. "Or are we speaking in general terms?"

Ella shushed him.

"You know, I'm starting to feel left out," Taylor said.

"Why don't you run on ahead," Liam said, nudging Little Taylor down the road. "I'll catch up to you in about an hour at our appointed spot, and you can 'capture' me then."

The tailor reluctantly went off by himself.

"Ella," Liam said, looking her in the eye. "The Sword of Erinthia needs to be in our hands—not Briar's, not Rauber's, not anybody else's. Until it is, nobody is safe. So I'm going to get it. And I'm not endangering the rest of you in the process."

Ella grabbed his hand and started leading him back toward the palace. "Come," she said. "If you really feel you don't need the rest of us, you can tell it to everybody face-to-face."

A short time later, Liam was standing in the garden trying to explain himself to Duncan, Gustav, Lila, Snow, and Mr. Troll. But they weren't buying any of it.

"We're a team," Gustav said. "If you go, we all go."

"People," Liam said, "this mission is no joke. For it to succeed, it will have to go off like clockwork."

Snow raised her hand. "I don't know how a clock works."

"Neither do I," Duncan added.

"It's just an expression," Liam sighed. "There's no real clock."

"Clocks are only make-believe?" Duncan gasped.

"But there's a big one right there," Snow said, pointing to the palace clock tower.

"People!" Liam said again, more forcefully this time. "You're missing my point. How are you planning to get past the Wall of Secrecy?" Liam asked in frustration.

"Hmm, what an odd question," Briar said as she strolled up, spinning a parasol over her shoulder. "I thought that's what all those catapults were for."

"It is," Gustav said. Liam shook his head vigorously, but Gustav continued. "Captain Cape-Head is just nervous 'cause we've never tested the catapults out. Let's give one a test run right now, and if it works, we're good to go."

"A reasonable request," Briar said. "But you'd better hurry up. I came out here to wish you all good luck, assuming you'd be on your way already. Half of you are still in your pajamas. You'll never make it to Rauberia by four if you don't start speeding things up." She turned and shouted to a silver-haired man in a teal military suit and dazzling mother-of-pearl helmet. "General Kuffin, ready a catapult for Prince Gustav."

"Aye, Your Highness," the general called in reply. He marched to one of the catapults sitting just outside the garden wall and had eight of his men tug and yank on various ropes to pull the arm of the machine into throwing position.

"Gustav, do you really want to do this?" Liam asked.

Gustav shrugged and grabbed a pair of flimsy-looking cloth wings. Just then the ground shook. Everyone looked up to see the early-morning sun blotted out by the frizzy-haired head of a scowling giantess.

"Monster attack!" General Kuffin yelled. Soldiers everywhere scrambled for their pikes and axes, ready to defend the palace. "Load the catapult, quickly," Kuffin barked. "The fiend is almost upon us."

A trio of soldiers heaved a heavy boulder up into the basket of the cocked catapult. "Fire!" one shouted as he cut the rope and let the spring-loaded arm of the machine fly upward.

Everyone watched, expecting the massive rock to arc toward the attacking giant—but it didn't. The boulder flew *straight* up. Far up. Very, very far up. And then it plummeted back down to smash the catapult into splinters and embed itself deep in the earth. Everyone turned and looked at Gustav.

"Well, I would've been wearing the glider wings," he said. He slipped his arms into the straps, and the wings tore in half. "Meh. I still would've been fine."

General Kuffin rallied his soldiers toward the next catapult, but everyone froze when they heard a soft, definitely nongiant voice calling down.

"Don't shoot!" Frederic cried. Maude crouched and lowered her hand to the ground to release her passengers. Frederic stepped off first, then took Rapunzel's hand to help her down from the enormous pinkie. "Time for me to introduce you to everyone," Frederic said as he saw all his friends running out to them.

Ella was the first to reach them. She picked Frederic up, swung him around, and planted a big kiss on his lips. Frederic stepped back, somewhat stunned. It was the first time Ella had kissed him since the night they danced at the ball.

And then a whole lot of things happened all at once.

Liam, who'd been racing to welcome Frederic, stopped in his tracks. Rapunzel, sheepishly trying to back away from Frederic and Ella, bumped into Gustav, who responded by yelping, turning around, and pretending not to see her. General Kuffin asked Briar what he should do about the giant, and Briar told him to shut up. Duncan spotted a toad he named Hoppin' John. And Maude cleared her throat, which sounded like the world's most disgusting thunder.

"Um . . . ," Frederic said, trying to get over the surprise of the kiss. "Obviously there's a lot to explain. For those of you who don't know her, this is Rapunzel." Rapunzel gave a modest curtsy that made Gustav roll his eyes. "She's a healer. She's going to wait here at the palace in case anybody comes back looking, well, like I did after our last adventure.

"And *this*," Frederic continued, gesturing skyward, "is Maude. She's going to get our team over the Wall of Secrecy."

At that moment, Liam didn't care about who had kissed whom; he couldn't help feeling proud of his friend. "Welcome back, Frederic."

And then, just to make sure no one changed his or her mind, Maude smashed the remaining catapults.

And so the plan for the Great Sword Heist was finalized.

1. Little Taylor, disguised as the Gray Phantom, delivers Liam and Frederic to Deeb Rauber and puts the two princes in the Bandit King's dungeon.

2. Duncan and Snow sneak into the castle, pretending to be clowns with the Flimsham Brothers Circus. Once inside, they will serve as lookouts.

3. While Mr. Troll causes a distraction at the front gates, Maude deposits Gustav, Ella, and Lila over the back wall—along with a rowboat.

4. They use the boat to cross the moat, then scale the back wall of the castle with grappling hooks.

5. On the roof, Lila goes down the Snake Hole to unlock the vault.

6. Exactly one hour after the start of the circus, Little Taylor frees Liam and Frederic from their cells so they can grab the Sword of Erinthia from the open vault.

7. When the show is over, everybody escapes hidden among the circus performers.

As soon as the last of the heroes had left for Rauberia, Briar Rose rushed to her bedroom. She glanced out her window, her eyes lingering on the malfunctioning catapult that most certainly would have killed Gustav. She tore herself away and darted to her vanity table, where she reached behind her mirror and pulled her diary from its hiding spot. She flipped past her annotated map of the Thirteen Kingdoms, past her list of evidence that connected the Jeopardous Jade Djinn Gem to the Sword of Erinthia, and stopped when she saw the heading "How to Get *JJDG*." Below it she'd scrawled dozens of ideas, all of which were messily scratched out except for one: "Use League of Princes."

It was under way.

Stay focused on the goal, she told herself. *Just like you always do. In a matter of hours you're finally going to get what you've been after.*

"Your Highness."

Startled by the unexpected voice, Briar slammed the book shut. But she relaxed as soon as she saw who had just crawled in through her window, looking filthy and haggard.

"It's about time you showed up, Ruffian," she scolded. "Do you have any idea how long I've been waiting for you to—"

"Save your badgering," the bounty hunter droned. "I don't have the patience for it right now. Days ago, back at your campsite in Sturmhagen, I spotted the Gray Phantom spying on you and the League, so I followed him. He passed through Rauberia on a shortcut into Flargstagg, which is where I caught up with him. And I was about to warn your husband when I was . . . *huff* . . . ambushed by those other princes."

"You were going to warn Liam that the Gray Phantom was following him?" Briar asked, her voice even tighter and more clipped than usual.

"No," Ruffian said. "I was going to warn Liam that the man he'd just hired *was* the real Gray Phantom."

Briar breathed in short, staccato bursts.

"And that's not all," Ruffian added. "I've also learned that Rauber isn't alone in his castle. His current guest is the Warlord of Dar. Your husband and his friends will be placing themselves in the hands of the most dangerous men in the Thirteen Kingdoms."

Briar hurled her journal at the wall.

"Your Highness?" Ruffian asked. "I do hope you will be sensible enough to call off your plans."

Briar stood up. "Not in a million years," she said with steely determination. "We're just going to have to move faster. Let's go."

PART III

STORMING
THE
CASTLE

19

THE VILLAIN PULLS
THE STRINGS

If someone does not tremble at your name,
try writing your name on a board. And hitting him with it.
— THE WARLORD'S PATH TO POWER:
AN ANCIENT TOME OF DARIAN WISDOM

"This is where we're supposed to meet Taylor?" Frederic asked, trying to walk casually as Liam led him along a rugged dirt path near the border of Rauberia.

"Yes," Liam hissed in a whisper. "Although if you keep asking questions like that, it will totally defeat the purpose of staging our kidnapping."

Just then Frederic fell to the ground, his legs suddenly bound together by a thick, winding thread. Liam hit the dirt a second later, tied up in the same way. The Gray Phantom leapt out from a crevice in the rocky mountainside, rolling a spool of red thread between his fingers.

"I see you both made it," the Phantom said. "All the better."

"Is that you, Taylor?" Frederic asked softly as the Phantom tied his hands together.

"Shhh," Little Taylor warned from behind the mask. "Rauber has scouts along these trails."

"But listen, Taylor," Frederic said. "It occurred to me that Rauber's men might search us before they throw us into jail, and there's something I don't want them to find. In my jacket there's a small vial of Rapunzel's tears. You should hold on to it."

"Rapunzel? The one who heals people?" Taylor said, reaching into Frederic's jacket and pocketing the vial for himself. "That's fantastic."

"People, we're supposed to be fighting," Liam whispered. "Darn you, Phantom!" he shouted for the benefit of anyone who might be listening. "You'll pay for this!"

Taylor tied Liam's hands and then punched him in the face, knocking him out.

"Hey!" Frederic protested. "You didn't need to hit him!"

"I know," said Taylor. He punched out Frederic as

well. Because he actually was the Gray Phantom. And he was a brutal madman.

Some of what Little Taylor had told the princes about himself was true. He really was a tailor (though one who got a kick out of "accidentally" poking his customers with needles). And Deeb Rauber really did rob him years earlier. But the theft only made Taylor realize how badly he himself longed to be a criminal. He wanted nothing more than to join the forces of the Bandit King, hoping to someday stand beside Rauber as his loyal number two. But alas, it was not to be.

Whenever the Bandit King had a recruitment drive, Taylor would try to earn himself a place in Rauber's army. And every time, Rauber would unceremoniously kick him out, scoffing at his choice of weapons before he ever got a chance to show anybody how well he could use them ("A needle and thread? Are you planning to terrify me by knitting a really ugly sweater?"). And the bandits always guffawed. But Rauber's incessant mocking never deterred Taylor; it only made him more intent on earning the Bandit King's respect. So he adopted the persona of the Gray Phantom and went on a streak of robbery, murder, and destruction—all to impress Deeb Rauber. Well, and because Little Taylor was an evil, soulless lunatic.

* * *

Deeb Rauber sat on his throne, looking a bit more genuinely king-like than usual. He had traded in his typical cotton pants and vest for a sleek black suit emblazoned with gold embroidery. He'd pilfered the outfit ages ago from a young Carpagian prince and, while it was still a tad too large for him, he felt it gave him a more mature look.

Vero was at Rauber's right hand, as usual, while Lord Rundark and his spike-covered bodyguard, Jezek, also stood by. When Rauber heard that the infamous Gray Phantom had come calling—with a gift for him—he made sure the Warlord was present to see him receive such an important visitor. Dozens of bandit guards looked on eagerly as the throne room's doors opened and the Phantom entered, dragging the bound-up princes behind him.

"Well, he's been unnecessarily rough," Frederic whispered into Liam's ear. "But at least he got us in."

"Holy snap!" Rauber blurted when he saw them. "If it isn't two of the people on my Top Ten Most Hated list. Seriously, look. Here's the list." He pulled a list of names from his back pocket and flashed it at them.

"This is a glorious day, men," Rauber announced, dramatically raising a jeweled scepter above his head. "For

326

I have recaptured two of my archenemies, Prince Lame and Prince Fred-stink."

"Actually, it was I who captured them," the Phantom said.

"Ah, yes, the Gray Phantom," Rauber said, pulling a bug from his hair and flicking it at Frederic. "I've been hearing

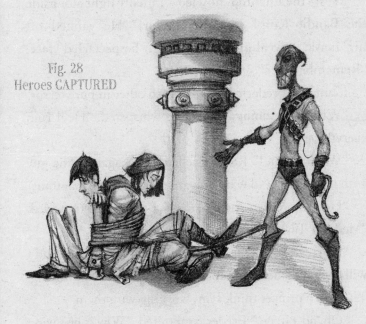

Fig. 28
Heroes CAPTURED

a lot about you lately. You've done some pretty nasty stuff. And now that you've brought me these wonderful little presents . . . well, there just might be a place for you in this organization."

"Do you mean it, sir?" the Phantom asked. "You will take me into your unstoppable bandit army? I can finally serve under the command of the glorious Deeb Rauber?"

"Okay, you're starting to weird me out," Rauber said. "Let's just give you a trial position and see how it goes."

"Yes!" the Phantom howled. "I finally fight alongside the Bandit King! I, Little Taylor!" He yanked off his mask, revealing his smiling, bespectacled face. "Remember me?"

Liam and Frederic looked at each other in pure terror.

"What is he doing?" Frederic whispered. "He'll ruin everything!"

"Waitaminute!" Rauber yelled. "You again? The guy with the string? No way. You are *not* the Gray Phantom."

"He is not even that good of a tailor," Vero added. "Medium Taylor does much better inseams."

"No, really, I am the Phantom," Taylor insisted. "And I will show you how valuable I can be to you, Bandit King. These two princes think I am working with them."

"Oh, no; oh, no," Frederic muttered. "Why is he saying that?"

Liam closed his eyes. "Because he's finally telling the truth. He really is the Phantom."

"They hired me to deliver them to you, believing I

would betray you and free them from their cells so they could rob your vault," Taylor said feverishly.

"Is this for real?" Rauber snickered. "You two goody-goodies were going to try to steal from me? Oh, that's rich. So, I'm curious: How did you two popcorn brains think you were going to get *into* my vault. I do keep it locked, you know."

"They know about the Snake Hole on the roof," Taylor gleefully explained. "They were going to have a troll distract your lookouts while some of their friends launched themselves over your Wall of Secrecy with catapults. But don't worry about that—I sabotaged the catapults."

"You fiend," Liam spat.

"So, Your Highness," Taylor said to Rauber, "I believe I have proven my worth. May I now officially count myself among the ranks of your loyal followers?"

Rauber leaned back in his throne and laughed. "Oh, Taylor, you leave me in stitches," he chuckled. "But seriously, no. Get out. I still can't get past the needle-and-thread thing. Lamest weapons ever."

Taylor looked heartbroken.

"Men! Escort this sorry so-and-so from the castle," Rauber said. He elbowed Lord Rundark. "Get it? Sew-and-sew?"

A dozen bandits approached Little Taylor, but the lithe little man wasn't going anywhere. He flipped, he kicked, he tangled, he pulled; and just as he'd done at the Stumpy Boarhound, he soon created a pile of much larger men hog-tied on the floor around him.

Lord Rundark stepped toward the panting tailor and applauded. "You are a master of String-Chi," the Warlord said. "It has been ages since I've seen someone with such vicious talent. You *shall* be part of this bandit army. A general, in fact."

"Hey, wait!" Rauber jumped up, standing on his throne, and wagging his finger in Rundark's direction. "You can't just—" Vero tapped the Bandit King on the shoulder and subtly shook his head. "Um, I mean, you can't just tell the guy he's a general without me giving him the official 'welcome aboard' sign." Rauber stuck his thumb up his nose and wiggled his fingers. "There," he said. "Now you're a general. I guess." He made a face at Rundark behind his back.

On the floor, Frederic squirmed over to Liam and whispered in his ear, "This is not going well."

Vero hoisted the bound princes to their feet and pushed them out the door, with Taylor skittering giddily after them.

"I assume you will cancel this circus now," Rundark said to Rauber.

"Cancel it? Why?" Rauber asked.

"There is an attack planned against your fortress, and you seek entertainment? Do you care at all what your men think of you?"

"My men think I'm awesome," Rauber said. "I think your men think I'm pretty awesome, too." He nodded at Jezek. "What about you, Spike? I'm awesome, right? Anyway, you heard the Phantom: There *was* an attack planned on my castle—an incredibly stupid one that never would have worked, by the way—but it's already been sunk."

"You have no concerns about this invasion?" Rundark was both fascinated and repulsed.

Rauber patted the Warlord on the shoulder (standing on his throne in order to reach). "Rundark, I had no idea you were such a worrywart," he said, smirking. "Look, if it'll make you feel better, I'll tell the archers at the front gate not to get spooked if they see a troll. And I'll put a bunch of extra guards at the back wall to look out for catapults. But the guys I put out there are gonna have to miss the circus; and if they ask about it, I'm telling them it was all your fault."

Simmering, Rundark walked away with Jezek right behind.

"Only a few hours until the circus, sir," Jezek said.

"The last few hours in the reign of King Rauber," Rundark said with a sneer.

The dungeon level of Rauber's castle was an unholy mix of torture chamber and candy factory. It contained, for instance, literal licorice whips. Its bleak stone floors had been intentionally splashed with syrupy beverages so that your feet made a sticky, ripping sound with every step you took. That alone was enough to drive Frederic crazy as he and Liam were led to their cells. He cringed as they passed a device designed to blow powdered sugar into a prisoner's eyes, one that dunked you backward into molten caramel, and another that force-fed people spoonfuls of dry cinnamon powder.

They turned and entered a dead-end corridor lined with cramped and clammy stone cells. Standing in the center of the cellblock, waiting for them, was a masked figure, vaguely human in shape but approximately the size of an ogre.

"Gentlemen, I would like to introduce you to Wrathgar, our dungeon master," Vero said politely. "He will be, as we say in my country, your *host*."

Wrathgar snorted steam from his nostrils.

"Does he have horsetails hanging from his face?" Frederic asked in disbelief.

Vero leaned over to him and whispered, "It is meant to be a mustache. You would be wise not to question it."

"Leave," Wrathgar barked at Vero and Taylor as he grabbed the princes by their heads and shoved each of them into his own separate cell and slammed the doors. He tossed his key ring onto a high nail at the dead-end wall of the cellblock and proceeded to stand there breathing. Both Liam and Frederic shrank, wondering how anyone could make the simple act of breathing so terrifying.

"Oh, hey, I almost forgot," Taylor said to Vero as they made their way back upstairs. He reached into his shirt and pulled out a small glass vial. "Magical healing tears from Rapunzel herself," he said. "You think the Bandit King would want these for his treasure collection?"

"Perhaps." Vero took the vial from him, tucked it into his own vest, and flashed a gentlemanly smile. "Have no fear. I will take care of this for you."

20

A HERO ACTS
LIKE A CLOWN

*The best disguises are so good, you won't
even recognize yourself. To avoid forgetting who you are,
you may want to consider disguising as yourself.*
— THE HERO'S GUIDE TO BEING A HERO

The Flimsham Brothers Circus was founded
generations ago by Jacques and Dmitri Flimsham,
twin boys who entertained houseguests by making their
younger brother, Rufus, jump through a hoop with a
ball balanced on his nose—and tossing him a small fish
afterward as a reward. As word spread, the Flimshams
added more acts and began charging admission. They
built themselves some homemade stilts, brought in a
neighborhood girl who could climb tall lamps, and even

trained the tiny fishes to jump into Rufus's mouth on their own. Eventually, this bit of weekend entertainment turned into a full-fledged traveling circus.

But it didn't become a huge hit until years later, when the circus was under the management of the slick and stylish Stanislav Flimsham, who also served as ringmaster. It was Stanislav's love of sparkle and dazzle (or "sparzle," as he put it), combined with his knack for finding truly unusual acts (like his famous jousting chickens or El Stripo, the tiger that spat human babies into the audience), that made the Flimsham Brothers' show the most renowned circus in the Thirteen Kingdoms.

Children all over would gather along the roadside to watch the circus caravan roll by: twenty glittering, rainbow-colored wagons driven by burly, heavily sequined men. The kids would keep their eyes trained on the passing windows, hoping for a glimpse of a shimmery top hat, a bouncy clown wig, or a flickering striped tail. Duncan had giddily done so several times in his own youth.

Those familiar old "happy bubbles" welled in his belly as he hid behind a large boulder in the woods, waiting for the circus caravan to come up the road. He had to remind himself that he and Snow were not there to watch the circus but to infiltrate it.

As they were instructed to do, Duncan and Snow had dug a huge hole in the road and covered it up with piles of long, dry reeds. And the lead driver steered his wagon straight into the trap. The right front wheel crashed down into the pit and snapped right off its axle. As the driver slid from his seat to take a look, the entire caravan came to a standstill.

Stanislav Flimsham threw open a door on the side of the lopsided wagon. "What happened?" he asked, feeling his hair to make sure his slick black pompadour was still in place.

Fig. 29
Stanislav
FLIMSHAM

"Lost a wheel," the driver groused. "This may take a while."

"Well, be fast about it," Stanislav said nervously. "You know who we're performing for today. We can't be late." He called for the other wagon drivers to come up to the front of the line and help out.

With that distraction in place, Duncan and Snow scrambled down to the wagon that was helpfully labeled

CLOWNS in huge pink letters. Duncan walked up to its back door, on which hung a small sign that read DO NOT DISTURB. He knocked anyway. The door opened, and a short man wearing a curly green wig poked his head out. "Which part of 'Do Not Disturb' do you not understand?" the man asked.

Duncan thought about it. "Turb," he answered.

The green-wigged man slammed the door in his face. Duncan knocked again. "Mr. Clown, we would like to make you an offer," he said, pulling a sack of coins from his belt. "My wife and I would like to trade places with you. I can't really say why—although I can assure you it has nothing to do with stealing a magical sword from the Bandit King. We'll make it worth your while, though. By giving you money."

The clown looked indignant. "Are you trying to bribe me?" he asked. "You think *I*, a master of the slapstick arts, will let *you*, an untrained nobody, perform in my place during this afternoon's show?"

"Me *and* my wife," Duncan added helpfully.

The man looked as if he'd just swallowed a mouthful of rancid yogurt. "Have you never heard of the Clown's Code of Honor?" He slammed the door once more.

"So was that a no?" Duncan asked through the door.

"Yes," the clown snapped. "I mean, no. I mean, yes, the answer is no. You're deliberately trying to confuse me."

"How many of you clowns are in there?" Snow asked, stepping up alongside her husband.

"There are four of us," the green-haired man answered, angrily throwing the door open again. "But we are all clowns of honor. None of my fellow artists will agree to your dirty payoff either."

"You clowns!" a sharp voice hissed from behind them. It was Briar Rose. "And I mean that to be an insult, not an observation."

"Who the heck are you supposed to be?" the clown asked.

Briar clocked him over the head with her golden gavel. The clown fell from the back of the wagon and landed in a heap on the dirt road.

"Princess, I told you to wait," Ruffian the Blue admonished as he ran up.

Duncan was perplexed. "Why are you two here? Does Liam know about this?"

"Of course he does," Briar tossed off as she climbed into the wagon and Ruffian hurried in after her.

Snow poked the clown on the ground. "He's unconscious," she said.

"Don't look at me," Duncan said. "I'm not going to kiss him."

Just then three more motley-clothed clowns were hurled from the wagon: two women and a man, each knocked out. Ruffian climbed back outside.

"Behind that boulder," Ruffian instructed. "Hurry. Before all the drivers return to their wagons." He, Duncan, and Snow dragged the four unconscious clowns out of the road.

"When exactly did Liam change the plan?" Duncan asked.

"He didn't," Ruffian said. "Princess Briar did. I'm sorry to have to do this." He pulled a rope from his belt and proceeded to tie Duncan and Snow together.

"Excuse me, Mr. the Blue," Snow said. "It's going to be a lot harder for us to dress as clowns when we're tied up like this."

Ruffian placed gags over both of their mouths and went back inside the clown wagon with Briar.

After several minutes of sitting in the dirt tied up, Duncan finally said, "I don't think this is really part of the plan." (Although, through the gag, it sounded like "Ah ro rih rih eh reeree rah oh ruh rah.")

Snow, who understood him perfectly, replied, "I think you're right." ("Ah rih roh rah.")

Thankfully for you, the reader, they didn't need to communicate like this much longer. Because Rapunzel appeared, slipping out from behind a nearby rock.

"I'm so glad you showed up," Snow said as soon as the gag was pulled down from her mouth. "I've been meaning to ask you what you use to get your hair so thick and silky."

"Um, I was going to ask if you were all right, but I'm guessing yes," Rapunzel said.

"Briar knocked out all the clowns and tied us up," Duncan said. "I'm not totally positive, but I believe she might be up to something"

"That's why I followed her and the hooded man," Rapunzel said. "Frederic warned me about Briar. He was afraid she might double-cross you all. So when I saw her sneak out of the palace, I knew I had to follow. Which is crazy! I don't really know what possessed me. I'm a peaceful person! I grow turnips and take care of elves with pinkeye! I shouldn't be here."

"That's okay, Punzy," Duncan said. "Snow and I can take it from here."

"Where are we taking it?" Snow asked.

"Where are we taking what?" Duncan responded.

"Whatever you're talking about."

"What was I talking about?"

"Lunch, I hope. Because I am starving."

"Okay," Rapunzel said with resignation. "I guess I'm sticking with you two a little longer."

"Wonderful. So what do we do now?" Duncan asked, then quickly blurted, "Wait! Don't tell me. Of the three of us here, I'm the one who's a real hero. I'll figure it out."

"Why don't we just continue with the original plan?" Snow asked.

"Hmm," Duncan mused. He pulled out a piece of paper and a quill and jotted down a note for his book: "A real hero listens to his wife." He put the paper away and announced, "Let's do it. We've got some perfectly good clown costumes right here. They happen to have clowns in them; but, hey, you take what you can get."

Duncan, Snow, and Rapunzel swapped outfits with three of the unconscious clowns. "I should be healing this woman, not stealing her clothes," Rapunzel sighed as she put on a roomy white one-piece jumpsuit with rainbow-colored fluff balls down the front. "I will come back and cry on you," she whispered to the clown.

After Snow changed into a baggy purple-and-blue striped shirt, baggy orange pants, and a pink cap, Duncan, who dressed behind a shrub for privacy, jumped out and asked, "How do I look?"

"Dunky, I thought you were going to put on the clown's clothes," Snow said, disappointed.

"I did," Duncan said, looking down at himself.

"They look just like your old clothes."

"Not the belt, though," Duncan said, shaking his hips and making a jingling sound. "It has bells!"

Just then the wagon train began moving again. The trio ran to catch up with the last wagon—the one marked ANIMALS—and jumped on board before it got moving too fast. They found themselves in a dark, cramped space surrounded by dozens of wild creatures, not all of which were in cages—including a nervous-looking pig and a monkey fondling a handful of darts.

"This should be a fun ride," Duncan said.

"Hey, look," Snow said, yanking a tray of berries away from a very sad bear cub. She smushed a raspberry with her fingertip and then touched it to her nose to make a bright red dot on the end. "We can't be clowns without makeup!"

After the circus rolled through the front gates of the Wall of Secrecy, the wagons parked in the open courtyard, and when the performers spilled out, nobody paid attention to the three new clowns with big berry-red circles on their noses and cheeks. It helped that the Flimsham clowns were a notoriously cliquish bunch who rarely socialized with the other circus folk. Most of the acrobats and lion tamers couldn't tell one clown from another anyway.

Duncan, Snow, and Rapunzel blended into the crowd of acrobats, dancers, and trapeze artists as they crossed the large wooden drawbridge toting crates of props and pushing wheeled cages full of wild animals. Once inside the castle, the circus troupe was led into a massive indoor amphitheater, where they began setting up for the show.

Duncan excitedly watched husky men walk by carrying insanely tall ladders, barrels loaded with lit torches, buckets of trick-performing ferrets, and other assorted armfuls of weirdness. Unable to restrain his curiosity, he peeked through the curtains to look out on the "stage," which was at floor level, with rows of tiered seating rising up around it. Hundreds of bandits had already filed in, hooting and belching as they took their seats. Many were brawling over who got to sit in the front row "splash zone." None of Rundark's Darian henchmen were present, however; they were all out patrolling the halls of the castle as the Warlord had instructed.

The shouts and grunts of the circus audience suddenly hushed as Deeb Rauber himself arrived. The Bandit King entered a roped-off private viewing area, which contained only three plush, red velvet seats. He took the center chair for himself, and Lord Rundark—who already looked nauseated by the unruly behavior of the bandits around him—sat down to his left.

"Interesting fellow," Duncan muttered. He, Snow, and Rapunzel made their way through the bustling backstage area. Behind a large stack of monkey-treat crates, the trio found Ruffian and Briar Rose. Briar was wearing a lime-green jumpsuit with bright yellow ribbons flowing from the arms and legs, a tiny pointed hat sitting way up on top of her immense mound of auburn hair. Ruffian was sporting a curly blue wig, an oversize polka-dot bow tie, and his cowl—hood up, naturally.

As soon as Briar saw Duncan and the others, she smacked Ruffian on the arm. "Can't you do anything right?"

"Aha!" Duncan shouted triumphantly. "We've caught you!"

Briar got right in his face. "You fools! I was trying to keep you safe. Do you have any idea what you've just walked into? You'll get yourselves killed in here." She turned to Rapunzel. "And *you*! Actually, who are you again?"

"Rapunzel."

"Well, you shouldn't be here either," Briar said, still sounding rather growly.

"Let me show you something," Ruffian said. He walked over to a small rip in the curtain and pointed out through the hole. "That monstrous man seated next to the Bandit King?" Ruffian said. "That is Lord Rundark, the Warlord of Dar, widely known as the cruelest, most vicious tyrant in the world. Lord Rundark is far more dangerous than the Bandit King."

"My goodness," Duncan said. "If the Warlord of Door is here, we need to warn Liam and Frederic."

"And Gustav and Ella and Lila," added Snow.

Ruffian glared at Briar. "The young girl is here?" he asked angrily.

"Everybody shut up and let me think!" Briar screeched. "I came in here with a purpose, and all you losers are getting in my way."

"Well, let me get out of your way," Duncan said. "I'm off to warn the others about our homely new enemy. It's what a true hero would do." He dashed off, shouting,

"Good luck, Snow! I'll be back!"

"Fantastic," Briar grumbled, stamping her foot.

"These things take forever to get started," Rauber complained, fidgeting in his seat. He was eager for the first act but even more eager for the last, during which he planned to invite Rundark onstage and present him with an exploding "trophy" that was filled with elephant dung and packets of colored dye. *Let's see how scary Rundork is when he's covered with rainbow poop,* Rauber thought. *My men will laugh him out of the castle. And I'll swipe his crazy skull helmet as he goes.*

He was chuckling to himself when Vero tried to sit in the private box's only remaining seat. Rauber shot out his hand and blocked the chair.

"Eh, sorry, Vero," Rauber said. "The Gray Phantom gets the good seat today."

Vero frowned. "But, sir, I have something—" He began to reach into his vest, but Rauber cut him off again.

"No can do, man. You're out, Phantom's in."

Vero narrowed his eyes and walked away. The glass vial remained in his vest. Little Taylor rushed past him and plopped eagerly in the seat.

A loud, sudden explosion caught everyone's attention

as Stanislav Flimsham was blasted out of a cannon. The red-robed ringmaster arced through the air, landed in a forward roll, stood up, leaned his head back, and spat a geyser of spark-spewing fireworks from his mouth. He was promptly hit in the side of the head with an old shoe thrown by a bandit in the audience.

"Boo!" the bandit jeered. "Do something exciting!"

Flimsham loosened his collar a bit, checked his hair, and took a deep breath. "Ladies and gentlemen . . ."

A tomato smashed onto his shoulder.

"Well, wait, let me see. . . . Okay, just gentlemen!"

Someone tossed an iron that landed very close to the ringmaster's toes. "Just *men*?" he tried. "Does that work? Men? Okay . . . Men! The time has come! Allow me to introduce the world's only circus with sparzle: the Flimsham Brothers Circus!"

The crowd spat and grumbled as a quintet of acrobats cartwheeled onstage with their pants on fire. The circus had begun.

Backstage, Snow fretted about Duncan's disappearance.

"Stop biting your nails," Briar said.

"I wasn't biting my nails," Snow said defensively. "I was tapping my teeth."

"Oh, well, by all means, carry on then," Briar said drily.

She glanced around and took note of the various exits. When the time was right, she'd need to make her move— no matter how dangerous it was.

There was a round of booing as the acrobats came running offstage, dripping with what appeared to be clumps of mayonnaise. One of them was in tears. Two sparkly hatted women gulped and pushed a cart full of kittens onstage for their juggling act.

"Hey, you clowns should really be rehearsing," one of the acrobats said as he wiped mayo from his eyes. "You guys go on in less than an hour, and this crowd is a real killer."

21

A Hero Gets Dumped

The bigger they are, the harder they fall.
So I suggest being small.
— The Hero's Guide to Being a Hero

When you're more than a hundred feet tall, it's not easy to find a good hiding spot. Luckily for Maude, Castle von Deeb stood in the shadow of the great, crooked Mount Batwing. The giantess poked her head out from behind the mountain, taking a peek at the fortress below.

"Watch what you're doing, Big Mamma!" Gustav snapped. "They'll see you!"

Maude pulled her monstrous head back behind the peak. She raised her hand up to her face so she could scowl directly at Gustav, who sat with Ella and Lila in a small wooden rowboat on the giantess's palm.

"Did I ever tell you about the last time an uppity knight called me a rude name?" Maude hissed at the burly prince. "I crushed him between my eyebrows."

"Why is Big Mamma a rude name?" Gustav asked. "It's factually accurate."

"Oh, so you're a smart guy, eh?" Maude sneered.

"Who are you calling smart?" Gustav growled back.

"Hey, call a truce," Ella admonished. "We need to work together."

"Yeah, yeah," Maude said. "I'm just a little on edge. I haven't crushed anything in a while. And I've got this boat right here in my hand. . . ."

"Maude, let me take a look again through the spyglass," Ella said. The giantess held the boat out at an angle that allowed Ella to see past Mount Batwing to the castle and barren fields below. "The circus has been inside for well over an hour now. The show must be starting soon. And I don't know why there are so many guards lined up along the back wall. We were only expecting two."

"Any sign of Awful Clawful yet?" Gustav asked.

"No," Ella said. "I hope there's nothing wrong. Oh, wait. There he is! Mr. Troll is making his way toward the front gates now."

"This is it." Lila said. She and the others all flipped

up the collars on their black thieves' outfits. "Time to get stealthy."

Mr. Troll rumbled out from behind his rock, roaring and pounding his big fists into the dry, cracked earth. He waited to hear shouts of "Troll!" echoing across the wastes. But none came.

He tromped straight up to the Wall of Secrecy and saw ten bandit archers with their bows drawn and arrows trained on him, all of whom had been warned by Rauber to expect a troll attack. Suddenly there was a whistling sound, and Mr. Troll felt a sharp sting in his right arm. He looked over and saw an arrow sticking out of his thick, mossy hair. "Hmm," he grunted. "This not good."

Ella put down her spyglass in frustration. "I don't get it," she said. "There are still like twenty guards along the back wall. Why are none of

Fig. 30
Mr. Troll, STUNG

them running off to stop the troll?"

Gustav grabbed the spyglass and looked for himself. "Whoa, there are a bunch of bow-and-arrow guys on the front wall, and they're shooting at Furface."

"What are we gonna do?" Lila asked.

Maude let out an exasperated groan. "This is the problem with you humans," she said. "Always asking 'What are we gonna do?' Just do something."

And with that, Maude stepped out from behind Mount Batwing. Everyone in the rowboat crouched down, clinging to their seats.

"Stop! The lookouts will see you!" Ella shouted to her. But before the startled watchmen could even raise their bows, the giantess swiped her free hand along the back wall, scooping them all up. Then she simply tossed them away. The screaming bandits sailed through the sky, over Mount Batwing and out of sight. They probably landed somewhere in Jangleheim.

"See? Taken care of," Maude said. "You people need to learn to trust me."

"Maude, we can't start a war out here!" Ella cried. "We need to *sneak* inside. This is a *stealth* mission!"

"Who brings a giant on a stealth mission?" Maude asked, frustrated.

Suddenly a long drawn-out howl from Mr. Troll reverberated through the mountains. "I'm on it!" Maude said.

She then dropped the boat—and its passengers—over the Wall of Secrecy before bounding to the front of the castle in two enormous steps. The boat crashed to the ground. Gustav reached out with his big arms and caught hold of Lila before she was thrown from the craft. "Gotcha, Spunky!" he said. Then he busted right through his wooden seat and landed on his back with a groan.

"I think I hate giants even more than dwarfs," he grumbled.

"Thanks for the save," Lila panted. She looked around. "Where's Ella?"

"I'm okay," Ella whispered, crawling to them from the dirt pile she'd landed in. "Come on, let's get this boat into the moat, quick. Before someone spots us."

"Um, got a plan B?" Lila asked, looking down. A crack ran along the entire bottom of the rowboat. "I don't think we're getting across in that."

"Maybe it's not as bad as it looks," Gustav said. He and Lila stepped out, dragged the boat over to the moat, and shoved it into the water. It sank instantly.

Ella stared at the two-hundred-foot-wide moat before

them. Ominous ripples disrupted the calm every so often—telltale signs of bladejaw eels lurking just below the surface. "Anybody here know how to fly?"

Up by the front gates, the bandit archers were ready to release another volley of arrows at the invading troll. But they never got their shots off. None of them was prepared for the shock of seeing a one-hundred-foot woman running at them. They all gaped at Maude.

The giantess brought her arm back, ready to take a big swing and swat as many bandits off the wall as she could. But a bite on her toe from Mr. Troll stopped her.

Maude leaned down and whispered to him: "What's the deal? Why'd you nibble me?"

"Giant Lady need stick with plan," Mr. Troll said. "Can't mess things up for friends inside."

"I don't care about those tiny, whiny pips; I want some action," Maude said.

Mr. Troll considered himself a pretty good judge of character, especially when it came to other monsters. He could tell right away that this giantess was not the thoughtful, reasonable type of monster that he was; she was more the rampage-and-wanton-destruction type. He was going to have to keep her in check if he wanted Angry

Man and the others to succeed. "Troll promise plenty of action if Giant Lady do what Troll say."

"What've you got in mind?" Maude whispered.

"Giant Lady fight Troll," he said. "If bandits watch *us*, bandits *not* watch friends inside."

"You know, I like you, troll," Maude said. "You remind me of a young ogre I wish I hadn't crushed."

Maude slammed the ground, causing Mr. Troll to fall flat on his back. He sprang up and punched the giantess in the shin. She tried to stomp on him, and he scratched at her bare foot.

Up on the wall, the bandits looked on in amazement. "Now, that's something you don't see every day," one said.

22

A HERO HATES SEAFOOD

You may have heard the expression "I'll be there with bells on." This should not apply to stealth missions.
— THE HERO'S GUIDE TO BEING A HERO

Gustav grew uncharacteristically queasy looking at the impromptu tightrope that Ella had rigged up. It stretched from their side of the moat—where it was tied around a petrified tree stump—all the way across to the far rocky shore where the barbed metal end of their grappling hook was firmly lodged.

"In case you didn't realize, there's a reason why I wasn't put on the circus team," he said. "I'm not the nimblest guy in the world."

"Have you got a better idea?" Ella asked.

"Even if I could keep my balance on that thing," Gustav said, "I'm too heavy. As soon as I step on that

356

rope, it's gonna snap."

"You'd better go last then," Lila said. She hopped onto the tightrope and speedily skittered across to the far side. She bounced to the ground and gave a perky wave to her friends across the water.

Ella turned to Gustav. "See?" she said.

"Yeah, but I'm like forty of her," Gustav said.

Ella stepped onto the tightrope and held her arm out to balance herself. "Sorry, we're out of time—and options," she said to Gustav. "Lila and I will have to handle this without you. Just make sure you find a good hiding spot and join up with us when the circus is on its way out."

Ella started her slow and cautious trek across the moat, moving one step at a time, pausing every yard or so to check her balance. She tried not to look down at the swirling, bubbling waters only a few feet below.

Without warning, a silver, snake-like shape exploded from the water. A bladejaw eel leapt up in the air and arced right over the rope, mere inches from Ella's toes.

"Whew," she breathed. "That was close."

Then another eel burst upward with a splash, this one flying right between Ella's feet. She flapped her arms like she was trying to take flight but couldn't keep herself up. She lost her footing and tumbled toward the moat.

Lila gasped and covered her eyes, but hearing no splash, she quickly looked up again. Ella was hanging under the tightrope, her arms and legs wrapped around it.

"I'm okay," Ella said confidently.

But Lila realized she was wrong. "Your braid!" she called out. Ella's hair was dangling downward, the tip of her braid dunking into the moat like a fishing line. And the dark, undulating forms of bladejaw eels were swimming at her from both sides.

"Starf it all," Gustav cursed. He picked up one of the loose oars that had fallen from the rowboat and stepped gingerly onto the tightrope. He took dainty tiptoe steps

Fig. 31
Ella DANGLING

(well, dainty for Gustav, which meant he stepped as if he were squashing a beetle rather than squashing a rabid rat). He had almost reached Ella when the eels started jumping again.

Ella swung her body left and right to avoid the toothy mouths diving for her, but in doing so she sent Gustav into a spin. He performed an unintentional pirouette, then slipped, dropped downward, and landed sitting on the rope with his feet sloshing into the water on either side. He swung his oar— *Swish! Fwap!*—knocking away one eel and then another. But the momentum of his third swing sent him flipping down into the same dangly, under-the-rope position as Ella.

Ella began inching her way along the rope, dodging leaping eels as she did. "Shinny out of here," she said urgently. "Fast as you can."

"I don't shinny!" Gustav growled. An eel landed on his face. He shook it off and started shinnying after Ella.

They were only about ten yards from the far side. "We're gonna make it," Ella said, just before an eel flew by and chomped her braid clean off.

"That's okay!" Ella said, blinking drops of murky water from her eyes. "I was thinking of cutting it anyway."

Another particularly large and sleek eel flew out of the water, aiming to make a snack out of Gustav's ankle.

Gustav saw it coming and deftly lifted his foot out of the way.

"Ha!" Gustav gloated. The eel missed his leg, but its machete-sharp teeth instead clamped down on the tightrope itself. He peered back and saw the creature hanging from the rope by its fangs—he could have sworn the thing was smiling at him. And with a snap of its jaws, the eel cut the tightrope in two. Gustav and Ella hit the water with a tremendous splash.

The eels were on them in seconds, snapping at their arms and legs in a ravenous fury. The water was such a chaos of splashing and kicking and swatting and snapping, they could barely see which way to swim. Then suddenly, they felt themselves being tugged toward the shore. Someone was reeling in the rope. Gustav and Ella held tight as they were towed up onto the rocky bank of the moat. They collapsed on the ground, exhausted, sore, and wounded in multiple places—but happily alive.

"Lila," Ella said. "You pulled us in. Thank you."

"I had some help," Lila said.

Ella and Gustav looked up to see Duncan, wearing clown makeup, standing behind Lila.

"Hello," Duncan said.

"What are you doing here?" Gustav asked.

"Not that we're complaining," Ella added.

"Well, I sneaked out of the circus to go look for Liam and Frederic," Duncan said. "I soon realized that I had no idea how to get to the dungeon, though, so I was just sort of wandering around the halls. The Bandit King has some really fun stuff in there: a moose head wearing a hat; a big, tall, stuffed grizzly; a clock shaped like a cat where the tail wags back and forth. . . ."

"Duncan!"

"Oh, and anyway, I just happened to be passing by a lovely picture window when I looked outside and saw Liam's sister having some trouble fishing. Only she wasn't fishing. She was trying to pull you out of the water. But you probably know that part. Anyway, it's all a great coincidence, isn't it? I feel like my old luck has returned."

"Don't start with the magical luck nonsense again," Gustav groaned. "There's no such thing."

"Oh, yeah? Well, how would you describe Duncan showing up just in time to save you from the eels?" Lila asked him.

"Not *lucky*," Gustav said. "Something else. Um. *Fortunate*!"

"Synonyms, Gustav," Lila said, shaking her head. "Synonyms."

"Whatever, Duchess Dictionary," Gustav grumbled.

"I think you mean 'thesaurus,'" Lila said.

"Are you *trying* to be as annoying as your brother?" Gustav snarked.

"Duncan," Ella interjected. "You said you wanted to warn Frederic and Liam about something. What?"

"Oh, well, we were backstage with Briar—"

"Briar followed us?" Ella snarled. "I knew that witch would try to double-cross us."

"Oh, but that's not even what I wanted to warn everybody about," Duncan said. "Ruffian told us that there's a guy here who's even scarier than the Bandit King."

"The Bandit King's not scary," Gustav said.

"Well, this other guy definitely is," Duncan said. "He's got some kind of skeleton on his head. Possibly a goat. Or maybe a swamp pig. Either way, it was definitely dead. And toothy. But anyway, this guy is the Lore-ward of Dar."

"The Lore-ward of Dar?" Lila asked. "The man in charge of chronicling history and folklore for the kingdom of Dar?"

"No, it was scarier than that," Duncan said, scratching his chin. "Let me see . . . Oh, it was the *Warlord* of Dar."

"Wait," said Ella. "You're telling us the Warlord of Dar is in the castle? The most bloodthirsty tyrant in the world?"

"Meh. I could take him," Gustav said dismissively.

"This is serious, Gustav," Ella said. "No way the Warlord travels alone. And if he's brought a squad of Darian soldiers with him, we could be in for a real fight. Duncan, go back in the way you came. See if you can find Little Taylor. Tell him about the Warlord and tell him to release Frederic and Liam right away." She stood tall. "The rest of us will continue as planned. Maybe we can still get the sword and get out of here before anything else goes wrong."

Duncan nodded and hopped back in through the open window.

Lila looked at Ella and Gustav. "Are you guys sure you can go on?" she asked. "No offense, but you look pretty bad."

Ella's clothes were torn in several places, revealing bright red tooth marks in her flesh. Gustav looked even worse; his pants had been turned into a pair of ragged shorts, and his legs below them were a painful-looking blur of dark cuts and bruises.

"I'll survive," Ella said.

Gustav took off his black overshirt and tied it around his waist to provide a little more leg coverage. "I feel great," he said, ignoring the pain. "I know for a fact that none of my brothers has ever survived a bladejaw eel attack. Or walked a tightrope, actually."

"I'm happy to see you've got your priorities straight," Lila said. She patted him on the back and unintentionally made him wince. "Sorry!"

"No, it's nothing," Gustav said. "Just a little indigestion. I should never eat burritos before a quest. Hey, don't we have a wall to climb?"

Back in the amphitheater, a pair of conjoined twin animal trainers were sticking both of their heads into the mouths of a two-headed lion.

"Boooooring!" yelled a heckler in the crowd. Somebody tossed a wooden leg at the performers.

As excited as Little Taylor was to finally be sitting at the right hand of the Bandit King, he was also getting antsy. "Excuse me, sir," he said to Rauber with a deferential bow. "I think I need to use the facilities." And he stepped out into the hall.

Elsewhere in the castle, the spiky-armored Jezek marched down glistening marble corridors, keeping an eye out for anything suspicious. But it was his ear that caught something. "What was that noise?" he muttered to himself.

And then he heard it again: a tinny jingling. The thick-bodied Darian ran in the direction of the sound, turned a corner, and found himself standing face-to-face with Duncan. Duncan froze.

"You're awfully far from the theater, aren't you?" the bodyguard said. "You look lost."

"And *you*," Duncan replied, "look like a pineapple."

"What are you doing here?" Jezek asked, growing quickly impatient.

"Answering your questions."

"You know what I mean. Why did you leave the circus?"

"I haven't left the circus. I just *joined* the circus. And it's marvelous! You should join, too. I'm sure they'd have a place for a human pineapple."

"Are you trying to make me angry?"

"No," said Duncan. "If I were trying to make you angry, I'd probably do something like this." He pulled a small, round jingle bell from his belt and tossed it at Jezek. With a tinkle, the bell bounced off the bodyguard's forehead. The man snarled and bounded toward Duncan, who turned and ran back the way he had come.

As he zipped along, Duncan plucked off more tiny bells and whipped them over his shoulder at Jezek. The tinny jingling did nothing to stop the raging juggernaut. Duncan tried to turn a corner, but his soft felt shoes skidded on the shiny marble floor and sent him hurtling into the belly of a towering stuffed grizzly bear that was standing on a decorative pedestal in the corner.

"Excuse me," Duncan said to the long-dead bear, and then crouched between the animal's legs. Jezek was barreling toward him at top speed, a vicious grin on his face. Duncan flung his last bell at him.

Jezek laughed. "How are you going to stop me with a little bellleeeeoof!" The bodyguard stepped directly onto the rolling bell, tripped, and landed face-first in the arms of the stuffed grizzly.

Duncan scrambled out from behind the bear, giggling. "It looks like he's hugging you."

Jezek tried to pull himself free, but the spikes on his armor had firmly planted themselves into the stiff, stuffed animal, and he only succeeded in ripping the entire bear from its pedestal. He and the bear turned as one and began lumbering toward Duncan in what looked like a mockery of a waltz.

"Eek! You're still coming!" Duncan leapt back out the window he'd only just come in through. Jezek tried to squeeze through after him, but doing so while attached to an enormous grizzly proved difficult. Halfway through the window, Jezek—and the bear—got stuck.

"Come back here," the bodyguard groaned as he struggled to unjam himself.

"No, thank you," said Duncan. He grabbed hold of one of the two ropes that were hanging along the wall next to him and began climbing up.

Halfway up the wall, Gustav, Ella, and Lila, who were on their way to the roof, noticed Duncan below them. They paused and waited for him to catch up.

"I should probably just make a little sign that says 'What Are You Doing Here?' so I can hold it up whenever I see you," said Gustav.

"I got forced back outside by a big hedgehog man and a dead bear," Duncan explained.

"That sounds about right," said Lila.

"Shush now," Ella warned. "We're almost at the roof. Remember, this is a stealth mission."

Gustav pointed down at Duncan. "Yeah, those candy cane pants are real stealthy."

"Hey," said Duncan. "At least I got rid of my jingle bells."

A few minutes later, they climbed up over a rain gutter onto the stone slab roof of Castle von Deeb.

23

A Hero Knows How to Count

Avoid capture at all costs. Dungeons are horrible,
dirty, smelly places. They're cold. They're cramped.
And don't even get me started on the room service.
—THE HERO'S GUIDE TO BEING A HERO

"Fifty-eight, fifty-nine—nine!" Frederic muttered, barely above a whisper. "One, two, three, four . . ."

"Frederic, are you okay?" Liam asked. He pressed his face up to the bars of his cell door, trying to get a better look at his friend across the way. "What are you doing?"

". . . fourteen, fifteen—shhh!—seventeen, eighteen . . ."

"Frederic, we haven't even been here for six hours," Liam said. "Have you gone stir-crazy already?"

Liam wouldn't have been surprised if Frederic had lost his mind. *And it would be my fault,* he thought. *I can't believe the mess I've gotten us into, storming the Bandit King's*

*castle with such a half-baked plan. It all went wrong because
I couldn't give up trying to be a hero. Because I couldn't admit
the truth about myself. Because I couldn't—"*

". . . forty-five, forty-six, forty-seven . . ."

"Frederic, I'm sorry, but I'm not in the best place right
now, mentally, and I think your counting is going to push
me over the edge."

". . . fifty-eight, fifty-nine—ten!"

With a click, a door opened down the hall. They'd been
hearing that sound on and off ever since they were locked
in the dungeon, and they knew what it meant: Wrathgar
was back.

The enormous man lumbered into their cellblock,
walked over to Frederic's cell, and gave the door a kick.
Frederic curled up into a tiny ball. Wrathgar stepped
across to Liam, who looked down to avoid eye contact.

The dungeon master smiled, revealing a mouth full of
green, stained teeth. He spat into Liam's cell, then turned
and marched back out of the cellblock. When the prisoners
heard the sound of the door closing, they started breathing
again. Frederic leapt up.

"Ten minutes!" he said. "Exactly ten minutes!"

"What?" Liam asked.

"Our jailer is incredibly punctual," Frederic explained.

"Over the course of the day, it began to feel to me that there was a very regular interval of time between Wrathgar's check-ins. So I counted them out. It's always exactly ten minutes every time."

Liam sighed. "Congratulations, Frederic. You can tell time."

"If we know how long he'll be gone," said Frederic, "we know how long we'll have to escape."

"That's incredibly optimistic of you," Liam muttered. "But knowing the timeframe doesn't matter much if there's no way out of these cells."

"The keys are right there on the wall!" Frederic said, pointing to the key ring hanging on a nearby hook. "It's like he's *daring* us to take them."

"Maybe he is," Liam said soberly. "I don't think we should try anything we'll regret."

"Nonsense," said Frederic. "We just need to figure out how to get them."

"There's no way," Liam said. "It's pointless."

"What's wrong with you, Liam?" Frederic asked. "You're acting like you don't want to escape."

Liam sighed. "I want *you* to escape, Frederic," he said. "But I don't know about me. Maybe I deserve to be locked up."

"Look, Liam, you're being too hard on yourself," Frederic said. "So your plan didn't come off exactly as you'd hoped. That still doesn't mean—"

"That's not it, Frederic," Liam said, his voice heavy. "I've . . . I've done a horrible thing."

"'Horrible' is a strong word," Frederic said. "I'm sure that whatever you've done doesn't rise to that level."

"I knowingly left two innocent men in jail," Liam said.

"Okay, yes, that's horrible," Frederic said. "But I'm sure you had a good reason."

"I didn't want them to tell people I'm not a real hero."

"Mm-hmm, yeah—not a good reason," Frederic said. "Care to elaborate?"

"In Avondell's dungeon, I met two actors who revealed to me that my rescue of Briar's parents back when I was a kid—the incident that first made the world think of me as a hero—was all a hoax," Liam said. He leaned his forehead against the cold iron bars. "They've been rotting in there for ages, and I should have freed them immediately; but I was too scared to have people find out I'm a fraud. I thought about all the mistakes and blunders I've made, and I wondered if I was even capable of being a hero anymore. But when I discovered Briar's plot, I thought it was the perfect opportunity to test myself. I bet all my friends' lives on it. And I failed."

"Wow. And I thought *I* had issues," Frederic said, rubbing his hands against his temples. "You seriously believe that you're not a real hero just because you didn't save the lives of a king and queen *when you were three*? You think that one false story negates all the good deeds you've done over the course of your life? I've never met— or even heard about—anyone who has performed more heroic deeds than you. But maybe you're right. Maybe you're not a hero anymore. If that's the case, though, it's not because of some silliness that was faked back when you were a toddler. It's because you abandoned those two innocent men last week."

Liam was silent.

"No one is defined by a single act," Frederic said. "Whether it was years ago or weeks ago. We're all given chances to change, to make up for things we've done wrong. It's how we handle those opportunities that really matters. For most of my life, I ran and hid from anything remotely dangerous. Does that make me a coward now? No. If I'm a coward now, it's because I was just curled in a ball, crying, when a scary man looked at me wrong. But you know what? The next time we see Wrathgar, I could stand up to him. I'm not saying I'm going to—I'll probably just cry again—but I *could* stand up to him. And so could you. And you'd be a hero again."

Liam nodded. "You're right: This isn't just about me. I have people counting on me," he said softly.

"And you're not going to let them down," Frederic said.

"No," Liam said, straightening up a bit. "Not without a fight."

"There you go!" Frederic said, unable to suppress a grin. "That's the Liam I'm looking for!"

"That's right." Liam stood and puffed out his chest. "I'm Liam of Erinthia! Getting out of tough situations is what I do best!"

"Huzzah!" Frederic thrust his fist in the air. He was smiling like a crazy person.

"We still have a few minutes before Wrathgar comes back. Let's get out of here," Liam said. He gripped the bars of his cell and looked Frederic in the eye. "But I don't think I can do this alone. Frederic, I need your help."

If Liam had wanted to pump Frederic up, he couldn't have said anything more effective than those last five words. Frederic rubbed his hands together and did what he always did when he found himself in a puzzling predicament—he asked himself, *What would Sir Bertram the Dainty do?* They would need to use some sort of tool to reach the keys. But the bandits had taken away everything they had, leaving them with only the clothes on their backs. Aha! That was it!

"My clothes!" Frederic said excitedly. "*In Sir Bertram the Dainty and the Case of the Loathsome Laundress*, he ties together a string of silk neckties to help him reach a flask of magical fabric softener. If he isn't able to get it in time, all the noblemen's suits will be coarse and uncomfortable. But luckily—"

"What's your idea, Frederic?" Liam asked.

"The gold braiding on my jacket—if I can rip it off and unravel it, I'm sure it will be long enough reach that key ring."

"Sounds good to me," said Liam. "Get ripping."

Frederic took off his jacket and tried tearing the gold braiding that ran up and down the sleeves. "Urgh, the stitching is really tough," he said. He yanked and pulled with all his might, even trying to stand on the jacket for leverage. "You know who would be really

Fig. 32
Frederic
RIPPING

helpful to have down here right now? Little Taylor."

Then they heard the clicking of the door down the hall.

"Stop ripping," hissed Liam. "It's Wrathgar."

Frederic hastily stashed his crumpled jacket behind his back and hummed as the dungeon master stomped into the cellblock.

"What are you hiding?" Wrathgar asked.

"It's just my jacket. I was hot," Frederic said. He dabbed his forehead with his shirtsleeve. "I mean, *whew*."

Wrathgar marched over to Frederic's cell and, like a human eclipse, blocked all light from entering. "I don't believe you," he said.

"Why?" Frederic asked. "Just because we're in a cold, clammy dungeon? Haven't you heard of nervous sweat?"

Wrathgar glared at Frederic until the prince's legs went wobbly. "Give it to me."

Thoroughly cowed, Frederic squeezed his jacket through the bars and handed it off. Wrathgar checked it inside and out, squeezing it and sniffing it. When he was satisfied there was nothing out of the ordinary about it, he wiped his mouth on the garment and tossed it into a corner, far out of reach of Frederic's and Liam's cells. Then he turned and left again.

As soon as they heard the door click shut, Frederic

said, "We can still do this, Liam, but I have to ask you to sacrifice your cape."

Liam unclipped the long blue cape from his neck and gave it a bittersweet caress. "You've served me well, old friend."

"Ten minutes, Liam," Frederic said. "I'll keep count. Thirty-one, thirty-two, thirty-three . . ."

Liam ripped his cape into three long strips of fabric, which he twisted and tied together to form one long, makeshift rope.

Upstairs, Falco was scouting the halls on guard duty. "Get me out of here!" he heard a voice cry. He turned a corner to see Jezek wedged into an open window with a stuffed grizzly. With some effort, he pulled the bodyguard free and managed to pry him from the bear. He raised a quizzical eyebrow at Jezek.

"Something's going on here," Jezek said. "There's a mad clown on the loose. It could be part of that invasion the Phantom warned us about. We have to tell the Warlord."

They sped for the amphitheater but stopped short when they saw a group of Rauber's men racing toward the castle's entryway.

"What's happening?" Jezek asked as the bandits ran by.

"A troll and a giant are having a fight!" one called as he disappeared over the drawbridge. "It's way better than the circus!"

"I'll check it out," Jezek said to Falco. "You tell the Warlord about the clown." Falco nodded. They dashed off in opposite directions.

Reaching his arm out between the bars of his cell, Liam flicked his cape-rope at the keys on the wall—for the fiftieth time. And once again, it missed.

"Crud," he grumbled.

"That's six minutes, Liam," Frederic said. "Come on—you can do this."

"Yes, I can," Liam said, and flicked again. This time the heavy knot he'd tied at the end knocked into the key ring and bumped it off its hook. The keys hit the stony floor with an echoing clatter.

"... forty-four, forty-five—excellent!—forty-seven ..."

"Okay, now to bring them over to me," Liam said. He whipped his cape-rope outward and, miraculously, landed the knot right through the center of the key ring. Frederic bounced with joy.

Liam slowly and carefully began reeling in the keys.

"Three minutes left," Frederic said. "Two, three, four, fi—"

The familiar click of the door sounded from down the hall, followed by approaching footsteps.

"No," Frederic said. "He's early!"

"Early?" Little Taylor asked as he stepped into the cellblock. "You were expecting me?"

At the mere sight of the man, Liam's hands curled into fists.

"Oh-ho! What's this?" Taylor said, grabbing the key ring off the floor and yanking the cape-rope away from Liam. "Were you two naughty boys trying to escape? The Bandit King is going to love me even more when I tell him about this."

"You're despicable," Liam hissed. "You've already sentenced us to death with your betrayal; why are you down here now? To rub our faces in it?"

"Yes, actually," Taylor said. He twirled the key ring on his index finger. "You see, I was sitting there at the circus, right next to the Bandit King. I'd gotten exactly what I'd always wanted. I should have been completely content. But I wasn't. Something was still eating at me. And then I saw Deeb Rauber throw a teapot at a sword swallower.

It broke the man's nose, and Rauber just cracked up. He laughed with more glee than anyone I've ever seen. And it hit me that that's what I was missing: I hadn't gotten the chance to laugh in the faces of my victims. So I'm here to do it."

He burst into a bout of heaving, horsey guffaws.

"You're completely insane," Liam said.

"Ha! You're the ones who are insane," Taylor said. "I played you guys perfectly. You know, when I first spotted you all camping out by that tower in Sturmhagen, I almost did you all in right then and there. But then I heard you talking about your plan to rob the Bandit King and how you were going to hire an accomplice to help you do it. I raced straight to the Stumpy Boarhound and made sure I was the one you chose. Part of me can't believe it really worked. You fools honestly thought that I would betray the Bandit King—the most amazing villain who has ever lived—so I could help a couple of Prince Charmings?"

"You know, when you showed up just now, I was still kind of hoping you might have come to help us," Frederic said sadly.

"Oh, yes, *that's* going to happen," Taylor drawled sarcastically. "I, Little Taylor, the Gray Phantom, have come down here to set you free, just like we'd planned. I'm going to unlock your cages and then the three of us can go rob Deeb Rauber's treasure vault together."

He was so enjoying his little performance that he didn't notice Wrathgar enter the cellblock behind him (right on time, by the way). And unfortunately for Taylor, the dungeon master had only heard the last couple of things he'd said.

"So, you're a traitor," Wrathgar said. "I knew there was something I didn't like about you."

"Ah, no, wait, you don't understand," Taylor stammered. "I wasn't really going to let them out."

"The keys are in your hand," Wrathgar said.

Instinctively, Taylor dropped the key ring and pulled out his spool of thread, rapidly reeling off a piece to use as a weapon. Wrathgar reached out, picked Taylor up by the face, and hurled him into a nearby stone wall. The wall collapsed and crushed him completely. All that was left of Little Taylor was a tiny spool of thread that rolled from the rubble and came to a rest against Wrathgar's heavy black boot.

"Hmm, guess I threw him kinda hard, huh?" Wrathgar said with a shrug. "Oh, well."

Both Liam and Frederic turned a pale shade of green.

Fig. 33
SPOOL,
ownerless

Wrathgar picked up the key ring and clipped it onto his belt. He grabbed a stool from the corner, brought it to the center of the cellblock, and sat down. "Now I stay here," he said. "No one is leaving these cells."

24

A Hero Smells a Rat

The element of surprise can offer a hero great advantage
in battle. The element of oxygen—also important.
— The Hero's Guide to Being a Hero

Deeb Rauber strongly believed that rooftops were for recreation. The roof of his very first hideout hosted a regular thumb-wrestling tournament; the roof of his last castle held a combination dueling arena/suntan deck; and now that he was a genuine king, his rooftop could have passed for a carnival midway. Dozens of small shacks rose up from the wood-and-stone roof, some of which were used for official bandit business like dagger storage and loot sorting, while others—like the dunk tank and the face-painting booth—not so much. Walkways ran between these mini-buildings like a grid of streets, all leading to the large, central, carved-ivory dome (stolen from the legendary Our Lady of Fancy Domes Cathedral in Hithershire), which housed the main stairwells.

Ella, Gustav, Lila, and Duncan slinked through a narrow passage between a facility for the de-fingering of gloves and a shack with a sign for "spitball moistening."

"I can't believe how much stuff is up here," Lila whispered.

"I think I saw a place that makes funnel cake back there," Duncan said. "I was very tempted."

"Just keep looking for the snake handler," Ella said.

"Yeah," Gustav added. "No matter what, we should still be able to find a thirty-foot snake. It's not like you can hide an animal that big."

"Hold up," Ella whispered urgently as she paused outside the corner of a workshop dedicated to mending torn loot sacks. Just around the bend was the big dome, and before it stood a man whom they instantly guessed to be the snake handler (the sixty-three snake tattoos covering Madu's body kind of gave it away). The Darian opened a small wooden door in the wall of the dome and, pulling on a rope inside, reeled up a large basket.

"What's he doing?" Gustav asked.

"It's a dumbwaiter," Lila whispered. "We have them at the palace back in Erinthia. There's a long shaft they use to send food and messages up and down between floors."

"And rats apparently," Gustav said as they watched Madu lift a squirming brown rat from the basket by its tail. He held the wriggling rodent up to his nose and sniffed it.

"King Moonracer," Duncan said.

"Don't get too attached," Ella warned. "My guess is that King Moonracer is going to be lunch for the snake."

Duncan shrugged. "Circle of life," he said.

"Where *is* the snake?" Gustav asked. He was growing agitated as they watched Madu walk around, toying with the struggling rat—swatting at it and poking it with his finger. After a minute or two, the tattooed man stuck out his tongue and took a big, long lick across the rodent's matted fur.

"I've seen enough," Gustav said. "I'm taking this wacko down now. Stuuuuuurm-haaayyyy-gennnnn!"

He burst out from behind the workshop and charged headlong at Madu. As Gustav tackled him to the ground, the surprised

Fig. 34
FEEDING TIME

Darian dropped the rat, which quickly scampered off.

"Run, King Moonracer, run!" Duncan yelled.

"Where's the snake?" Gustav demanded to know as he pinned Madu to the stone floor. Ella drew her sword and rushed to his side.

"How did you get up here?" Madu rasped.

"Where's the snake?" Gustav asked again.

"Never mind the animal," Ella said. "We just need to know where the Snake Hole is."

"No way," said Gustav. "I came here to fight a giant snake, and I'm not leaving until I fight a giant snake. Now, where is it?"

"Gustav, we don't have time for this," Ella said. "More bandits could come along any second."

"I think I found the hole," Lila called from a few yards off. There was a small metal hatch in the floor surrounded by crisp, translucent shreds of molted snake skin. Ella and Duncan ran over to Lila as she turned a wheel on the hatch door and lifted it to reveal an eighteen-inch-wide shaft that ran downward into pitch darkness.

"Nice job, Lila," Ella said. She pulled a coil of rope from her belt. "You ready to head down there?"

Lila nodded and began tying one end of the rope around her waist.

"Starf it all!" Gustav griped. "Last time I was supposed to fight the dragon. But *that* didn't get to happen! This time I was supposed to fight the giant snake. And we can't even find the stupid thing!"

"You want so badly to see the snake," Madu snickered from underneath him. "I would hate to disappoint you." Suddenly he began to spasm and squirm. His skin appeared to crack all over, turning into thousands of individual scales. His nose went flat, his eyes turned yellow, and his entire body began to elongate.

"Oh, man," Lila said. "That guy doesn't just *take care* of the snake. He *is* the snake."

With a slurping sound, Madu's arms were sucked into his torso, and his legs fused together, blending into one monstrous tail. Within seconds there was a thirty-foot-long, sand-colored serpent slithering out of Madu's empty vest and kilt. The creature swayed, raised its scaly head, and flicked a long, forked tongue at Gustav's dumbstruck face.

"What are you slack-jaws doing?" Jezek barked at the gawking bandits on the ramparts of the front wall.

One timidly pointed at the battling troll and giantess.

"I see them, fool," Jezek said. "Why are you standing

here watching them? It's all part of the invasion we were warned about. You men have bows—shoot them."

"Um, you know, sir," one of the bandits began. "We did shoot a couple o' arrows into the hairy one, but he didn't seem to be hurt by 'em. And the big one? I don't know if it's really worth us wasting ammunition."

Jezek looked out at the monsters. "Trolls are tough, but not invincible. It'll go down eventually. As for the giant . . . We may need a little something extra." He took two bandits aside. "You know those crates of sleeping potion that were left by the castle's previous owner? Go grab as much as you can. We're going to need a lot."

Down on the ground, an arrow hit Mr. Troll in the shoulder. "Hey, where that come from?" the monster asked.

"Those cockroaches on the wall are shooting at you again," Maude said.

"Giant Lady better look at self," the troll said. "Arrow Men shoot at Giant Lady, too."

Maude craned her head around to see seven arrows sticking out of her back. She hadn't even felt them. "Well, look at that," Maude said. "You're not still going to tell me we can't fight back, are you?"

Mr. Troll scratched his furry chin. "Okay, Troll and

Giant Lady fight back. But no crushing. Need to make fight last as long as possible."

Maude shrugged. "Better than nothing. Okay, let's wreak some havoc."

Thwack! The tail of the giant sand snake smashed into Gustav's chest and knocked him backward. With a gurgle, Gustav slid down the side of the dome and landed on his hands and knees.

"Hurry, hurry!" Ella urged. She held one end of their rope as Lila, with the other end tied around her midsection, slipped feet-first into the Snake Hole.

"Wow, snakes must have super–night vision or something," she muttered. "I can't see a thing." She could barely move a knee or elbow without banging a wall. Claustrophobia had never been an issue for Lila in

Fig. 35
Giant SANDSNAKE

the past, but then again, she'd never been shoved into a seemingly bottomless hole that was barely wider than her body. It was beginning to creep her out. But she took a deep breath, thought of Liam, and continued to inch her way down the shaft. Then she heard Ella cry out from up above.

And Lila began to drop. She screamed, plummeting downward, before jerking to a stop.

"Don't worry, Liam's sister!" Duncan called down to her. "I've got the rope!"

"What happened to Ella?" Lila shouted upward, relieved but slightly worried (the way many people feel when Duncan comes to their aid).

"She and Gustav are fighting with the snake," Duncan yelled down. "But they're not doing very well. The snake knocked Gustav through the wall of that sack shop. He crawled out with a burlap bag over his head. I wish our lives weren't in mortal danger right now, because normally that would have been hilarious."

"Duncan, please hold on tight," Lila said. She shimmied downward as fast as she could in the dark, tight tunnel, her heart beating faster with every crash, shout, and groan she heard from above. Then her feet hit the bottom.

"I'm here," she said, not even sure if Duncan could hear

her from that far down. "Gotta find the lever." She tried to crouch down and banged her head into the wall of the far-too-narrow chute. "I don't even have room to bend in here," she grumbled. She poked around in the darkness with her foot, and it smacked into a stick that was jutting from the bottom of the shaft. "Aha!"

With both feet, Lila shifted the lever from one side to the other. Immediately, a series of mechanical gears and gizmos creaked into action.

Five stories below—beneath Gustav and Ella fighting for their lives, beneath Stanislav Flimsham preparing to announce his world-famous clown act, and just a few corridors away from Liam and Frederic staring in despair at their barely human jailer—the door to Deeb Rauber's vault clicked, trembled, and swung wide-open.

25

THE VILLAIN GIVES
TWO THUMBS-DOWN

They say laughter is the best medicine. Destroy the clowns!
—THE WARLORD'S PATH TO POWER:
AN ANCIENT TOME OF DARIAN WISDOM

"Do we have to go on?" asked the leader of a team of jittery bear-back riders, cowering behind the curtain in the amphitheater. One set of performers after another had been subjected to heckling bandits throwing everything from rotten eggs to crowbars.

"Of course you do!" barked Stanislav Flimsham, whose stomach was doing more flips than his acrobats. "Do you want us all to be killed? Now get out there!"

Trembling, the bear-back riders took the stage. Even the bears looked nervous. Stanislav turned to his brother,

Armando, who handled the circus paperwork.

"Why did you ever book us to play here?" Stanislav asked.

"They promised a really great buffet table backstage," Armando answered. And he ran off before Stanislav could hit him.

Stanislav turned, cupped his hands to his mouth, and called out, "Clowns! You're on next!"

When the bear riders left the stage a few minutes later, bruised and dizzied from being pelted with pebbles, they were followed only by an uncomfortable silence. A dead minute passed, and the bandits began growling and chopping into the railing with their axes.

Finally, Stanislav ran onstage.

"Fear not, fear not, my good, um, men," he said. "For now you are about to be entertained as you have never been entertained before." He raised his arms in the air. "Send in the clowns!"

Nothing.

"Send in the clowns!" he cried again. The ringmaster licked his lips nervously. "Prepare for a big surprise," he added, his limp pompadour sagging onto the side of his head. "You never know what these clowns are going to do.

Or apparently when they're going to do it."

Backstage, Briar peered at the secret pocket watch she'd hidden in the belt of her clown costume. *The vault should be opening any minute,* she thought, and she quietly stepped away from the others, heading toward the rear exit. She was reaching for the door that would lead her out into the rest of the castle when Rapunzel's hand landed on her shoulder.

"You're off to do something horrible, aren't you?" Rapunzel said. "I hate making judgments about people without really knowing them, but I have to say, you do not give off good vibes."

"You don't understand," Briar said impatiently. "The vault's going to be open any minute now. I have to get down there."

"No, you don't," Rapunzel said. "Frederic and Liam will take care of that."

"What else am I supposed to do? Go out there and perform a clown act?" Briar scoffed.

"That's exactly what you're going to do," bellowed a leopard-skin-wearing circus strongman who had come up to them along with Armando Flimsham. "You clowns think you're better than the rest of us," the strongman said.

"But if we've got to go out there and survive this audience, so do you."

Hands on their shoulders, he turned both women around and steered them back toward the stage.

Ella hunkered down into the sword-fighting stance Liam had taught her, but seeing as she was facing off against a thirty-foot snake, proper fencing posture wasn't all that helpful. She swung at the snake, but the creature easily curled its body to avoid the blow and rammed her in the chest with its flat, scaly head. Ella tumbled backward. She lay flat as the snake rose up over her. The beast's mouth opened, and Ella could see the venom dripping from its fangs. But the monstrous animal only let out a gurgle of shock as Gustav grabbed it by the throat.

He dragged the creature to the edge of the roof and tied it into a tight knot around an iron railing. The snake hissed and spat angrily.

"Ha!" Gustav crowed. "I beat you, stupid snake!" He raised his fists in victory and marched back and forth, howling like a troll. This was the first time Gustav had ever actually bested a monster in battle, and he couldn't wait to rub it in his brothers' faces. Even Rapunzel would look at him differently after this, he thought.

"Gustav made the big snake into a pretty bow," Duncan called down the hole to Lila. "Let's get you out of there, Liam's sister!"

Lila had never been happier to hear anything in her life. But as soon as she felt Duncan pulling her upward, she yelled for him to stop.

"Wait!" she cried. "When I take my foot off the lever, it starts sliding back. I think the vault's gonna close again the moment I leave this hole."

Ella ran over. She looked at the stopwatch Liam had given her to keep track of time. Unfortunately, watches don't respond well to being dunked in moats full of bladejaw eels— it had stopped working. "Well, I *think* it's been about an hour," she muttered. "Which means Little Taylor should be letting the guys out of the dungeon any second now. Hold on a few more minutes, Lila."

Fig. 36
LILA, descending

Lila began gasping for breath, praying that those minutes would pass quickly. As she often said, she was great with heights. But as she had only recently discovered, she was not so great with depths.

The curtain parted and the four "clowns" were unceremoniously shoved onstage. Snow spun around under the candle-powered spotlights, taking in three hundred of the angriest faces she'd ever seen. She fell, dizzy, into Rapunzel's arms.

Not that Rapunzel was feeling any more comfortable in front of such an audience. She'd never even seen a circus before. She had no idea what clowns did. Caper? Frolic? Engage in acts of whimsy? While she puzzled over what those terms might even mean, she noticed Briar and Ruffian whispering conspiratorially.

The crowd began to grumble.

"Snow," Rapunzel said softly. "You've got to do something. Be a clown."

So Snow tripped Briar, knocking her onto her backside.

"How dare you?" Briar snarled. But the audience laughed.

Briar stood up, and Snow knocked her back down again. Bigger laugh.

"Stop that," Briar hissed. She grabbed Snow's ankle and yanked her to the ground. Biggest laugh yet.

But Briar wasn't amused. *I can't let these fools waste my time any longer,* she thought. *I came here on a mission of my own, and I'm going to see it through.* She stood up and stomped over to the side of the stage. She tossed a basket of juggling balls, colored scarves, and other clowning toys to the others. "Here," she snipped. "You want to put on a show? Put on a show."

Then she marched offstage.

Snow rifled through the basket of toys and picked up a wicker hoop. "What do you think we do with this?" she asked Rapunzel.

But Rapunzel was too distracted by Briar's sudden exit. "Good luck," she said to Snow. And she darted offstage as well.

Snow stood there holding the hoop in her hand. She looked to Ruffian for a hint of what to do next, but the bounty hunter was standing statue-still, like he was on guard duty. So Snow tossed the hoop over his head.

She got a chuckle from the crowd. So seven more hoops quickly followed. As well as anything else Snow could find to throw at him.

Ruffian sighed.

"Finally, something enjoyable," Rauber said as he kicked his feet up onto the railing in front of him.

"I am so glad you're being . . . entertained," Rundark remarked with obvious disgust.

"See the way the big, grumpy-looking clown just stands there while the little, energetic one keeps bouncing stuff off his face?" Rauber said, grinning. "It speaks to me."

Lord Rundark crossed his arms. *How pathetic,* he thought, *that some of the last breaths you take will be wasted on laughter.*

From a few seats away, Vero saw Falco run into the amphitheater. The scout was headed straight for Lord Rundark, but Vero grabbed him first.

"What is it, Falco?" Vero asked.

Falco started swinging his arms and doing a goofy dance. Then he pointed out to the hallway.

"A circus monkey has escaped into the castle?"

Falco shook his head. He clamped his fist over his nose like a ball, made a triangle in the air over his head, and waddled back and forth.

"There is a big-nosed unicorn pretending to be a penguin?" Vero tried.

Falco shook his head again, gnashing his teeth in frustration.

"Why the Warlord insists on using a man who does not speak as his messenger, I will never know," Vero said.

Falco pointed out at Snow and Ruffian, then back at the hallway.

"Clowns!" Vero said, proud of himself. "There is a clown out in the castle. Oh, yes, now that you mention it, some of the clowns appear to be missing. It is, as we say in my country, *suspicious*. Falco, go wait in the hall. I will inform the Warlord."

Falco ran back out, but Vero went straight to Deeb Rauber. He whispered in the Bandit King's ear. Rauber's eyes widened. Something strange was going on outside. Had he been too cocky, too quick to dismiss the League of Princes and their assault on his castle? He leapt from his seat to follow Vero.

"You are leaving?" Rundark asked.

"I hate to blow the surprise, but I'm gonna be a special part of the final act," Rauber said haughtily. "I gotta head backstage and get ready. Enjoy the show."

"Oh, I will," Rundark said.

Slinking through the halls of Rauber's castle, Briar froze when she heard footsteps from around a corner. She ducked behind an ogre-size suit of armor and saw two bandits open a closet door and start pulling armfuls of clinking glass bottles from a crate inside.

"Think this is enough?" one bandit asked the other.

"It'll have to be," the second bandit responded. "I can't carry any more'n this. We'll come back for another batch if we need to."

"I think that seems likely," said the first. "We're talking about taking down a giant."

They've seen the giant? Briar thought. *Better move fast.*

As soon as the two bandits left, Briar rushed over to the closet. On the floor sat a wooden crate labeled SLEEPING POTIONS — PROPERTY OF Z.

Fig. 37
POTIONS

I don't know who this Z is, Briar thought as she picked up one of the flasks of pinkish liquid and swished it around, *but I thank him for this little gift.*

Out by the front gate, archers on the Wall of Secrecy continued to rain arrows down on Maude and Mr. Troll. But now Rauber's men also had to dodge the large chunks of rocks that Mr. Troll hurled at them.

"HWAH!" Mr. Troll grunted as he slung another heavy rock upward and knocked his fourth bandit from the wall. "Ha-ha! 'Nother one down."

Maude, who was on her knees, hunched over to provide cover for the troll, grabbed another huge boulder and crushed it into dozens of smaller rock bits. "You sure I can't just kick down the wall?" the giantess asked.

"Battle be over too fast," Mr. Troll said. "Troll and Giant Lady can't let Arrow Men go inside. Got to give friends enough time to get shiny sword. This very important part of—"

"Less talk, more rocks," Maude interrupted.

"Oh, yeah," Mr. Troll said, and chucked two more huge hunks of stone.

Maude grabbed another boulder to break up but suddenly stopped. "Hmm," she said. "I'm not sure why, but I'm suddenly feeling tired."

"What Giant Lady tired for?" Mr. Troll asked. "Troll doing most of the work."

"Guess I'm just not as young as I used to be," Maude said.

"Heh-heh," Mr. Troll chuckled. "Nobody young as used to be. That scientifically impossible."

Up on the wall, Jezek had been instructing the archers to dip their arrows in sleeping potion before launching them. The last twenty arrows to hit Maude had all been tainted. And more were hitting her by the second.

"Seriously, troll," said Maude, struggling to her feet, her eyelids fluttering. "I think I'm going to . . ." With a thunderous thud, the giantess fell flat onto her back, and a massive dust cloud cloaked everything.

"How much longer?" Lila wailed from the bottom of the Snake Hole. The tight space was feeling tighter by the second, and she feared she was about to stop breathing altogether.

"I think another five minutes or so should be plenty of time," Ella said. "Assuming everything has gone according to plan down in the dungeon."

"Um, guys?" Duncan called.

"What is it, Duncan?" Ella asked.

"The snake is gone," Duncan replied.

Ella and Gustav turned around to see that, indeed, the giant sand snake was no longer tied around the railing.

Gustav growled and stomped his feet.

"Did you see what happened?" Ella asked.

"Well, first it squiggled, and then it wriggled, and then, I believe, it jiggled—"

"Duncan!" Ella shouted.

"It turned back into the man with lots of drawings on his body," Duncan said. "And then he ran to the other side of the dome."

"Stay with Lila," Ella said, drawing her sword. Then she and Gustav ran in the direction Duncan had pointed—where they found themselves face-to-face with Madu. And Vero. And Falco. And Deeb Rauber. And two other random bandits whose names, frankly, aren't worth mentioning.

26

A Hero Tells It Like It Is

If you want something, the best way to get it is to just ask.
If that doesn't work, you can always fall back on
a fully armed twelve-person assault team.
— The Hero's Guide to Being a Hero

Down in the dungeon, squatting on the cold, booger-encrusted floor of his dark cell, Liam suddenly stood bolt upright. He'd been struck by an idea. An actual idea. For the first time in more than a week. Was it a good idea? He didn't know. He was still having a hard time trusting himself. But when he looked across the cellblock at the pitiful state of his friend, he knew he had to give it a try.

"Frederic, how long do you think the circus has been going on?" he asked.

"Huh?" Frederic said, looking up. "A little over an hour, probably. Why are you asking me this right now? So openly?"

"Yes, what *do* you care about that worthless show?" Wrathgar asked, sitting stone-still on his stool.

"So you think the others have probably succeeded by now?" Liam asked Frederic.

"What others?" Wrathgar asked.

"Liam," Frederic said out of the corner of his mouth. "You-know-who is sitting *right there*."

"He knows I hear him," the dungeon master said. "What are you up to?" He leaned forward on his seat, his eyes darting from one prince to the other.

Liam ignored him. "Well, Frederic, I'm going to assume our friends have succeeded in their mission," he said. "Which means it's time for us to get out of these cells. Here, catch!" He stood and brought his arm forward as if he were about to throw something.

Wrathgar jumped up, toppling his stool, and stepped in front of Liam's cell. Liam quickly hid his hands behind his back.

"What are you playing at?" Wrathgar barked. "Show me your hands."

Liam brought his arms forward but kept his hands cupped together.

"You must have heard how much I *love* smart-aleck prisoners," Wrathgar said. "Open them! Before I open you."

Liam parted his hands just the slightest bit.

"Show me!" Wrathgar raged.

Liam held his hands right up to the cell door and uncupped them, revealing a miniscule flea sitting in his palm.

"Huh?"

When Wrathgar pressed his face up against the bars to get a better look, Liam yanked both long, ponytail-like strands of the dungeon master's mustache into his cell and tied them together.

"I did it!" Liam shouted triumphantly. "I've got him trapped. Now to get the keys." Aiming his fist squarely between the bars, Liam punched the huge man in the face.

"OWWWW!" Liam howled, shaking his aching hand. "His skull is *so hard*!"

Fuming, Wrathgar whipped his head backward. The knotted facial hair ripped away. Both Liam and Frederic gasped.

"Rraghh! It's going to take *days* to grow that mustache

back," Wrathgar snarled. Too angry to bother with keys, he tore Liam's cell door straight off its hinges and tossed it into the corridor with a sonorous clang. Liam pressed himself up against the back wall of his cell. He was cornered.

"You die now," Wrathgar said.

And then the dungeon keeper felt a thin, pointy finger tapping at his back. "Hey, Ugly," a voice called from behind him. As he spun around, Briar splashed her bottle of sleeping potion into his face, dousing him with the pinkish liquid.

Fig. 38
WRATHGAR, raging

"What the—?" Wrathgar fell onto the floor, snoring.

"Briar!" Liam shouted. "Why are you dressed like a clown? What are you even doing here?"

"Saving your sorry butt, apparently," she said. "Oh, and *you're welcome*, by the way."

"Quit the charade," Liam said. "You snuck in here to get to the sword before us."

"Then why aren't I already in the vault?" she shot back.

"Because you saw Wrathgar and knew he'd get in the way of your escape," Liam said.

"What did you do to him, by the way?" Frederic asked, peeking out of his cell.

Briar held up the tiny bottle. "Sleeping potion."

"You just threw it at him?" Liam asked.

"What was I supposed to do, offer it to him in a teacup?" Briar snapped.

"Never mind. I guess we're all working together now," said Liam. He crouched down by Wrathgar. "Ella and Gustav should have the vault open by this point, so let's grab the dungeon keys and get Frederic out of there."

"Nah-ah-ah," Briar said. She placed her curly-toed shoe on Liam's shoulder and pushed him away from the snoozing dungeon master. "You see, I trust you about as much as you trust me. You and I are going to get the sword *first*. As long as you behave yourself and don't try to double-cross me along the way, we'll free your friend on our way back."

"And if I don't agree?" Liam said, staring her down.

Briar waved the potion bottle in his face. "Thirsty?"

"Just go," Frederic said. "We don't have time to argue. I don't know how long Wrathgar will be out."

Liam and Briar dashed off together.

Outside, the dust was finally beginning to settle around the Wall of Secrecy.

"I think I can see the giant again," one of the archers called out, peering through the thinning cloud of dirt particles to spy Maude lying unconscious on her back. "Yep, still down."

"Hit it with a few more to be safe," Jezek ordered. "Anybody see the troll?"

"Um, I do," one bandit reported. "He's bouncing."

Mr. Troll had climbed up onto Maude's big belly and was using it as a springboard, sending himself higher upward with every bounce, until finally he launched himself at the wall. He soared through the air and landed on the ramparts, where he immediately tossed two of the bandits down a long flight of steps to the courtyard below.

"Shoot it! Shoot it!" Jezek yelled.

"Sir, I'm sorry to have to be the one to explain this to you," one archer said, "but we have bows and arrows. They're made for long-range combat. *Long*-range. They don't work so well when the enemy is right in front of you. For that you need *melee* weapons, by which I mean swords and clubs and other such things that you could use for close-range fiiiiiiiiiiiii—"

And Mr. Troll tossed him off the wall.

Like a shaggy green whirlwind, Mr. Troll whipped through the archers, howling and snapping their bows to pieces.

"It's you and me, Troll!" Jezek shouted. He flexed his neck. "Let's go."

Mr. Troll dropped the archers he was holding and nodded at Jezek. "Troll like that."

On the circus stage, Ruffian paid no heed to the balls and rubber chickens bouncing off his head. Briar was paying him to keep an eye on the Warlord, so that was all he was doing. He was growing increasingly disturbed, though, by Deeb Rauber's absence. If the boy was headed where Ruffian thought he might be . . . well, Briar's instructions didn't matter much anymore.

Without a word, Ruffian turned and walked backstage. The rolling pin Snow threw in his direction landed harmlessly on the ground.

Snow looked up from her basket of chuckable goodies. She was entirely alone onstage. And three hundred bandits, plus the Warlord of Dar, were watching her.

"I found it!" Liam shouted as he spotted the vault, its thick steel door wide-open.

"Yes!" Briar shoved past Liam to run ahead.

"Oh, no, you don't," Liam cried, grabbing her clown-suit ribbons and pulling her back. They wrestled each other through the threshold of the vault and tumbled into deep piles of gold and jewels. Treasures were scattered everywhere, priceless artifacts lay haphazardly on their sides as if they were toys carelessly tossed into a closet by an untidy child (which is basically what had happened to them). There was no mounted glass case for the Sword of Erinthia here—the priceless artifact had simply been plopped into a random bucket of coins. But at least it was easy to find.

"Get off me," Briar snapped as she and Liam rolled on the floor.

"You won't get that gem," he spat back.

Briar reached for the sword, but as she did, Liam snatched the bottle of sleeping potion from her.

"Ha!" Liam shouted. "Ha! Ha! And once more, *ha!* Your plan to ruin my plan to ruin your plan just backfired." He flicked the bottle at her, spattering her with all of the remaining sleeping potion.

Fig. 39
The SWORD, finally

Which was two tiny drops. They dappled the front of her clown suit harmlessly.

"Crud," he grumbled. "I thought there was more in there."

Briar reached over and plucked the Sword of Erinthia from its bucket. "Don't be sad that you're a loser, Liam," she said. "Be happy you're married to a winner like me. Now, shall we leave?"

And that was when the vault door suddenly slammed shut, locking them inside.

27

A Hero Invites the Villain to Drop In

Never regret anything. (If that turns out
to be bad advice, I sincerely apologize.)
—The Hero's Guide to Being a Hero

Lila was standing on the switch in the pitch blackness. Humming to herself. Trying not to panic. "It's just like having my eyes closed," she told herself. She closed her eyes. "Yeah, see? Nothing scary about having your eyes closed." Then she opened her eyes, saw that it was just as dark, and wanted to cry.

Suddenly she felt herself being jerked upward. The rope was being reeled in from above. As soon as her foot came off the lever, it snapped back into its "lock" position. Gears turned, poles shifted, and five stories below, the vault slammed shut. But Lila didn't care anymore. She was finally getting out of that horrible hole.

"Thanks, Duncan," she said as her eyes readjusted to the sunlight. "So, what happened with Ella and the . . ."

"Hello, my little wagon driver," Vero said. "I did not expect to find *you* at the end of this long rope."

Lila gasped. Ella, Gustav, and Duncan had their hands tied behind their backs, held against the dome at sword point by Madu, Falco, and the two other random bandits. Deeb Rauber looked on.

"Don't worry," Ella yelled. "It'll be all right."

"Put a sock in it, cousin," Rauber said. He strode back and forth in front of his new prisoners, his hands clasped together behind his back and his nose high in the air. "You know, Ella, you and I are family. If you wanted to come visit my new place, you could have just asked. I would have had a nice little room made up for you—*in the dungeon!*"

He laughed. The two bandit foot soldiers laughed with him. Vero, however, did not; he had noticed how Madu and Falco rolled their eyes at Rauber's corny joke.

"What's wrong, Vero?" Rauber asked, cocking an eyebrow. "Sense of humor gone dry?"

"Oh, no, sir," the swordsman responded. "Perhaps something was just lost in translation, yes?"

"Whatever. Tie up the girl," Rauber said. Vero held Lila's hands behind her back and bound them together.

"Who is the, uh, young lady, anyway?" Rauber continued.

"I'm Lila, Liam's sister. And I hope you realize that if you do anything to me or my brother, your sorry excuse for a kingdom will be at war with Erinthia."

"I wouldn't be so sure about that," Rauber retorted. "It'll kinda depend on how the bards decide to tell the tale. I'm a very popular villain. And the League of Dunces are not very popular heroes."

Snow was frozen in the spotlight. She'd been doing so well, she thought. But that was before she'd been left alone. Now what was she supposed to do? She wasn't used to having to make decisions on her own.

The audience was booing. "Bah! It's starting to stink again," yelled one burly bandit, and he hurled an empty grog bottle at Snow.

She raised her hand and, with astounding finesse, caught the bottle. Not knowing what else to do with it, she threw it back at the bandit. It smashed across his face and knocked him off his seat.

The crowd roared.

Another bandit shouted, "Catch this, clown," and winged a mealy apple at Snow. She spun around and caught it easily, then whipped it back at him. Several audience members began throwing vegetables, flatware, and other various doodads at Snow; and—with twirls, flips, and hops in between— she caught and tossed back every one. The bandits were laughing and clapping as Snow bounced around the stage, using those gifted arms of hers in a juggling act with the entire audience.

Fig. 40 AUDIENCE, PARTICIPATION

"I didn't even know I was good at this," Snow said, grinning uncontrollably. "But I'm really good at this!"

The only person not amused was Lord Rundark.

Frederic was pondering the possibility of trying to reach Wrathgar's keys with a stretched-out sock when he heard footsteps running toward the cellblock. He braced himself for the worst.

"Rapunzel?"

"Frederic!" she said in a horrified whisper as she ran to him. She stopped when she saw Wrathgar lying in her path. "Is that a person?"

"Yes, a mean one," Frederic said. "Whatever you do, don't cry on him."

They briefly filled each other in on their situations as Rapunzel crouched beside the fallen dungeon master and gingerly unclasped the key ring from his belt. She ran to Frederic's cell and tried one key after another, until finally the door opened and she threw her arms around him, her cheeks smearing his shirt with berry stains (not that he minded at that moment).

"Hurry," he said. "We need to catch up to Liam and Briar."

Together they darted through the dungeon corridors until they reached the vault.

"Oh, no, it's closed," Frederic said.

"I guess Lila never got it open," Rapunzel said.

Then they heard muffled voices from behind the thick steel door. Very unhappy voices.

"No," said Frederic. "She did."

* * *

"We wouldn't be in this predicament if you'd been smart enough not to hire the Gray Phantom," Briar snarled, kicking over a stack of gold doubloons.

"I could have gotten the sword out of the vault in time if you hadn't been so bent on reaching it before me," Liam retorted.

"Who are you kidding? You'd have been smashed to bits by that monster if I hadn't come along."

"I'd rather be back in a cell with him than locked here with you! What have we done all this for? How do we know the Gem even works?"

Briar placed her thumb against the large orange stone at the base of the blade. "Punch yourself in the face," she said.

Liam punched himself in the face.

"Satisfied?" Briar asked. She was about to remove her finger from the Gem but kept it there. "Tell me how you really feel about me."

"You are the most horrible person in the world," Liam said. "You've destroyed my life. I wish I'd never kissed you and woke you from that spell. I've made a lot of mistakes over the years, but that was by far the worst. The world would have been better off without you."

Briar slid her thumb off the Gem. She suddenly had a terrible taste in her mouth.

"Why did you even bring me and my friends into this?" Liam cried. "Why did you ask us to get the sword for you?"

"Because I expected you to fail!" Briar blurted out. "I wanted the Djinn Gem. I wasn't sure exactly what I would do with it when I got it—maybe take over the world, maybe use it to get the husband I wanted, maybe just use it to play mortifying jokes on people I don't like—but all that really mattered was that I *wanted* it. I couldn't send just anybody to retrieve it for me. If I hired a professional thief or mercenary—even Ruffian—that person might have kept the Gem and used it for himself. I had to make sure *I* was the one to steal it. But I couldn't just break into the Bandit King's castle on my own. I needed a distraction. And who is more distracting than the bumbling League of Princes? I recruited you to do this, Liam, because I knew you would mess up royally. That's what the League does. And while you and your pals were causing your inevitable chaos around the castle, I could sneak in and grab the sword on my own."

"You wanted to sacrifice us all along," Liam muttered in disgust.

"*Wanted* to, yes—past tense," Briar said. "But then you and your friends just *had* to prance around me all week, being all admirable and oddly respectable, and flaunting your worth as human beings. Making me feel guilty about sending you to your dooms. And making me realize that whatever I might have done with the Gem would be child's play compared to what Rauber—or, heaven forbid, the Darians—could do with it."

"You expect me to believe you've had some sort of change of heart?" Liam said, almost laughing.

"I expect you to believe I'm smart enough to realize I was wrong. Don't think I haven't struggled with this. I don't like you, Liam. And it's obvious you and all your friends can't stand me. Yet I didn't leave you to the mercy of the muscle-bound maniac out there. I saved you."

"And left Frederic behind!"

"You know what?" Briar snapped. "You don't believe me? Here!" She took the Sword of Erinthia by the blade and held it out to Liam.

Liam looked at her strangely.

"Here," she repeated. "Take it. If you really believe I'm out to destroy you, take the sword from me."

Liam reached out and took the sword by the handle. Briar let it go.

"Happy now?" Briar asked. "Go ahead. Take control of my mind. Make me run into a wall or bash my head against that solid gold chamber pot over there."

"No," Liam said.

"Why not? You hate me."

"But I'm not like you."

Briar sighed and plopped down into a giant sack of coins like it was a beanbag chair. "You're insufferable, you know."

Up on the roof, Deeb Rauber was still monologuing. ". . . and that's why villains get all the glory. And that's why, even *among villains*, I get the most glory. And that's why I, even among the *top ten youngest villains*—"

"I am sorry to interrupt, sir," Vero said, looking out into the distance. "But that troll you told your men not to worry about—I believe he is on your wall."

"You'd better be wrong about that," Rauber said. Vero tossed him a spyglass, and he peered through it. "Holy cripes! The troll's on my wall! Why haven't they killed it? Oh, for crying out loud, it looks like it's beating my guys! Argh! Someone's going through the spanking machine for this! Vero, over here now!"

Vero ran to Rauber's side. The Bandit King began

shouting a long list of complex orders at him, pointing in seemingly random directions, and occasionally jumping up and down. While the Bandit King ranted and raged, Ruffian appeared from behind a tattoo booth (having ditched the wig and bow tie). He slipped silently over to Lila and drew his sword.

"Please don't kill me," Lila whispered.

"And deprive the world of the most promising young bounty hunter I've seen in years?" he replied as he cut her bindings.

"I knew you weren't all bad," Lila said, flashing him a sly grin.

"You knew no such thing," he returned. He grabbed her by the hand. "Come. We're escaping over the side."

Lila pulled away. "Not so fast, Ruff. I'm not leaving my friends behind."

"You need to get to safety. And stop calling me that."

"Look, Ruff," Lila said. "You claim you're not a villain. Prove it to me."

Ruffian huffed. "Fine," he said. "Hide over there and don't come out." He pushed Lila behind a rain barrel and charged at Rauber's men. Taking them by surprise, he flipped through the air and delivered a pair of flying kicks to the chins of the two unimportant bandits.

"You!" Ella shouted. "I never thought I'd actually be happy to see you." Ruffian slashed through her ropes and handed her a sword.

"Take care of your friends," he said to Ella, and turned to fend off an attack from Falco.

Swinging a fat broadsword, Madu leapt into the fray. Ella ducked, and Gustav smashed the tattooed Darian between the eyes with a powerful head butt.

"Free my hands," Gustav said as Madu hit the ground and began morphing into his snake form. Ella cut Gustav's ropes and handed him Madu's fallen sword before she charged out to attack Vero.

As Ruffian's sword clacked against the blades of the three foes he was dueling at once, Gustav turned to free Duncan. But before he could, the giant sand snake barged in between them, whipping Duncan to the ground and coiling around Gustav.

"Well, well," said Vero. "It is quite the predicament you have put me in, yes? I have never before dueled a lady. It seems inappropriate, no?"

"I'll let you be the judge of that," Ella said. And she lashed into him.

"I am impressed," Vero said. "You have had training,

no?"

"Yes, from Liam," Ella said. "Liam of Erinthia." She jabbed; Vero sidestepped.

"The fellow in the dungeon?" Vero said. "Oh, I would have liked to have dueled him then. Too bad he is most certainly dead by now."

The comment caught Ella off guard, and Vero's sword slashed across her cheek, drawing blood.

"I am sorry it had to come to that, dear lady," Vero said. "Would you like to surrender now?"

"Not a chance," Ella growled. And she kicked Vero in the gut.

Lila could not just crouch there watching her friends fight for their lives. She grabbed her rope and stepped out from behind the rain barrel to help. But Deeb Rauber was waiting for her.

"You know, I don't normally allow girls inside my castle," the Bandit King said. "But maybe I'd make an exception for you."

"Eww, are you flirting with me?" Lila winced.

"What's flirting?" Rauber asked. He'd never blushed before in his life; but he felt his cheeks getting strangely warm, and he didn't like it. "Look, I just thought you seemed pretty tough for a girl. A compliment from the Bandit King is incredibly rare, you know. You should be groveling in thanks."

"That's likely," Lila snarked.

"Never mind!" Rauber snapped. "I should have known better than to try to talk to a girl." He pulled a dagger from his belt and pointed it at her.

Duncan lay on the ground, desperately trying to untie the ropes that bound his wrists together. Suddenly he heard a squeak.

"King Moonracer, you came back for me!" he cried. The rat skittered behind him and gnawed through the ropes, freeing him. "Woo-hoo!" Duncan shouted.

He ducked into the tattoo booth and emerged a second later with a handful of long, pointy needles. He charged at the giant snake and rammed twenty needles at once into its scaly body. The snake's head darted upward in shock, and its grip loosened just enough for Gustav to wriggle free of its serpentine clutches.

Before Duncan knew it, though, he was trapped. The snake reared up and flicked its forked tongue in Duncan's face, while Falco crept up behind him.

"Duck!" Gustav shouted. And astonishingly, Duncan

did not start looking for signs of waterfowl; he crouched down just as Gustav grabbed the snake by its tail and began spinning in a circle, swinging the long creature around like a huge propeller. With a whoosh, Madu's thick snake head sailed over Duncan and whammed into Falco like a mallet, sending him hurtling into a nearby candy booth. Gustav let go of the snake, which flopped to the ground in a dizzy stupor.

"How'd you get free?" Gustav asked Duncan.

"King Moonracer."

"The rat?" Gustav said. "How'd you manage that?"

Duncan smiled and showed Gustav the piece of cheese that was in his hand.

"Where'd you get the cheese?" Gustav asked.

"I always have cheese," Duncan replied as if answering the silliest question he'd ever heard.

Vero charged at Ella with a series of frenzied slashes, finally knocking her weapon from her hand.

"You are good," he said. "But I think you must agree that I am simply superior." He knew he had defeated this fascinating woman and couldn't resist the urge to show off just a bit. As he came in for the final blow, he spun gracefully, his long ponytail flowing out behind him. Ella grabbed a handful of flapping hair and jerked Vero off balance. As the swordsman stumbled over, she brought her knee up into his face.

"Capes, ponytails—they're all the same," Ella said. She looked down at Vero, who was on his knees, cradling his broken nose. "Never underestimate a woman again."

"Dis I will nod do," Vero mumbled in a stuffy voice.

Deeb Rauber was sneering at Lila, flashing his dagger in her face.

"Nice pocketknife," Lila mocked. "I suppose they only let the *big boys* play with real swords."

"It's not a sword; it's a dagger," Rauber whined. "And I'm pretty sure you know that. You're just trying to make me angry."

"Ooh, what happens when you get angry?" Lila said, surreptitiously dropping the loop of her rope in front of her. "Do you turn into a whiny brat? 'Cause, in that case, I think it's

Fig. 41
DEEB, angry

already happened."

Rauber took a step toward her. As soon as his foot landed inside the circle of rope, Lila yanked her end. The loop closed up like a noose around Rauber's ankle, and he fell flat on his back. Lila ran for the Snake Hole, dragging the Bandit King behind her.

"Ow! Ow! Hey! Stop!" he cried as he was pulled along.

Heaving with all her might, Lila yanked Rauber to the edge of the hole and gave him a good, solid shove with her foot. The Bandit King slid headfirst into the Snake Hole. Lila slammed down the metal lid and scanned the rooftop. Gustav, Ella, and Duncan had all gathered together and seemed to be okay for the moment. She waved to them.

"Okay, Ruff," Lila called. "We can go now."

Ruffian easily knocked out the last two bandits as if he'd just been waiting for Lila's say-so.

"Hold on," he said, swinging her onto his back. With Lila clinging tightly, he ran to the rear edge of the roof, dove over the side, and skidded briskly down the rope that was waiting for him.

Vero staggered groggily to his feet. Ella and the others were nowhere in sight, but he heard a strange, muffled sound: his boss's voice shouting from the depths of the Snake Hole.

"Vero! Vero, get me out of here!"

Rauber was trapped at the bottom of the dark tunnel. Upside down. With his shoulder jammed painfully against the vault lever.

The vault door clicked and swung open suddenly, bonking Frederic in the nose. He staggered backward as Liam and Briar burst from the vault.

"Thank goodness," Liam said, and then did a double take. "Rapunzel?"

"Long story," Rapunzel said.

"Liam, you got the sword," Frederic said excitedly.

"Yes, the big hero has the prize," Briar said impatiently. "Now, can we leave before someone finds us down here."

The quartet ran through the dungeon corridors, past a door marked KNEE-SKINNING ROOM and a complicated-looking device labeled ARMPIT HAIR PULLER. They passed a cupboard-size door in the wall, and Frederic stopped to peek inside.

"It's a dumbwaiter," he said. "Climbing up this shaft won't be easy, but I doubt we'll run into any bandits along the way."

"It's worth a try," Liam said. Briar shoved her way to the front of the line, crawled into the dumbwaiter shaft, and began hoisting herself up the rope.

"We need a fast way downstairs," Ella said as she, Gustav, and Duncan ran around the dome on the castle rooftop.

"How about the dumbwaiter thingy?" Duncan suggested.

He ran to the dome and opened the dumbwaiter door.

"Sounds good to me," Gustav said, climbing in.

Ella followed, with Duncan close behind. "I just hope this rope holds all of us."

Snap! It didn't.

"Ack!" Briar screamed as Gustav's eel-chewed backside came falling at her. In a cacophony of shouts and groans, one body after another crashed together, and everyone landed in a heap at the bottom of the dumbwaiter shaft.

"I didn't do it," Duncan said.

"Oh, great," Briar moaned. "It's the clown."

"Briar?" Ella asked angrily. "Did you cut the rope to trap us?"

"Yes, it was all part of my plan to trap you *on top of me*," Briar replied sarcastically.

"Ella?" Liam squeaked from somewhere beneath her.

"Cape-Man?" Gustav asked.

"Gustav?" Rapunzel called up.

"Rapunzel?!" Gustav shrieked.

"Why do I always end up on the bottom of these pileups?" Frederic moaned.

"Hold on, everybody," Liam said. "Let's squeeze out of here first and then sort things out."

Slowly and painfully, they tumbled one by one onto the dungeon floor.

"You okay, Blondie?" Gustav asked. "You're supposed to be back in Avondell."

Rapunzel nodded. "I'll survive." She smiled at him sweetly. "Thanks for asking."

"Well, you know, you're here to heal us," he said. "If *you* get hurt, who's gonna heal *you*?"

Gustav's cheeks burned red. He was awkwardly trying to look anywhere other than at Rapunzel.

"Wait, where's Lila?" Liam asked nervously.

"Don't worry," said Ella. "She's with Ruffian."

"Oh, good," Liam said. "Wait? Is that good?"

"Where's Little Taylor?" Duncan asked.

"You don't want to know," said Liam.

"I'm okay, too," Briar said loudly. "Thanks for checking,

everybody."

"Well, how do we get out now?" Frederic asked.

"Hey, I've got a *crazy* idea," Briar said, losing patience. "Why don't we go back the way we came in?"

The group rushed toward the stairwell door.

"Ella, when did you cut your hair?" Liam asked as they ran.

"Wait!" Rapunzel cried as they passed the cellblock. Everyone stopped. "Where's that unreasonably large man?"

The floor in front of Liam's old cell, where Wrathgar had been lying unconscious, was now bare.

"Oh, that's not good," muttered Frederic.

The dungeon master stepped out of the shadows. "If you thought I was mad before," he said, "you haven't seen anything yet."

28
THE VILLAIN WINS

*If your followers are not listening to you, it had better be
because you've cut off their ears.*
— THE WARLORD'S PATH TO POWER:
AN ANCIENT TOME OF DARIAN WISDOM

At the sight of Wrathgar, the first thought that went
through Gustav's head was *Gotta make sure Rapunzel
and Frederic get out okay.* But what he said was "Where
have you been hiding this guy? This is the fight I've been
looking for!"

He took a step toward the dungeon master, and
Frederic tried to hold him back. "Gustav, wait, you don't
know what he's like."

"Based on the look of him, I've got a pretty good idea,"
Gustav said. "You guys get out. I'll take care of the Masked
Marvel."

He drew his sword and charged at Wrathgar.

"No," Liam shouted.

But it was too late. The dungeon master grabbed Gustav's sword by the blade and twisted it out of his hand. In a second, Wrathgar's enormous hand was wrapped around Gustav's throat.

Liam held up the Sword of Erinthia. "Stop!" he shouted.

Wrathgar went right on squeezing.

"Why . . . are . . . none . . . of . . . you . . . leaving?" Gustav gurgled to his teammates.

Liam tried again. "I command you to drop Gustav."

Wrathgar lifted Gustav off the ground by his throat.

"Are you touching the gem?" Briar asked urgently. "You have to be in contact with it!"

"I am!" Liam snapped in frustration.

Gustav started gasping for air.

"Give it up, Liam; it's not working," Ella said, and leapt at Wrathgar with her sword. With the back of his hand, the dungeon master knocked Ella up against the wall. Her weapon flew from her hand as she slid to the floor.

"Drop him!" Liam shouted, twisting the sword. "C'mon, drop him!"

Gustav's face turned red, then a sickly blue.

"You're not doing it right," Briar said.

"Yes, I am," Liam shouted. "It's just not working!"

When Gustav went limp, Duncan first let out a mournful cry. Then he got angry. He held his fist in front of him and ran straight at Wrathgar.

"Syllllll-vaaaaaaah-riiiiii-aaaaa!"

Wrathgar flicked a single finger at Duncan and send the petite prince hurtling into an empty prison cell.

"He'll kill them all," Frederic gasped.

"Give me the sword, Liam," Briar said.

"No," Liam snapped, keeping his focus on Wrathgar. Sweat pouring from his brow began to mix with tears in his eyes. Gustav wasn't moving.

"You were right, Liam," Briar said with a sudden realization. "In the vault when you said you weren't like me, you were right. You're too good. You can't connect with the malevolent power in that gem. But we know *I* can. Give me the sword."

Liam looked away from Wrathgar and locked eyes with Briar. There was a pleading look on her face that was unlike anything Liam had seen from her before. She held out her hand.

"Trust me."

He gave her the sword.

Briar turned around to face Wrathgar and rubbed her finger over the odd orange jewel at the base of the blade. The dungeon master's body suddenly went stiff. He opened his hand and let Gustav fall to the floor.

"He's not breathing," Frederic cried. Rapunzel hurried to the fallen prince and ran her hands over his chest. She began to weep.

"I'm fine, I'm fine," Gustav wheezed, waving her away. "Quit it. You're getting me wet."

"Thank you," Frederic said to Briar.

Liam said nothing. He ran to help Ella and Duncan back to their feet.

Gustav marveled at Wrathgar, who still stood frozen in place. "You're controlling him?"

Briar smirked. Suddenly, Wrathgar danced a jig.

"Hmm. He's got better rhythm than I would have thought," Frederic said.

Duncan ran up next to Wrathgar and capered alongside him.

Liam's eyes lit up. "He's our ticket to freedom," he said. "Briar, make him lead us out. We'll all just follow behind, like we're his prisoners. Can you make him do that?"

"Darling, I can make him do anything," Briar said. "With this sword in my hand, I have complete control of that brute. He is my puppet."

"The sword can do *that*? Sweet!" cried a reedy voice from behind her. Deeb Rauber emerged from the stairwell, along with Vero, Falco, Madu, and a dozen other bandits he'd gathered on his way down.

"So, Sleeping Beauty, huh?" Deeb Rauber asked, taking stock of the group before him. "I have to say, even when I heard the Prince Charmings were staging some sort of '*heist*,' I never expected to find you involved."

He and his men were blocking the only exit from the dungeon. Briar, Liam, and the others had all gathered behind the frozen Wrathgar.

"I'm just reclaiming what is rightfully mine," Briar said.

"You mean you're trying to steal what belongs to me," Rauber corrected.

"Actually, it belongs to *me*," Liam re-corrected.

"Technically, *us*," Briar re-re-corrected.

"I'm already bored by this," said Rauber. "Boys, get that sword!"

Vero and the bandits rushed at Briar, but didn't make it very far. Wrathgar snapped into action. He held one arm straight out to each side and barreled through the hallway, mowing down every bandit between him and Rauber. The

Bandit King himself was short enough to duck under the armpit of the mesmerized brute and avoid the attack.

"Holy gnome nuggets!" Rauber yelped.

Wrathgar snatched Rauber by his shirt collar and carried him off into the cellblock kicking and screaming.

"Help me!" Rauber shrieked.

Vero stood in a daze and staggered over to aid his boss. He struggled to pry Wrathgar's fingers open.

"Let's get out of here before they're all up again," Frederic urged.

Liam grabbed Briar by the arm and tugged her toward the stairwell.

"It stops working if I lose sight of him," Briar said.

"Do you plan on staying down here with him forever?" Liam asked.

"Give me one second," Briar said. *Destroy all the bandits,* she thought.

Wrathgar went berserk. He tossed Rauber aside and began pounding on his former allies. The bandits had no choice but to fight back in order to stay alive. They all leapt on the dungeon master, hoping that together they could take him down.

The heroes didn't stick around to see what happened next. Together, Frederic, Rapunzel, Gustav, Ella, Duncan,

Liam, and Briar ran up the steps. As expected, the moment the stairwell door shut and Briar could no longer see Wrathgar, her power over him was broken. She hoped the other bandits would be so caught up in fighting him that they wouldn't realize they no longer had to, but she knew it would only be a matter of minutes before Rauber and his men would be after them again.

Throughout Snow's lively act, Lord Rundark sat seething as he waited for Rauber's "surprise" finale, during which he planned to turn the tables on the boy. Rundark knew this would be the best way to ensure the loyalty of the bandit army: first showing them that Rauber's childish pranks had no effect on him and then slaughtering the boy in front of them. It would work out perfectly—as long as he was able to wait patiently for the end of the circus. But that was proving difficult.

The more the Warlord saw the goofy grins on the bandits all around him and listened to their riotous belly laughs, the more his temples began to pound and his teeth began to grind and his fingernails began to rip into the velvet arms of his chair. The Warlord was prone to fits of violence, but he could usually rely on the calming advice of a trusted follower to prevent him from going over the edge. Unfortunately, that trusted follower had been Redshirt, whom Rundark had tossed out a window the day before.

The audience went wild as Snow caught a cinnamon bun with her teeth, and Rundark couldn't take it anymore. He stood up, stepped over the railing, and strode out onto the stage.

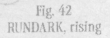

Fig. 42
RUNDARK, rising

A plate that one of the bandits had thrown to Snow came flying in Rundark's direction. The Warlord caught it and hurled it back—straight through the body of the bandit who had thrown it. The laughter died out instantly.

"This ends now!" Rundark bellowed. He grabbed Snow before she could run.

"Put her down! She's the best performer we've got!"

cried one of the circus strongmen as he and three fellow weight lifters ran to Snow's defense. As each of the musclemen got close to him, Rundark slammed, punched, or kicked him to the ground. None of them stood back up.

Snow looked up at the Warlord and trembled.

"You call yourselves a bandit army," Rundark said to the crowd. "You are nothing more than a gang of unruly children. But I will change you. I will make you into real villains. The time has come for you men to learn the true power of fear."

* * *

With the Sword of Erinthia still in hand, Briar led her group down long, echoing corridors, searching for an exit.

"There's the way out," Gustav said as they spotted the main entry hall.

"But Snow is still at the circus," Duncan said.

"Follow me," Briar said, heading away from the exit. She brought them around several winding corridors, heading deeper into the center of the castle.

"I think the theater was this way," Rapunzel said, pointing to a gargoyle-festooned archway.

"No, it's through here," Briar insisted. "I remember these doors." She marched past Rapunzel and headed for a pair of large wooden doors with images of laughing cherubs carved into them. To her surprise, everybody followed her, and she wondered for a second if she were somehow controlling them all with the sword. *No, that's not it,* she thought. *They trust me.*

The group flung open the double doors and charged into the backstage area. All the performers were gathered at the curtains, gawking in horror at the stage. The heroes rushed in for a look. At center stage, Lord Rundark held Snow White over his head as if he was about to break her in two.

"Snow!" Duncan screamed.

But Lord Rundark did nothing to Snow. He didn't move at all. After a terrifyingly long pause, he set her down on her feet and sent her backstage.

"Hurry along, young lady," Rundark said, patting her on the back. "And thank you for letting me be part of this wonderful circus of yours."

In the stands, six hundred eyeballs simultaneously bugged out.

"You've got Rundark?" Liam whispered to Briar as Snow ran into Duncan's waiting arms. Briar nodded.

Lord Rundark started stiffly clapping his hands. "And that's the end of our show. Let's hear it for the Flimshams!"

A few bandits offered tentative applause.

"Now the circus people will leave the castle," Rundark continued. "And no one will get in their way."

"Nice," Ella said. "But what happens once we're out of the room?"

"Good point," said Frederic. "The Warlord has got to come with us."

"Obviously," Briar huffed. She clutched the sword tightly to her chest, and Rundark walked backstage to join them. The real circus performers all scattered as the mesmerized Rundark led the team of heroes toward the rear exit. Lila and Ruffian ran up and joined the group.

"What's going on?" Lila whispered, clutching Liam's hand. Liam held his finger to his lips, and Lila decided she could ask questions later.

The path to the exit was clear, save for one thing: El Stripo.

The tiger was curled on the floor next to a big bowl of water. Its faded orange fur sagged loosely on its thin and feeble frame, and it still had no teeth. The animal had trouble keeping its eyelids open.

All heads turned to Frederic.

"Well, okay, now I feel a little silly," he said sheepishly. "Let's move on."

Outside the building, the group crossed the drawbridge,

weaved a path through empty circus wagons in the courtyard, and headed for the Wall of Secrecy. Any bandit who might have stopped them stepped aside at the sight of the Warlord.

"I think this is going to work," Frederic whispered.

"Look, on top of the wall!" Gustav suddenly shouted. He pointed up at Jezek and Mr. Troll, who were still wrestling on the ramparts. "We've gotta get Furface down with us."

"Of course we do," Briar muttered, rolling her eyes.

Lord Rundark rolled his eyes, too.

"He's part of the team," Gustav insisted.

The group stopped.

"Hey, you up there!" the Warlord shouted.

"The man's name is Jezek," Frederic told Briar.

"Hey, Jessie!" Lord Rundark called.

"Jezek!" Frederic corrected.

"Jezek!" Rundark called again. "Stop fighting! Leave that hideously unkempt creature alone!"

"Could you repeat that, sir?" the bodyguard asked, holding Mr. Troll in a headlock.

"You heard me, Jazzy," Rundark shouted. "Let the walking carpet go."

"You don't sound like yourself," Jezek said.

Crud, thought Briar.

"Crud," said Lord Rundark.

"Something's not right," Jezek said, dropping the troll and running to the stairs that led down to where everyone was gathered. But trolls don't like being ignored. Mr. Troll rammed Jezek from behind. The bodyguard crashed, bumped, and clattered along one hundred stone steps, landing in a heap at the bottom.

Mr. Troll bounded down the stairs, jumped over the unmoving Jezek, and joined up with his teammates. They were fifty yards from the gate when they heard a shout.

"Stop them, you idiots!" Deeb Rauber darted out of the castle and stood on the drawbridge with the entire bandit army behind him. "Don't let them escape!"

The bandits rushed forward, but Rundark raised his hands and yelled, "Stop! I am your true leader. Do not interfere."

The bandits stopped.

"Rundark's been hypnotized, you idiots!" Rauber shouted. "Get after them now! Or every one of you sits in the Tack Chair!"

The bandits charged at the heroes.

"Freeze! All of you!" bellowed Lord Rundark.

The bandits stopped.

"You dare to think that I, the Warlord of Dar, am so weak that I could be hypnotized?" he snarled. "That I can be controlled like someone's puppet?"

"Don't listen to him!" Rauber hollered. "They're making him say that! Listen to *me*! I am your leader!"

"Is he?" Rundark asked. "Is that mewling little piece of spittle your leader? Do you all take orders from a petulant child? Or do you listen to a ruler like me?"

There was a harsh, uncomfortable silence as hundreds of bandits looked around, unsure of what to do.

"Stop them all!" Rauber ordered. "Including Rundark."

"Step aside and clear a path," Rundark demanded.

And the bandit army made their choice. They lowered their weapons and stood down.

"Aaaaaaaargh!" Rauber screamed.

"Everybody run—now!" Liam said. And the group hustled toward the gate.

Just then, Vero and Madu appeared on the drawbridge. It didn't take them long to figure out what was going on.

"No one's listening to me!" Rauber cried. His face was beet red, his eyes watery.

"Madu, get the sword," Vero said.

In a blink, Madu transformed into a thirty-foot-long sand snake and zipped across the rocky courtyard. Just as Briar reached the gateway and stepped out beyond the Wall of Secrecy, the serpent enveloped her and yanked her back in.

"Briar!" Liam shouted. He dove and managed to snag the tip of Madu's long tail. With Briar coiled under its chin, the snake slithered speedily back toward the castle, dragging Liam behind it. "Use the Gem on the snake!" Liam shouted.

Briar shook her head. "I'll lose Rundark," she wheezed.

As the serpent slid onto the drawbridge, Liam lost his grip and rolled into Vero, knocking him over.

"Give me that sword," Rauber yelled. He tried to wrench the weapon from Briar's hand, but despite still being wrapped up in endless yards of snake, her grip was insanely tight. She and the boy yanked back and forth until finally Madu ended the tug-of-war. The snake bit down, sinking its long fangs into the back of Briar's hand.

"Yes!" Rauber shouted, waving the sword in the air. "I win!"

At that moment, just beyond the front gate of the Wall of Secrecy, the Warlord of Dar blinked his eyes; his mind was his own again. And he knew exactly what had happened to him. During his years of battle and conquest, he had developed a thirst for knowledge as well as for blood. He'd read every ancient scroll and historical manuscript he could pry from the stiff fingers of a corpse. There wasn't a tale of evil sorcery or black magic that Lord Rundark wasn't familiar with. And he easily recognized the effects of the Jeopardous Jade Djinn Gem.

"Guys," Ella said, watching the wicked smile spread across Rundark's face. "He's evil again."

"Out of my way," Rundark barked, shoving Ella to the side and charging, rhino-like, back toward the castle.

On the drawbridge, Liam gasped when he saw Briar slumping woozily in the sand snake's clutches. He snatched Vero's fallen sword and rammed it through the tip of the giant reptile's tail, pinning the creature to the drawbridge. As the serpent hissed in pain, Liam pulled Briar free and tossed her over his shoulder.

Rauber spotted Liam running for the gate and decided to test out his new toy.

"Hey, everybody! You think Rundark is bad?" he yelled. "I'll show you bad! Liam, freeze!"

Liam kept running.

"Do as I say! Obey me!" Rauber shouted, but to no effect. "Is there a button or something?"

And then Liam finally stopped. But he stopped because Lord Rundark smacked him and Briar to the ground, where they were promptly surrounded by a dozen bandits. Liam looked in horror at Briar; her green face was swollen, and her breath rattled, the snake venom coursing through her veins.

"You honestly thought you could usurp me?" the Warlord said as he reached Rauber on the drawbridge. He wrapped his hand around the blade of the Sword of Erinthia. "It seems I have already won. Your men have chosen me. And I didn't even have to kill you. Although I still will."

Rauber squinted at Rundark, trying to focus all his concentration on the man. "I command you to jump in the moat," he snarled defiantly.

"So ignorant," Rundark said. He easily wrested the sword out of the Bandit King's hands, then threw the boy to the ground and stepped on his head to hold him in place. The Warlord dug his fingernails behind the orange stone on the hilt and pried it loose. "It's only the Gem that matters." He casually tossed the rest of the sword into the moat.

Liam took Briar's limp hand and held it tight.

"And now," Lord Rundark said, holding up the jewel, "let me show you how a warlord uses the Jeopardous Jade Djinn Gem."

Just then: "Stuuuuuuuuurm-hayyyyyyyy-gennnnnnnn!"

Gustav burst into the courtyard, riding Seventeen. And Ella was right beside him on her horse. Duncan and Snow followed, both astride Papa Scoots Jr. And Mr. Troll took up the rear, his long arms flailing. The group galloped straight at the circle of bandits that surrounded Liam and beat them away. Ella pulled Liam up onto her horse, while Gustav scooped up Briar. Just as quickly as they'd entered, they spun their horses around and began racing back out, knocking away any bandits that tried to stop them.

Then suddenly, Ella pulled up on the reins and brought her horse to a halt.

"What are you doing?" asked Liam.

Wordlessly, Ella turned the horse around and began trotting *toward* the castle again.

"It's Rundark," Liam called out. "He's using the Gem on her! Ella, snap out of it!"

Ella stopped her horse just before the drawbridge. She hopped off and yanked Liam down after her.

Rundark licked his lips. "Bandits of Rauberia," he shouted. "Let me demonstrate for you the real difference between heroes and villains. Heroes have lines they will not cross. But a true villain—a successful villain—will do whatever he needs to in order to win."

Ella drew her sword.

"Ella, it's me," Liam pleaded. "Don't do this."

A bandit tossed a sword to Liam. He caught it and faced Ella, who was in the dueling stance he had taught her.

Bandits cheered—and heroes gasped—as Ella launched a vicious attack on Liam. Liam danced around to avoid her blows but refused to raise his sword against her.

"Fight back," Rundark said darkly. "It's only going to get more difficult."

Ella's swings came at Liam faster and harder. Liam had no choice but to defend himself. Swords flew so rapidly, the onlookers could barely see them. Until finally the duelers reached a standoff, the tip of Liam's sword aimed at Ella's throat, the point of her sword pressing into his. He peered desperately into her eyes, hoping for any sign of the real Ella.

"You had better deliver the final blow, prince," Rundark called. "Because if you don't, in three seconds *she* will."

Liam closed his eyes.

Duncan suddenly gasped and turned to Snow. "You have to be a hero, honey," he said.

"One!" Rundark called.

Duncan dug into his saddlebag and handed an oddly shaped rock to Snow.

"Two!"

"It looks just like Frank!" she said.

"I know," Duncan said. "I'll be sad to lose it. But this is important. Show me your trick."

"Three!"

Snow squinted, brought her arm back, and hurled the dwarf-shaped rock with all her might. The stone smashed into Lord Rundark's raised hand, knocking the magical jewel from his fingers.

Ella blinked.

"No!" the Warlord cried as the Djinn Gem flew into the air, over the moat. He reached out in a desperate attempt to snatch it before it hit the water and found himself teetering precariously on the edge of the drawbridge. Deeb Rauber sat up. It would have taken him no more than a single finger to push Rundark into the killer-eel-infested waters, And that is exactly what the boy did.

Lord Rundark splashed into the moat and disappeared into the murky depths. Everyone watched and waited. A second later, the Warlord resurfaced. Grinning wickedly, he raised his arm out of the water and showed off the hunk of orange jade in his hand.

But his celebration was short-lived.

Below the surface, a bladejaw eel bit into his leg. And

then another. And another. Rundark's howl turned into a gurgle as the carnivorous fish swarmed him, pulling him down into the depths. Soon, the only part of him visible was his right hand, the Jeopardous Jade Djinn Gem still clutched between its fingers. And then a particularly large eel leapt out of the water and slipped its toothy mouth over the Warlord's hand like a glove—gem and all—before sinking back underwater along with any remaining sign of Rundark. The splashing slowed. Then all was silent.

While the bandits stood there stunned, the heroes took the opportunity to zip through the gates and gallop to safety.

"All right," Deeb Rauber said to the bandits as he climbed firmly to his feet. "Who's ready to listen to me now?"

"Everybody stop!" Liam shouted as soon as the group was safely out of sight of the castle. "Briar needs help fast."

"Yeah, she's not looking so good," Gustav said, dismounting from his horse, with Briar dangling limply in his arms. "I mean, she looks sort of zombie-like on a good day, but she looks particularly bad right now."

"It's the snake venom," Liam said. "Rapunzel!"

Frederic and Rapunzel, who were riding together,

caught up with them. As Gustav set Briar down, Rapunzel rushed over to her.

"I hope I'm not too late," she said.

The others gathered around as Rapunzel crouched next to Briar. Ella was such a tangle of emotions, she wasn't sure how she should feel. She looked to her companions for a clue. Duncan and Snow were embracing, their eyes locked on each other in silent support. Frederic's eyes were cast upward—and Ella knew him well enough to understand that he was feeling guilty for some of the words he'd used to describe Briar in the past. Liam's watery eyes were focused very intently on his dying wife. And Rapunzel's were closed tightly, until she managed to squeeze out a single tear.

There was a humming sound, and Briar's body began to quiver. The greenness faded from her face, returning her complexion to its normal ghostly white. She opened her eyes to the entire team staring down at her.

"Ugh," she grumbled. "It was bad enough when I woke up to just Liam's ugly face. Give a girl some space! I can't believe I have to breathe the same air as you losers."

"She's fine," Liam announced.

"You're probably wondering how our horses got here," Duncan said, obviously eager to offer an explanation. "The answer is them." He pointed over to Frank, Flik, and Frak, who were waiting nearby in an open-topped wagon.

"How did they know to come here?" Liam asked.

"I told them, sir, Your Highness, sir," announced Smimf, who appeared with a *whoosh*. "Princess Briar hired me to deliver the message to them this morning."

Liam didn't know what to say. He turned to Briar, but she was sitting against a boulder with her eyes closed, exhausted.

"Hey, what 'bout Giant Lady?" Mr. Troll asked, pointing out into the clearing at Maude, who lay like a heaving mountain in front of Castle von Deeb. "Can't leave her there for Arrow Men."

"Smimf," Frederic called. "I have one more message for you to deliver."

He sent the fleet-footed boy off, and a short time later the ground rumbled as Reese stomped into Rauberia, lifted his mother gently off the ground, and carried her back to Jangleheim.

By that time, though, everyone else was well on their way home.

"Did we win?" Duncan asked. "We didn't get the Djinn Gem."

"But nobody else got it either," said Liam. "And that's

probably the best of all possible—" He stopped short when he felt something he wasn't prepared for.

Briar, sitting behind him on his horse, wrapped her arms around his waist and rested her weary head on his shoulder.

29

A Hero Doesn't Know Where to Go Next

When facing unbeatable odds,
just think of yourself as unbeatably odd.
— The Hero's Guide to Being a Hero

Soon after they left Rauberia, the team came to a crossroads. Everyone stopped. Except for the dwarfs, who raced past in their wagon, ducking low as they went by (Snow had sworn to banish any dwarf she *saw*, so Frank and the gang had been making a concerted effort to stay out of her line of vision).

"Well, where do we go from here?" Frederic asked. No one responded. "I didn't mean that as a trick question, you know."

"Well, *we're* heading home to Avondell," Briar said.

She tapped Liam on the shoulder. "Aren't we?"

Liam looked over to Ella.

"Where are *you* going, Frederic?" Ella asked.

"Me?" Frederic asked, surprised. "I don't know."

"I'm going back to my cottage," Rapunzel quickly threw in. "You know, because of my work. I'm sure I have patients waiting for me."

"Oh. Well, I think maybe—" Frederic began.

"I'll ride with you, Goldilocks," Gustav said to Rapunzel. "I'm heading in the same direction anyway."

"Ah," Frederic said softly. "Well, as I was saying, I'm, um, heading home to Harmonia. I suppose."

"And I'll ride with you," Ella said. She glanced at Liam to see if he had anything to say.

He didn't.

"Well, Snow and I are going home as well," Duncan added with a bittersweet tone. "So, I guess this is good-bye. For now."

"Yes, for now," Liam said, trying to sound like he believed it.

The group split up, riding off in four different directions.

The very first thing Liam did upon returning to Avondell was to free Aldo Cremins and Varick Knoblock, the wrongfully imprisoned actors. Then he addressed the public and revealed the truth about his origins. He assumed this would make people hate him again—and he was correct—but he also knew it was the right thing to do. He was a hero, after all.

Even if he was a hero everybody hated.

You might think that the two people who hated Liam most in the world were Cremins and Knoblock, but as it turned out, those two forgave him pretty quickly. Thanks to a new song by Reynaldo, Duke of Rhyme, the pair gained instant fame, which, in the end, is all any actor really wants.

But Liam still felt quite mopey after the whole episode. He sat around the palace for days with his head in his hands. Occasionally, he'd kick at a pebble or absentmindedly tug at a loose thread on his cape, but other than that, he didn't do much. One day, he walked down to

Fig. 43
LIAM,
re-imprisoned

the palace prison, stepped into cell 842, and pulled the door shut behind him.

Lila decided not to return home.

"My parents won't even notice I'm gone," she told Ruffian.

The bounty hunter was crouched by a tree in the woods, examining scrapings on the bark. He had quit working for Briar and gone back to freelance person-finding. He'd already been hired by a duchess to locate the thief who had run off with a tray of her fresh-baked tarts.

"You're exaggerating," he said to Lila. "Surely they will miss you eventually."

"No, seriously, they don't care about me at all. I asked this chambermaid friend of mine to put on one of my dresses and show up whenever my parents throw a banquet or something. They won't realize it's not me."

"That still doesn't explain why you're following me while I am trying to work."

"I'm your apprentice. Show me your tricks. Why are you checking out that tree bark?" She crouched down beside him.

"This scrape here was made by a wagon wheel, which may not necessarily—wait! Why am I telling you this?

You are not my apprentice. I don't need an apprentice."

"Sure you do," Lila said.

Ruffian narrowed his eyes. "Why would you even want to learn to be a bounty hunter?"

"Because you said I was good at it. I don't get much in the way of positive reinforcement back home."

Ruffian lowered his head. "I can think of few things more irresponsible than taking on a twelve-year-old as an apprentice."

"Actually, Ruff," Lila said with a grin. "I'm thirteen."

"Since when?"

"My birthday was the same day as Liam's wedding. Everyone kind of forgot it, but I understand. There was a lot going on."

Ruffian looked into Lila's eager eyes. For some reason, the girl admired him—liked him even. And she reminded him so much of his own daughter—the one missing person he'd never been able to find.

"Come," he said, leaving the scene of the crime. "There's something you need far more than a lesson in tracking down fugitives."

"What's that?" Lila asked, disappointed.

"A cake."

* * *

"So, Ella," Frederic said as they made their way back to Harmonia. "I've been thinking about . . . well, us."

"Frederic, you're a wonderful person," Ella said, looking uncomfortable. "I care about you a lot."

"Oh, I know you do," Frederic said. "And believe me, it's mutual. But . . . when the Warlord forced you to duel Liam, I couldn't help thinking how glad I was that it wasn't me. You would have killed me. Not intentionally, of course! It's just that, well, what I'm trying to say is . . . I'm not the type of guy who can keep up with a woman like you. You and *Liam* are so well matched. You should be with him."

"Hold on! Who says I want to be with Liam?"

Frederic's cheeks went red. "But I thought . . . I mean, *everybody* thought . . ."

"Look, I like Liam. A lot. But he and I may be a bit *too much* alike. I don't respond well to being told what to do all the time; and, in case you haven't noticed, Liam can get a little bossy. I haven't completely forgiven him for the rotten way he treated you before the mission."

"Really?" Frederic said, surprised. "Because he and I are all good now."

"Are you telling me I have to forgive him?" Ella asked

pointedly. "Did I not just explain how I feel about people telling me what to do?"

Frederic recoiled. "Um, well, uh, it's just that—"

"Relax, Frederic, I'm joking," she said with a laugh.

Frederic loosened his collar. "You see, this is what I mean about you and me—not completely compatible."

"But even if we're not husband and wife, we'll still be great friends, right?" Ella asked earnestly.

"Always," Frederic said. "I'm certainly not casting you out. You're still staying at the palace with me. If you want to, that is." He smiled shyly.

"I do. Thanks." A few days later they reached the royal palace in Harmonia. As they entered, King Wilberforce came running. He threw his arms around Frederic.

"I didn't believe it when they told me you'd returned," the king said. "How are you? Let me look at you."

Frederic was touched. He wiped a tear from his eye.

"It's good to see you too, Father," he said. "I'm sorry if you were frightened. To be honest, I was afraid you wouldn't want me back."

"This is where you belong," King Wilberforce said.

"I'm so glad you feel that way," Frederic said.

"But *you*," Wilberforce snapped, turning on Ella. "I can't believe you have the gall to step foot in my palace!"

"Sir?" Ella asked, shocked.

"Father, what are you doing?" Frederic asked, aghast. But he was ignored.

"This is twice now that you've led my son into near death," the king hollered. "You think you're so brave. You laugh at danger. You're just like—"

The king stopped himself. The veins in his temples throbbed visibly.

"Just like who?" Ella asked defiantly. "Frederic's mother?"

"You're a blight on this family!" Wilberforce shouted. "On this *kingdom*! You are forbidden to see my son ever again! Leave Harmonia at once!"

Frederic was trembling, reduced, in his father's presence, to that same old quivering child again. All he could do was mumble, "I'm sorry."

Ella marched out of the palace and straight to the stable, jumped onto her horse, and sped off.

"And now, my son," Wilberforce said. "You can finally settle down into the life your parents intended for you."

That was too much for Frederic to handle. "Not my *parents*," he said sharply. "You. *Just* you! Mother would have loved Ella, and you know it. She would have loved Liam, too. And she would have wanted me to be like them.

She would have wanted me to stand up to you!

"I let Ella down just now. But I'll never do it again. You need to listen to me now and understand me clearly: Every choice I've made, *I've* made. Ella didn't *make me* invade the Bandit King's castle. Liam didn't *make me* attack an evil witch. No one has ever *forced me* to do anything. Except you."

"But . . . . but . . . ," the king stammered. "I do it because I worry about you."

"You'll have to get over it," said Frederic. "I'm leaving." He paused. "Just as soon as I pack a few things."

Frederic gathered some essential belongings—a money pouch, his hairbrush, several spare suits, baby powder—and walked out of the palace. He looked upon the vista of open countryside before him. He could go anywhere now. Anywhere he wanted. He was terrified.

Duncan and Snow turned their woodland estate back over to the dwarfs, who were grateful to have a space of their own again. To show their appreciation, Frank even consented to let Duncan "stroke his beard for good luck."

Duncan and Snow moved back into Sylvaria's royal castle, which made Duncan's family very happy. They held a big dinner to celebrate his homecoming (although they served nothing but asparagus casserole). Duncan was given the seat of honor at the head of the long—but virtually empty—table in the castle's bland, undecorated dining hall. Snow held his hand, while his parents beamed at him adoringly. Mavis and Marvella wore homemade signs on their heads. Mavis's said WELC, and Marvella's said OME HOME, DUNCAN! YOU'RE OUR HERO!

"Speaking of heroes," Duncan said, "I think I've decided to rewrite my book."

"Oh, but Dunky, you've already put so much work into it," said Snow.

"I know. But I fear the advice I've got in there now isn't very good. We followed most of it on this mission, and things didn't turn out so well."

"Maybe you just need to go on some more adventures to learn more about heroing," Snow suggested.

Duncan's eyes widened. "Does this mean you *want* me to go on more adventures?"

Snow gave him a coy smile. "Only if I can go with you," she said. "And only if they're not *too*, too dangerous. Besides, you've seen what I can do. I'm awesome!"

King King let out a sad, low moan.

"What's wrong, Dad?" Duncan asked.

The king looked up (in his sudden sorrow, he'd let his face drop into his casserole). "You've only just moved back in, and you're going to leave again already," he said.

"Oh, not right away," Duncan said. "I think this castle will be our home for a while."

"Huzzah!" said King King. Queen Apricotta bounced in her seat. The twins began drumming the table with asparagus stalks. Snow rubbed Duncan's head playfully, and he began to blush. There were at least five people in this room who definitely considered him their hero.

Mr. Troll became quite a celebrity, thanks to Lyrical Leif's newest story-song, "The Troll and the Giant." The tale told of a brave troll who defended the castle of a young king against the attacks of a vicious giant.

"It not so true," Mr. Troll told his fellow monsters at Troll Place. "But least Troll is good guy in story."

The trolls danced and cheered. And then headed out to steal more vegetables from nearby farms.

"Turnip soup?" Rapunzel offered Gustav the pot, after spooning her own portion into her solitary bowl.

"That all you ever eat?" he grumbled.

"I've been telling you for days now, you don't need to stay here," she said, lighting a few extra candles. "I'm fine by myself. You don't need to watch over me."

"I know," Gustav said. He walked to the window and stared out into driving rain. "But, you know . . . you went through a lot of rough stuff during that heist. You looked a little freaked out after. So I figured you could use the company."

Rapunzel chuckled. "You barely speak," she said. "If you're here to provide company, shouldn't we at least try having a conversation?"

He glanced over his shoulder at her. "What are we gonna talk about? Turnips?"

Outside the cottage, Frederic approached slowly on horseback, holding his sopping jacket fruitlessly over his head. As lightning flashed, he saw Gustav's burly silhouette in the window. *I knew it was foolish to come here,* he thought. Frederic turned his horse around and rode back the way he'd come.

"Why not talk about the real reason you're here, Gustav?" Rapunzel said. "Like maybe you feel lost without the League of Princes? Or perhaps you're afraid to go home and see your brothers again?"

She was right on both counts, but there was no way Gustav was going to admit that. "Hey, I'm not afraid of *anything*," he said, spinning to face her. "Least of all my brothers! And see? This is exactly why I don't like talking

Fig. 44
FREDERIC, alone

to you: You always think you know what's going on inside my head."

"Oh, I would never even pretend to understand you, Gustav. I just want to help. It's my nature."

"Yeah? Well, it's *my* nature to . . ." He paused and cocked his head like a curious beagle. "Well, I guess I want to help people, too. Just not in a wimpy way like you do."

"I'm so glad you appreciate my life's work," Rapunzel sighed.

Gustav grinned. "Was that sarcasm, Blondie? I guess I have been rubbing off on you. Anyway, you're right: You *don't* need my help. But somebody out there must. So what am I sitting around for?" He grabbed his bag (which contained nothing but knives and beef jerky) and headed out the front door.

"Where will you go? What will you do?"

"Wander the countryside, I guess," he said. "Fight off monsters, rescue farm families. You know, hero stuff."

"And you're leaving in the middle of a downpour? I mean, I want you to go, but you can wait until the storm stops."

"I'm not afraid of rain," Gustav said, his long, wet hair already matted to his forehead. He raised his fist to the sky and jokingly shouted, "Do your worst, clouds!" He laughed and looked back to Rapunzel in the doorway. She was laughing, too. And oddly, Gustav's heart beat a little bit faster.

"By the way," he said. "Thanks for saving my life."

An hour after Liam shut himself into Avondell's prison, Briar found him there. "What are you doing, you idiot?" she asked.

"I belong here, don't I?" Liam said. "Besides, you and

I don't like each other. This marriage is a prison sentence anyway."

"Oh, spare me the drama," Briar said, folding her arms across her chest. "You'll make me regret what I just did."

Liam eyed her suspiciously. "What did you do?"

"I just came back from having the Archcleric annul our marriage. You can leave."

"What do you mean?"

"Clear the wax out of your ears, Liam the Blue. I've had our marriage annulled. It's like it never happened. We're not married anymore."

"Why would you do that?"

"Why do you care? It's done. Haven't you ever heard that expression about gift horses? If someone gives you a horse, ride away on it fast before they can ask for it back."

"What's in it for you?" Liam asked.

Briar threw open the cell door (which had never been locked to begin with). "I'm done with you, sweetheart. You serve no purpose to me anymore. In fact, at this point, having you as a husband is only a negative. For one thing, you're not very popular. And who knows? Someday I might meet a guy I actually *want* to spend time with. You know, as opposed to you. Whom I do not care for. At all. I just want to be clear on that point." Briar was used to being *worshipped*—whether out of fear or false admiration—but lately she found herself wondering how it would feel to be *liked*. Or even loved.

"So get out of here," she said. And with that she walked away.

"Wait," Liam said. But Briar was already gone. And he wasn't sure exactly what he'd wanted to say to her anyway. Over the past few weeks, there was nothing he'd wanted more than to have Briar out of his life. So now that she'd granted his wish, why did it feel so strangely bittersweet?

Don't waste your time thinking about it, he told himself. *Just go. Before she wants her gift horse back.*

Dazed (but elated), Liam left the prison. He gathered a few things—a money pouch, his sword, a spare cape— and stepped out through the front gates of the palace into the early-summer sun. He couldn't remain in Avondell, and he wasn't going to return to Erinthia. He had no idea where he was going. But he was free.

29½

◆━┤┝━◆

THE VILLAIN
SHEDS A TEAR

Before you close this book, there's one more set of events you should know about. But we need to jump back in time a little bit—to the moment the heroes were escaping on horseback through the front gate of the Wall of Secrecy and Deeb Rauber was victoriously addressing hundreds of stunned bandits on the drawbridge of his castle.

"All right," Rauber said. "Who's ready to listen to me now?"

As it turned out, not everyone in attendance was listening. As Rauber went into a long, grandiose speech about why he was the one true ruler of Rauberia, he didn't notice three people silently slip away from the proceedings.

The first was Wrathgar, the dungeon keeper, who had

emerged from the castle just in time to see Lord Rundark go underwater. Wrathgar went to the edge of the moat and peered in. Silently, he began walking along the water, looking down into the murk every few feet or so. Eventually, he turned the corner and went around to the side of the castle, out of view of the rest of the crowd.

Vero saw Wrathgar go and ducked off to follow him; and Madu, who had returned to human form, pulled the sword out of his foot and hopped along.

On the shadowy side of the castle, Wrathgar continued to stare into the moat. Finally he saw what he'd been searching for: a bubble. The enormous man got onto his knees and looked closer. More bubbles.

As Vero and Madu rounded the corner, they saw Wrathgar thrust his arm down into the dangerous waters and pluck out the mangled, eel-ravaged body of the Warlord of Dar. Rundark looked so terrible, it's best you don't even try to picture it. But if you really need to, think of your kitchen trash can the day after Thanksgiving.

Vero and Madu approached.

"Dead?" Madu asked.

"Might as well be," Wrathgar replied. "There is a faint wheezing. Hear it? But it won't last long. Even a man such as Lord Rundark cannot overcome this kind of damage."

"Does that mean we all work for that kid now?" Madu asked, nauseated by the thought.

"Perhaps not," Vero said. He reached into his vest and pulled out a small glass vial. "The Bandit King, he cannot command the respect of a real army. I have seen this now. But the Warlord, he is a different story, no? You asked me to choose whom I would follow. I have made my decision."

He tipped the vial and poured Rapunzel's tears onto Rundark's body. With a low hum, the Warlord began to vibrate. His wounds closed up. His breathing stabilized. And he opened his eyes.

Lord Rundark saw the three faces hovering over him, and his lips peeled back into a wicked grin. He raised his right hand, which still had an eel clamped over it. He ripped the eel off and opened his fingers. In his palm sat a large glowing piece of orange jade.

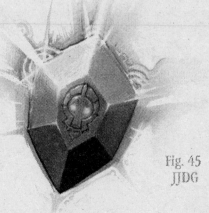

Fig. 45
JJDG

◄ ACKNOWLEDGMENTS ►

Once again, heartfelt huzzahs to all those who aided me during the writing of this book. Thank you to my wonderful and talented wife, Noelle Howey—without your moral and editorial support, this story may never have made it to print. Thanks also to my biggest fans, Bryn and Dash—Bryn, your wise input is always welcome; Dash, I hope you appreciate that this sequel came much closer to featuring actual ninjas. Thanks to my insightful and ever-enthusiastic editor, Jordan Brown, as well as Kellie Celia, Deborah Kovacs, Casey McIntyre, and the rest of the wonderful crew at Walden Pond and HarperCollins. Thanks always to my tireless agent, Cheryl Pientka, and everyone at the Jill Grinberg Literary Agency—I'm so glad I've got you all in my corner. Thanks to Neil Sklar, Brad Barton, and Christine Howey—suggestions from each of you were essential to crafting this tale. Thanks also to my mom, dad, and brother—having you cheering me on means everything. I want to give a very special thanks to David Wagner, Erik Singer, Cori Lynn Peterson Campbell, and Lulu French, who gave virtuoso performances as Gustav, Frederic, Ella, and Zaubera (respectively) at the very first live staged reading of *Hero's Guide* scenes—as well as Bronson Pinchot for his amazing turn as *everybody* in the audiobook. And a big, important thank you to Milo Ruggiero for coming up with the name Smimf, my favorite name in the whole series. I'd also love to thank every blogger who promoted *Hero's Guide* and every reader who has recommended it—you're all awesome! Finally, thank you, Todd Harris—I'm the luckiest author in the world to have you bringing my characters to life. Here's to many future collaborations!

And now, a sneak peek at Book 3:

THE HERO'S GUIDE TO
Being an Outlaw

1

AN OUTLAW IS NEVER AROUND WHEN YOU NEED ONE

"**H**arrumph."

King Wilberforce was in a foul mood, as he had been ever since Prince Frederic had stormed out of the palace months earlier. His son had never lashed out at him like that before. And to think it was simply because he had banished his son's fiancée. What choice did he have? Ella was a bad influence. He couldn't even keep track of how many times she had nearly gotten Frederic killed. Exiling the girl was what any good father would have done.

At least that's what Wilberforce told himself as he sat on his velvet-cushioned throne grumbling in a positively unkingly manner. Apparently forgetting his rule that "a proper man never fidgets," he absentmindedly fiddled with the dozens of glistening medals that adorned his finely tailored purple jacket. His normally stiff, right-angled shoulders began to dip into a position that came dangerously close to resembling a slump.

"Harrumph," the king grunted again.

"Your Highness?" asked the tall, thin, well-mannered man standing before the throne. "I mean no disrespect, but I feel the need to remind you that I am . . . here. Unless, of course, you summoned me only so that you would have someone at whom you could grunt. In which case, by all means, Your Highness—grunt away."

"I don't understand the boy," Wilberforce said, half mumbling. "You're his valet, Reginald. You know him better than anyone. Why would he go? What's wrong with him?"

"Perhaps part of the problem, Your Highness, is that you refer to him as 'the boy,'" Reginald said. "Frederic is a grown man."

"Who acts like a boy," the king responded. "Why would he feel a need to go off in search of *adventure*?" He snarled the word as if it were a curse. Before Reginald could respond, the king rambled on. "Do I not provide enough entertainment here at the palace? We hold royal balls every other week. Banquets! Bard concerts! Frederic never even stopped by the royal art gallery to see the new series of cat portraits

I commissioned for him. One of them shows a kitten in a hammock; Frederic loves that sort of thing."

"Perhaps, sire," Reginald finally interjected, "the prince was looking for more of a challenge."

"Challenge?" The king pshawed. "As if that boy could handle a challenge. He's got no backbone, no determination, no drive. Why, I gave him a custom-made backgammon set last year. After *one try*, he whined that it was too hard to play."

"To be fair, Your Highness, I believe his difficulty with the game was due to the *round dice* you forced him to use. They never stopped rolling."

Wilberforce arched an eyebrow. "You expected me to give my son those pointy-edged, cube-style dice? He'd lose an eye."

"Well, if you are going to be such a stickler for safety, why not give him dice the size of honeydews," Reginald said dryly. While he technically served the king, his loyalty lay with the prince he'd practically raised from birth. "After all, regular-size dice are a dangerous choking hazard."

"You're being cheeky with me, aren't you, Reginald?"

"Cheeky, sire?" the valet replied.

"You're giving me cheek. Sass. Cheeky sass."

"I would never dream of it, Your Highness. Look at all

those medals on your chest: Best Posture, Team Solitaire Champion, Silkiest Mustache. I have nothing but the utmost respect for a monarch with so many . . . *amazing* accomplishments to his credit."

"Cheek!" Wilberforce bellowed. "Cheeeeeek!" He stood and pointed toward the exit, his arm as stiff as a road sign. "I want you out, Reginald. Leave at once."

"The room?" Reginald asked. "Or the palace?"

"Think bigger," the king sneered.

"The kingdom then. As you wish." Reginald bowed his head. "Someday I hope you realize that just because your wife died as an adventurer doesn't mean your son will, too. You need to let Frederic make his own choices. Otherwise you will only drive him farther away." He turned and walked out.

Wilberforce leaned forward in his throne. "If you find Frederic out there . . ." But Reginald was already gone. The king slouched back in his seat and added—to no one— "Take care of him."

He unpinned one of the medals from his jacket and took a look at it. WINNER: CRUSTIEST LOAF, HARMONIAN BAKE FAIR. He tossed the award angrily to the floor and went back to brooding. Sometime later, the door opened and Wilberforce quickly straightened up as an attendant stepped in.

"Sorry to disturb you, Your Highness," the attendant said. "But there's someone here to see you."

Frederic! Wilberforce thought. *He's come home.* "Send him in. Right away."

"Your visitor? Um, he's got some friends with him," the attendant began.

"Yes, of course, I should have figured he'd still be traveling with those ne'er-do-wells," the king said hurriedly. "But we'll deal with them later. Just get the boy in here."

"Boy? But—"

"Go! Let him in!"

The attendant scrambled from the throne room. Wilberforce worked his face into a welcoming smile, almost trembling as he waited. But a moment later, he frowned and cocked a quizzical eyebrow as his visitor entered the chamber. It was not Frederic. It was a tall, broad-shouldered, scar-faced man with some sort of monstrous skull sitting on his head like a helmet. And he had ten more equally questionable characters standing behind him, all brandishing nicked, battle-worn swords.

King Wilberforce shrank back. "Who . . . who are you?" he whispered.

"I am Rundark, Warlord of Dar and ruler of New Dar," said the stranger. His thick, braided beard rattled against his armored chest as he spoke. "And I am here to make an offer to the king of Harmonia."

Now, if Frederic had been there, he certainly would have warned his father about Lord Rundark, the vicious and brutal dictator who had nearly destroyed the League of Princes that past summer. Frederic could have told his father about the Jeopardous Jade Djinn Gem, the mystical artifact that gave Rundark the power to control people like human puppets. He might even have mentioned how Rundark—and the Gem along with him—were supposed to have been swallowed by a school of hungry bladejaw eels. But at that moment, when Frederic could have been very, very helpful to his father, he was many miles away, passing out at the sight of a hobgoblin with a splinter in its toe.

2

AN OUTLAW FAINTS
AT THE SIGHT OF BLOOD

Frederic wasn't always helpless. Sure, he'd grown up in a palace with spill-proof goblets, padded bathtubs, and servants who wiped his nose for him; but those days were long behind him. Well, okay, a few months behind him. But in that time, Frederic *had* changed. He was now a man who had battled witches, negotiated with giants, and escaped from dungeons. He had proven he could be brave—when he had an ally or three at his side, that is. Working solo was still a challenge for him. And sadly, there was not a friend in sight when the hobgoblin lifted its crusty foot and wiggled its fat, infected toe in his face.

As Frederic's head hit the dirt and consciousness slowly faded away, his mind replayed the events of the previous three months, the pitiful chain of events that had brought him to this point.

It all began when Frederic walked out on his father. He marched out through his palace's arched marble gateway, his head a dizzying swirl of emotions—shame at having let Ella get banished, pride at having finally stood up to his father, anxiety over the prospect of leaving his royal comforts behind forever. But he had a plan: Go see Rapunzel. The long-haired healer from Sturmhagen had an easygoing warmth that made Frederic feel calm and comfortable whenever he saw her. She got his jokes, she made the best turnip soup he'd ever tasted, and she'd saved his life twice. Just thinking of Rapunzel made Frederic feel like everything was going to be all right.

Unfortunately, seeing her didn't have quite the same effect. When Frederic finally reached Rapunzel's cottage in the deep woods of Sturmhagen, he noticed that she was not alone. Through her kitchen window, he spotted the familiar, broad-shouldered silhouette of his friend Prince Gustav. *I shouldn't be surprised,* Frederic thought. *Gustav was* her *Prince Charming, after all.*

"Good for him," Frederic said aloud, trying to convince himself he really felt that way. He turned his horse around, trotted back into the forest, and began . . . wandering.

He spent several days on the shores of Lake Dräng with

Reese the giant—but he didn't like the way Reese's colossal mother, Maude, licked her lips when she looked at him, so he decided to move on. He got a warm welcome at Troll Place, but the "bed" that Mr. Troll constructed for him—a splintery piece of wood precariously balanced between two jagged rocks—didn't even come close to his comfort standards; so he politely told his host that he had an important appointment elsewhere. He tried Duncan and Snow White's estate in Sylvaria, but learned from the dwarfs that the couple had moved out.

"I suppose you'd like to know where they went," Frank the dwarf said, somehow making it sound like an insult.

"Yes, I would," Frederic replied.

"Just what I thought," Frank grumbled. And he walked away.

Frederic had no doubt that if he showed up on the doorsteps of Avondell Palace, Liam would offer him a room. But Liam's wife would be there, also—and Briar Rose was not a person with whom Frederic cherished the thought of being roomies.

After thirteen weeks on the road, and with nowhere else to go, Frederic headed back to Harmonia. He arrived outside the palace at twilight but couldn't bring himself to actually reenter the gates. Instead, he led his horse, Gwendolyn, a few yards away, where he laid out a blanket and sat down against the palace's wrought iron fence, gently caressing the gold-braid tassels that hung from the shoulder pads of his baby-blue suit. Eventually his eyelids drooped. But before he got a chance to dream about warm peach tarts and cardamom ice cream, he was awakened by a strange blue light mere inches from his face.

"Fairy!" he shrieked, before jumping to his feet and attempting—fruitlessly—to climb the fence.

"Wrong thing! Wrong thing!" he heard a twinkly voice call as he slid down the iron bars and landed gracelessly on the grass. He turned around and got a better look at the creature that had terrified him—a tiny woman, bathed in bluish light, hovering three feet off the ground. Frederic began to breathe a little easier.

"I, uh . . . I don't know if you were trying to tell me that I was *doing* the wrong thing or that I had *called* you the wrong thing," Frederic said softly, "but in either case, I think the latter is true. You're *not* a fairy, are you?"

The little blue woman smiled, her silvery antennae twitching. "Wrong thing. Wrongety-wrong."

"If I'm not mistaken, you're a sprite," Frederic said, remembering Rapunzel's description of her otherworldly helpers.

"Right thing!" the sprite squealed, and she flew loops in the air.

Frederic grinned. "Sorry about my initial reaction," he said, his cheeks reddening. "I've never actually met a sprite before. I thought you might be a fairy, and fairies make me nervous. Not that I've ever met a fairy either. But my friend Liam had a run-in with a very nasty one. You know the Sleeping Beauty story? Anyway . . . pleased to make your acquaintance. I am Prince Frederic." He bowed.

"Of coursety you's Frederic," the sprite said with a giggle that sounded like sleigh bells. "Frederic is skinny like candy cane. Frederic wears clothes with golden spaghettis. Frederic never touchety dirt. You's Frederic. Just like Zel say."

Frederic frowned. "Is that really how Rapunzel described me?" Then he perked up. "No, wait. That doesn't matter! Rapunzel described me! She sent you to find me?"

"Right thing!" The sprite mimicked his bow, hovering in midair. "Blink," she said.

"Blink?"

"Blink!"

"Um, okay." Frederic blinked his eyes.

The sprite shook her head and chuckled. She pointed to herself. "This is Blink."

"Ah, your *name* is Blink. Well, Miss Blink, why did

Rapunzel send you to me?"

"Zel needs helpety-help. Too many forest peoples been hurt lately. Zel said you help. Comety-come."

"I'm not sure how much help I'll be," Frederic said. "I mean, I'll go, of course. But I'm not exactly a skilled medic. And seeing as Rapunzel has magical healing tears anyway, I just wonder—"

"Comety-come!" Blink squeaked loudly.

"Right away!" Frederic sputtered as he folded his blanket and placed it neatly in Gwendolyn's saddlebag. "Uh, Miss Blink? You wouldn't happen to know if there's *another* man, um . . . helping Rapunzel already? A very large man? With long, blond hair and questionable hygiene?"

"You not understand 'comety-come'?"

Frederic hopped on his horse and followed the sprite all the way back to the cottage in Sturmhagen. He was relieved to see that Gustav was not present. Rapunzel, however, was not there either.

"Is anybody home?" Frederic called out. His answer came in the form of a second blip of blue light zooming up to his face—another sprite, male this time.

"You's Frederic," he said. "Skinny like candy cane."

"Yes, that's me." Frederic sighed. He climbed down from his horse. "Is Rapunzel about?"

"Zel's in forest. Too many patients. Busety-busy," the sprite rattled off. "You wait here."

"I can do that," Frederic replied. "But, in the meantime, I suppose . . ." And then he realized that both sprites were gone, having already zipped off among the thickly clustered pines that lined the small valley. He took a deep breath. "Well, I suppose I'll make myself comfortable."

That was when the hobgoblin limped out of the woods. Dripping with what was either sweat or slime, the rust-colored creature shambled toward Frederic. It was only half the prince's height; but something about its long, pointed ears, bulbous nose, and jagged teeth told Frederic that this was not a creature to be messed with.

He ran into the cottage and slammed the door. But

the thing outside began to knock. "My toe," the hobgoblin moaned. "Hurts. So. Much."

"Uh, Rapunzel's not in right now," Frederic said. "I'd be happy to take down your name and contact information."

"Help me," the monster sniffled through the door. "The golden lady says all who come to her cottage will be healed. Please."

Frederic's mind turned to thoughts of his favorite fictional hero. He asked himself, *What would Sir Bertram do?* No matter what kind of challenge he faced—be it an orc using uncouth language or a baroness eating her entrée from a dessert plate—Sir Bertram the Dainty remained calm, levelheaded, and, above all, polite. There was no question as to what the dandy knight would do in this situation.

"Okay," Frederic said. "Let's . . . uh, see what we have here." He opened the door and cautiously stepped outside to see the drippy monster wobbling on one leg. "A hobbling hobgoblin. Heh. Try saying that five times fast. Well, I will hazard a guess that there is something wrong with your foot."

"Yes," the hobgoblin said. "Look!" It slapped its damp hands on Frederic's shoulders and raised its bare foot toward the prince's face, flaunting the three-inch-long shard of broken, splintery wood stuck in the fat flesh of its big toe.

That's when Frederic passed out.

THINK YOU KNOW YOUR FAIRY TALES?
THINK AGAIN.

BOOK 1

BOOK 2

BOOK 3

Don't miss a second of the hilarious, action-packed adventure series from Christopher Healy.

WALDEN POND PRESS
An Imprint of HarperCollinsPublishers

www.harpercollinschildrens.com • www.walden.com